D1106086

NOT UNTRUE & NOT UNKIND

NOT UNTRUE
& NOT UNKIND

ED O'LOUGHLIN

THE OVERLOOK PRESS
New York

This edition first published in hardcover in the United States in 2010 by

The Overlook Press, Peter Mayer Publishers, Inc.
141 Wooster Street
New York, NY 10012

Manufactured in the United States of America
ISBN 978-1-59020-295-1
FIRST EDITION
10 9 8 7 6 5 4 3 2 1

To Nuala

Talking in Bed

Talking in bed ought to be easiest,
Lying together there goes back so far,
An emblem of two people being honest.

Yet more and more time passes silently.
Outside, the wind's incomplete unrest
Builds and disperses clouds about the sky,

And dark towns heap up on the horizon.
None of this cares for us. Nothing shows why
At this unique distance from isolation

It becomes still more difficult to find
Words at once true and kind,
Or not untrue and not unkind.

Phillip Larkin

NOT UNTRUE & NOT UNKIND

I

Ten years ago I became a hero, and when I came home my old paper took me on again. They thought I'd be an ornament. Ten years now working four shifts a week, six hours a shift and six weeks off each year. If you can call it working. At any rate, I get paid.

It took me a while to get used to it here again, this northern estuary. Why do I say that? I'm still not used to it. It rains a lot, and there always seems to be a wind. The days and nights mill round like mismatched fighters, short and long, long and short, from summer to winter to summer again: it would make you feel dizzy. Then in September they rest for a while, leaning together, equatorial evenings, and next comes October, when the trees drop their leaves before a sky filled with remote patient light – the light of a highveld winter, following me halfway round the world. Nights come early, the low buildings shrink from them, and I remember that most of this city is built on silt, and that out past the sea wall the waves are still hissing. It's time then for the kids to light fireworks and bonfires, to hold the perimeter, keep the living from the dead, until November relieves us with its numbing east wind.

By then the basin behind my house is crowded with migrant birds driven down from the far north. People throw bread in the water, and the ducks and swans reward them with hustle or grace. Each to his own.

This town is, you might say, a forgiving place. Big enough to hide in, small enough to support a familiar cast of tramps, screamers and congenital syphilitics. Here people call them 'characters' and give them freedom of the streets. And the streets are full of stories – other people's stories, not my own, and for ten years now that's been fine with me. When I came back from Africa they wanted me to write again, but I told the interview panel, with a straight face, that for the time being I'd prefer to explore avenues of production and management. From time to time I still churn out the odd worthy think piece – global affairs; the big picture; filler, really, rewritten from the wires – but mostly I just mess with other people's copy, working backbench on the night shift.

It seems, though, that Cartwright may have screwed things up for me. Hugh says he needs someone to replace Cartwright, to put manners on the newsroom, and he seems to think it's me. Nor is my boss alone in this belief: there is a story going around that Cartwright was secretly grooming me, had been for years back, without my knowing it. And even now, knowing him as well as I did, having seen him at his weakest, as nothing at all, even I have to admit that Cartwright was somewhat uncanny. The evening he died a strange wind blew from the south and pasted rain and red mud onto every flat surface and every parked car. The rain was still falling as I left the police station, and streaks of wet dirt swallowed the blood spots on Cartwright's folder when I took it from hiding in his old leather bag. I needed to see it again, right there on the street, outside the police station.

I went into a bar – not the usual one, this would need some privacy – and opened the folder and started to look through it. Later, when I stopped reading for a while, the TV in the corner was talking about a storm in the Sahara, dust blown thousands of miles by freak currents in the air. I ordered another drink, just for stage business, though the bar was almost empty. At the other end of the counter a barman was reading the evening newspaper in the glow of a fake carriage lamp. An old man stood in the hallway, just inside the open door, the smoke from his cigarette curling into his eyes. Above the door a fan of glass had stained the evening sky dark mauve. I've seen that before, I thought, and I remembered Katey, and a thunderstorm.

Cartwright's folder was still open in front of me, at a page clipped from the *New York Chronicle*'s magazine, dated ten years ago. Most of the page was taken up with a single colour photograph, a picture I hadn't seen since it was taken. I looked at it again now.

In the photograph Fine has his arm around Tommo's shoulder and the two of them are leaning against a blue Mitsubishi. Funny. I don't remember it being that colour. I could have sworn that it was green. Tommo is frowning a little, his arms folded across his chest. He thought it unlucky for colleagues to take each other's pictures.

Fine is smiling, but with that faintly puzzled look which, for years now, has been all that I can see of him. It was the look that just about saved him from seeming too arrogant. To the left stands little Charlie Brereton, the image on his T-shirt still stained with blood and snot. Behind him, beyond the Mitsubishi, appears the cab of an old Bedford army truck, punched through with bullet holes. The crude swastika painted on its door seems to grow from the back of Brereton's balding head, and he is leering at the camera like he means to start a fight with it. Off to the right, just a little apart from Fine, stands Beatrice. She is staring at the camera, staring out of the photograph. She is staring at me. I took the picture, with Tommo's favourite camera.

I closed the folder and thought for a while. More people had come in – a girl and a boy, a group of young men in suits with hot red faces, two ladies with shopping bags looking for gin. I had to stare past the TV so as not to seem alone. It was talking about the dust again. I put the folder back into Cartwright's bag and leaned it against my stool, and then I had another drink, and I was halfway to the next bar – the usual one, where I was going to meet Hugh to arrange Cartwright's funeral – before I realized that I'd left the bag behind me. It was night now, still raining, and the wind picked at my collar and slid fingers up my sleeves. I stood for a while on the corner, watching the cars wash past, and then I turned and limped back and found the bag where I'd left it, at the corner of the bar. The place was quite crowded now, so I stayed for another drink.

I could just as easily leave Cartwright out of this. He never went anywhere, the twisted old fucker. He never knew any of the others. But he's forced his way into it, dust reassembling itself. Beatrice stared at me, and I took her picture. It seems I can't escape that. And then there's the joke, which I'll have to learn to savour: years after I stopped caring, after I gave up all the play-acting, I find that someone else was watching all along.

*

3

Tommo's favourite camera was a manual 35-millimetre single-lens reflex, old-fashioned even then. When Fine talked me into taking that picture Tommo had to show me how to turn the focus and aperture rings, and how to balance the exposure in the viewfinder. I suppose that by rights the *Chronicle* should have paid me for that picture when they published it, but I never went after them for money. After all, the snap was taken on Tommo's film, which the *Chronicle* had paid for, and the *Chronicle* did fly me out of there, in the end, after Armitage showed up. And it was Armitage's piece that made me famous, or at least famous enough to land a cushy job back home. So no complaints there.

We read from left to right. Charlie Brereton stands on the left. He's even uglier than I remember him – I must have got used to him in the end – but his face is the one I'm drawn to first, avoiding the other frozen gazes. Seeing him again I still can't help smiling.

Charlie Brereton was maybe ten years older than me, balding and squat, with a flattened nose and heavy shoulders, and if he hadn't been almost a midget he'd have looked like a thug. Which would have really pleased him; he came from a good home in Warwickshire and spoke very proper English, but he liked to toss in the odd glottal stop when trying to impress. He had a way of worming his way to the front of a crowd or the middle of a conversation, and when he got there he stayed there, bobbing up and down like a cork in a stream. He always pushed in.

Right, so: to begin. Charlie Brereton looked like a gargoyle, and the first time I met him he lent me a pen. I was newly arrived in eastern Zaire, standing at the back of a United Nations press conference at the Hôtel des Grands Lacs in Goma, flapping my notebook, digging in my pockets, and a pig-ugly little Englishman leaned over and handed me a biro, then took another for himself from a leather satchel that lay at his feet. The pen he lent me was covered in teeth marks, even though you weren't supposed to put anything in your mouth or near it, what with all the cholera in town. I tried to thank him but he waved me away, face screwed up so he could listen to the briefing. Every minute or so the UN spokesman had to stop talking while an Ilyushin or a C-130 passed over the terrace on final approach, flying so low you could smell the spent fuel. In those mornings the air on the terrace would still be cool from the night. The evening sun would find gold in the dust from the volcano. At night you could see the fan of red light that rose from its crater, the cherry on the cake.

It was my first foreign story and to me none of it looked real – the light, the volcano, the polythene-green banana trees, fat Warsaw Pact freight planes sinking down from the sky. Our own Beechcraft had dropped from clear air into a cloud of black dust and when the ground appeared again I was born into another world. Dazed people wandered zombie-like along the runway; the pilot had to gun his engines to scare them off so we could land. In the long grass by the airstrip Rwandan refugees squatted down in the first rush of illness, beside the dying and the dead. Cargo jets bumbled around the apron on their fat bellies, unguided, looking for clear spots to vomit their loads, while the boys from the town played dare in the wash from their engines: how close can you get before you're blown off your feet? Inside the terminal the Presidential Guards and the customs agents fought for the chance to shake down the passengers. I heard later that the airport was charging each aid plane seventeen hundred dollars in landing fees. Outside, bright nylon bell tents had sprung like fungus around the satellite feed-point and the French army's briefing tent, and just beyond the shiny new coils of razor wire the refugees, hundreds of thousands of them, were shuffling north towards the UN's new camps. Underneath the wire, only feet from the tents, lay little yellow cylinders bundled in straw sleeping mats. The bundles lay in two files, one on either side of the road, stretching with occasional gaps for thirty miles north past Katale. They were the hardest things of all to believe in. Mummified by cholera, they didn't even smell.

The story had been strewn along the floor of the Western Rift Valley like rubbish in a run-down theatre. The cone of Nyiragongo was a black plug blocking the valley to the north. To the south stretched Lake Kivu, its deep waters saturated with deadly gases waiting to fizz up and kill thousands. To the east, almost lifelike, loomed the high green hills of Rwanda, and off in the west, when

5

the day was clear, you could see the jagged black heads of the valley's far rim. A few years later this scenery came apart at the seams and buried half the city under liquid lava. I watched it on TV, the British world service.

Given that much of it is gone now, what's the point of describing Goma as it was back then? I could be imagining it, not remembering. I could be making it up. Anyway, let me say that there were rusting tin roofs and shuttered lock-up stores and workshops, and mottled one- or two-storey concrete commercial buildings with rusted steel rods sticking up from the roofs. There were shanty towns built of sticks and cardboard and flattened tins, broken streets in the commercial quarter, littered waste ground in the once-grand traffic circles where flowers flamed on unpruned flamboyants. By the lakeshore stood the big residential compounds left by the Belgians, surrounded by gum trees and wood or steel fences. And everywhere there was the sweet sick smell of human sewage and the toc-toc of machetes cutting living trees for firewood. Hutu soldiers, disarmed now but still in their uniforms, lurched about with their arms around each other. You couldn't tell if they were drunk or merely dying.

After a few days of this the Zairean army woke up and chased the refugees out of town into the new UN camps, returning the city to its filthy street kids, its market women in proud twists of cotton and its sharp-eyed hipsters in high-waisted jeans. They rushed about on foot, on motorbikes, shopping for food, looking for work with the aid agencies, for advancement, for a gathering of souls, a street parliament where they could get drunk on talk of politics or find someone to buy them a Primus in one of the invincible bars whose music jangled, all night long, through all the shifting curfews. I'll bet they're there yet, most of them, building again on the lava flows.

I'd been in town for two days already when Brereton found me. We got talking after the press conference, and it turned out that he was already an old hand in Johannesburg, my next destination, where I was hoping to set myself up and find some freelance strings. It was Brereton who invited me to Mitzi's Bar. You might say he inducted me; I'd never have found it myself – a real Belgian restaurant, in a place and time like that.

The dining room and bar were full of foreigners, mostly press but with a fair number of aid workers, and Brereton ducked and barged his way to the corner of the bar. He bought us each a beer and took a long, silent drink, and then he lit a cigarette and turned to face the room, his elbows hitched up on the counter behind him.

'See those people over there?' he said after a while, nodding at a group of older men. They wore neatly pressed jeans and short-sleeved shirts and cotton waistcoats with lots of bulging pockets. Laminated ID cards hung on chains round their necks. 'Network pussies. From the States. See the one in the middle, with the bush hat and the combat boots and all the knives and pouches and stuff on his belt? The fucking survivalist? He's actually a satellite technician for 24/7 News. He never leaves the feed-point.'

'Ah,' I said wisely. I was already terribly impressed by Brereton. I'd seen his byline in a big London paper.

Brereton was looking past me now. He had to lean out from the bar to do so because I was at least a head taller than him. He fixed his stare on a big round table where a heavily tanned man in a blue polo shirt was addressing a circle of listeners. Some of them were taking notes.

'And that', said Brereton, 'is Michael Brady, from Alarm International. He's telling them that the Western countries should all send soldiers into Rwanda right away to rescue these poor Hutus from the evil Tutsis. I don't know where he gets that from – the French, I suppose – but he's been saying it all week. And some of these idiots are actually filing it. They're no-budget hacks who could only get here because Alarm flew them out for free and is putting them up and driving them around the place. In return they give it wall-to-wall coverage about all the black people it's saving and about all the money it needs to raise to save more. Most of these idiots will never go near the genocide story. It would only confuse their readers back home.'

I lit a cigarette while I thought about what he'd said; it helps to build confidence, I don't care what they say.

'Well, you know,' I said slowly, 'I came here from Nairobi on a free flight with Think of the Children. They're letting me sleep on the sofa in their compound. And they let me use their office for free, otherwise I'd have no way to file. I can't afford a sat-phone of my own.'

Brereton stared at me for a long moment and then his face broke out in a triumphant leer. 'I know,' he said. 'I saw you at Think's compound yesterday when I went to steal some biscuits.' He raised his glass to me. 'Jambo karibu.'

We stood by an open window looking out over the gate of the compound. A little group of bundles lay in a row on the other side of the dark laneway, the straw flaring yellow whenever a car pulled in. There were six of them, two adults and four children, judging by their size – a whole family, perhaps. When we left the bar that night Brereton staggered across the lane and gave names to each of them. I can't remember what he called them. Next day they were gone.

Brereton had just made a name for himself, somewhat late in his career, by filing from inside Rwanda when the killings were still going on. He was now getting so many hard-news commissions that he could no longer do much feature stuff – his bread and butter when he'd been a part-time stringer. He passed one such assignment on to me, to help me get started. It was a story about Sun City, for his newspaper's travel section, and a lens monkey came with the job. Brereton had found him a couple of weeks before, on a jaunt to Angola, and wanted to give him a try.

So I first saw Tommaso Capaldi in Johannesburg, standing outside the Hard Times in Melville, where he was waiting for me to collect him. He looked very young, square-faced and stocky, with sweat shining in the short dark hair that seemed to grow from a third of the way down his forehead. He wore thick glasses with grey steel frames, grey flannel trousers and a blue blazer that strained against its brass buttons, revealing elongated ovals of off-white shirt-front. Dark hairs spilled out around the cuffs and through the top button of his shirt. Slung round his neck was an old-fashioned wind-on camera with an old-fashioned manual lens, the sort of eccentric gear that Brereton had taught me to associate with his 'Leica pikeys', the glamorous rich kids who lark around in shitholes pretending to be freelance photographers. But he certainly wasn't dressed like one. He looked more like the inmate of a halfway house for child molesters. I soon learned that Tommo did have all the monkey gear stashed away in his shoulder bag – the electronic camera bodies and auto-focus lenses, the scanner and the flashguns – but he was happier when he could just work with his manual Nikon. He said he liked the weight of it, and that it did what it was told. I'm sure he was telling the truth: unlike a lot of snappers Tommo didn't choose his equipment to be noticed. Tommo didn't like to be noticed at all.

We were halfway to Hartbeespoort before I dared to ask him about his clothes.

'I reckoned we'd be going to the casino,' he replied, after a short pause. 'The brochure says you're supposed to dress smart or they won't let you in.'

He had a very quiet, gentle voice. It overcame his Australian accent the way water wears down rock.

'Here that just means that you can't go in barefoot,' I told him. 'You look like you're in a Welsh choir.'

He laughed, not embarrassed. 'It's my old cricket blazer, actually. I had to pick the crest off the pocket last night.'

The road to Sun City threaded through the sharp ridges of the Magaliesberg, past Hartbeespoort dam and then across the thorny plain of the North West Province. We took a wrong turn some-where in the Boer badlands between Brits and Rustenburg, and it was already dusk when we drew onto the final stretch of highway to the Pilanesberg hills. The spring rains had yet to reach the highveld and the wind from the dry scrub blew plumes of dust across the road. Tommo was reading out extracts from a travel guide.

'It says here that under apartheid this was all a black homeland. I guess because it's such poor soil.'

There was a long pause and I glanced over. He was experimenting with his lips. 'Bop – bopoo – bopoo-tast, no, tstat, tswana. Anyway, everyone called it Bop. Gambling was banned in South Africa, but they allowed it here because this was supposed to be a different country. An enclave. Great. I love enclaves. Ever been to Hong Kong?'

He loved enclaves; I loved resorts. I always want to believe in them, at least while I'm there.

From the entrance gate a narrow road led up into the dry volcanic hills, running alongside a monorail that carried day-trippers from the car park to the resort. As we drove along the road the thornbush on the hillsides gave way to trees and flowers watered – Tommo read aloud – by a giant pipeline stretching for scores of kilometres across the dry scrub. Buildings of glass and concrete were sunk into the side of a green, narrow valley threaded with golf courses and artificial woods and lakes.

The new hotel stood at the head of the valley. Built from moulded cement and hidden steel, it was a mishmash of motifs lifted from Great Zimbabwe, pre-Columbian America and ancient Persia, Egypt and Greece. As I handed the keys to a parking valet we heard a strange hiss and thud above us, followed by a steady roar. Great flaming jets of gas shot up from turrets on the roof.

The resort manager had told me on the phone that we could work wherever we liked as long as we didn't upset the paying guests. Tommo wanted to start as soon as we'd checked in, and when he came down to the lobby I saw that he'd got rid of the blazer and swapped his glasses for contacts. Now when he smiled I could see a sly joke in his eyes.

It was a weekday night, quiet, and in the casino the massed slot machines chattered and winked at the outnumbered patrons like the whores in a Nairobi nightclub. Tommo paused for a long minute on the edge of the slots pit, scanning for prey, then dived in among the clamouring machinery. I watched as he stalked an old white lady who was spreading her custom across three slot machines. She wore rhinestone spectacle frames and clutched her handbag in her armpit as she mechanically fed each machine in turn. She seemed to be hypnotized, but whenever another customer strayed too close to her patch her elbow clamped tightly on her handbag and the rhinestones flashed menace in the variegated lights.

Tommo moved to the end of her row, then gradually stole towards her. He would stop, pretending to study a dial or pull a handle, whenever she turned towards him to feed her left-hand machine, and then he would advance in short rushes whenever she turned to her right again. By the time he was three machines away from her he must have judged that he was on the edge of her critical area, and, just as she fixed her stupefied gaze on the dials in front of her, he lifted his camera and clicked off a frame. He was already strolling away from her, suddenly relaxed, when she realized that something odd had happened, her head jerking around in confusion.

'I reckon that one'll do,' said Tommo, joining me.

When he showed me the print a few days later I saw that her face was lit from below like a Halloween mask. Coloured lights shone out of focus in her rhinestone glasses, and behind them the whites of her eyes glinted crazily in deep black shadow. Her mouth was half open and a shiny tongue poked out through her lips. The image was grainy and unclear because of the bad light, which had turned yellow on the film. I liked the picture so much that I asked Tommo for a print of it – I must have left it in Johannesburg, with all my other stuff. But the travel editor wouldn't use the shot. She told Tommo that it was much too noir to use with a holiday piece.

We ate in a French restaurant and afterwards we took the shuttle back to our hotel, ordered cigars and signed them to our rooms. We smoked the cigars on the deserted terrace, drinking whiskey. Above us the gas jets thundered into the night, vaporizing hordes of beguiled insects. Sprinklers blew a fine mist in the shrubs across the moat, drawing scent from the dry leaves, and the lights of the resort, spilling down the valley, shone a second time in the still surface of the swimming pool. But the moon had not yet risen, and above the valley ancient outcrops waited in the dark.

Tommo took long pulls on his cigar and the glow lit his face through the thickening ash. He told me that he'd packed in a staff job with a big paper in Sydney because, like a lot of people, he wanted to travel all the time, and have adventures, and do great work. But he was learning already that in Africa great pictures are ten a penny, that what he saw as his art (he didn't actually say that, because he was quite modest for a snapper, but you could read between the lines) could be a commodity, space-filler, like the stuff that the likes of me churned out to illustrate his snaps. Provided you got up early for the soft light, provided you physically made your way to the scene, Africa would line up haunting images for you the way a beggar shows off her sores. As a trainee in Australia, Tommo had always admired his paper's star photographers when they came back from their foreign jaunts with harrowing images of starving children and broken lives. But he'd just been on his first trip to a shithole, central Angola, combining his own freelance work with a paid NGO assignment, and disillusionment had set in.

'It was the same picture, over and over again,' he said, waving the cigar slowly. 'The kids stand and stare at you with their big eyes and you try to angle them up in a classic composition or with something gimmicky in the background . . . I'll tell you what I'll do next time. Next time I'm going to bring an inflatable vulture and put it in the back of every frame.'

'Wouldn't it be easier just to scan your pics into your laptop, then Photoshop the vulture in digitally?'

'You don't get it. The vulture has to be analogue. It's standing in for me.'

I laughed. 'Great. Another angst-ridden photographer.'

It was late. We were the only ones left on the terrace. A waitress came to bus away our empties and we ordered one last round. When she was gone I spoke again.

'So if you're fed up already what are you going to do for the rest of your time here in Africa?'

'Oh, I didn't say I was fed up.' He laughed again. 'It's still worth doing, I suppose. Even for the sake of curiosity. And, then again, maybe it does help people. Gets the charity funds flowing, human rights, whatever. Puts it on the record.'

'What record?' I asked, and instantly felt smug.

He laughed, gently, in the darkness. 'Oh, I don't know. Maybe it's like in that show on the telly. You know – "The truth is out there."'

In Africa the sun beats down hard most days, flattening shadows and bleaching out colours, and photographers have to be out at dawn and dusk to catch their few short minutes of sweet light. So Tommo got up at 4.30 next morning to trek into the hills, while I was up at eight to have breakfast with the manager. By lunchtime I'd already finished all the interviews I'd set up for the day and because I was bored I went looking for Tommo. I'd decided that I liked him.

I found him lurking in the leisure centre, which was already busy with customers. The arcade was infested by white kids from the timeshare villas up the valley, bickering and shouting while they waited for their parents to come out of the casino, beaten for another day. Large white men with moustaches and pudding-bowl haircuts and oddly patterned shirts barged back and forth in twos or threes, followed by thin, bitter women with dry hair and red wrinkled skin. The black customers dressed more formally and came in wary couples or as lively parties of day-trippers. Their well-mannered children stood aside, baffled, watching the white kids scream.

Tommo and I were beginning to find ourselves hilarious: we at least were being paid to be here. The leisure centre was walled with fibreglass rocks and plastic grottoes with fake bushman paintings, and we exchanged a look of silent victory when the old lady from the night before came waddling past us, her handbag still clamped to her armpit.

'I know – let's go to the wave pool!' said Tommo. 'Some idiot might be trying to surf in it, like in that picture in the brochure.'

The wave pool was fan-shaped, fringed with palm trees and artfully placed boulders. At its wider end was a beach of white coral and sand, while the thin end of the wedge lapped into a cave set in a fake rock face. Every minute or two a mechanism inside the cave would hiss and convulse, and a large but listless wave would spread across the pool. A few kids were splashing about in the shallows while their parents lay on towels and recliners by the beach. Waiters in white jackets went back and forth with trays, and the shouts of the children in the pool were answered by the screams of other kids shooting down water slides in another phoney rock face to the right. Tommo led me to an awning by the bar, then stopped to study the beach.

'No surfers, then . . . Pity . . .' he mused. 'Hang on, though, what's this?'

A tall young woman was wading out into the shallow water, dressed in a red swimsuit. Her face was turned away, and all I could see of her was straight brown hair, pale skin and a slender figure. She wore pink flippers on her feet and inflatable red water wings around her upper arms.

Tommo was giggling. 'What the hell is she wearing those floaties for? She's a bit long in the tooth for that kit . . . Right. I'm having a go.'

He ambled off into the palm trees. I ordered two beers and sat on a bar stool and watched the young woman splash her way out into the centre of the pool, then turn on her back and float. The wave machine had been dormant for several minutes, and her arms, buoyed by the water wings, made slow easy circles. Finally she stopped moving altogether and bobbed alone in the water, eyes closed against the sun. Then behind her the wave machine, which had only been biding its time, produced a sudden mighty whoosh, and I watched her struggle to turn over so she could meet the wave face down. But her beach toys seemed to hamper her, and she was still on her back when the wave rolled over her, and when it was past I saw her splutter to the surface, trying to clear the water from her nostrils and eyes. She staggered out of the pool, and I lost sight of her behind a boulder.

The afternoon was hot and I began to feel sleepy. I wondered where Tommo was. Perhaps I could go for a nap. For a pleasant moment my eyes began to close.

Then a woman screamed, and faces snapped up all around the swimming pool.

'You! What the fuck are you doing with that camera? Get out where I can see you!'

I thought of getting out of there, but if Tommo was in trouble, then so was I: I'd breakfasted with the manager that morning, for God's sake. I pulled myself to my feet and moved towards the commotion.

Just beyond a clump of boulders and rubbery bushes stood the woman with the water wings, her face livid. Tommo was cowering in front of her, half hidden in the fronds. Another woman sat bolt upright on a beach towel a couple of yards away, hugging two frightened little boys and staring in dismay. Beyond them, on the path at the back of the fake beach, two security guards were standing and watching. One was talking into his radio.

'Give me that camera!' the woman shouted again. Her accent sounded familiar.

Tommo dithered, then found a voice. 'It's all right, please. I'm a press photographer. I'm just . . .'

Her voice trampled him like an elephant. 'A *press* photographer? What kind of press photographer sneaks around in the bushes taking pictures of women? I'm calling the manager.'

Reluctantly, I took off my sunglasses and stepped forward, hands spread in a gesture of calm. 'Excuse me, madam, but I think there's been a mistake here,' I said, as smoothly as I could. 'This gentleman here is a professional photographer who's on an assignment for us.'

I glimpsed adoration on Tommo's face. Then the woman rounded on me. 'Oh, yeah? Who's "us", so? Are you the hotel management?'

I blinked. I'd hoped to flit in and out of this as a nameless angel of reason.

'No,' I said slowly, 'I'm his boss' – I was careful not to catch his eye – 'and he's working for me on this assignment. I'm writing a travel article, and I've asked him to get pictures of people here enjoying themselves.'

'Oh, yeah? So why was he secretly trying to photo me in my swimsuit?'

Unconsciously she gestured towards her body. My smile was

painful as I fought to keep my eyes on hers. The slightest downward glance could be fatal.

Tommo had come out from the bush and stood meekly, his hands holding his camera behind his back. He looked up and muttered something, then dropped his head again.

She turned on him. 'What did you say?'

He raised his voice. 'I said it was the beach toys.'

'Beach toys?'

'I wanted a picture of you wearing the flippers and the floaties.'

For the first time she seemed taken aback. She looked at me, at her friend with the small children, then back to Tommo. 'Is that your thing? Rubber flippers? Christ.' She paused, staring at Tommo's reddening face, then added more quietly: 'Good job I didn't have a snorkel.'

A smile was creeping across the face of the woman on the beach towel. Her arms relaxed, and the little boys wormed their way around to face us, eyes wide with wonder. The standing woman put her hands on her hips, staring at me, and the water wings squeaked against the sides of her breasts.

It seemed the right moment to get rid of my smile. 'No, seriously. I really am a reporter and he's working with me. We're just looking for offbeat stuff, and I suppose you looked a bit unusual. That's all it was. I promise you, we're not perverts.' I paused. She was still staring at me. 'Well, I'm not anyway. Tommo might be. I haven't known him very long.' Tommo gave me a pained look.

'Why didn't he just ask me if he wanted a picture?' she demanded.

Tommo cleared his throat. 'Even if you said yes you wouldn't have been able to stop yourself posing. It would have been a set-up, not spontaneous. I don't shoot set-ups.'

The two security guards were inching away from the scene, decided. The young woman studied Tommo for a moment and then for the first time I saw her smile.

'If you don't mind my asking,' I said, 'why *are* you wearing water wings? Don't you know how to swim?'

She stopped smiling and looked at me appraisingly. Then she

nodded to the woman on the beach towel and the children in her arms. 'They belong to Ben and Conor. I wanted to see what they felt like. I haven't worn them since I was a little girl.'

Her name was Katey. She taught civil engineering at the University of the Witwatersrand, high on the ridge where Johannesburg was born. I moved into her little house in nearby Melville, an old miner's house with a green tin roof and pressed-steel ceilings, and we lived together there for almost two years. The house had two bedrooms, two bathrooms, a living room and a kitchen, and out the back was the small, square brick room where Bountiful the maid lived with her boyfriend. The garden was mostly lawn, thank God, but twice a month Thembo came all the way from Sebokeng to pull the weeds, mow the grass and smoke dagga in the blind spot behind Bountiful's room. In time I learned that when Thembo was there I should open the porch door noisily and wait a few moments before I went out: it was embarrassing for both of us when I caught him doing nothing.

The garden was bounded by a six-foot wall made of painted concrete panels, but most of this wall was hidden by the trees and bushes that grew up inside it. Once Katey went out with a plant book and tried to identify them all. The sausage tree was easy, as were the syringa, the bottlebrush, the bougainvillea and the jacarandas, but she soon got fed up and went back to the porch. At a mile above sea level our little banana tree would never grow beyond chest height and, unlike the berry bush – the one that Katey couldn't find in the book – it would never bear fruit. For what seemed like half the year the berries dropped into our pool, clogging the filter, and whenever we went away for more than a couple of days we'd come back to find the pool transformed into a black stagnant sump, stirred only by larvae. I never worked out the right mixture of chlorine and acid, so even at its best the pool was green and murky, and when friends brought their kids to the house we had to drag a wire fence around it so they wouldn't fall in. If the house had been ours, not rented, we'd have filled the pool in, and as it was we hardly ever swam there. When I left the house for the last time the water wings that I'd bought for Katey as a joke were still lying in the corner of the back porch, where she'd let them drop two years before. I'd always meant to pick them up.

2

Hugh called me into his office yesterday and sat me down on the sofa away from his desk. He looked very grave. He said he wanted to talk about Cartwright, and I found myself staring past him at the roof slates and chimneys outside the window. On the other side of the courtyard a clump of dock leaves grew from a gutter. The leaves were nodding in the wind.

The police must have worked out by now that something was missing; anyone could have seen that just by looking at the bloodstains in Cartwright's front room. It turned out, though, that Hugh was asking me to take over Cartwright's old job. I felt better when I heard that, though not very much. Why the hell would I want to be Cartwright?

He was a nasty piece of work: most people learned that on the first meeting. He wasn't tall or strong, or physically striking in any way apart from his limp. His hair seemed a little too dark, maybe, and the skin of his face, although lined, was strangely soft and pink. What really worried you about him was his looming stillness. He was like one of those giant boulders you see in the American desert, perched on narrow pinnacles of rock, that make you think, 'It may not have fallen in millions of years, but now's as good a time as any, and I'm standing right beneath it.' Cartwright didn't blink much, and his voice was horribly soft and mild.

Like a secret policeman, Cartwright had survived several regime changes at the paper through efficiency, hard work and sneering loyalty to the strongman of the day. He could never hope to be editor – he scared the directors too much – but his dominion covered three whole floors, from the caseroom right up to features. He found me in the newsroom on my first freelance shift, even though they'd hidden me in an out-of-the-way corner. Without saying anything Cartwright picked up the typescript I'd set on my desktop – yes, it was that long ago, just; our paper has always been the slowest here to modernize – and read the first paragraphs. Then he smiled into the air above me, walked over to the newsdesk and rammed the typescript down on the spike. I found out later that his nickname was 'Vlad'.

He wandered off, talking quietly over his shoulder. 'Too clever for us, Mr . . . Simmons, is it? Write it again, and this time please lead with the principal facts. We don't want anything clever. Remember, history gets written from newspapers. And we are a journal of record.'

A journal of record, for the love of God. And from a man of his age too . . . And I soon learned that it was worse than that: Cartwright had taken it upon himself to keep notes and files on his fellow employees – or at least those who were junior to him. He'd a whole cabinet stuffed with his dossiers, and you knew someone was in trouble when you saw Cartwright lurking about with one of these under his arm. His chosen victim would be dragged across the street to the café – for privacy, Cartwright said – but he knew that half the people in the office used to hang out there. Once he had you in the café he'd buy you one non-alcoholic beverage of your choice, sit you down, cough once or twice and open your file, and inside the file he'd have lots of clippings and typescripts of stories you'd written. And all of this was done off his own bat, in his own time; he hadn't been told to do it by anyone higher up, and whenever he tried it with the senior reporters they'd tell him to fuck off.

Well, I for one won't be keeping any records. Cartwright's desk, still vacant, is opposite mine in our little alcove off the newsroom. Like Cartwright I have special computer access that allows me to spy on the minions while they write and edit. I never bother, of course; that would be too much like work, and I allowed Hugh to rescue me only on the understanding that there wouldn't be too much of that. Because I work mostly night shifts, all the real decisions have been made before I walk in the door. I just sweep up a bit, a little light polishing. The only major headache I have is when there's a late-running story and reporters come looking for advice.

Some bother me more than others. There's a hulking oaf called Ted Hetherton who always, always drops his intros – the very crime that Cartwright pulled me up for that first day. I tell him to vary his game but he never does. There's Niamh Hanrahan, the social affairs correspondent, whatever that is, who twice came to me with questions of ethics. There's a crime reporter, Harry McDowell, who files perfectly straight and balanced pieces but then insists on coming up to me afterwards muttering about all the conspiracy angles and mad rumours he's been forced to leave out. And there's Lucy Viner, who seldom has any problems but who talks to me all the same. Sometimes late in the evening, when she's finished, she stops by my desk on her way to the door. They all drink in one of those new palaces down on the river, and she says I really should drop by some night. I make a joke and dodge the invitation. She's very assured. It worries me a little that some evening she might happen to walk into the late bar where I sit with my strangers. Seen in the dim light and mirrors, she could look like several people I used to know.

I wonder what Lucy and the rest of them would think if they knew what Cartwright had filed away on me. I'd flattered myself that I was past caring about stuff like that, but Cartwright's folder has taught me otherwise. I almost feel grateful to him, the prying old bastard. He's given me something to hide from again, and hiding is almost a game.

'Hot Metal' they call me behind my back here, though the old lead type was gone before my time. Perhaps it's because I seem old school to them, though most of them here aren't much younger than me. Or perhaps it's because of that rumour that I set off detectors at airports. Which I would, as it happens, if I ever travelled any more. The other day Lucy Viner asked me why I never go away on holiday. I laughed and told her I'm frightened of terror- ists. Fact is, I reckon I've done enough travelling. I've chosen my ground.

I was never a natural nomad, not like some of the others. Most of my friends in Africa had been dislocated in childhood, shunted about a bit; it seems to me that once you've lived in more than a couple of places in your early years you'll never be able to settle fully, you'll always be dogged by the stranger you were. This doesn't apply to me – I come from a long line of settled country folk, had my own reasons for running off to Africa – but I'm thinking of people like Tommo. Before he was seven years old his family had taken him from Italy to Scotland to Australia. No one loved Australia more than he did – he was always going on about it, if you let him – yet he'd left it, and, for all his yakking about the Blue Mountains and the Top End or wherever, I never once heard him talk about wanting to move back.

Brereton's father was a former British army officer who had tried and failed at several lines of work before taking a job as a farm manager near Mount Kenya. He'd recently married a much younger woman, he needed to make good, and the Mau Mau rebellion was supposed to be over. Things worked out okay for a while, his wife told the police, until one morning he went out to the paddock and found the cattle had been hamstrung. Fearing for his wife's safety, she said, he sent her off to Nairobi, and the last time she saw him he was sitting on the porch with a self-loading rifle. When the search party arrived they found no sign of a struggle, but Brereton's father was never seen or heard from again. He hadn't even known that his young wife was pregnant; neither did she, at the time. Brereton's mother remarried (rather too quickly, Brereton hinted once, a little more drunk than usual), a man who managed a neighbouring farm, and as a kid the young Charlie was dragged around after them to Bulawayo, Durban, London and, latterly, Poole in Dorset. His mother died there when he was still rather young. How many times and in how many ways can a person be exiled? No wonder Brereton spent so much time on the road, or turned out the way he did.

Or consider Beatrice. She was a diplomat brat, educated at expensive international schools in four different countries. She spoke perfect English and – as far as I could make out – perfect French as well. She told me her father had been a military attaché at the French embassy in Washington when he met her mother, who was some kind of writer. That's about as much as she ever told me about herself, directly.

Once, early on in the affair, I told her that I liked her name, although I'm not sure I did really. She said that her father had called her after some place where he'd once served in French Indochina, years before she was born. I said it was a strange name for an army post, and she laughed and said that her full Christian names were Beatrice Gabrielle Huguette Dominique Eliane. Well, there was a coded warning for me; what a pity I didn't work it out at the time. I suppose it's easier now, what with all these new search engines. But I'll bet Fine picked up on the names straight away, if she ever bothered telling him. Fine knew everything. You could see it in his face, although to be fair he usually did try to hide it.

It still bothers me a little that I knew who Fine was before I even met him. It was almost as if he were famous, though he wasn't, back then.

It was a year after I came to Africa, and Tommo and I had just gone overland to Rwanda after finishing up a story in Burundi – the one that got poor Vincent killed. In those days when you went to Rwanda you had to go to the information ministry in Kigali and give them two passport photos, and they'd staple one of the photos to your temporary press card and staple the other into a big register that they kept on a desk. You could look through the register while you waited for your card to be issued. It was a good way to find out who was around at the time.

News was slow in Rwanda just then, so there was only one other photograph in that day's page in the ledger. I suppose it was the name of the *New York Chronicle*, printed beneath the photograph in the clerk's careful writing, that made me look twice at the photograph. The black and white face was handsome, though not remarkably so. It suggested that its subject's hair was dark blond, or perhaps light brown, and that he wore, or perhaps affected, a look of faint puzzlement. That's how I've always remembered him. It's how he looks in that photo I took. Apart from that expression, I've always found it difficult to bring Fine to mind. I never could decide

23

about him. I never could work out if his hair was blond or light brown.

Tommo pulled the ledger round towards himself and flicked to the previous day's page. He leaned forward for a moment, to read without his glasses, and then he looked up at me and laughed. 'Guess what!' he said. 'Jesper Jansson's in town!'

We found Jansson's tent in its usual place on the roof of the Hôtel des Mille Collines, tied between a ventilation stack and a clump of rusty aerials. A sat-phone was set up beside it, and the warm breeze ruffled a stack of French comic books just inside its flap. The childhood smell of old tarpaper rose from the warm roof, laced with Turkish tobacco, and we followed our noses, dodging chimneys and wires, until we came upon Jansson himself. He was sitting high on the parapet and smoking a cigarette, looking out across a long valley of green treetops and red earth and silver roofs, his cameras set on the wall beside him and his feet dangling in space. At the foot of the hill, obscured by the trees, the cars of early evening were yapping and growling around the Place de la Constitution. Children played noisily in a neighbouring compound, and off behind the hotel somewhere two dogs were engaged in a barking duel. Brereton, who had been there in April '94, told me once that when the Tutsis captured the city, putting an end to the massacres, they had to send parties to shoot all the strays. The masterless dogs had grown insolent, and much too fat.

Tommo called Jansson's name, and he turned and gazed sadly down at us before he allowed himself to smile. He always looked like a solemn child until he smiled or frowned and showed you where his lines were hiding. He had brown hair, rather dark for a Finn, but grey Baltic eyes.

'I'm pleased to see you,' Jansson said formally, the way he spoke when he was sober or very drunk. 'I've just ordered beer. I will order some more. And have you both eaten?'

We followed Jansson back to his tent, where he switched on his sat-phone and called the bar downstairs to order up room service. It took him ages to get the order right; his famous year in Paris had done little for his French.

Waiters brought up food and beer, and after Jansson gave them a very big tip they went, unbidden, and found us some bar stools in a storeroom by the lift. We put our plates and our glasses up on the parapet and ate looking out over the valley.

Not for the first time, the Amalgamated News agency didn't know what to do with Jansson, so it had parked him in Rwanda while it worked out his next move. They could have sent him back to his wife and kids in Jo'burg, I suppose, but his bureau chief wanted to keep him as far from the office as possible. And Jansson didn't seem to mind much. He was the purest nomad I ever met.

Jansson made another thirty-dollar call to room service, and we took what was left of our old beers, now warm, and moved to the other side of the roof to watch the sun sink into the hills. Night thickened in the east. It was still too hazy for the stars to appear but the strobe of an aircraft moved noiselessly in the high western sky. Beneath us lights were coming on up and down the valley, shimmering through the gently waving branches. Dark figures drifted slowly along the road beyond the hotel gate, strollers taking part in the vast, continent-wide promenade by which Africans mark their single soft hour of twilight. Below us, somewhere in the shadows by the car park, someone was listening to the British world service on a short-band radio, its hiss transformed by distance into comforting white noise, the screams of the day soothed to a murmur.

Tommo and Jansson were deep in their own conversation, talking about ethics and techniques and workshops they'd been to – photographers are always going off to workshops and exhibitions and conferences to talk about stuff like that. I don't know why. You never hear about reporters doing anything like that. We just get on with things. A chair scraped somewhere behind us and I thought it was the waiters again until a figure loomed beside me, and I looked around and saw the face from the register. He had a laptop bag over his shoulder and a sat-phone under his elbow, still in its carry-case, and he stood there looking slightly awkward, as if he didn't know whether to be shy or annoyed at finding us there. In one hand he was dragging along one of the bar stools that we'd left on the other side of the roof. Finally he made up his mind and offered me his hand, the one that was clamped to his side at the elbow, and he muttered that he was Nathan Fine and that he was from the *New York Chronicle*. I already knew that, of course, but I wasn't going to tell him.

So we all talked for a while, the usual thing, trying to work out what stories the other guy was doing. The world turned black and the city lights steadied as the breeze died away. Jansson heard his sat-phone ringing on the other side of the roof and he went off to answer it. The waiter brought more drinks and we shared them with Fine while he set up his own phone: he couldn't find a satellite from the window of his room.

Fine pressed the on button and now I could see his face dimly in the green light from the LCD. He looked up, hesitated a moment and then asked: 'Your friend Jesper . . . What's he doing with that tent?'

'He sleeps in it, mate,' said Tommo. I could hear the amusement in his voice.

There was a pause. 'Why?'

'Jansson says he's had malaria so often that he's sworn he'll take no more chances,' I said. 'The tent has a built-in mosquito net.'

'And the hotels let him do that?'

'He does a deal with the managers. He pays for a room on the top floor so he can lock his stuff there and use the bathroom and whatever.'

There were a few moments of silence while Fine fiddled with his aerial and studied the read-out, finding the satellite. Then he spoke again. 'So why doesn't he just put up the tent in the room and sleep in it there? It's small enough. He could pull the fabric back and use just the net.'

Tommo laughed. 'That's a good question,' he said.

'Maybe he has some other reason for sleeping on roofs?'

'Who knows?'

We left Fine to make his calls. On the way back to the stairwell I saw Jansson, a pale shape in the darkness, crouched behind the ventilation stack and murmuring as if to himself. You could tell from how quiet he was that he was talking to his wife. They never shouted when they were together, either. They just stared at each other in uncomprehending misery.

This was Tommo's first trip to Rwanda so he wanted to visit one of the sites they'd preserved. I'd seen it before so I stayed by the car and watched him pick his way up the hill through drifts of rags and bone and hair. It was difficult not to step on them.

Tommo didn't take any pictures that day. We were the only visitors, and the curator followed Tommo at a distance until he got to the cluster of low brick buildings that once had been a school, and then the curator held back and let him go inside alone. It was worse in there, I remembered; you could make out children's hand prints in the black smears on the walls. And then the curator followed Tommo down the hill to the car and wanted to tell us all about what had happened there and of course we had to listen, there was no getting out of it. The curator spoke very quietly, and you could see in his face why he needed to explain.

Back at the hotel we found that Jansson had gone, leaving a little wedge-shaped carpet of cigarette butts pointing to the place on the roof where the tent had been. An empty whiskey bottle stood on the parapet, a forlorn sentry, and Tommo picked it up and turned it over in his hands a couple of times before sadly replacing it. He cheered up, though only a little, when he saw a note on the floor of our room, just inside the door. The note said: 'I have to bail. Talk to Fine. Jesper.'

We found Fine in the hotel bar that evening. He sat by the wall in a corner near the door, as far as he could from the girls roosting on their bar stools. They were tall and slender, with long necks and oval eyes, and Brereton swore to me once that some of them were transvestites. I don't know how he would know that. I couldn't tell.

Fine stood up to greet us. He seemed shy again, like the night before, and as he talked he couldn't help spreading his palms before him, smiling on one side of his face as if he were spieling on behalf of someone else, someone he didn't quite believe in.

He said that there was a feature he wanted to do in Zaire but he had no one to take the photos. When he called his paper the night before, after we'd met him, they had told him that Amalgamated News was offering to hire out the services of someone called Jansson, but when he returned to the roof to talk to Jansson himself Jansson said he couldn't do it: his little girl had fallen ill and he had to go straight back to Johannesburg. Jansson had recommended that Fine take Tommo instead. Jansson had said that Tommo was the best young freelancer around.

Fine paused, eyebrows raised, and lowered both hands to his beer glass. For a moment he glanced at me and then he looked back at Tommo, who was sitting on his stool trying not to look too pleased with himself. Any snapper would have been delighted to shoot for the *Chronicle*, but for Tommo praise from Jansson counted even more.

He'd the sense to say nothing, though, so Fine gave me another look and then finished his pitch. He was going to travel to Goma, he said, to do a story about the mountain gorillas. Because of all the recent trouble it was months since anyone had seen them, but the conservation agency was prepared to lay on a trip for the man from the *Chronicle*. He was going to rediscover the gorillas, Fine said, and he gave a little laugh.

As he spoke he glanced at me once or twice, but I just sat there, smiling blandly and inwardly calculating. How many words would I get from this story, who could I sell them to, and how much would I get paid for them? And would anyone help with the expenses? Who would pay for the car?

'Sounds good,' I said loudly, and Fine turned to me reluctantly. There was no way to withdraw an offer he hadn't made.

'I reckon I'm in too, then,' said Tommo.

And that did it. We were both secretly thrilled, of course. We'd always wanted to see the gorillas.

The Goma representative of the international conservation agency was a Fleming who had lived in the Congo for most of his life. His mouth was always smiling. He showed us a poster on the wall of his office, a close-up of a gorilla's face with the words *Protégez Moi* printed across the bottom. In Kenya, he said, President Moi's goons had called to the agency's Nairobi office to beat up the staff and seize all the posters. He giggled like a schoolboy. A picture of Mobutu hung above his desk on a wall that was otherwise bare.

The Kivus were almost peaceful right then, and for a change there was no curfew. Think of the Children threw a big party in its compound that night, so Tommo and I were still pretty drunk when the Fleming called for us at four the next morning. Fine was okay: he'd gone home early. The Fleming took the wheel of our jeep and drove us north for an hour through forests and refugee camps and fields of weeds and lava slag, until we turned right onto a dirt road pointing up towards Visoke. The jeep churned up steep wooded tracks, slipping and spinning in the fresh mud, until we came to a halt a couple of hundred yards below the park warden's hut on the last open meadow. The long grass shone with yellow flowers and the valley below lay clear in the morning air, electric-green forest creeping out onto lava slabs, smoke wisping from the crater, but behind us the jagged Virungas were combing the clouds. A tracker and a guide were waiting for us, and two park wardens with long Belgian rifles, and we had to sign a book and pay the hundred-dollar tourist fee and fifteen dollars for nature tax and something upfront for the guides, and then they led us up to the abrupt edge of the cloud forest, dripping like a shower curtain.

We smoked and drank too much, Tommo and me. As we hauled ourselves up the steep track, if that's what it was, a stinking paste of dead leaves and writhing insects slid away beneath our feet. We had to grab at twigs and roots to pull ourselves upwards, and often just to stop from slipping back, and thorns tore our hands and ants bit us to distraction. Fine seemed all right, though; he was up front with the trackers and the wardens, talking to them in French, asking them about their work and their families. From what little I could hear above the sound of my own heart and lungs, Fine seemed to think that maybe this was a life they'd chosen from a big range of options. I don't think they knew what to make of him, all these personal questions. You could see they were embarrassed, giving short little answers and polite little laughs. I think even Fine could see that, but it wasn't going to stop him. It made me wonder who he was talking to.

The Fleming took the lead, forcing the pace as if he weren't twenty years older than any of the rest of us. He smoked filterless local cigarettes and every now and then he'd stop to light one and we'd drag ourselves up level with him, and he would flash us a quizzical smile as we dropped to the ground and then he'd be off again in a cloud of sulphur.

By the time we reached ten thousand feet Tommo and I were finished, blown by the climb, sick from drink and dehydration, and I almost didn't notice when Fine finally stopped talking. Then I saw him with the guides, right in front of us, crouched down and listening, and the Fleming was pinching off the end of a freshly lit cigarette. I heard nothing for a while, and then there was the sound of branches breaking all around us in the wet undergrowth, followed by a symphony of farts.

The big male didn't like us much but he couldn't find the energy to chase us away, so most of the time he sat with his back turned to us and arms folded huffily, half turning from time to time to shoot us cutting looks. It might as well have been an actor in a suit. The Fleming told us not to stand up tall or catch the chief's eye – he might take that for a challenge – and every few seconds one of the guides would cough apologetically, the way you do to let a stranger know you don't mean to be a bother. The infants played chase through the branches above us while their mothers foraged through the undergrowth, often invisible, their presence revealed by the breaking of twigs and wind and the smell of rancid armpits. Every few minutes the male would grunt and move off a few yards, and when he did the whole band would drift slowly on in the same direction, keeping station around him.

The rules said you could have only one hour with the gorillas. The time came – after only minutes, it seemed – when the Fleming put up his hand to hold us where we were. Then he turned, looked past us, and leaned over to whisper: 'Here's the other one. He's never far behind.'

Another adult male, smaller than the first, came slowly through the bushes. He looked around him, stared into my eyes for a moment, and then began to feed, fully exposed at the other end of a tiny clearing. Tommo squeezed past me, raising his camera: none of the other gorillas had presented itself so well, clear of all the undergrowth.

'He's the chief's younger brother,' whispered the Fleming, 'but he's now too big to stay with the family. The chief chased him off last year.'

Apart from the chief the other gorillas had all ignored us, but this one was fascinated by Tommo, or perhaps by his camera. He kept inching towards him, sniffing the air, and every time the gorilla drew nearer Tommo would back away, like the rules said you had to, but every time the gorilla followed him again. Tommo had to make a little half-circle, edging backwards, to avoid being caught between the gorilla and the edge of the clearing. When he was free, almost back on the trail again, I saw him fiddle with the controls of his camera, and then he set it carefully amid the thick branches of a low bush, its wide-angle lens pointing back at the gorilla. Then Tommo backed towards me, muttering 'timer' from the corner of his mouth, as if he didn't want the ape to hear.

The gorilla advanced in another little bound, reached the camera, stared at it, sniffed the lens, and then stretched out a hand and gingerly poked it. The camera, caught in the bush, pivoted round, and then the timer clicked and the motor drive whirred and the gorilla panicked and bolted off into the undergrowth, ripping through the bushes.

Somewhere behind us Fine cleared his throat. 'So I guess it's true what they say about snappers, Tommo,' he said. 'A monkey really could do your job.'

I had a print of that photo on my wall in Johannesburg. Perhaps the landlord kept it, when he cleared out my things. It doesn't matter; I can still see it clearly. Tilted to the left, the wide-angle image squeezes all three of us into one corner of the frame – Tommo refused to crop it, of course. I'm on the left of the group, sweating and grinning, while Tommo, unbalanced as he backs away, looks like he's falling into my arms. On the right stands Fine, arms folded and eyebrows raised, half smiling towards the camera. It would be an amusing picture even if you didn't know the story behind it. Fine told Tommo that he should submit it for a world press award, or perhaps for one of those gimmicky art prizes they like so much in London. But Tommo refused: he said that as far as he was concerned the gorilla owned the copyright.

3

So that's how Fine comes into it. A chance meeting, a kid somewhere with measles, and you can be stuck with someone, one way
or other, for the rest of your life. I suppose I'd have met Fine
anyway, sooner or later, because he was coming to work out of
Johannesburg. But what if he'd met some other people first, in
some other hotel or airport – would he have imprinted on them
instead? Might we have been spared one another? Most of the other
American bureau chiefs lived a sedate life of tennis games and
dog-walking, and polite dinner parties with diplomats and ministers
and business tycoons. If Fine had hooked up with his true peer
group first, would we ever have done much more than nod to each
other at press conferences? But the *Chronicle*'s Nairobi correspondent had fallen sick, and Fine had been sent out early to fill in for
her, before taking up his own post in South Africa. And so by
chance we were the first to discover him. And after that Fine always
preferred to work with us, on the cheap side of the beat. Years later
Armitage told me that their bosses had been worried when they
heard about the sort of people Fine travelled with: they thought
Fine had too much future to be allowed to stray so far. Armitage
said there'd been a lot of debate about giving Fine the bureau in
the first place, him being so young by the *Chronicle*'s reckoning. But
Fine had quickly vindicated his selection, fulfilling his representative
role on the Jo'burg cocktail circuit (he was careful not to invite
most of us more than once) and boring himself stupid with set-piece
interviews with presidents and ministers. And there was no denying
how good he was. Only Laura Guenther ever had better story ideas
than Fine had, and she was just a snapper.

There used to be a joke in the trade back then. The joke went as
follows: 'How many Bosnia correspondents does it take to change

a light bulb? You don't know? (Voice rises angrily.) Well, of course *you* don't know! *You* weren't there!'

Laura had been there, Beatrice too, at a time when I was still hiding from Cartwright. That's how they knew each other. Laura had also done the Gulf War, Central America, her pick of assignments for magazines in Germany and the States. I should have been overawed by her – actually, I was – but she took to me from the start. It helped that I was the first colleague she met after she arrived in South Africa, but she was under no obligation to keep me on her books, not even after I helped her move into her new house in Johannesburg.

Laura had chosen a bungalow that stood in an overgrown garden at the end of a long driveway in Parktown North. The house was built of grey concrete slabs, with glass walls and matt-steel window frames, and inside each room a brushed-steel dimmer switch controlled access to the desired quantity of detached cold light. I see it now as unfurnished, as it was when I helped her move into it, and again three years later, when I helped her move out. The rooms were all decorated alike – eggshell plaster walls, pale, slightly scuffed oak floor tiles. The first time I saw them the rooms were softened by a layer of dust and a musty smell, just enough to remind you that people had once lived there; the house had been unlet for a long time. The lounge, which fronted on a long patio, was soaked in grey light from the autumn evening. It wasn't cold, but when I turned on the light switch I almost shivered. Then I heard Laura come in behind me, struggling with the first of her suitcases, and I had to go to help.

You might have thought that Laura would repaint the place but she liked it as it was. Above the fireplace in the lounge she hung a large abstract weaving made of sisal yarn, ochre and brown and burnt orange, which seemed to suggest sections cut from a globe, and during her stay she gradually lined the walls with African sculptures and masks and utensils, each carefully poised on its own hardwood plinth. Fixed in sterile light from hidden fittings, the art works stared sadly back at you, like specimens pinned to a card.

Laura didn't buy a lot of furniture – she never knew for sure if she would be around much longer, because her people were always trying to relocate her to places they cared about – but what she did buy was in keeping with the house: square and spare, in dull earth colours, always a little too hard. Each of the two bedrooms contained a double futon, an occasional table, a bedside lamp, two chairs and a single smaller version of the weaving that hung in the lounge. Bushes grew up outside the bedroom windows, staining the daylight an undersea green. I suppose she must have liked that too, or she would have had the bushes trimmed.

We had first met in Cape Town during parliamentary briefing week. I was driving along beneath the elevated section of the N1 motorway, where it runs on stilts above the commercial docks, when I saw a woman walking on a deserted footpath. She was staggering along in an easterly direction, wearing what looked like a trouser suit, her shoulder drooping under the weight of one of those bucket-sized telephoto lenses that you usually only see on the touchline at sporting events. Every few steps she'd slow and half turn and throw a look back over her other shoulder, then she'd pick up the pace once more. The late-afternoon traffic was thundering on the highway overhead but down on the derelict fringes of the docklands the traffic was slower and light. I drove right past her and then, thinking she might be in trouble, I stopped my car and reversed back along the empty road. Pieces of litter scuttled away in the wind from Table Mountain, paper crustaceans seeking the sea. As I wound down my window she pursed her lips and frowned. She was tall, with short reddish hair and broad shoulders, and her flared shirt sleeves revealed wrists and forearms dark with freckles.

'Hello,' she said briskly. 'You are parked in my shot.'

'Your what?'

'My shot. I'm doing a portrait.' Her accent was German.

I pulled my head back into the car, using the mirrors to check all around me. Then I looked back at her. She was still staring at me, head to one side, lips pursed in vexation.

'There's nobody else here,' I said.

She shook her head impatiently and waved an arm in the direction of Signal Hill. I leaned forward to look up through the windscreen. There, high on the rearing ramp of the unfinished motorway, black against the failing sun, a distant figure raised a hand, held it aloft in what seemed to be interrogation and then wearily let it drop again. I turned back to the stranger. She was propping her heavy lens up on its monopod, squinting through her viewfinder.

It seems that Laura had fallen in love with those films they used to make years ago, the ones that followed tiny figures as they made their way slowly across vast, uncaring landscapes of stone or sand or concrete, driven by stark impulses of greed or revenge. It was not those emotions in particular that interested her, I realized later, but the illusion of distance: in those days directors filmed their subjects from halfway round the world. And they showed you things; they didn't tell you about them. Which is perhaps why Laura never told me what she knew about Beatrice. Why else would you hold back a story like that?

People were always rising against Mobutu, had been for decades, but in a place like the Congo it was easy not to notice. Then the new lot – Tutsis, Rwandans, Che Guevara retro-groupies, whoever they were meant to be – captured Bukavu and laid siege to Goma, and we had to launch ourselves at the story in the usual headless dash.

The Kigali-based agency people were first to the Rwanda–Zaire border, as you might expect, and the Nairobi crowd was there half a day later, on charters from Wilson airport. Next, through Entebbe or Wilson or Kenyatta, came the Johannesburg contingent, and the firemen and bigfeet and freelance explorers arrived two or three days later, a stream of cars and jeeps coming westwards from Kigali, through the green hills and down to the lake.

It had been a while since Africa last hosted such a parade of stars. From New York came UBC's Kitty Krauser, who had wept on air for the children of Sarajevo. 24/7 sent Bob Reilly, who could claim to have covered the fall of Saigon, albeit from a ship out to sea. The Brits had so many people fighting to cover the story – radio and television, news and current affairs, reporters based in London, Jo'burg, Nairobi and Abidjan – that they couldn't decide who to send, so they sent all of them. Alas in vain: they all were bigfooted by Timothy Drysdale, who arrived last of all in his own chartered KingAir. Drysdale wrote bestselling books about his excursions, finding hope amid the darkness.

There were many others whom we didn't know at all. France, Italy, Germany and Spain contributed TV celebrities of their own, tanned middle-aged men and sleek, expensively dressed younger women. Most of the big papers and magazines also sent out star reporters with orders to seize the story from their people in the field.

The arrival of so many new people on our patch was intimidating, of course, and it was heartbreak for those who were bigfooted; Polly Vermeulen came all the way from Jo'burg to freelance for 24/7, only to be dumped when she got there because some New York staff producer decided to come out himself. But there was one consolation, the only one that counted: watching them arrive at our hotel in Gisenyi we knew that our story was big-time once more.

By the end of a week the old hands agreed that this was the biggest story on the beat since the Goma refugee crisis of two years before. We were now the custodians of this ancient history, and for a day or two the newcomers would sit round us on the terrace by the pool, cramming themselves on our background – even Fine could set himself up as an expert by now. Brereton, who was already a tribal elder, went around telling people how back in '94 he'd seen the hotel's pool filled with slaughtered bodies. I'm not sure if this was true, but I do know that nobody swam there, though one or two people fell in. Much of what we said would come back to us later, in mutant form, on the TV in the bar or in other people's stories. A couple of times I recognized myself as an 'informed source': it was like feeding bone meal to cattle. But most people had no choice but to turn cannibal: the Zairean rebels, or the Rwandan army, or whoever it was who now held Goma and was still supposedly fighting for the outskirts and the airport, had closed the border, and we were all stuck in Gisenyi in Rwanda, two miles away on the wrong side of the frontier, waiting to cross.

Beside the hotel a stretch of coarse grass ran down to the edge of the lake, beyond which the water hazed seamlessly into the horizon. After breakfast you could drive or stroll along the lake-shore to hang around at the border post, distilling news from gossip. The road ran between tall trees infested by fish eagles and, on the landward side, rows of big mansions, alpine follies built for the Belgians long ago.

It was the rainy season, and at the border you could watch the black and grey clouds build over Rwanda, blurring the banana trees high on the hills, then sliding down to the lake. The cool wind gave warning, and when the squall lines hissed in, seeming to pick up speed at the last instant, like tracer rounds, there was always time to find shelter, a tree or a doorway, from which to watch them pass.

The Zairean side of the border was blocked by a gang of empty-eyed children whose ancient Russian sub-machine guns were held together with string and insulation tape. Beyond their striped wooden boom the road into Goma was lined with Ugandan trucks trapped by the war. Their drivers slept all day wherever there was shade from the sun and shelter from the rain, the wind off the lake picking at their clothes. Close by, a group of brightly dressed Rwandan market women sat quietly on the steps of the Zairean emigration office, their sacks and trays empty, patiently waiting for the border gods to raise the boom and let them go home. Their Congolese counterparts sat only a few yards away, stranded with us on the Rwandan side, identical but opposite, as if trapped in a mirror. The boom was designed only to stop vehicles; the border was unfenced; if the two groups of women could touch at one point, why should anyone care if they quietly melted into each other then drew apart once more, like the globules in a lava lamp? But the teenaged gunmen kicked viciously at any woman who strayed close to the line. Mzungus could go right up to the border but were careful not to put a toe across it. African states, however hollow, are jealous of the borders that the Europeans left them.

As evening fell and the sun sank towards the wall of the Western

Rift Valley, its light would pour along the road that led towards Goma, and the trees on either side of the road seemed to form the entrance to a tunnel, or the barrel of a gun. And every now and then a mortar round would fall to the north or the west, shaking the earth, beyond the avocado trees with their unripe fruit and the cinderblock walls and the tin roofs of Goma, hanging from the rain clouds by thick ropes of smoke.

It was on such an evening that Beatrice showed up. A squall had turned to drizzle, and Fine and I were sheltering under a tree out in no man's land, by the frontier boom. Tommo had gone off with our jeep, looking for cigarettes, and we were waiting for him to come back for us. We didn't want to walk back in the rain. Jansson was there too, sitting on a stump and waiting for a lift back to the hotel with his TV colleagues, Extrastrong and Rasheed. They were packing up their camera gear, shutting down their border watch for another day.

From time to time a big cold drop, flushed by the breeze from the lake, would ricochet down through all the leaves and branches and penetrate our clothes. The sound of an engine rose in the east, but when the car came around the bend in the Corniche it was only a Kigali taxi. It stopped thirty yards away, beside the shuttered Rwandan customs office, where a sentry hugged the shelter of the porch. Off to the left you could just make out several more border guards posted under the trees, given away by the gleam of wet ponchos.

The taxi stood there for a couple of minutes, engine idling, the sound loud above the pattering drops and the low drone of voices. Then the passenger door clunked open and a woman got out. She stepped clear of the door, holding it open, looking around her, and then she spotted our group in the shadow beneath the avocado tree. She said something to her driver and took a camera and a black canvas satchel from the car, closed the door and came walking towards us across the mud and weeds of no man's land. I heard Jansson mutter something to himself in Swedish or Finnish – he was a bit of both – and then she stopped in front of us, beyond the sheltering branches, blinked the drizzle from her eyes and asked rather loudly if anyone knew Laura Guenther.

So Fine said yes, and he was telling her about the hotel, and which room Laura was in, while behind me Jansson grabbed my elbow and used it to lever himself to his feet. The stranger was trying to understand Fine's directions as Jansson stepped up to her with an odd expression on his face – it might have been a smile – but she didn't seem to notice him, so he stood there for a few moments more and then he reached up and touched her shoulder, and she turned and saw him and didn't say anything more.

'Hello, Beatrice,' said Jansson. 'I didn't know that you'd be here.'
'Jesper,' she said.

Then her expression too became something like a smile, and she abruptly placed one hand on his shoulder and pulled him forward a couple of inches and kissed him on both cheeks. The gesture was performed quickly and almost formally, the way a distracted aunt might say hello to you, and then she stepped back and Jansson was left holding empty air as he turned around to smile at us.

'This is Beatrice,' he said. 'She's an old friend from Bosnia.' And he proceeded to introduce us all in turn, even Extrastrong and Rasheed, who were in a hurry to get back to the hotel. South Africans don't take well to the rain.

Jansson got to me last and Beatrice took my hand, still trying to look interested. Her hair was dark but the drizzle had coated it with a film of fine silver. Her eyes seemed to be blue, or perhaps they were green, shifting to blue in the last light: there was something in their composition that confused me. She wore jeans and a T-shirt, now greying in the rain, and I watched her raise her arms to hug herself. Standing there like that, poised but blinking, beginning to shiver, she looked like a child forced to swim in the winter, working up nerve for the plunge. And that's how she's stayed with me. Perhaps it seemed to me then that I'd be someone who would help her.

'If you want,' I said, 'I can take you to Laura. But you'll have to give Fine and me a lift to the hotel. Our friend has abandoned us, and we're scared of the dark.'

She didn't reply for a second or two, still hugging herself but no longer shivering, and I was beginning to feel as if I'd made an improper suggestion when abruptly she nodded.

'Sure,' she said. 'There's plenty of room in my taxi.'

When I looked round for Jansson he'd already gone. I suppose he must have left with the TV crew.

For six years Extrastrong Hlongwane and Rasheed Williams had covered the Zulu troubles for Amalgamated News, tearing up and down the N2 from Port Shepstone to Pongola. The Zaire thing was supposed to be a reward for their heroism, their first trip away from South Africa, but when they arrived the chief producer in the field, who'd flown out from London, gave them the job that none of the agency's other crews wanted. Every morning, when all their colleagues were still in bed, they had to drive down to the border post, set up their camera and stay there, all day long, just in case something happened.

Rasheed really hated it. He was a nervy guy from the Cape Flats who always had to be operating and he couldn't sit still for more than two minutes, not even sober. Extrastrong was tall and slender, with a long thin nose and a sad patient smile, the kind you see painted on medieval saints. He was always giving Rasheed errands to run, just to keep him occupied. He'd send him off for cigarettes, or sweets, or back to the hotel for fresh batteries that he didn't really need, and as Rasheed went trotting off, happy again, Extrastrong would smile to himself and turn back to his camera, set up on its tripod. Folded around the camera, fixing the world through its big wide-eyed lens, Extrastrong looked like an anglepoise lamp.

The morning after Beatrice turned up Extrastrong and Rasheed drove down to the border very early, and before Extrastrong had set up his sticks or Rasheed had time to get bored someone shouted across the boom at them and told them the border was open again. Which is how Amalgamated News scooped all the other agencies that day by moving the first TV shots from Goma, when the streets were still empty apart from a couple of fresh corpses and the debris from the looting. We were pretty quick off the mark ourselves –

Fine had told Tommo and me to pay our hotel bills the night before, just in case, he said innocently, we needed a fast getaway – but by the time we made it across to Goma the streets there were already full of people cheering and dancing and singing, celebrating whatever it was that they hoped had got better.

A lot of people wrote up the story that night as 'the liberation of Goma', even though the rebels had controlled the town for days before they let us in. The locals did seem pleased to see us. Doors flew open and the streets filled with people, and there was ululating and cheering and backslapping, and young men punched fists in the air and sang the praises of Laurent Kabila and Paul Kagame and Yoweri Museveni, smiling with their mouths and casting little darting looks at the stony-faced gunmen watching from the corners. Old men in shirts and ties planted themselves in front of us and made long, inaudible speeches, while the girls stood to one side and simpered demurely.

Before it left, the Zairean army had used dynamite and RPGs to blow open all the bank safes in town, so the people were dancing on streets paved with money, Zairean notes too worthless to pick up. The bottom layer was compacted and slippy with damp but the notes above rustled free in the breeze, gathering in gutters, sticking to the blood that seeped from the corpse in the roadway outside the government bank, a soldier once, who now lay on his back under a shroud of dead money, elbows bent back and hands raised to the sky. Tommo looked at him a few moments and then he clicked off a couple of frames and that was all he had time for because we heard a horn blaring close by, just round the corner, and then yet another commandeered lorry swung into view, bearing down on us, its open back crowded with men and boys, chanting and singing, and behind it came yet another contingent of dancers, waving white rags and green branches, singing and chanting, and then the lorry got stuck in the crowd and its passengers jumped down and the crowd swelled and surged and closed over the dead man and the carpet of money. The air was thick with the breath of the people and the heat and dust of the approaching noon. Hands reached out and rocked us and shouts filled our ears.

All this time we were losing the advantage that Fine's foresight had won for us. TV cameras were bobbing above the crowd now, and Timothy Drysdale appeared near by, up on a truck-bed, doing a stand-up.

Fine grabbed Tommo and me and shouted so we could hear him above the racket. 'We have to move on. Every hack in Gisenyi is going to be here pretty soon. The TV people will all have this story on-air by tonight. We need something else for tomorrow morning.'

'Like what?'

Beatrice pushed her way through the crowd to stand in front of us, elbows drawn in and notebook hugged to her chest. I smiled at her as Fine steered Tommo and me to the edge of the crowd.

'For one thing, we could head out to the northern edge of town and see what's happening there,' he proposed. 'I heard last night that there's still some fighting near the airport. We could go and have a look.'

We had come to a stop on the edge of the crowd, near where our jeep was parked. Tommo was slowly reloading a camera, threading the film through the spindle.

'You think we should go looking for bang-bang?' Tommo asked, his words as careful as his motions. Then he snapped the back of his camera shut and peered at Fine.

'I just think we should find out what's out there,' said Fine.

'There's nothing out there,' Beatrice said loudly, and we all turned to look at her. She seemed to feel a little awkward, standing off to one side, still hugging her notebook, and I wondered for the first time what she was doing there alone.

She spoke again. 'I've just been to the airport with Laura and Charlie. There's nothing to see there apart from a couple of burned planes. There's some shooting to the north, but the rebels have a roadblock outside the airport and they wouldn't let us past.'

Fine was already turning towards the jeep. 'Let's go anyway,' he said brusquely. 'I need the colour.'

Tommo went to follow Fine. I stayed where I was, facing Beatrice.

'So where are Laura and Brereton now?' I demanded.

'I don't know. They were here with me a few minutes ago, and then Jesper Jansson turned up saying something about a palace, and then they all rushed off in Laura's car. I didn't go with them. I wanted to get some more interviews.'

So much for Bosnia, I thought. Imagine missing your lift for the sake of a vox pop . . . And then I understood what Beatrice had told me and I quickly took her arm and led her to where Fine and Tommo were waiting by the jeep.

'Fuck the airport,' I announced. 'We need to get to the president's palace. But we better move quickly. Brereton's already ahead of us, with Laura and Jansson.'

Fine still stood there, one foot on the running board, frowning fiercely, but Tommo, opening the passenger door, was starting to laugh.

Tommo had claimed snapper's privilege so I sat in the back with Beatrice. I always feel sick in the back, but rules are rules. We took to the residential streets that wound round the bottom of Mont Goma, working always to the west. The streets out here were narrow, overhung by trees, and the further west we went the fewer people we saw. They kept close to the walls, avoiding open spaces, or peeped out from doors as we passed. We drove past the compound of the gorilla conservation agency. Its gate had been broken open and a thick slick of discarded papers and broken furniture spewed out into the street, a cratered obstacle course between the sagging fences. Beatrice was asking questions about the town and its history. I let Fine answer most of them, even though he'd little right to do so.

We got back to the main road and turned left at the Stade de l'Unité. A group of people who were huddled in front of the hospital stood up to watch us pass. We came to the place where the road forked left for the lake, right for Mugunga refugee camp and whatever was left of the war. The shacks and booths of the Marché quarter were shuttered and silent, the junction deserted except for a couple of Rwandan sentries who blankly watched us pass.

We turned left. The road now ran between big modern villas

that stood in walled compounds on lava too new for the trees to have colonized. Some of the villas were only half finished, built with siphoned-off aid money. Bright fans of rags and plastic flowed out into the road from twisted steel gates. Then the walls fell back from the roadside and we were out in the open once more, in grey light, with the lake gleaming coldly on our left. The wind from the lake skittered leaves and litter across the puddles and dirt. The volcano had withdrawn behind its clouds.

Fine felt his way from bend to bend, stopping at intervals to put his head out of the window and listen. Off to the west a little way an engine started up, raced, grew louder, still invisible beyond a gentle curve, and we looked at each other, and then Laura's jeep burst into view. Brereton was leaning out of the passenger-side window, laughing and waving something, a piece of green and gold cloth, and Fine honked our horn and flashed the lights so that Laura braked and the two cars came to a stop beside each other.

The cloth in Brereton's hand was a silken Zairean flag with golden tassels. From the back of the jeep Jansson was beaming at us, but he had to keep pushing back a heap of clothes and junk that was trying to topple into his lap from the seat beside him.

'Off to the palace, then?' asked Brereton, his leer widening.

'We thought we might look in,' I said. 'You've been there?'

'Oh yes.'

'Any good?'

'It was when we were there.'

'Well, we'd best be off, then.'

'I reckon you had.'

Fine floored the accelerator, and moments later the president's compound came into view round the bend, a clump of low white buildings set among wide lawns and ringed by spiked steel railings. I remembered the garish circus trailer with the lions painted on its side, parked inside the railings, but now its windows were broken and a black smudge showed where someone had tried to set fire to it. Beyond the trailer the presidential limousines and ambulances still stood in a line but they were up on blocks now, their hoods propped open and wheels removed.

Fine parked the jeep on the gravel in front of the railings and we all got out. The double gates gaped open, unguarded now except for a machine gun that sat on the tarmac between them, propped up on its bipod, its barrel pointing gamely north at the volcano. Its hinged breech cover was twisted sideways, half torn off, a bright groove gouged in the dull metal, and the butt of the weapon rested in a puddle of jelly, black round the edges, cherry-red in the middle. A few spent cartridges glinted in the gore, from which dark drag marks led off towards the palace for a few yards before petering out on the lawn. The gatehouse was abandoned, its windows splintered. An open case of grenades sat on the floor inside the door.

'You'd think someone would be guarding this stuff,' said Fine.

Nobody answered him. A vehicle was moving somewhere in the west, towards Lac Vert, and a dog barked back along the lakeshore.

From the gateway the coarse but well-trimmed lawn stretched off towards the villa's French windows, and as we swam slowly across the grass I anchored myself to the lake and the sky and the three figures around me. The windows had been smashed open and white curtains wafted in and out with the breeze, like breath in cold air. We stopped outside and looked at each other, and then we went in.

The villa's interior was made of plaster and plastic and fine marble, and it contained a lot of overstuffed furniture with fat silk throw cushions, and gilt rococo chairs, and bits of polished brass. In one room two huge ebony masks, the gods of lost kingdoms, flanked a whimsical painting of a Victorian child in a sailor suit. Here and there bright patches on the plaster showed where other artworks had recently hung between the art deco light fixtures, their undersides grey with the husks of trapped insects. There was a smell of furniture polish, mixed with that of the wet grass outside.

The president's vast bedroom was flooded with pale light from a row of tall windows. Over the bed a quilted silk headboard was mounted with gold-look knobs marked 'television', 'radio' and 'hi-fi'. The bed itself was dressed in white and gold cotton and silk, each heavy sheet, bedspread and pillowcase embroidered with the president's initials. There was a ruffled indentation on one side of the bed where someone had recently lain. Brereton, most likely. He'd want to be able to say he'd done that. The adjoining bathroom was dominated by a giant marble bath in the shape of a scallop shell. Around it stood bottles of bath oils and huge flasks whose labels showed names like Chanel, Gucci and Yves Saint-Laurent.

I was alone in the bathroom, although I could still hear Fine and Tommo laughing somewhere down the hall. The room darkened; another squall on the way. The light changed again, and cold wind gusted in through an open window, stirring perfume in the air. Then the perfume faded and the air smelled again of furniture polish and carpet shampoo, and as the first rain spattered against the window I remembered a wet afternoon, many years before, when I had taken shelter in a church in the countryside, empty and almost abandoned. And then the palace made sense for a moment. In all his years as president, Mobutu had stayed here only once, decades before, but in this nation of all-consuming rot the palace on Lake Kivu was tended and clean. The president and his retinue processed to Switzerland, to Kinshasa, to the Côte d'Azur, to Gbadolite, but here in Goma the lawns were trimmed and weeded. Until that morning, maybe, or the day before, somebody had dusted the icons and polished the furniture, aired the beds and washed the cars, believing that one day he would return. The crystal bottles stood like offerings around the empty bathtub. Who had arranged them there?

Fine appeared in the doorway. 'Come on,' he said. 'Let's get moving before somebody else gets here.'

He disappeared and I went back into the bedroom. The closets and drawers were already open, their contents messed up or spilled on the floor. Rooting through them I found a few old shirts, some bed linen, old magazines – a couple of ancient *Playboys*, French editions of *Vogue*. Torn wires stuck out of the wall by the bed: the room had already been picked over once, quickly, by serious people, probably the guards before they fled, and then again by Brereton and the others. I went over to the bed and began to strip away the sheets.

'Jesus!' Tommo called, somewhere down the corridor. 'This room is full of booze! How did Brereton miss this?'

I half turned to reply and found Beatrice leaning in the doorway, watching me. She was so close that for the first time I could see what it was that made her eyes seem so strange: the irises were comprised of flecks of pale blue, with a ring of much darker blue around them.

'You can have some of these pillow cases if you want,' I told her. 'They've got the president's initials on them. There's nothing else here apart from some perfume in the bathroom, but I doubt if that's real.'

She pushed herself away from the doorframe and sauntered into the room, swinging her arms up together. It seems to me that she might have been frowning, but it was often difficult to tell with her, even later, when I knew her much better. I straightened up, a bundle of sheets swinging in either hand, but she'd vanished into the bathroom.

'You do realize that by rights all of this stuff belongs to the people of Zaire?' she called, her voice echoing off the tiles. I couldn't place her accent. Only her voice registered, and I'm pretty sure I can hear that still.

'It's the thing to do,' I replied after a pause, raising my voice so she could hear me. 'It's a story to tell afterwards.'

She reappeared in the doorway, her arms piled with perfume flasks. 'To tell who? . . . I'm pretty sure these are real. Can we put them in your pillowcases?'

Outside the squall had passed but a wet wind was spilling from the highlands. A half-dozen soldiers in Kagame-brand wellingtons were huddled in the shelter of the gatehouse, watching through what was left of its windows as we came across the lawn. Tommo and Fine were waddling ahead with a heavy crate of bottles swinging between them, but when they saw the soldiers their pace slowed and Beatrice took the lead. She was carrying one of my clinking pillow cases, smiling brightly, and as we trudged past the gatehouse she gave the soldiers a cheerful greeting and moved on towards our car. We were out of the gate, almost clear, when a voice called after us. A soldier had stepped out of the gatehouse and stood there, waving one hand palm downwards. He looked a little older than the others and his rifle was slung muzzle down to keep out the rain. He took a step or two after us, out of the lee of the gatehouse, and then he stopped, shivering in the wind. The faces of his comrades stared from the window behind him, indifferent with fatigue. The soldier considered us, his face screwed up, anxious, and then he spoke, very politely, in good mission-school English. Could we please tell the other mzungus not to come here again, he said. There were Interahamwe near by, and the area was not safe. And besides, he said, someone had been looting. He looked sadly at my bundle. Looters, he said, could be shot.

4

The story picked us up and hurled us five miles westwards and then it stranded us again. The Rwandans and their local friends had put up roadblocks all around the town, sealing it off from the camps where the Hutu militias held out. Once again there was nothing to do but sit on our dateline and wait for the story to move. Each day clouds scoured the valley with rain and fidgeting wind. The black dust turned to mud, and in the centre of town the street parliaments, reconvened after the fall, had to renounce the privilege of the open sky and find shelter in doorways and porches. The Congos they built in the air, republics of the breath, dissolved in the rain and scattered with the wind. The trading women gathered up their goods, the children sprinted, and the colours of the street gave way to grey. Beads of rain ran along broken guttering and dropped heavily onto concrete and mud, and there was nothing to be done but lean away from the wind and shiver, waiting for it all to pass. Driving through the centre of town one evening, close to curfew, I saw with a shock that the sheltered edges of an apparently empty street were lined with standing figures, and that I was being followed by scores of calm, curious eyes.

The mortars mostly fell in the intervals between the rain showers, dropping from the sky onto the western edge of town. The Hutus in Mugunga camp were taking long-range potshots at the antennae and beacons on top of Mont Goma; perhaps they thought they were still in use. Or perhaps they had nothing else to aim at; they can't have been able to spot where their rounds fell; they must have been firing blind. But our hotel lay on the line between Mugunga and Mont Goma, and that very first evening a mortar round dropped a hundred yards off and killed an old woman as she washed in her hut. All the same, nobody wanted to check out. The only other hotel open at that time was the Grands Lacs, three miles south-east and well out of mortar range, but it was stinking and flea-infested, without lights or running water, and our manager had assured us that the shelling would be light.

We did the hospitals together, and the aid agencies, and we wrote analysis, and rewrote diplomatic stuff from New York and Paris and Washington, but when all that was exhausted Fine and Laura grew restless. Me, I was happy to hang around and wait for the herd to move. It was Laura who suggested sneaking out past the roadblocks, to check the rumoured attacks on the northern refugee camps. And Fine's fixer said he knew of a track that might not be guarded.

Rain was washing against the window when my alarm went off that morning. The alarm tone began as a low, insistent coo but swelled to a high spiteful shriek. I couldn't credit it. Tommo was moving now too, a light stabbed on, and we greeted each other dumbly with a glance of sick dismay.

I dressed in silence, then sat on my bed and watched Tommo as he used a knife blade to cut the top from a plastic bottle half full of water. Then he poured in instant coffee and powdered creamer and stirred it all up with the blade. Tommo couldn't live without caffeine, however revolting the means of delivery. Finished, he sat on his bed and stared hopelessly out of the black rain-swept window, sipping his cold, clotted mixture. It looked like something you might use to worm a sheep.

Leaning forward very carefully, I picked up his discarded knife, unfolded the bottle opener and prised the top off a warm bottle of cola. I took a box of pills from my bag, swallowed four and wordlessly passed the box to Tommo. He took it without speaking.

There was a knock on the door and Fine's voice called quietly: 'Are you two ready?'

I opened the door. Fine was wearing a rain jacket and carrying his gear. He wrinkled his nose in the air of the room.

'Jesus. What time did you call it a night?'

'After two,' said Tommo flatly. 'We were just going to bed when Jansson turned up with a litre of whiskey. He'd just finished filing.'

'You should know better by now than to drink with that guy. There's no way I'm going in the same car as you two. You stink of rancid booze.'

I found my first words of the day. 'Then we'll take the Hilux. You can fuck off in Laura's car for all I currently care.'

Fine smirked and vanished.

The lobby was empty apart from two servants dozing on straw mats. It was mercifully black outside as we assembled in the car park. Rain ran down my face and onto my waterproof and I leaned against the tailgate of the twin-cab Toyota, waiting for Fine to take charge. Tommo and Brereton were flattened against the wall under a protruding eave, and there was also something in a green rain cape that must have been Beatrice. Behind me somewhere Fine and Laura were talking to Fine's fixer, Sylvestre. He used to be a professor of moral philosophy, back in the days when state wages were paid.

Footsteps squelched in the mud, and Fine raised his voice just enough for all to hear. 'Tommo and Owen are disgusting this morning so I'm going to ride with Laura and Sylvestre. We'll go in front because Sylvestre knows the way. Beatrice can come with us in the Trooper and Owen and Tommo can take Brereton in my Hilux. He stinks as bad as they do.'

'That's too many people for the Hilux,' I said, after a short pause to think. 'It's four, with that driver you hired. Four is too many – we have to take all our gear in the cab with us. It's too wet to leave it in the back.'

I could almost hear Fine's smirk. 'I paid off the driver last night. He'd only turn into a pain in the ass a couple of miles up the road if he thought there might be trouble. One of you should drive. It's safer that way.'

I knew that Tommo would refuse to drive: he couldn't see in the dark, even when he was sober.

'I think I'm still drunk,' I told the tailgate.

'Me too,' said Brereton.

'Then I'll drive the Hilux, if you like,' said Beatrice's voice. 'I prefer driving. One of you can go with Nathan and Laura.'

'Fine with me,' said Brereton, and he put his stuff into Laura's jeep. Even with four of them there would be room for him to stretch out in a corner of the back seat.

I watched, head on one side, as Beatrice shifted her bags into our Toyota. Fine, after a moment's hesitation, stepped in to help her.

We had to slide our gear in under Tommo, who had already fallen asleep across the length of the rear seat, pillowing his head on his camera bag. Beatrice got in the driver's seat and started checking the gear box, working that extra little lever that they put into four-by-fours. She seemed to know what it was for.

There were hints of grey in the sky to the east as we followed Laura's jeep out of the car park. There were now a few lights on in the hotel. At one ground-floor window I could see Jansson, trying to peer out past his own reflection. The engines must have woken him. Or perhaps he was still drinking. I tried to feel guilty about giving him the slip but I only felt sick. Laura had insisted: no wire people could come with us. We should keep this story for ourselves.

We drove east towards the town until we reached the junction by the hospital and then we doubled back west on the road towards Mugunga. Beatrice's face was green in the light from the instruments. After a few hundred yards Laura's tail-lights drew apart and grew larger, then moved together, then vanished, and in the cone of our headlights we saw her jeep turning off the tarred road into a narrow opening between black silent shacks. We followed onto a narrow path, barely visible in our dimmed lights as a smooth stain on the buckled lava slabs. The huts fell behind, and bushes and thin trees rose up through the slag of recent eruptions, crowding in around us. Travelling at little more than walking pace, climbing steeply now, our car began to buck and roll and lurch. The heater in the dashboard was on full, its jets directed upwards to demist the window. Despite the ragged motion I soon fell asleep.

When I opened my eyes again it was no longer raining but a heavy sky was camouflaging day. We had stopped, and Laura's jeep was standing in the road twenty yards ahead, the wind snatching puffs from its exhaust pipe. We were already well past the airport, back on the paved road where it climbs steeply northwards from the lake, into the high saddle where the sleeping and waking volcanoes lean together. To the south the town and the lake were hidden in the mist. Beatrice sat calmly in the driver's seat, her hands in her lap.

'Why've we stopped?' I asked.

'Checkpoint. Let's hope they don't know we're not supposed to be here.'

A dark figure walked slowly around the back of Laura's jeep, then stopped at the front on the passenger side. We waited two minutes, then Laura's car moved off and Beatrice let the clutch out. The roadblock was the usual symbolic structure, two sticks and a piece of string, guarded by three sad-looking kids wrapped in damp greatcoats, their rifles held under the skirts. Beatrice waved to them and they nodded in reply.

Tommo was unconscious in the back seat. Apart from my headache I felt much better now: all I needed was some more pills. I took two from the box in my pocket, and as I got ready to wash them down I glanced over at Beatrice and saw the corner of her mouth turned up.

'You two had fun last night, did you?' she asked.

'Last night was great. This morning is the problem.' I swallowed the pills and took a swig of water.

To the right invisible claws tore at the mist and a forested hillside oozed through the slashes, shockingly green. A couple of hundred yards off the road, on a bare slope, stood a square of tatty gum trees.

'That's the old Belgian cemetery,' I said, pointing for her. 'The last time the volcano really went off, back in the seventies, it killed hundreds of people around here. One of the main lava flows destroyed a whole village and then came to a stop right at the edge of that graveyard. The villagers decided that dead Europeans have really strong magic.'

'Nathan told me about that last night.'

'Really? Fine told you that? It was me who told him.'

She smiled again, without looking at me, intent on the roadway.

After a while I dared to speak again. 'That mountain up there is Karisimbi. Some mountain gorillas still range on the upper slopes, and sometimes they get within a few miles of the refugee camp. You can see the line where the refugees have cut away the forest halfway up the foothills to get firewood. Another year or two and the gorillas will be gone for good.'

Beatrice said nothing but she peered through her window. The road climbed and turned, and then the land fell away to our right, plunging down to the foot of the mountains.

'We're there,' I said.

Ahead Laura's vehicle was slowing, and I could see Fine and Brereton in the back seat, their heads craning to the right. I reached back and shook Tommo. He sat up, groggy, and followed our eyes.

'Christ,' he said. 'This place has changed.'

From the roadside on our right a cascade of blue plastic swept in long waves down the slope until it washed into a far-off tree line near the foot of the mountains. The UN engineers had sought to impose order on the camp by trigonometrical survey, carefully measured sectors dividing the hillside like Mercator lines, but within these subdivisions thousands of tiny lava-block shells had burst organically out of the slag. The huts, tens of thousands of them, protruded from these broken pods like electric-blue polyps in a jagged black reef. Here and there larger white or green tents rose above the huts – schools, clinics, food stores – and sheets of white plastic screened pit latrines blasted from the rock. Beyond it all, seeming to lean over it, were the sleeping volcanoes and their violent green forest. The attack would have come from there. It had left the camp desolate.

Laura's jeep came to a stop and Beatrice, looking past me at the huge, abandoned camp, almost drove into the back of it before braking suddenly.

'You need to watch out for that,' advised Tommo. 'In places like this Laura likes to take out the fuse for her brake lights. It's so she can drive in the dark without any light showing. Apparently they used to do that in Sarajevo. On account of the snipers.'

Beatrice reached for a cigarette and lit it.

Laura had stopped at a point where the road rose above the camp. We disembarked and stood in a row on a low stone wall, watching in silence. Black specks swirled against the grey sky. A thick trail of rubbish led from the camp across the road and up into the forest on the flank of Nyiragongo. The rubbish was alive with rats, sleek grey ones, sniffing and scurrying among the discarded cooking pots, abandoned buckets, flour sacks and clothing. Above them, the hawks and eagles circled, awaiting their chance.

Sylvestre watched Tommo as he braced his elbows on the truck to steady his long lens. Sylvestre was a small, tidy man, who wore a dark grey suit and a white shirt and leather shoes. He could have passed for thirty if it weren't for the grey in his hair.

'It is a good picture?' he asked, then coughed politely.

'Not really,' said Tommo, talking through his camera. Then he lowered it and turned to smile sheepishly at Sylvestre. 'This kind of photo has to have people in it to give it some meaning. Human scale. Otherwise it's just real estate.'

Brereton went first, leading the way along a winding path that went in among the huts. We made lots of noise and picked our steps carefully, avoiding the deeper drifts of garbage where more than the wind might be rustling. The shelters closed in, plastic sheets stretched over frames of bent branches. The huts seemed to generate a heat of their own, saturated with the refugee smell of sweat and old cooking oil. I ducked to look into one. Inside it the diffused daylight shone blue through the plastic like the light in an igloo, cold as charity. The full UN-issue refugee kit – the metal pot, plastic bucket, sacks of rice and USAID bulgar wheat – was still stacked along one wall. Cotton clothes hung from a string. They really had left in a hurry. For a moment I let myself wonder about them, and then I heard Brereton's voice calling and I quickly turned away.

Brereton was standing on the edge of a clearing a few yards wide, a sort of firebreak between the huts. The ground here was formed from twisted and broken skins of lava, with weeds sprouting from the pockets where dust could collect. Beyond the clearing rose a long wall of white plastic sheeting, the screen for a pit latrine. An upright pole supported the wall in the centre, dividing it into halves. The left-hand section thrummed to the wind's touch, but the right-hand panel was beaded with rain, stretched taut and round by heavy objects leaning against it from within. The gusts wafted a sweet and sour smell from the latrine.

'We'd better have a look,' said Laura quietly.

Brereton was the first to move. He pulled his hands from his pockets and, using them for balance, picked his way slowly across the uneven ground around the side of the latrine. There was no path here, just jumbled blocks of lava left over from the blasting, new weeds growing up among them. Brereton rounded the corner of the latrine and came to an entrance, a flap of loose plastic, then paused to consider it. The rest of us bunched up behind him. The smell from the latrine was almost choking. Brereton looked around at us once more, pulled the front of his shirt over his face, then peeled back the plastic flap and took a step backwards, leaning for a moment against me.

Fine craned in to look. 'How many are there?' he asked after a while.

'Hard to say,' said Brereton slowly. 'Twenty or thirty. There'll be more down the hole.'

A rat slithered out from among the heap of corpses, briefly disturbing a cloud of bored bluebottles, then bolted into the dark rectangle of the latrine. I looked away. Brereton glanced at me but said nothing. I found myself looking at Beatrice, who was standing several feet back with Tommo and Laura. She was staring back at me, and I turned to the door again.

'How do you think they died?' It was Fine's voice.

'Hard to say,' said Brereton again.

'The women and children look like they've all been macheted,' said Fine, almost conversationally, 'but the men all look like they're shot . . . You'd think it would be the other way around . . .'

Fine stood to the right of the doorway, holding the neck of his T-shirt up over his mouth and nose. Brereton turned and walked a few paces off and lit a cigarette. He stood looking out across the camp, hands rammed deep in his pockets. Tommo and Laura were fingering their cameras and waiting for the scribblers to have their fill. Beatrice stood with them.

The ripped bodies sprawled ludicrously across each other in torn, oily clothes. Thick steel-grey maggots writhed wherever they had found a way inside. I let my gaze slide over the mass without focusing on detail, looking without seeing, a trick to be learned, the way an actor avoids the faces in a crowd. A child tried to implore me but I refused to catch her eye.

Beatrice pushed in beside me. She was completely still, holding her sweatshirt over her face tightly with both hands. All I could see of her was her eyes. They moved around intently, not like mine, not skimming, and for a moment it seemed to me almost as if she were searching for someone. And it occurred to me right then, thanks to that, thanks to Beatrice, that these people must have had names once. I waited beside her until she had seen enough and turned away.

'Are you all right?' I asked her.

She looked up at me quickly, eyes puzzled above her mask.

'Sure,' she said, and I felt her hand touch my elbow. 'How about you?'

It was necessary for us to try to count them. I heard Fine muttering to himself, then he stopped, perplexed.

'Has anyone seen the other half of this baby?' he asked. 'We mustn't count it twice.'

Tommo and Laura moved in to take their shots and the rest of us went a few yards upwind. Sylvestre followed the snappers to the doorway, stared in for a moment and then came to join us. In his dark suit he had at first reminded me of an undertaker, or a priest, but he seemed only a novice priest now, or an apprentice undertaker.

Brereton lit another smoke, tossed the match away and turned to us. He gestured with his cigarette. 'Someone's coming,' he said.

A woman was picking her way slowly towards us along the rubble-strewn firebreak. She was very old and small and thin, wrapped in what looked like a military greatcoat, and the brim of a man's felt hat came down about her ears. She used a stick for balance, and as she came closer, picking a path through the rocks and the rubbish, I could see her eyes flitting from us to the ground and back. Her coat was many times too big for her, and a faded cotton skirt showed in the few inches between its hem and her bare splayed feet. You could tell she had never worn shoes.

It seemed to take her for ever to close the gap between us. I don't know why we didn't go to meet her. Perhaps it would have seemed presumptuous. And then when Tommo and Laura swung their lenses up at her we all had to move further away from her. It wouldn't do to get in their shot: she was the only thing moving in the camp apart from us and the wind and the rats.

When the old woman was so close that we could hear her breathing, she stopped, placed both hands on the end of her stick, straightened her back and began to talk to a point in the sky just over our heads. Her voice was a high-pitched murmur. She didn't look at our faces, and certain phrases were repeated, like a refrain or a prayer.

Sylvestre was polishing his glasses on his shirt, head to one side again. 'She is speaking Kinyarwanda, which is hard for me to follow,' he told Fine, who had moved to stand beside him.

The old woman was still talking, ignoring the translation. Sylvestre listened again, his face screwed up. 'She says that she wants to take her granddaughter home to Kibuye with her. She says the soldiers said she cannot stay here.'

'Ask her which soldiers told her that?' said Fine, glancing back towards the road.

Sylvestre translated, and the old woman spoke again. 'She says the new soldiers. They said she must go back to Rwanda.'

'Ask her if she knows who killed these people,' insisted Fine. 'Was it the new soldiers?'

More murmuring.

'She says she does not know. There was shooting in the camp and then she ran away and did not see who did it.'

'Ask her if the Interahamwe killed these people.' Fine was sounding impatient. The old woman looked up for a moment when she heard the familiar word, but then her eyes seemed to slide away into the distance.

59

'She says she does not know. She ran away with everyone else. The others ran into the forest but she left her granddaughter behind and had to come back for her. She says she wants to take her to their home in Rwanda.'

'Sure, yes, Kibuye. Right. Ask her if there is anybody else who was here when it happened.'

'She says her granddaughter is at their hut.'

'Let's go talk to her, then,' suggested Brereton. 'This old doll is out of it.'

The old woman led us in among the huts, moving so slowly that I kept stepping on Beatrice's heels. We wove in and out for about a hundred yards until we were close to the road again, and then abruptly the old woman stopped, threw a quick look back at us, turned into one of the low stone enclosures and came to a halt. In the door of the hut lay a thin oblong package, wrapped in a straw mat.

'Fuck,' said Brereton, and we all came to a huddled stop behind him.

Flies crawled lethargically over a large dark stain at one end of the rolled-up mat and a pair of small, bare feet protruded from the other, with the dirty lace fringe of an old cotton skirt. The smell was not so bad this time; it's like that sometimes, with children.

Fine cleared his throat. 'Ask her if this is her granddaughter.'

Sylvestre said nothing. The old woman stood over the bundle, staring up the hillside towards the road, and began murmuring once more. There was a whirring noise. Laura and Tommo had found all the scale they could ask for.

'She says her granddaughter is all she has since she left Rwanda two years ago, and God has told her that she must take her back to their village,' said Sylvestre. Then he raised his voice. 'It is good for people like this to be buried in their own place,' he explained. 'It is like their religion.'

Nobody said anything. Sylvestre spoke to the old woman again and she looked around at us now as she answered, as if becoming really aware of us for the first time as people.

'She asks if you can take them to Rwanda.'

We all looked at each other then. I may have rolled my eyes. For a few moments Fine seemed lost for a reply.

'Tell her we're very sorry but we can't do that,' he said finally. 'Tell her the border is closed. Tell her the humanitaires will come soon and they'll bury the kid.'

As Sylvestre translated, the old woman pulled herself taller and spoke again, staring at Fine.

'She says the humanitaires will do what they did to the rest of her family when there was cholera. They will bury her granddaughter in a trench with many others and then fill it in and no one will be there and no words will be said for her.'

Brereton had been wrong, then; she wasn't entirely out of it. Sylvestre was hunching forward now, so that he didn't have to look at her as he listened and translated. Then I saw that Beatrice was peering around the circle of faces, her eyebrows raised.

Brereton noticed her and shook his head emphatically. 'No way,' he declared. 'Even if the border was open, which it's not right now, there's no way they would let anyone carry a dead body across.'

Fine looked unhappy. Laura and Tommo were still shooting pictures of the old woman with her dead grandchild.

'What if we just took them to the border?' demanded Beatrice.

We all stared at her. Fine cleared his throat carefully.

'That's a really bad idea, Beatrice. At the first roadblock they'd want to know why we were carrying a dead body around. It'd take hours to talk our way out of it, and we've got our own jobs to do. Besides, that body has been dead for a few days now.'

'We can't just leave them both here,' said Beatrice flatly. It struck me how she said it – she sounded almost bored, like a policeman or a bureaucrat stating a rule.

'Too fucking right we can,' protested Brereton. 'Everybody else in Africa has.'

Beatrice didn't look at him. Laura was standing off by herself now, hands in her pockets. I don't think she was even listening any more.

'We have to help them,' said Beatrice, and calmly took out a cigarette. I watched her hands. They were perfectly steady.

Brereton looked furious; Fine and Tommo dismayed.

Sylvestre exchanged some words with the old woman then turned to us again. 'She says that if the girl cannot go back to Rwanda, she wants to bury her in – how do you say it? – terre sacrée?'

'Holy ground,' Beatrice said.

'Yes. Consecrated.'

'I thought you said they had their own religion?' Brereton demanded.

Sylvestre ignored the sarcasm in his voice. 'People here can believe in many things at the same time. She says the girl can be buried in holy ground, even if it is here in Zaire.'

Fine seemed to come to life again. 'It doesn't really change the basic issue,' he protested. 'We're not driving around through roadblocks with a corpse in the back of our car. This is very sad, but it's not our job to make it better.'

Beatrice exhaled sharply. 'So we're just going to *interview* her and then leave?' she asked, and there were red spots in her cheeks.

'Of course,' snapped Brereton. 'Do you know any other way to get the job done?'

Brereton and Fine were right, there was no doubt about that. We all had deadlines coming up. So we stood there for a while, some glaring, some looking at the ground. Tommo had gone to stand with Laura, abdicating. Maybe the situation was hardest for Fine. He always wanted people to have dignity, and things like that. I looked from him to Beatrice. Behind her the old lady stood watching us. The wind gusted for a moment and her coat flapped about her like the broken wings of a bird.

'We can take them to the Belgian cemetery,' I heard myself say. 'It's only a couple of kilometres back along the road, before that last roadblock. That must be consecrated ground.'

Brereton exploded. 'You're being fucking stupid, Owen.'

He had my complete sympathy, but I was looking at Beatrice and she was looking back at me. I went on: 'We can put her in the back of our Hilux, and the old woman can ride with her. We leave them at the cemetery and that's our bit done.'

62

'Who's going to bury her?' demanded Brereton.

I shrugged. 'We'll have done our bit if we get her to the cemetery. It's not even much out of our way.'

The old lady's hut was only a few yards from the road. Tommo directed me as I backed the truck onto a narrow path between the twisting walls. It led right to the back of the hut. Then we all stood and watched, not knowing what to do, as the old woman tried to lift the body up in her arms. Her knees sagged before she had raised it even halfway off the ground and the bundle dropped back to earth again. There was the crack of bone on rock. How long had it taken her to drag the child up here from the pit latrine? Maybe she was stronger then. The flies were buzzing loudly now.

'We have to do it for her,' said Fine, and he reached out and gently steered the old woman away. He took up a stand at the corpse's head, but for a few moments no one else moved. Beatrice was the first to step towards the dead protruding feet. She needed both hands for the job, so this time there would be no way for her to hold anything over her face. She was pale, and I saw her staring at the bare feet and the faded cotton skirt. Fuck her, I thought viciously. As she stooped over the feet I reached out and pulled her quite roughly aside.

Fine nodded to me from the other end of the bundle. He was white. 'A quick lift on three,' he said, 'then put her head-first into the truck. For the love of God don't let her slide along the truck-bed or the matting might come undone. I don't think I could stand seeing that.'

The body weighed nothing, and it scarcely sagged in the middle as we cradled it into the back of the truck. I kept my hands beneath the straw matting, which at my end was free of stain. I tried not to breathe until we were finished. I didn't look at Fine.

When we were done the old woman climbed up beside the body, uninvited, as if this were an everyday routine for her, and sat on a wheel-arch. The others hammered the tailgate shut while Brereton went back to Laura's jeep and returned with a bottle of Jameson's. Beatrice poured water from a bottle onto Fine's hands and then mine, and then we poured some of the whiskey onto them and rinsed them off again. Fine took a small nip, but I still couldn't stand the thought of whiskey.

The graveyard lay a couple of hundred yards east of the road, along a rocky track across open ground. The wooden gate was off its hinges and we had to rip it clear of the weeds so we could drive the truck inside. The headstones bore French and Flemish names, almost illegible, untended and crusted with moss. There was almost no soil here – they must have had to drill down into the lava when digging the graves, like the UN with its pit latrines. The location had clearly been chosen for its view. Beneath us the land fell away to the lake and great beams of misty light fanned down onto the water from beyond the steel-wool clouds. In the cemetery we were still shaded, but ten miles to the south the tin roofs of the town, caught in the light, were red, green or silver. The baby cone of Mont Goma stood out from the lakeshore precise and clear like a figure from a geometry book.

We backed the Hilux in through the gate and the others followed us on foot. I got out of the truck and waited for Fine. 'You and me may as well unload her,' I said to him. 'We've already picked her up once.'

'Where are we going to put her?'

There was so little soil here that the old woman would struggle to hide the child from the birds, let alone whatever burrowing things would come from the forest at night.

Brereton, who had wandered off into a corner, spoke up. 'Some of these graves over here look more recent,' he said. 'They've built up the sides with rocks and then shovelled soil and gravel over the top.'

All around the edges of the graveyard were loose stones that had rolled free from the top of the wall. Beneath one tree we found a spot that had some soil on it and we began to gather the rocks in a heap beside it. The old woman had climbed down from the truck now, and after watching us for a couple of minutes she slowly joined in. In a few minutes we had assembled enough rocks to build a low cairn.

The old woman watched as Fine and I took the body and lowered it onto the ground beside the heaped stones. Then we began covering the body with rocks, piling them gently around and over it until nothing of the straw bundle could be seen. The wind was hissing in the trees.

Laura placed her last rock on the pile and then straightened up. 'We need to head back now,' she said, matter of fact. 'I've a deadline to meet.'

We all looked at Beatrice. She was standing by the old woman, beside the cairn. 'What's she going to move the soil with?' she asked, and for some reason she looked straight at me. 'Is there anything we can give her?'

There was a folding shovel tucked behind the rear seat of the Hilux, along with the towrope and jump leads and other odd gear. I took it out and gave it to Beatrice, and she opened the blade, screwed down the locking mechanism and handed it to the old woman, who took it without expression.

'Has anyone got anything she can eat?' asked Beatrice.

Brereton had a box of those revolting high-protein biscuits that the charities hand out to starving people. He had somehow acquired a taste for them and would steal them whenever he could. He put the biscuits on a headstone, away from the damp ground, with a couple of bottles of water.

'Tell her we have to go now,' said Fine. 'Tell her we're sorry we can't help any more but we have to go because of our work.'

'Tell her not to worry,' said Brereton acidly. 'Tell her her story will be told.'

The old woman began to slowly twist the shovel in her hands. In my mind I saw her inching along an empty road, coat flapping in the wind, no better than a ghost, utterly unwanted. The odds were excellent that she would not see Kibuye again, assuming she ever even tried to leave the graveyard. She might, if she were very lucky, encounter a little more of what passes for charity somewhere, but the odds were excellent that no one would ever be kind to her again, or touch her without violence. Fuck Beatrice, I thought again. What right did she have to involve us in this?

Fine and I went back to the Hilux to disinfect our hands again and this time I took a pull from the whiskey bottle, already half empty now. The old woman seemed to have forgotten us. Slowly she scraped some loose dirt from the surrounding lava, shaped it into a small pile then scooped it onto the bare stones that formed her granddaughter's grave, again and again, slowly and carefully. It would take a long time.

We stood for a few moments, watching the story of the old woman and the dead child sliding away from us, and then we turned and began to move back to our vehicles, slowly and quietly, and for the first time I was reminded of a funeral. We were back at the truck when Beatrice abruptly stopped, grabbed Sylvestre's arm and pulled him back towards the grave.

When I caught up with them the old woman was bent over, frozen halfway through her cycle, staring blankly at Beatrice. Beatrice had taken her shoulder in one hand and in the other she held a hundred-dollar bill.

'Please, Sylvestre,' she said, quickly but steadily. 'Tell her she can use this to get a priest to come and say prayers, or whatever she wants. There must be a priest up here somewhere.'

Sylvestre looked away, then answered himself. 'She has not asked you for money. I don't think there is any priest nearer than Goma, and he wouldn't dare come out here. Anyway, a hundred dollars is too much.'

'It's the smallest I have.'

She pushed the bill into the old woman's hand, where it gripped the shaft of the shovel. The old woman looked at it, let it fall to the ground and then began to dig again.

'Come on,' I said to Beatrice, and I touched her forearm. She followed me to the car and this time she didn't look back.

Tommo was waiting for us, leaning against the back of the truck.

'She'll be all right,' he said to Beatrice.

Laura and Fine were waiting by their jeep for Sylvestre to join them. He took a few steps towards them, then turned and looked at Beatrice.

'I forgot to tell you,' he said, 'but the old woman said to thank you. She said she'd say a prayer for you.'

Beatrice turned away and got into our truck. Tommo and I looked at each other and then looked back to Sylvestre, but he was already walking towards Laura's car. It was nice of him to lie.

At dusk people would move out onto the hotel veranda and set up their satellite-phones facing the lake. The aerials sprang up along the concrete floor in precise alignment, plastic flowers to a man-made sun. They had big yellow stickers on them warning you not to stand in front of them when the phones were in use. The radiation could make you sterile, or give you cancer, but the waiters refused to believe this until Laura got Sylvestre to tell them in Swahili. After that we had to go inside to get our drinks.

I sat and listened to Brereton talking to his office.

'I don't think it's a news piece as such,' he was saying, hunched over his handset on the lip of the veranda. 'It'd have to have a colour lead. If we wanted to make it news we'd have to know who killed them, and who they were. The fact that somebody butchered some poor bastards in Zaire again isn't in itself going to jump off the page. It could have been either side.'

He paused to hear the answer, then went on: 'I mean, of course I'll lead with it, but it's a colour lead, not a news lead. That's what I'm saying.'

Another long pause.

'I can talk about the trip, and the fact that hundreds of thousands of refugees have gone missing, and that where we've found one massacre in one quick visit there are likely to be others that we didn't see. But it can only be speculation. And I'll take in the updates from the town itself, and the aid situation, and you can mix in the diplomatic stuff there, if you don't mind. I've no idea what's happening in your world.'

Pause. 'No, the rebels claim to be on a ceasefire and the town's quiet right now. I don't know if the Hutus are still shelling from Mugunga or whether they're also on ceasefire. There's no way of talking to them. Most of what we're hearing from them is actually coming out of Paris and Kinshasa.'

He looked around, then called over to me: 'Hey, do you know if we're still being shelled?'

Before I could answer the concrete shivered and from somewhere towards Mont Goma there came a sharp smack and thud as the air flew open, then slammed itself shut again.

'We're still being shelled,' Brereton said into his handset. There was another long pause, then he said goodbye and switched off his phone.

'Well, that last bit impressed them,' he said, and moved to join me where I sat with my back to the wall. 'Should be worth a grand on my next expenses claim.'

The sky was almost clear and the sun shone low and red over the valley and the lake. Here where I am now, this northern estuary, the winter evenings come early and summer ones hang late, remote eastern clouds lit up on the edge of night by the last of the western sun. But on the Equator the night whispers up like the tide round a sandbank, then closes in with a rush.

The others would all be done soon but I still had a feature to write. The news piece I had sent earlier was no longer enough for them; some advertising had been cancelled and there was space left to fill. It would have to happen now, before I went to sleep. And I was very tired. I'd tried to sleep for an hour when we got back but the scenes from the camp flickered against my eyelids. So I got up again and sat against the veranda wall and drank coffee with the others, watching them work, waiting for the sun to disappear beyond the valley. That would have to be the signal. Jansson and Tommo, both having filed off Jansson's sat-phone, were packing their computers away. Jansson had already forgiven Tommo and Laura for leaving him out of their adventure. Lights came on in the dining-room window. I thought I saw a bat brush the water. The sun was gone and the darkness welled up from the lake. I got up and went inside.

I was alone now with the blank gaze of the computer screen. I tried typing in all my notes but there weren't enough of them to help me stare it down. I went out again, ordered enough coffee for three and brought it back to the room, and it was cold long before I finished drinking it.

I had already used up most of my facts in the news piece. I had nothing left to feed the beast except for the old woman, and who knew what she might mean? She kept sliding away from me just as I was about to set her moving again. Could she be hammered home with a big theme? There was something there about acceptance, perhaps, or maybe something sacramental for the spiritually inclined. I fumbled in my bag of tricks from college. *King Lear*, was it? *Antigone*? The burden of love, that whiskey priest and his fucking donkey? But really he had nothing to do with it. Too literary. Too Catholic. And, besides, I'd used him before.

The screen grew whiter and brighter, the room darker, and my head screamed at me in pain and spite. My eyes clouded and my throat tightened and I realized I was about to cry. Unfair, unfair. Tommo could just dip his day in chemicals and then hang out in the bar. As for Laura, it would be worth being shot at all your life, from one shithole to another, if it meant not having to sit alone for hours in a badly lit room, picking scabs off your brain. Snap and send, that's all the photographers ever had to do. Why couldn't I do that?

But, then again, why not? Send the old doll out to bat, unpolished, just as found. That might do it. Straight up straight down, no drop no spin, type it up around whatever notes there were. Strictly kosher, third-person stuff. I looked at the screen and saw that its glare had softened, and now I also saw patterns in the straggling notes and half-formed sentences. They might do. I started to type.

5

Katey wore cotton summer dresses that showed off her figure, and even in the dull heat of December I found myself admiring her. When she caught me looking she would smile, like she used to, but now the joke was private, reserved for her own growing need.

The rebellion had moved west from Goma off into the forest, perhaps never to emerge again, and when I flew back to Johannesburg Katey met me at the airport. She told me that Wits could not renew her contract and asked what I thought she should do. I said I didn't know. It would be hard for her to find a new teaching job in South Africa, she said, and, even if she did, it would be even harder to get a new work permit from Home Affairs. I said she was probably right. I was getting plenty of work, back then, what with all the interest in the Congo. One of my strings was even talking about giving me a proper written contract, although I hadn't found time to tell Katey that yet.

One afternoon just before Christmas we went shopping together at the big mall in Sandton. As the escalator carried us down from the scorched rooftop into the chill of the mall I saw goose bumps forming on her upper arm. We'd left it late, and the mall was much quieter than usual: everyone in Jo'burg comes from somewhere else, or thinks they do, and at holiday-time they go back to their villages, or the beaches where their forebears came ashore. The mall was decorated with imported fir trees and drifts of phoney snow. Toffee-apple carols cooed knowingly from the PA system, and Katey and I came to an unspoken agreement that we would take this flake of a day and preserve it in plastic, a souvenir snow globe from our life together. I'll take it out and shake it now.

Our first stop was at the camping store on the upper level of the mall. There were no customers and only one clerk was on duty, a muscular blond kid with a tight T-shirt and round, dull eyes.

When we walked in he was standing behind the counter nodding compulsively to the flat bass thud of a techno track on the shop's PA. His eyes were fixed on a point in the air between the counter and the wall, and Katey had to cough loudly before they came goggling round to bear on us.

'Yah, can I help you, lady?' he asked her, and I saw Katey smile at him through her instant dislike.

She wanted to buy a present for her brother, she said; could he suggest some new gadget that might appeal to an outdoors type? Maybe something that was new on the market, and fun? A look of low cunning stole across the kid's face, only to be shooed back into hiding by the blinking of his eyes. We watched, fascinated, as he fought to compose himself.

'The present to give this X-mas is this thing here,' he said, pointing to the glass countertop in front of him. 'A lot of people is going for this GPS this year. It's a satellite machine that tells you where you are in the bush. If you have one of these, you can never be lost, and now they is making them so small they is hand-held, and very cheap.'

'The price tag on this one says 4,500 rands. That's almost a thousand dollars.'

'Yah, but they used to cost a lot more.'

'My brother lives in Dublin. Why would he want one of those?'

'A lot of people is buying these in Natal. You can use them on your boat as well.'

'Not Durban. Dublin. It's in Ireland.'

The music was still pounding and the kid's limbs began to jerk again as the prospect of a big score drained slowly from his brain.

'Ireland, yah?' he said. 'I would love to go the UK.'

Katey's smile broadened and she leaned on the counter, arms pressed down and shoulders raised. Her dress rose up her legs. I wandered into a corner and picked up a folding shovel. Its mechanism was jammed by cheap green paint.

'How about these multi-tool pen-knife thingies here? How much are they?' Katey spoke loudly and slowly, pointing down through the glass counter. Painfully the kid assembled another span of attention.

'These here is 250 rands, but they is the old model. These here is 350. They is the latest one.'

'They look a bit bigger.'

'Yah, and they have been upgraded as well.'

'Upgraded?'

'Yah. More functions.'

'Amazing . . . What else is new this year?'

The kid thought hard, then pointed to a display of imported American flashlights. 'These here is the top of the range. You see they have different sizes, from these little key ring ones up to this one here that takes four big batteries. Now they have just made a new one that takes five big batteries. It's a very powerful torch.'

'I'm sure. This one here?'

'No, that's the old four-battery one. Actually, the five-battery one we haven't got any more. It sold out very quickly. Everybody wants one.'

'Shit.'

'Yah. But I can order for you if you like.'

She bought a multi-tool – one of the older ones. I put the shovel back and we left the store. It was lunchtime and the crowd had thickened. A group of young Indian girls walked past and I saw one of them look at Katey, then nudge her friends. We went into a couple of clothes stores and Katey picked fiercely through the racks and rails. She frowned over an off-white cotton top with thin shoulder straps, holding it up before her and twisting from side to side in front of a mirror, singing to herself. She caught me smiling at her, smiled back for a moment, then put the top back on its rack.

Katey said she was hungry so we went to one of the bistros lining the pastiche Venetian square on the other side of the mall. The December sun was almost directly overhead, and fat dusty pigeons clustered torpidly in a thin band of shade. Intermittent water jets spurted in sequence from vents hidden in the paving at the centre of the square, and a plump little child ran shrieking from one jet to the next. When the fountain switched off he trotted around aimlessly for a minute, then charged in among the pigeons, screaming. They dragged themselves reluctantly up into the hot thin air then settled again a few yards away. Ignoring the weather, Katey ordered a carafe of red wine and a large portion of ribs, and ate them messily with her fingers. I had a sandwich and drank two beers. When we had paid we stood up to leave and Katey looked flushed. We took the escalator down to the lower floor and were eddying in a slow flow of people when Katey grabbed my arm.

'Let's go look at a luggage shop,' she said suddenly, 'just from the outside.'

The nearest one was three shops along and we loitered near the door, examining the bags, cases, rucksacks, satchels, trunks, wallets and suit-carriers arranged in the window. Inside, a tiny woman was perched behind the till, reading a paperback. There were no customers.

'Look at the size of that suitcase,' whispered Katey, pointing to a huge leather case hanging on the back wall. 'You could put everything you ever needed into it and just take off. Just pack up and go. Imagine.'

'It's not so bad here,' I said, and turned to walk away. A few yards on Katey caught up with me and took my arm again.

'There's nothing I like in this place,' she said. 'I'll finish my shopping when I get back to my parents'. There'll still be a couple of days left. Let's just stock up on booze for now.'

In the bottle store Katey took a trolley and started loading it with liquor. I stepped into the refrigerator for a case of Windhoek and the chill air bit through my shirt. When I came out again Katey was picking through the wine racks, pulling out an assortment from some of the more expensive South African vineyards. We were on our way to the check-out when she squealed and veered off towards a display of vodka coolers in the middle of the aisle.

'Alcopops! Let's get some of those! Just for a laugh.'

The check-outs were manned by a pair of short and very plump women in floral shop coats. Customers were few and they sat behind their counters, enfolded in their bulk and dignity, talking quietly in Sesotho. They didn't look up at us when we unloaded our trolley, but when the check-out lady saw Katey's vodka coolers sliding down the rubber belt she gave a long 'Ehhh!' and then laughed.

'You are both children,' she said. 'I should not be serving you at all.'

We put the bottles into the trolley and took the lift up to the roof. The sun was strong enough to suck moisture from the summer ground. North towards Pretoria I could see the high white clouds darken and lose their definition until they blended into a towering wall of slate and mauve. The looming storm front was topped by another crest of white and gold, impossibly high and distant. Somewhere over Midrand a light aircraft banked noiselessly between us and the storm, and for a moment its wings flashed in the sunlight. The concrete shimmered in the wide gaps between the parked cars, and a blast of hot air struck my face when I opened the car door.

We put the bottles on the floor behind the front seats and Katey started the engine. On Rivonia Road the traffic was light and we got a clear run of green robots all the way to Rosebank. Katey put the air-conditioning on, but I opened the window and hummed to myself. We turned right down Bolton Road and carried on straight along Emmarentia, then right onto Carlow Road.

Fourth Avenue was almost dead. A couple of Zimbabwean pedlars sat in the shade of a shop front on the corner of Seventh Street, listless behind their cunning wire ornaments, hoping for a last sale. A few customers in designer sunglasses posed under umbrellas outside the Question Mark, self-consciously drinking beer. At the end of the avenue Mzwandile, the local parking guard, was standing in a shady patch in his yellow high-viz vest, disputing with some cronies. Soon he'd be gone too.

We pulled into the driveway and Katey went straight into the house, leaving me to fetch the shopping from the car. On my second trip I heard the noise of the shower and I was sitting on a lawn chair in the back porch when she walked past me, still dripping, wrapped in a towel. I watched two louries cackling at each other in the large bush that dropped berries in the pool, then picked up my book and started to read. Katey reappeared and sat on another chair beside me. She was wearing a different dress. I felt her look at me for a while before she finally spoke. 'I wish you were coming back for Christmas with me. I don't like to think of you here by yourself.'

I put my book down. 'I won't be by myself. I'm going round to Laura's place. There'll be a few others there too.'

'Christmas doesn't make sense in this climate. It's a winter thing. You need darkness and cold. You said that yourself.'

She stood up and moved to the French window. When she spoke again her voice was low and almost bitter. 'It doesn't matter what my parents think of you. We'd have a room to ourselves and the run of the place. But there's no point arguing with you now, is there?'

I didn't answer and after a pause she went inside. I picked up my book but put it down again a couple of minutes later when I heard the music. She was playing one of my old cassette tapes from ten years before. She always played sad music when she wanted to cheer herself up quickly. No patience at all.

The storm was much closer now. I went into the kitchen and drank some water, then put whiskey and ice in a glass and came out onto the porch again. Beyond the suikerbos tree at the end of the garden, beyond the koppie crest across the low valley, the sky had the blue-black menace of a loaded gun. Lightning arced from one horizon to the other. The birds were still singing in the trees but their voices sounded muted and the wind was rising in the branches. I counted elephants until I heard the gruff concussion in the sky. The storm was about five miles away.

The music shut off and Katey came back out and sat down beside me, drawing her knees up to her chin, exposing the backs of her legs. She lit a cigarette.

'It looks like a really big one,' she said. 'Please get me a beer.'

When I came back out the sky was flickering with discharges from one horizon to the other, like a faltering neon tube. The storms formed every other afternoon at this time of year, sometimes more than one a day, but Katey was right: this one would be special. I felt the catch in my breath, the same feeling you get as a kid in the queue for a roller coaster. The birds were silent now as the thunder swelled around us. I looked at Katey. Her eyes were wide and she stared out at the sky, the beer can lodged between her knees and her chin, where it would leave a mark. She looked at me and smiled quickly.

'I hope it doesn't put the power out again. Have you unplugged the fax?'

I went inside and heard the first scattered drops of rain pinging on the tin roof. The staccato volley steadied into a deafening roar and when I returned to the porch the trees were being thrashed by the storm. The iron smell of the wet garden rose up around us and I saw hail picking flecks of flower off the bougainvillea in the corner of the garden. The wind in the trees, the rain and the hail on the roof and in the leaves, all moaned and hissed and rattled together, while above them the thunder tore like freight shifting in a sinking ship. Then the garden turned white and in the same instant a great ripping explosion made us jump in our seats.

'That'll be the cell-phone tower on D. F. Malan!' exclaimed Katey. 'Isn't this great?'

Her face was full of her excitement. The storm was swaggering about the city with gleeful fury now, tearing the air. The thunder rolled continuously, chasing the lightning about the sky, and the hail had turned to a sheet of crushing rain. Surrounded by this elemental violence, shielded only by tin and two-by-four, we felt the savage pleasure of the fly upon the wheel.

The storm lasted another two hours, and when it finally passed it was early night and the crickets were singing. By then Katey had gone back inside and I was reading again, and when I looked up the skies above were clear. To the north, though, something black was crawling up the sky, swallowing the watery stars. Another storm was coming. Sometimes they seemed to waltz around each other for days on end.

Katey and I drove to Heinrich's for dinner that night. Most of the other decent restaurants had already closed for the holiday so Heinrich's was almost crowded. We'd been there only half an hour when I heard a familiar voice outside the security gate and looked around to see Tommo with Brereton and Laura. The place was short-staffed because of the late season and I went to the door myself to buzz them in off the street. Heinrich moved a couple of businessmen from the booth so we could make up one party. I welcomed the company.

Tommo was celebrating. The *New York Chronicle* had just called him to ask if he was interested in a contract. There would be prestige, a big retainer, plenty of travel and guaranteed expenses. He wouldn't even have to give up filing for his freelance agency in London, so long as the *Chronicle* had first call on him. After two years of largely self-funded assignments, travelling in bush taxis, risking his own cash, Tommo had finally made it. It came as a complete surprise to him. Fine hadn't mentioned anything about the offer, although it was obviously done on his nod. So we slapped Tommo's back for him and then he slumped in his chair and tried to raise Fine on his cell phone as we ordered him champagne. Fine's phone was switched off so Tommo left an abusive message. The champagne arrived.

I drank more wine and half listened to them talking. Laura too would be gone for good soon, although she was fighting hard to stay. Soon Brereton would be the doyen of the foreign press corps, and I reckoned he would never leave.

I looked at Katey, who was happily arguing with Brereton about something that neither of them cared about. Her voice was raised to drown an interruption and she waved a cigarette imperiously in the air. I knew that she wouldn't come back in the New Year.

Someone from the *Chronicle*'s picture desk called Tommo on his cell phone, and while he was out the back talking to them the front door buzzed again and after an interval Beatrice appeared in the vestibule. Fine was behind her. She was wearing a blue party dress and her hair was tied back behind her head, which made her look younger. She smiled when she caught me watching her but Fine seemed taken aback to see us all there, and he hesitated a moment before he followed her over to our booth.

'What's this I hear about you hiring Tommo?' I demanded of Fine, while Beatrice sat down beside me. Reluctantly Fine sat down on the edge of the booth, squeezing Beatrice against me, and picked up the wine bottle. At the other end of the booth Brereton and

Katey were now shouting at each other while Laura, who sat between them, was sitting back and laughing.

'My desk said that if I wanted to do more features I needed a regular snapper,' Fine said casually, pouring a glass for Beatrice. 'I gave them Tommo's name but they had other people in mind too. It wasn't up to me.'

'Bollocks. Have you seen him since he heard?'

'No. He left a message on my phone earlier, though.' Fine poured a glass for himself.

'He's here now,' I said. 'You'll see him in a minute. He seems pretty pleased about it. Why I don't know. I'd hate to have an arrogant bastard like you for a boss.'

Fine laughed. 'Boss? I'm just a client. I'll let him do all the planning and just follow him around. He sees stories much better than I do.'

'Well, I hope you'll still let us borrow him from time to time.'

'Sure. You can all play with him so long as you put him back in the box.'

Beatrice wanted to know what I was going to do for the holidays and I gave them the line, which happened to be mostly true, about how I had to stick around this year because the accounts people at my main string hadn't bothered paying me for Goma before they went off on holiday. Fine smiled when I said that and I was suddenly angry with myself for telling him.

'I'm flying back to the States tomorrow,' he said, looking past us. 'I'm meeting up with Rachel in New York and then we're heading to her folks' place in Colorado. We have to start planning the wedding.'

Tommo came back to the table, and Brereton and Katey broke off their argument to join in a toast to him and to Fine. Then the pair of them sat down together to talk shop and I turned to Beatrice. 'You look like you've been out somewhere.'

'Nathan took me to a cocktail party. There were some people there he wanted to introduce me to.'

'Oh, yes?'

'ANC people, diplomats, people like that.'

'Not much of a date, then.'

She smiled. 'No.'

Networks of fine channels ran from the corners of her eyes and made little deltas in her cheeks. On the edges of her lower teeth there were the faint beginnings of new nicotine stains. She took a packet of cigarettes from her bag and handed me one.

'And how have things been since you got back from Goma?' I asked. 'How are you settling in?'

'Not too bad. My people were pretty happy with the stuff I sent. They've offered me a retainer.'

'Is that your people in France or your people in the States?'

'In the States. My French paper doesn't have any money. They think I should work for the love of it.'

'Some of my bosses are like that too.'

Katey turned to look at Beatrice, absorbing her with a single bright, ingenuous glance.

'You're Beatrice, aren't you? I've heard about you,' she said pleasantly. 'You were in Goma too, weren't you? It sounds like you all had an interesting time.'

Beatrice smiled back. 'Yes, very interesting. It was my first time there. I've only just arrived in Africa.'

'Yes, Laura was telling me about that. You write, don't you?'

'That's right. You too?'

Katey shook her head and laughed. 'Oh, no, not me. Nothing as interesting as that. I teach at Wits. Civil engineering.'

'I don't think I've ever met a woman civil engineer before.'

Katey's smile became even sweeter. 'That's why I do it, you see. I get to meet lots of boys.'

It was well past midnight when Katey announced that she wanted to leave. I told her to go ahead, I'd get a lift back with one of the others. She looked back at me for a moment and then spoke very quietly, so that none of the others could hear her.

'It's my last night, Owen. You know that.'

The others looked up as we gathered our phones and cigarettes and stood up to go.

'You're off early,' said Beatrice.

Katey smiled at her again. 'Yes. Indeed we are.'

'Well, goodnight, then,' Beatrice told her. 'And happy Christmas, if I don't see you again.'

'You won't. Happy Christmas.'

It was only a short drive home and Katey took the wheel. She yawned a lot. The yellow sodium light rose and fell, rose and fell, as we swung along between the pools of darkness. Katey looked beautiful, I thought, with something like shame. We were almost home before she spoke again. 'Do you think there's something going on with Nathan and that Beatrice?'

I looked at her. 'No. Why would there be?'

'No reason. It just occurred to me.'

I turned in my seat so I could look at her directly. 'He's going home to Rachel tomorrow. She's coming out to live with him in the New Year. They're getting married.'

Katey yawned again. 'Poor Rachel.'

The second storm had missed us but arc lightning flickered noiselessly in the clouds high above. Behind us the moon, almost full, was rising at the end of Fourth Avenue. As we got out of the car in our driveway I could hear the crickets and cicadas singing in the steaming gardens of the old mine houses along the street.

That night the usual impediments, the slight hesitations, sudden misgivings, deliberately missed cues – none of these intervened. But as Katey clung to me that last time I knew it was only an old idea that she was holding on to, and of course she knew this too. Later I got up to go to the bathroom and through the uncurtained window the lights of the city were hard and unblinking beneath the last stuttering splashes of arc light. Only the lightning and the clouds seemed to move, but as I watched them, hardly breathing, it occurred to me that we below were also in motion, drifting away from each other, silently receding into fields of electric stars. Katey was asleep when I went back to bed.

6

I should have kept a diary for the time I was in Africa. It would have come in handy, now. Fine kept one, which wasn't surprising, him being from Yale, a serious American, and it certainly proved useful in the end. And Tim Drysdale made a fortune by turning his three-week assignments into epics of suffering and hope, with titles he stole from an English lit. poetry course.

I did try to keep a diary when I first went to Johannesburg but it didn't last for long. It's a very good idea: write up your journal every night, store it away, and after two or three years you have the guts of a memoir, full of incident and insight, skilfully weaving the thread of your adventures into the ever-changing tapestry of this great and troubled continent . . . We've all read them. I read Drysdale's again last night, in my newspaper's library, or at least the bits that mattered. The Charlie Brereton character is particularly good in it. Lovable fucking clown.

I'd tried keeping a diary before, when I was a kid, having read a lot of books about other kids who kept diaries, or collected stamps, or who knew the names of birds and trees. Of the three, keeping a diary seemed the easiest option, though it soon defeated me. What do you say to the blank pages? Who do you meet there? A diary, like any other story, needs a hero, and I never found one. And the A4 hardback volume I bought at the CNA in Melville – with its sharp edges and its tide tables for the Cape of Good Hope, two pages to fill for each day of the year – it didn't fit well in my baggage. It was a relief when I managed to lose it.

Hugh has asked me twice now whether Cartwright kept a diary, or left any word for us. He seems to think it's the kind of thing that Cartwright would have done. I told him no, which is true, more or less. You might say that this newspaper was Cartwright's diary, for the forty years he worked here. He thought he'd get to keep it. Talk about clutching at straws.

Hugh seems upset now that Cartwright is gone. He seems to blame himself, which I find pretty funny, and to ease his guilt Hugh has made me his chief mourner; Cartwright had no people of his own. I was the natural choice for the job because I shared Cartwright's office; because I'd known Cartwright for almost as long as Hugh had, ever since Hugh and I were in the newsroom together and Cartwright – in his prime then – used to bully us; because I've little else to do with my time and Hugh knows it, even if he's too polite to mention it.

So lately I've been getting rid of Cartwright. I've looked through his things, made arrangements for the funeral, paid the bills that I found in his house. It'll soon feel like he was never here at all. Hugh had a notion to hold some kind of tribute for him, last week, when he was still quite emotional, but he dropped it when I told him that no one else cared.

When I started out at this paper the editor was a pompous, insecure man named Partridge. He was the kind of backroom operator who'll call a spade a digging implement and then, when you aren't looking, get someone else to hit you with it. That someone was usually Cartwright. He used to refer to Cartwright as his 'man on earth', as if he, Partridge, were not himself sitting there behind his expensive blinds in a 25 × 20 foot glass box at the back of the newsroom, decorated with bound volumes of *Le Monde Diplomatique*, a shelf of hardback classics and a lucky-bag assortment of Aquinas, Spinoza and Nietzsche. He used to fumble his books absent-mindedly whenever he had visitors; he'd even perform for the copy-boys, if they hung around too long. Sometimes you'd look over and see the blinds in the glass box twitching. The buildings manager told me, much later, that Partridge had once asked him about installing two-way mirrors.

Cartwright was the ideal henchman for Partridge, not only because he liked bullying women and children but also because he could never become editor himself; he terrified half of the directors and the rest of them detested him. None of them was qualified to appreciate his skill, but to Partridge his usefulness was plain: Cartwright would be loyal because otherwise he would get the shove, and Partridge knew that Cartwright knew that Partridge knew that Cartwright had nowhere else to go and not much else to do. Partridge didn't really understand newspapers, as later became plain, but he knew a fair amount about human weakness.

But Partridge in turn could survive as editor only as long as he was content to stay in his cage and leave the real work to Cartwright, and a time came when hubris overwhelmed him and he started trying to put out the paper himself. One Friday night, after Cartwright had gone home, Partridge decided, without consulting any grown-ups, to remake the front page so he could put in the first few pars of a think piece he'd commissioned from some human rights lawyer he fancied. But it was a heavy news day, the front page was already full of real stories that couldn't be bumped, so to make room for this drivel Partridge told the duty sub to reset the page in tiny eight-point type. The next day even the directors couldn't help noticing that something looked wrong with the paper, and this led to questions about what Partridge had actually been doing for the previous five years. Not long after that he was promoted to the board, and Hugh came back from Washington to pick up the pieces. He was the youngest editor the paper had ever had. He still is.

I was already in Africa by the time Partridge met his downfall, but Hugh told me all about it. He said that it had looked at the time as if Cartwright would have to go too. Partridge's habit of constantly hiring new minions to pit against the old ones meant that the paper was now heavily over-staffed and there would have to be savage lay-offs. Cartwright had already been at the paper longer than anyone else and there was, moreover, a strong suspicion that he wasn't entirely innocent in the affair, that Partridge had been in some sense Cartwright's creature, and not just the other way around. So the board sent Cartwright on leave as a step towards firing him, and while he was gone someone told maintenance to clear out his stuff, including all the files he'd kept on everyone for years. The next day the security guards caught him out the back of the building, scrabbling through the rubbish skips to save as many records as he could. He was still clutching an armful of folders as they marched him out to the street.

It was game over for Cartwright, but then Hugh came back and saved him. A newly appointed editor gets three wishes, Hugh told me, and after a lot of spitting and moaning the board allowed him Cartwright as the price of two of them. I was the third, although that came sometime later.

The following week, when Cartwright presented himself in the editor's office, Hugh was so busy that he didn't even notice him. There were secretaries coming in and out with faxed congratulations and lunch invitations and bottles of champagne, and a couple of maintenance men were fussing about in the corner trying to dismantle Partridge's glass walls. Hugh told me it was the cough that got his attention; the cough was still the same. But when Hugh looked across the expanse of his new desk all he saw was a little old man with a diffident smile and a lot of greasy dandruff on the shoulders of his suit. It took Hugh a couple of moments to realize who it was. And when he did, said Hugh, his gut flooded with a churning sense of loss. It took him a few moments more to remember that Cartwright wasn't hovering over him out of choice, preparatory to striking, but was waiting for his boss to ask him to sit down. Then Hugh felt even worse, because he thought Cartwright might think he was throwing his rank at him. He could have thrown a lot worse, as far as I'm concerned, but that's Hugh for you. I don't know how he holds down that job.

Hugh put Cartwright to work on the backbench, quality control, which is where I found him when I came back myself: they put me in the same little office. Cartwright limped on his left leg, I on my right. He did home news, features and op-ed, I started on foreign news, business and sport. After a couple of weeks I was able to talk Cartwright into taking foreign off me, swapping it for features and op-ed. I had to work a bit harder but for me it was worth it.

For Cartwright the swap meant nothing in real terms; it was a sterile exercise in negotiation, because in practice he usually tried to check everything that went into the paper himself, regardless of whether it was supposed to be someone else's job to do so. I know that Cartwright used to check my own pages behind my back because sometimes, when I was using the edit trail to trace a fuck-up through the system, I would find Cartwright's digital fingerprints over my own. I reckon he was too old-fashioned to know that he left a trace on every computer file he looked at. Or perhaps he knew and didn't care. I don't know.

But I always knew when he'd found a howler. His chair would scrape slowly back and then his face would appear above the partition that separates our desks, wearing the same dreamy smile that had once terrified me. He would step away from his desk, staring vacantly across into the corner of the newsroom that was visible through the open arch of our alcove, and then his head would vanish again. If I leaned out sideways I could watch him lurch slowly towards the archway; sometimes he even hummed. But the archway brought him up short every time; he couldn't allow himself to go through it. Because Hugh, to protect his youngsters from bullying, had banned Cartwright from talking to the junior staff himself: if he wanted to query someone's work he had to go through their department chief. And if their chief was off duty then Cartwright had to go through me.

That's how I acquired my power over him. It wasn't much, but it was fun. I would secretly watch him as he scanned the rows of reporters and sub-editors, twitching like an old dog scenting rabbits, and then I'd duck my head before he could turn and catch me looking. His feet would shuffle across the grey nylon carpet, scuff-clump, scuff-clump, scuff-clump, and then his chair would squeak and his phone would click and a few seconds later his voice would start murmuring to the news editor or the sports editor or the chief sub or whoever it was, quietly putting the knife into someone. Or else the silence would continue and then the phone would click again, and then I knew that Cartwright needed me. His chair would creak, and a few moments later his dry little cough would sound behind me.

After only a little practice I learned exactly how much force was needed to swivel my chair around precisely one hundred and eighty degrees to face him. There was no cause to jump any more.

I should probably mention here that his points were almost always good ones. He wasn't petty or pedantic, Cartwright, he just had this ferocious urge to get things right. I would listen, nod politely, and then if I felt like humouring him I'd pick up my phone and talk to the culprit, enjoying the silence from Cartwright's side of the room. Sometimes – like the time when Lucy Viner was new and she fucked up and nearly got us charged with contempt in the High Court – I would nod wisely while Cartwright briefed me, and then, while he waited, I'd pretend to go back to what I'd been doing before. He would sit back in his chair and the air in the room would grow denser and hotter until finally I'd stand up, stretch myself slowly and make my way towards the arch – clump-scuff, clump-scuff, clump-scuff – across the industrial grey nylon carpet. Then I'd stop in the doorway and scan the newsroom for a few moments and plan my next move. I could stretch again, shrug and return to my desk; or turn in the wrong direction and head to the canteen; or just stay where I was and wait for somebody coming past to stop and chat to me. I might even go to find the offender, but only if I thought Cartwright wasn't looking.

I could have been crueller. I could have ignored him completely. But the truth was that Cartwright had got his hooks into me, back when he had them. I had to get it right, just to spite him.

7

It's a big place, the Congo; the maps you see don't do it justice. The Kivus have more to do with East Africa, with the Swahili Coast, than they do with Kinshasa, which is really a West African town – hotter, steamier, its currents deep and slow. Up north, along the border with Sudan, Arab horsemen still raid for slaves. Down south you meet the edge of the high, open plains that stretch, ever more arid, all the way to the Cape. In the middle is the forest, and only the rivers cut through that.

Hardly anyone thought that the rebels could make their way across all that vastness, with their stolen jeeps and their little rubber boots, up against the president's tanks and his Serbian gunners, his French spooks and his Ukrainian MiGs; hardly anyone was right. Mobutu's soldiers wouldn't fight, so the rebels came steadily westwards along the rivers and still had enough force left over to send a second column south along the old Katanga railway line. Their success made a lot of people look bad – not me, thank God, I was hardly anyone – and it posed a major problem for Fine.

It wasn't that he'd fucked things up; on the contrary, he was one of the few who thought Mobutu's enemies could go all the way to Kinshasa. At a stretch you might even say that it was Fine's war: Armitage told me later that when the CIA's Kigali resident wanted to support the rebels with money and guns and a US Navy spy-plane, he bombarded the White House with Fine's stories from Gisenyi and Goma, the ones about 'an African solution to an African problem'. But Fine then became a victim of his own success. America's secret adoption of the rebels enabled them to push west into the forest, where Fine was not allowed to follow: he was bureau chief for southern Africa only, and he made it to Goma only when he was filling in for the *Chronicle*'s Nairobi woman, who was often off sick. And everything west of the Rift Valley belonged to

87

the *Chronicle*'s West Africa bureau in Abidjan. So while the rest of us were flying off to Kinshasa to cover the downfall, poor Fine and Tommo had to stay in Johannesburg. For the first couple of weeks I got several e-mails a day from them, floating schemes to get back in the game, but by the time the airlines stopped flying to Kinshasa, and we knew that the end was near, the e-mails had stopped.

And by then the only people who mattered were the ones in Kinshasa. The city was now an enclave, a resort drawing to the end of its last jaded summer, and everyone knew what to do as the rebels drew closer, the season ended, the perimeter crumbled and the ship went down. Laura had a big room at a corner of the third floor of the hotel and there were parties there most nights; this was to be her very last trip with us, she was finally leaving, she knew she must put on a show. Brereton was always there, now. It took me a while to realize that they were sleeping together.

One evening Jansson appeared in Laura's room with a skinny little black guy with a grey moustache, horn-rimmed glasses and a white cotton boubou. They seemed to know each other from before, and when the stranger handed out his cards I read the name Douglass Tolbert McDonald II in spiky gold letters. He was sort of from Chicago, sort of from Liberia, and he said he was in Kinshasa to mark time until his diamond trade picked up again.

'Sierra Leone is all messed up right now – there's going to be another coup real soon with Taylor behind it, and he doesn't like me at all,' he confided to Beatrice and me one night. 'Things are bad here in Zaire too. Because of the war there ain't too many stones coming out on this side of the country. Since the rebels took Kisangani, the stones from there are all going east through Rwanda and Uganda, and so will the stones from Mbuji-Mayi, when the rebels get there. Which won't be long now.'

'You really think the rebels can capture Mbuji-Mayi?' Beatrice asked him. 'You don't think the FAZ will put up a fight to keep their diamonds?'

Douglass appeared in many of our stories as an 'informed source', but behind his back he was plain Diamond Doug.

He shook his head, smiling kindly at Beatrice. 'You see, "capture" is such a dramatic word,' he said, still shaking his head. 'I can see why you folks like it. But here's how it really works. Kagame's boys will get hold of the sat-phone number for the FAZ commander in Mbuji-Mayi, and when they're good and ready they'll give him a call. They'll tell him it's time for him to leave, and they'll probably lob over a couple of mortars, just as a formality. And as soon as they do that he'll be out of there, him and as many of his FAZ as can follow with all of the loot they can carry – actually, probably a lot more than they can carry. So me, what I'm going to do is I'm just going to wait here in Kinshasa and make a few side bets until the rebels come in cell-phone range. I've got some numbers of my own.'

'Aren't you worried about your safety?' asked Beatrice. 'It seems to me that both sides might think you're working for the enemy.'

Diamond Doug shook his head, smiling, and tipped his gin at her. He wore a gold Masonic ring. 'There you go again, young lady, misapprehending the situation. People like me and all these Lebanese and Israelis and Greeks you see hanging around in the restaurant, *we* are the financial infrastructure of this country. *We* are what they're all fighting for. If they mess with us, who's going to come here and hand them their dollars? You can't just walk into a Mercedes dealer in Nice and offer him a hundred kilos of coltan or a fistful of uncut stones. You need a middleman you can trust. And that's me.'

Douglass liked to sit out in the lobby, quietly watching the network people rushing back and forth, sipping coffee or gin in a business suit or boubou depending on the time of day. Sometimes, when we were pumping him for gossip, Douglass would deflect us with questions of his own. How much money could a freelance shooter make? What did we think of Tim Drysdale's reports? Was it true that Kitty Krauser was an utter bitch? He loved to pick up and examine pieces of our jargon, and I remember him sitting there one evening, smiling to himself and murmuring, 'Fifteen minutes to bird!'

Once, when Laura asked to photograph him, he flatly turned her down. 'Now, girl, the people who need to know me already know me,' he said, wagging a finger. 'They don't need to see my face in the papers.'

'Come on, Douglass,' Laura begged. 'I need some stuff for a story on the diamond trade. It'll only be published in Germany.'

He shook his head again. 'Nope. I've got plenty of friends in Germany. People I met in the old days.' He stared at her for a moment. 'Mind you, I don't hear so much from my old German friends lately.' He paused again. He was beginning to smirk. 'Not since they took down that wall.'

Sometimes he would disappear for a day or so, and the next time we'd see him he'd be with a group of FAZ brass or Lebanese businessmen, drinking beer by the pool. Then, by unspoken agreement, we would pretend not to notice each other.

Charlie Brereton used to sweat when he was angry, stressed or frightened, and I could smell his tension as I stood behind him in the darkened room. He was scarcely breathing, and I was careful not to touch him. When he spoke his voice was low and his eyes remained fixed ahead. 'Fuck it. May as well make a break for it, eh? There's not much future staying here.'

His eyes were dark hollows. I shrugged and nodded, though he couldn't have seen me. Brereton lifted his arms and twisted them slowly to ease his cramp. Then he lowered them and steadied himself for action.

'On three, then,' he said. 'One . . . two . . . three!'

I saw his body lurch to the right and in that same instant a door behind us burst open and light flooded in. Brereton's head jerked around to face the light, then jerked to the front again as the room exploded with crimson flashes and the sound of machine-gun fire. Brereton spun, his out-flung arm striking me in the chest. His mouth was dark and open, spewing obscenity. He remained bolt upright for a moment, then slumped back into the corner, against the wall, glaring into the softening light from the doorway.

'Rasher, you horrible cunt,' he moaned. 'Why can't you fucking knock before you enter? I was almost through to the next level.'

Rasheed smirked and reached inside the door to fumble the main light on. 'Sorry, bru. But I told you you should save it as you go along.'

Brereton closed the lid of his laptop. It beeped in protest. 'I do, but even if I get into that last room with full health and ammo the fire monsters still kill me before I reach the other side. Now I'll have to go back to that fucking imp room again to get more bazooka rounds.'

Rasheed wandered into the room and sat on the sofa, yawning. 'I could get you the cheat codes,' he offered.

Brereton shook his head emphatically. 'I don't want them. That would defeat the whole purpose of the game.'

'What's that, then?'

Brereton moved to the window and pulled back the curtains. The day was decaying over Kinshasa, and across the street a couple of thin young Lebanese men were leaning on a balcony, chatting to someone on the pavement below. Brereton fumbled with the window catch and slid it open. Warm, stuffy air invaded the air-conditioned room, carrying with it the stink of garbage and engine oil. The concrete canyon roared with the last cars trying to make it home before dark.

'I'm through with it for today, anyway,' said Brereton morosely. 'You stare into that screen long enough and even after you stop playing you still see the fucking monsters. Let's make some calls, Owen, and try to find something to do tomorrow. We could go to the parliament. It sounds like a laugh.'

Rasheed lit a cigarette. 'I can get you the cheat codes for that game. You get unlimited life and unlimited ammo and just blast away in God-mode.'

Brereton was still looking out the window. 'What's the fun in playing if you can't lose? That's not a game. It's just a . . . a pastime.'

Rasheed laughed. 'Don't tell me you keep score.'

Brereton looked around at us, puzzled. 'No. *Is* there a score in this game?'

'Sure there is,' said Rasheed. 'It comes up every time you get killed.'

'Oh. I hadn't noticed.' Brereton was watching the street again.

I went and stood beside him. A squad of Presidential Guards was sitting on the back of a Land Cruiser parked on the triangle in front of the hotel. They had tight uniforms and mirror sunglasses and they carried brand-new miniature Kalashnikovs and drum-fed grenade launchers. The street vendors and beggars kept well clear of them.

'There's a score,' said Rasheed, 'but it means fuck-all when you're only playing against the computer.'

'Course not,' said Brereton, and he went over and reopened the laptop. Its screen blinked back to life again as he peered into it. 'I wonder what my score is.'

The parliament building was a large box of rusty concrete, dirty glass and yellow marble. The Chinese had built it for the president to reward him for snubbing Taiwan, and it stood amid acres of crumbling asphalt like an unwanted gift, still in its soiled wrapping when the Christmas tree comes down. Four or five vehicles were parked in a cluster by the front steps, at the top of which a couple of bored soldiers were slumped in plastic chairs, their rifles discarded on the floor tiles beside them. The guards perked up when we parked our car at the foot of the steps but by the time we had reached the top they had sunk back into apathy. The sight of Laura and her cameras failed to stir them: not even the men of the Forces Armées Zaïroises could be bothered to pretend that this was still a strategic location. We tried to show them our papers but the older of the two just scowled and looked away again, waving us past with a flick of his hand.

Inside was a high, glass-fronted vestibule with broad staircases leading up to a gallery. Far above us greasy chandeliers hung like geometric fungi.

'It looks empty,' said Brereton. 'I told him last night we'd be here at 10.30.'

'Maybe we should ask someone,' I said.

'There's no one here to ask . . . What about those FAZ?'

We turned and looked back. One of the soldiers had left his chair and was stretched out on the tiles at the top of the steps, his beret covering his face. The other was fiddling with a transistor radio.

Laura crossed the echoing hall and tried a high double door facing the entrance. It was locked.

'Hello?' she called in French. 'Is there anybody here?'

Somewhere on the mezzanine above us a door creaked open. We froze, listening, until the echoes had subsided, and then we heard a new sound, footfalls, a pair of invisible heels clicking slowly along the mezzanine towards a point above our heads. The feet stopped just short of the balustrade and still we could see nothing.

Brereton and I exchanged glances, and when I turned back to the balustrade I found myself looking into the eyes of a grim-faced middle-aged man.

'Yesss?' he said, drawing out both vowel and fricative. 'May I help you, please?'

'Yes, please,' said Brereton brightly, blinking up at him. 'We are looking for Dr Ngandu, the speaker of parliament. He was supposed to meet us here.'

'You have found him, sir. I am Ngandu.' The head turned and moved towards the stairhead, looking down at us. 'I understood you were to come to my office.'

'I'm sorry,' said Brereton, 'but we didn't know the way. Your assistant told me we'd meet in the hall.'

Ngandu reached the top of the stairhead and halted. 'My assistant told me you were coming to the office.' He turned and shouted something short and violent over his shoulder. Another pair of shoes squeaked across the floor above. Ngandu stared in their direction for a moment and then turned back to us. He was a small, fastidious-looking man in a well-cut dark blue suit, its broad pinstripe at odds with a yellow collar and a startling red cravat. Brereton stood bolt upright and smiled and clasped his notebook in front of him with both hands, in token of suppressed excitement. Another man appeared at the stairhead with Ngandu. He was young and unflustered.

'This is Malingi, my assistant,' said Ngandu, not bothering to look at him. 'It was he who misdirected you.'

From behind his boss's back Malingi gave us a polite smile.

'Not at all,' I said; 'I'm sure we just misunderstood.'

'No, no,' said Ngandu, and he turned to glare at his assistant, 'professionals like yourselves do not make such silly errors. Alas, not everyone is so efficient . . .' He shook his head. 'Still, I am glad that you are here.'

'It's very kind of you to see us at such short notice,' said Brereton.

Malingi was studiously avoiding his boss's glare. Finally Ngandu sniffed and turned back to us, his expression softening. 'Please,' he said, 'let us talk in my office.'

We climbed the stairs and crossed the desolate mezzanine to a door that stood open. Inside were a few plastic chairs, a desk with an old telephone, a couple of filing cabinets, some framed proclamations and a portrait of the president. A long trunk-like wooden box lay across the back of the room. Paint was peeling off the walls, pale in the light of a forty-watt bulb. There was no window.

Dr Ngandu lowered himself slowly into his chair behind the desk. 'Sadly my official office is closed for renovation,' he said. He produced a weary smile, with the bloodless deliberation that seemed to characterize all his actions. 'But perhaps this room is better. It is better for us to avoid daylight, no?'

He raised his eyebrows at Laura, who was changing a lens on her camera. He seemed to expect an answer. Laura paused and looked back at him. 'I'm sorry?'

'The daylight. It is confusing for your apparatus. It is better to eliminate it and use artificial lights, no?' He raised a modest hand. 'I am used to being interviewed.'

Laura stared at Ngandu in puzzlement. Then the penny dropped. 'Oh, no, sir. Perhaps you are thinking of television, in the old days, when they still used film cameras. That is such a long time ago now. For stills photography light is not such a problem.'

Ngandu said nothing but continued to smile.

Brereton and I sat down and took out notebooks. Brereton went first, with a fat pitch to make him start swinging.

'So, Dr Ngandu, can you tell us about your duties as speaker of parliament?'

Malingi cleared his throat. 'As acting speaker, to be exact. The speaker resigned some time ago and the president has not yet seen fit to replace him. The speaker, if there was one, would be next in line for the presidency.'

Ngandu glared at Malingi again, but his face gave away nothing. Finally he turned back to us. 'My responsibilities are, of course, many,' he said, 'and the current difficult situation has greatly increased them. Not only must I run parliament as acting speaker but I am also expected to play a leading role – it would be fair now to say *the* leading role – in the mediation that is under way to avert catastrophe.'

Brereton leaned forward, genuinely interested. 'Mediation? Are you saying that you're in contact with the rebels?'

Ngandu leaned back in his chair and dropped his hands on the desk, staring at us in horror. 'No! Of course not! Why would you ask me such a question?'

Brereton was also thrown. 'Well ... you said you were mediating ...'

'Yes, of course I am. I am mediating between the president's office, the leader of the opposition and the former prime minister. It is already more than two weeks since parliament voted to dismiss Prime Minister Kengo and still he refuses to accept. Because of that we now have no properly appointed cabinet. It's anarchy!'

There was a long pause while Brereton and I scribbled diligently.

'Dr Ngandu,' Brereton resumed, 'many people in Kinshasa ask what is the point of talking about parliament or ministers when public servants haven't been paid in years and government services no longer exist. They say the only priority right now should be negotiating a ceasefire with the rebels before lots more people are killed.'

Ngandu waved his hand impatiently. 'Of course. And that will be the task of the new leader, when he is appointed, so he can organize elections. The rebels may be allowed to participate in them, subject of course to certain conditions.'

I was the first to stop writing. 'But Mr Kabila says his fighters are able and willing to take Kinshasa by force if they have to. He also says that Zaire will not be ready for elections for a long time.'

95

Ngandu smiled patiently. 'But of course. We are realists. That is why we need a ceasefire, to allow us time to prepare the people for democracy. A Western power – the French would be best – could monitor such a ceasefire and help us to rebuild our country. We will need substantial foreign aid.'

Brereton came in again. 'Do you really expect the rebels to just stop now on the point of total military victory and start negotiating instead?'

Ngandu's smile was undiminished, but its quality had changed. 'Mr Kabila should be aware that we will not surrender our precious sovereignty to foreign forces – to these Rwandans and Ugandans and other English-speakers who hide behind him. Our army will destroy these invaders if they attempt to go too far.' He paused, made a slow, conciliatory gesture. 'It would be better for him to seek an alliance with the democratic forces that already exist here in the capital. Soldiers should respect the will of the people.'

This was much better than anything we could have hoped for.

'So what exactly is the present state of affairs in Kinshasa?' asked Brereton, pen poised.

Ngandu leaned forward, suddenly animated again. 'It is disgraceful! Former Prime Minister Kengo – who, I should tell you, is in fact really a foreigner, his mother was a Tutsi – has refused to give back his official vehicles, and several other ministers are known to have sent theirs across the river to Brazzaville. It is not at all clear that we will be able to recover these vehicles, which should rightfully go to the next ministers.'

'I meant, who do you think should succeed President Mobutu?'

He smiled sadly. 'Ah. Now there you ask a question. The opposition leader Mr Tshisekedi has the support of many people here, but he is also little better than a foreigner, from Kasai.'

I said, 'What about the army chief of staff? Mahélé? People say he's still respected. Could he take over to ease the transition?'

Ngandu sighed. He swivelled his chair around, opened the long wooden trunk and bent down to fumble inside it. The box appeared to be empty but when the acting speaker straightened up again he held a thick volume loosely bound in leather. 'This is the constitution of the Republic of Zaire,' he proclaimed. He held the book higher, in one hand, and jabbed it towards us like a referee flourishing a yellow card. 'Nowhere in this constitution does it say that a soldier can take over the running of the state. Not Mr Kabila, not General Baramoto, not General Mahélé. No one!' He paused, the volume elevated above us.

'Of course not,' said Brereton smoothly. 'Not again, anyway. So tell me, who do you think will be the next leader of Zaire?'

Ngandu allowed the heavy book to sink back to the desktop, pursing his lips. 'In truth,' he said, 'many now think that the best outcome might be to appoint a compromise candidate, one who would enjoy respect both across the political divide and in the community at large. One who would have proven credentials struggling for democracy, but also experience of government.'

Brereton continued to look at him brightly. I waited, my pen poised over a page of doodles. Ngandu made a little embarrassed gesture with his hands and exhaled sharply. 'There are even those who say that I myself should be a candidate.'

Brereton smiled, but not too much. 'For the prime ministership or for the presidency?'

Ngandu shrugged, his face showing a hint of distaste for the question. 'It is too early to say. Of course, I am prepared to serve my country in any capacity.'

'Of course,' said Brereton.

'Of course,' I said.

It was time for Laura to start taking photographs. She took Ngandu out onto a corner of the mezzanine to get some sidelight from a window: Ngandu didn't want to go outside. Brereton went with them, still talking to Ngandu to relax him for the camera. I waited at the stairhead, lighting a cigarette. From where I stood, leaning on the balustrade, I could see out through the front door. It looked like both the sentries were asleep now. I heard footsteps behind me and Malingi joined me. He accepted a cigarette.

'I hope this interview was useful to you,' he said. He glanced over his shoulder. His boss was too far off to hear us. 'I am surprised that you take an interest in our parliament.'

'It might make an interesting story for us.'

'Interesting, but perhaps not very serious.'

I exhaled, and studied him through my smoke. The fibres of his white shirt were fuzzy from too much washing. 'Perhaps not, no.'

'So why did you choose to interview Dr Ngandu?'

I looked out the door again. A pied crow had landed near one of the sleeping FAZ. 'Someone gave Charlie his number so we decided to come out to see the parliament. Pity it isn't sitting, though.'

'It only really sits when there is a chance of a new cabinet being formed. There are hundreds of deputies and almost as many parties, all of them appointed by the president. They spend most of their time trying to make deals with him. Dr Ngandu has been trying to return to office ever since Mobutu fired him. He was minister of social welfare for almost a year. He was very rich for a while.'

'You don't seem to like him much.'

'I was hired by the previous speaker. Dr Ngandu would like to replace me with his nephew.'

'Why doesn't he?'

'Because his nephew refuses to take the post until government salaries are paid again. I come to work anyway. I have nothing else to do.'

Heels clicked behind us as Dr Ngandu shepherded Brereton and Laura over to the stairhead. They were discussing some important point of the Zairean constitution as we made our way slowly down the staircase and halted at its foot. Dr Ngandu stopped on the lowermost stair, extended a foot towards the ground and then, on second thought, retracted it. He gazed solemnly down at us from his vantage point.

'My friends, I am sorry that I cannot show you the great chamber of deputies, but, alas, it is locked today and the army has the key. I thank you for coming here to talk with us. It is important that the outside world understand that there are still those who are working for a lawful and democratic outcome . . . By the way, do you think that this interview will be used on 24/7? No? The British world service? A pity. Many people watch them in Kinshasa.'

The guards outside were sitting up now, resentfully squinting into the dark hallway in search of the source of the noise. Dr Ngandu noticed them and retreated up the staircase. His progress was slower now; his heels protruded beyond the steps, and I could see steel segs nailed into his soles to eke out the shoe leather. Between the metal plates ragged holes were patched with cardboard and the cuffs of his pinstriped trousers had been skilfully darned. He reached the top of the stairs and vanished, but as we escaped into the daylight I could still hear his heels, clicking off into the darkness.

8

Fine found a way back into the story, of course, right at the last minute. One night Tommo went over to Fine's house with a bottle of that bourbon swill that Fine claimed to like so much and Fine took out one of those big romantic Michelin maps ('eau doux à deux mètres', that sort of thing) and pointed at Katanga. Even thirty years on the name still had a ring to it – all that stuff with Moise Tshombe, Patrice Lumumba, the Wild Geese and Mad Mike Hoare. Mobutu hated the breakaway province so much that after his forces reconquered it in the sixties he renamed it Shaba, but now the rebels had taken most of it and changed the name back. Katanga was in the news again. And it could, at a stretch, be seen as part of southern Africa. The way in was through Zambia, and Zambia was on Fine's manor.

Next day Tommo sent me an e-mail to say that he and Fine were on their way to Katanga to cover the fall of Lubumbashi to the rebels. Fine said that if the story worked out okay and if they got enough good pictures they might even have a pitch at getting some spreads in the *Chronicle*'s magazine, the kind of space and treatment you could shoot for a prize with. Tommo thought it would be great fun if me and Brereton or whoever else could join them there. He reckoned that Fine thought so too.

Polly Vermeulen had arrived from Johannesburg on the last scheduled flight to land at Kinshasa, having picked up a freelance gig with the Brits. The great thing about having Polly around was that she never knew when to stop producing. Without her help I doubt if we would ever have worked out whom to visit and whom to bribe in order to assemble all the permits we needed to fly to Lubumbashi. It didn't do us any harm that Brereton was coming: Polly would do anything for him. When we left for the airport that morning she even lent us her private fixer to help with the officials. His name was Hubert and he was an old friend of hers from previous jobs in Kinshasa. A dapper man, not quite young any more, he wore pressed blue slacks and a crisp white shirt. He had a slow voice and thoughtful eyes and he was, when not otherwise engaged, a major in the Garde Civile, one of those African officers who might have gone a lot further in their service if they hadn't been so able.

Inside the airport terminal a strange silence was disturbed only by the diffused murmur of distant voices and by invisible men coughing in lonely offices with open doors. Hubert said that the night before a big detachment of Presidential Guards had arrived in trucks and jeeps and driven the hustlers from their temple. They were gone, almost all of them, the porters, hawkers, thieves, beggars, pimps, policemen, soldiers, vaccination officials and diplomats who used to hunt there in snarling, bickering packs. Apart from the Presidential Guards only passengers and essential staff were allowed in the airport now, and there were precious few of those.

Hubert took our passports and permits and bribe money and left us in the empty VIP lounge, and it was barely an hour later when he reappeared and took us to the aircraft. Waves of soaking heat broke round us as we waded across the shimmering tarmac. A silver and blue Antonov was parked on the opposite side of the apron, with a small group of officials and porters clustered in the shade beneath its wing. Beside the aircraft a fuel truck stood shivering in its own fumes. Off to the right a lone Hind and a row of dead C-47s commemorated the past glory of the Zairean air force, and beyond them loomed the president's private airliner, its doors left open to the void. An armoured car was parked in the shade of its wing, a soldier sleeping on its hull with his head pillowed against the turret. Beyond the Antonov, across the wide runway, was a strip of mown grass, then high elephant grass, then a line of palm trees, and through their trunks you could see the silver and green Congo – silver for the sky, green for the floating mats of hyacinth. The glimpse of the river made me feel thirsty.

The sun had leached most of the bitumen from the grey tarmac and a hot wind stung us with kerosene fumes. A dozen Presidential

Guards had posted themselves in a wide circle around the aircraft, their weapons held waist-high. They hid their eyes behind cheap sunglasses and their mouths were tight like traps. Two white men with white shirts and black and gold epaulettes were arguing with a plump official by the plane's cargo ramp. We set our bags down beneath the wing and sat on them and watched until one of the pilots threw his hands up and went stamping back towards the terminal, fumbling at a cell phone, with two junior officials trotting at his heels. The other pilot cursed in Russian or something and then he climbed inside the aircraft. Hubert yawned and went over to talk to the fat official, who was now leaning against the fuselage, his feet crossed, fanning himself with the manifest. The fat man laughed and shook Hubert's hand and then the junior officials all smiled at him, and the pair of them talked for a couple more minutes, heads together, before Hubert returned to us.

'There is a small problem with fuel,' he said calmly. 'These gentlemen here are from the airport authority. They have told the Russians that if they want to get fuel at Lubumbashi this afternoon they will have to pay for it here, in advance, in dollars.'

'Why's that?' asked Beatrice. She had settled on her rucksack, cross-legged.

Hubert lit a cigarette, ignoring the stink of fuel. 'The rebels are now very close to capturing Lubumbashi,' he said, shaking the match out and freeing it to the breeze, 'and the company is frightened that the rebels or the army or its own local agents will steal any dollars that are paid there. So they say, "Pay us here in Kinshasa, and we will radio our agents in Lubumbashi and tell them to give you fuel when you land there."' He exhaled carefully, then went on: 'But the Russians are cynical people, and they believe that when they get to Lubumbashi the authority's agents there will say they know nothing about this arrangement and will also demand cash for the fuel. The Russians think they will have to pay twice for the same fuel, and if they refuse their plane will be stuck.'

'So what?' I said. 'It's not their plane, is it?'

Hubert smiled thinly. 'Yes, it is. They took it with them when they left the Soviet air force. You might say it is their pension.'

Brereton was either snorting or laughing.

'The other problem', Hubert went on, 'is that the pilots say they do not have enough dollars with them this morning to pay for all the fuel needed to take them from here to Mbuji-Mayi and then on to Lubumbashi, then back again tomorrow. They were planning to pay for the fuel for the return journey with cash they will get from passengers wanting to leave Lubumbashi. It seems there are now many people there who want to get out.' He drew on his cigarette again. 'I think there will not be many more of these flights.'

'So if the pilots can't find a lot more cash in a hurry, then we can't fly today?' asked Brereton.

'That's correct.'

'So we're fucked, then?'

Hubert permitted himself another smile. 'I think perhaps not. The pilot has just gone to talk to the manager of the airport. The manager keeps some of his own private dollars in the company safe.' He tossed away his half-finished cigarette. 'I expect the interest will be rather high.'

A young man with shockingly blond hair and greasy overalls propped a ladder against the port engine of the plane and started attacking it with a wrench. A pilot emerged from the cabin and stood at the bottom of the ladder beside an open toolbox, shouting suggestions. Thick black oil was dripping from the engine onto the undercarriage and pooling on the ground, restoring a youthful black sheen to both tyre and tarmac.

The other pilot returned, followed – at a greater distance this time – by the two officials, who were smiling and shaking their heads. Fuel lines were attached to the aircraft and the workers began listlessly loading cargo. There were a few pallets of maize meal and flour, some boxes of sugar and canned meat, a couple of old-fashioned high black bicycles, some motor parts and a giant, tightly bound bale of second-hand clothing from charity shops, donated in Europe for resale in Africa. *Le Grand Méchant Look*, said a shirt flapping loose. The porters stacked the cargo at the rear of the cabin and when they were done the blond mechanic climbed in over it and tied it down with a plastic web net, then vanished into the cockpit. A couple of minutes later he reappeared, having swapped the overalls for a snazzy green flight suit, all zippers and pockets.

'Come,' he called to us, and paused, as if searching for words, and suddenly his face split into a smile of childlike pleasure. 'Flight is boarding now for Mbuji-Mayi and Lubumbashi!' His accent was like soup, all viscous vowels and chunky consonants.

We finished our cigarettes and Hubert shook our hands and wished us well, and while we were saying goodbye a half dozen civilians hurried across from the terminal and filed past us onto the plane, heavy with baggage.

The plane's passenger accommodation consisted of two benches made from canvas stretched over metal tubing running lengthways on either side of the cabin. There were no seat belts. Light entered the cabin through the open cargo ramp and through a long row of portholes. Smudged Cyrillic warnings were stencilled here and there on aluminium panels of battleship-grey, and the air smelled of oil and perished rubber and sour milk. At the rear of the cabin three foam mattresses were rolled up and tied to the bench with string; Beatrice had settled by them and I sat down beside her.

The door closed and immediately the temperature in the airless cabin began to soar. There was a building whine and a bark and one after the other the engines clattered into life, then throttled back into steady, flat-pitched drones, their propellers replaced by discs of finely diced light. The brakes snapped off, the plane lurched forward and we were moving. Across the cabin Brereton was gasping from the heat, and I could feel Beatrice's sweat meeting my own where our sides touched. The aircraft swung onto the threshold of the runway, slowing for a moment, and then the propellers changed pitch to claw holds in the air, the whole aircraft shaking, and we leaped forward, swerving from side to side, the wheels humming loudly on the tarmac, picking up speed, until the plane's nose lifted and the wheels fell silent and we were airborne. The line of trees fell away from the porthole and the great pool of the river stretched off to our left, brown water and silver ripples and yellow shoals and green islets, stepping stones to the far Brazza shore. I stole a look at Beatrice but she was twisted away from me, looking out of her porthole.

Far below there was an anti-aircraft gun, sitting out in the open near the end of the runway, no trenches or sandbags, its tiny crew lounging beside it. The aircraft turned right, still climbing, and the airfield was gone. Jets of white vapour began gushing from the roof panels and it was possible to breathe again. Beneath us was parkland scattered with blotches of a lighter green, ragged fields cleared for manioc. There was a concrete highway with cars and some tiny black specks on it, and a line of rusting pylons, and a while later there was a dirt road, and after that there were only microscopic red spider webs, foot trails joining little groups of huts half hidden in the forest, and then even these were gone. We were ten minutes from take-off and the plane was still climbing.

Beatrice leaned closer and shouted to me: 'I've never seen a real jungle before.'

'It's a lot nicer when you see it from up here,' I shouted back.

Across the cabin Brereton was already dozing. I let my head sink back against my porthole, closed my eyes and floated off into the dark comfort of the engine noise, and as I did I felt Beatrice shiver.

Sometime later the aircraft lurched and I woke again. The plane was banked hard over, leaning into a downward spiral, and the crew chief was standing over us, bracing himself against the side of the cabin and leaning forward to stare past Beatrice out through the porthole. He had plugged his headset into a socket above us and as he peered down I could see his lips moving. The aircraft began to buck, punching through a layer of turbulence, and from the pressure in my ears I knew we were descending. Brereton was peering out through his porthole.

'Mbuji-Mayi?' I shouted at him. He looked at me and shrugged.

The aircraft heeled until there was no horizon in the porthole, nothing but the green froth of the forest, and then another slash-and-burn clearing, then another, then some huts, then a dirt road, growing larger, and then the aircraft abruptly levelled off and the blue sky filled the upper half of the window again, smudged with lines of high white cloud. A concrete road flashed by, empty of traffic, and then there were clusters of tin shacks beneath palm fronds, stands of banana trees, warehouses, a glimpse of a dusty street of colonial buildings and then a concrete runway a couple of hundred feet below. Elephant grass grew up through the fence, through a roofless hangar, and through the dead and dismembered planes scattered around the perimeter.

It was past midday and the air near the ground was boiling with convection. We had to cling to the bench to keep from being hurled into the air. Then our descent levelled and the crew chief lurched across the cabin to peer out the opposite window, the spiral lead of his headset straightening out behind him. Through the porthole, beyond Brereton's grey face, I saw something green flash across the empty blue sky and then an unseen hand smacked the aircraft downwards, smashing it onto the runway, and the wheels bounced and for what seemed like long seconds we might have been motionless, frozen in time, and then the illusion of stillness came to an end as the aircraft struck the runway again. The plane levelled out, drifted, alighted, the tyres sucking down onto the tarmac. As the engines throttled back, the crew chief walked to the centre of the cabin and smiled all around him, like an amateur magician who has pulled off a trick.

'Welcome to Mbuji-Mayi!' he announced. 'Passengers for here please only to get off plane.'

The aircraft came to a halt on the edge of the apron, a hundred yards short of the low colonial-era terminal building where two Toyota pick-ups full of soldiers were waiting for it. The soldiers leaped from their trucks and crowded the steps to the door of the plane, jostling each other and shouting at the pilot who had casually wedged himself into the door. More soldiers were jogging from the hangars and the terminal, heading for the aircraft. A couple of civilians also appeared, staying clear of the crowd of FAZ, skulking like jackals at a hyena kill. The soldiers clustered around the door of the aircraft, toting their rifles uncertainly, like expiring passes. At the back of the cabin the crew chief lowered the ramp part-way to let the outside air in. The gap revealed a nearby fence of concrete posts and chain-linked wire, beyond which ran a deserted perimeter road, and beyond that again smoke rose from a distant tree line.

Brereton looked over at Beatrice and me, eyebrows raised, mimicking the gesture of lighting a cigarette. We climbed over the strapped-down cargo and perched at the edge of the ramp, our feet deep in a drift of spilled flour. The hard landing had torn one of the crates loose and it had smashed into the flour sacks, tearing some open, and flour was still trickling out onto the apron. It formed a snowy heap on the tarmac, turning black at the edges where it soaked up stray oil.

'So what are we doing here?' Brereton asked the crew chief. 'Nobody's getting on or off the plane.'

The airman lit his own cigarette before slowly replying. 'On the radio they tell us there are passengers here, but now they say some other plane took them. If we knew it was like this, we would not have landed.' He joined his hands in front of him in token of prayer. 'Now we must talk nice before we can go again, never come back here.'

A truck came careering down the road and screeched to a halt beyond the fence. The truck had NGO markings but a dozen soldiers jumped from it, abandoning it where it stood, half on the verge and half on the road. They came scurrying over the chain-link fence to join the group beside the aircraft. One of them fell on landing, dropping his weapon, and ran on a few yards before he hesitated, stopped, then went back to retrieve it.

A leader had emerged from the crowd and was shouting at the pilot in the doorway. He wore colonel's insignia and as he shouted he waved a plush leather briefcase in the pilot's face. The crowd outside hushed so that when the pilot answered his voice carried to us.

'This plane is not going to Kinshasa now.' The pilot waved an apologetic hand southwards. 'This plane is special charter for the Presidential Guard. We go now to Lubumbashi and unload the cargo, for Presidential Guard there, then we refuel and come back here again tomorrow morning. Then we can take passengers to Kinshasa, take you all, no problem.'

A soldier appeared at the tail of the plane, staring in at us through the gap above the half-opened ramp. He was a scrawny, sick-looking kid in filthy green fatigue pants and a ripped camouflage T-shirt. He might have been fifteen. The only weapon he had was a hand grenade. It was his symbol of office and as he stared at us, open-mouthed, he toyed with it absently, spinning it round a finger he had crooked through the pin.

The officer on the steps was shouting in English now. It seemed that apart from his mission to Kinshasa he also had orders to fly to Lubumbashi for a strategy conference. His staff would have to come too. They would all return that afternoon. He had to raise his voice when he got to that last bit because his soldiers were now jeering him.

Somewhere in the distance, off where the town would have been, there was a sound like a giant door slamming home, a thud at once sharp and dull. For an instant the new sound silenced the commotion outside as all eyes jerked towards its source. Then the explosion echoed off a distant row of hangars and heads snapped back the other way, like spectators at a tennis match. The shouting was louder than ever now.

'Fuck Lubumbashi, maybe we should stay here,' said Brereton, looking around at us. But nobody answered him.

The pilot in the door bent forward, talking quickly to the colonel. Another shell landed, this one a little further off but in the opposite direction. This time nobody looked around. The pilot straightened up, glanced towards us and nodded. The crew chief tossed his cigarette out onto the tarmac. 'We go now,' he said.

The cargo ramp ground shut, cutting off Grenade Boy's stare. The pilot in the doorway stepped back and a moment later the FAZ colonel scrambled past into the cabin. He was flustered, without his pistol or his beret, and he stood there for a moment in the daylight from the doorway, blinking in the unaccustomed gloom. Something flashed in through the open doorway and hit him between the shoulders and spun to the floor and the colonel gasped and arched his back in agony. The missile lay on the floor at the front of the cabin, in front of the civilian passengers. They stared at it impassively. It was the colonel's briefcase. In one quick move the pilot pulled the aluminium steps into the cabin and then he closed and sealed the door, his mouth no longer smiling.

The colonel stooped, wincing, to pick up his briefcase, then stumbled back along the cabin. The civilians watched him as he eased himself down on the bench. He put his briefcase on his knees, opened it and took out some documents, and the papers shook as he pretended to read them.

The port engine barked, scattering the soldiers beyond the wing tip. A few of them were shouting at the colonel's staff officers, who stood and ignored them, staring bitterly at the plane. Then the Toyotas began to move off and soldiers were fighting to jump on the back as they accelerated away. The officers were too slow and were left behind, jogging a few steps before giving up and turning to watch the plane again. The Antonov lurched forward and just as it did so someone ran past my porthole, checked himself just short of the spinning propeller, jinked and ran clear. Beatrice nudged me and pointed. It was Grenade Boy, now bare-chested, hugging his bundled T-shirt in his arms. It was stained white with flour.

At Lubumbashi we were met on the apron by a squad of angry Presidential Guards. They separated us from the Zairean passengers and marched us off towards a small building on the edge of the apron.

This airport too, like the one in Kinshasa, was eerily calm, silent apart from the drone of a generator somewhere off beyond the hangars and the voices of distant sentries carried on the wind. The FAZ colonel came with us. I suppose he had been told to. He walked briskly, chest out, swinging his briefcase just a little bit jauntily, but he was careful to keep between Brereton and me, and away from the Presidential Guards, who were stalking along in a cordon around us.

The guards took us to a low rectangular building with VIP stencilled on its wall in fading black paint. There was a veranda out front where a captain of the Presidential Guards was sprawled across a sofa. He seemed quite old for his rank, with a thin, pained face, but the daylight recoiled from the mirrors hiding his eyes. When the guards saw him, they drew themselves a little more upright than before and fingered their weapons and the captain raised a lazy hand and the soldiers made us all stop, standing there in the punishing sun, while the captain sat in the shade and took off his sunglasses and coldly looked us over, and then he put his glasses back on and he stared at the colonel for a while, still without saying anything. The colonel had looked as if he wanted to speak but before that blank gaze he silently wilted. The captain yawned, stood up and stretched, and then he barked a single word at us, 'papers', but when the colonel tried to hand him something from his briefcase the captain stared at him until he put it away again.

Beyond the veranda was a cool hall with tiled floors, grubby white walls, high dirty windows and rows of plastic benches. The walls were decorated with yellow tourist posters from the 1950s, the glass now missing from the frames. To the right was an open archway leading to a second, larger room, darkened by heavy red curtains. The arch was blocked by an armchair that had been pulled out from the wall. Wordlessly, the captain took all our documents from us, went into an office at the far end of the hall and closed the door behind him. When we got tired of standing looking at each other we settled on the benches. The colonel went into a corner by himself and opened his briefcase again. It had shiny brass hinges and was made of gleaming ox-blood leather that exactly matched the colonel's shoes. He took his papers out and began to read them again. His hand was steadier this time. But every now and then he would lower the papers a few inches while his face turned up to the light from the grimy window, and his chest would convulse in what might have been a sigh.

I finished my magazine and took out a book I had borrowed from Laura. It was a Congo travel guide from the 1950s, and it told you where to collect mail or cash cheques in Albertville and Stanleyville, and how many hours it would take to drive to Élisabethville from Fort Salisbury, and all the nice places to stay on the way.

Outside, the day softened and turned yellow and ibises shrieked horribly as they flew back to roost. It was now too dark inside to read. A radio went on in the office; somebody talking, scraps of high life guitar. The colonel seemed to be asleep in his corner, stretched out on the bench with his head on his briefcase, but you could see his eyes flash whenever he looked to the window. The hotel where Fine and Tommo were staying, where we'd hoped to spend that night, was becoming a dream to us. After a while I went out to the veranda. The guards were out of sight around the corner but their voices grew louder and harder, as if they were drinking. Long shadows betrayed the hollows and bumps in the runway, and fleshed out the skeletons of the aircraft sprawled on the perimeter. The ibises were gone. Off beyond the terminal a diesel generator clattered into life and a light came on in the window behind us. The passenger terminal became a broken chequerboard of yellow light, and a yellow wedge appeared on the veranda floor in front of me, pointing to the open door. Back in the trees fringing the perimeter fence I heard voices – male and female – and a transistor radio playing jangly pop. A cow lowed, and quiet feet and voices trailed dark shapes along the road.

When I went back inside the situation was not as I'd left it. Beatrice was alone in one corner of the room, the colonel in another, separated by three Presidential Guards who stood in the aisle between the benches. There was no sign of Brereton. The soldiers stood with their feet apart and shoulders back, rifles held stiff across their chests, the barrels swaying gently. One of them kept on nudging his mates and pointing at Beatrice, grinning and talking in a raised voice, as if for her benefit. His friends just stared at her as she sat there, ignoring them. I went and sat beside her, smiling at the soldiers. One of them laughed at me.

The door opened behind me and Brereton emerged from the office, followed by the captain. Brereton came and sat beside me.

'The captain has decided to inquire into our bona fides,' he said in a low voice. 'He thinks we might be spies. They're very angry about some photographer called Jansson. Apparently he landed here yesterday and went straight over to the rebels. I said I'd never heard of him.'

'How the hell did Jansson get here before us? This was the first plane in two days.'

'The bastard moves in mysterious ways.'

The captain was standing over us now. 'Les deux autres,' he shouted, 'la Française et l'autre.' It was only then that he seemed to notice his soldiers inside the room.

'Allez-y, sortez,' he shouted at them, and they stared at him, not moving, even when he repeated himself in what I took to be Lingala. Only when he shouted for a third time did they begin to turn and leave through the door to the veranda.

The office walls were bare apart from a dreamy-eyed portrait of the president and a map of colonial Africa with each European territory picked out in its own flat bright shade. Someone had stuck red and blue pins into the Kivus and down along the western shore of Lake Tanganyika, red for the rebels, blue for the FAZ. They seemed to have run out of pins far to the north of where someone had biroed *Lubumbashi* over the partially scratched-out *Élisabethville*. There was a wooden desk and a couple of plastic chairs, and a metal filing cabinet stood in the corner beside a glass door, through which could be seen a wide reception room, lit by moonlight through floor-length windows. On the desk lay an untidy pile of passports and travel papers.

The captain told us to sit down, then glided around the desk and dropped into a swivel chair, his eyes on us all the time. He removed his pistol from its holster, laid it down on the desk and picked up the documents, shuffling them slowly between his hands until he had extracted Beatrice's passport.

He opened it and peered inside, then placed it face down on the table and picked up one of her government travel documents. He tapped the document with one finger, staring at her. 'It says here that you were born in the United States.'

'Yes.'

'But you have a French passport.'

His eyes wandered across to meet mine and he gave me a tired smile. He cupped his hands on the desk and leaned forward, smiling to himself now. There was a half-empty bottle on a low shelf behind him.

'You will forgive me,' he said, 'but it is my duty as an officer of the Republic of Zaire to inform myself about those in my custody. You will appreciate this.'

'My father is French, my mother's American,' said Beatrice. 'I'm allowed to have two passports.'

'Where is the American one?'

'I don't have one,' she said quickly. I guessed she was lying.

He studied the travel papers before him in silence. Beatrice and I glanced at each other.

'The French are good,' he mused. 'They are our friends. I myself have studied their culture. But the Americans are not good for us here in Zaire.'

'I'm afraid I don't understand you,' said Beatrice.

The captain sat back in his chair and hunched his shoulders and then blew his cheeks out, as if he had, indeed, studied the French rather too closely. He spoke their language beautifully. How had he ended up here?

'I refer to this invasion by the Tutsis, who want to enslave our motherland and steal its wealth,' he said, speaking slowly, as if explaining for children. 'America supports them, even after all our president did for the Americans to fight the communists.' His tone was mild, his smile condescending, the smile of a schoolteacher taking his time. 'So people like you come to spy on us, pretending to be French.'

He was thin, and without his sunglasses he did not look well. The beer would have got to him quickly. Beatrice sat stiffly in her chair, still smiling politely.

'We are reporters,' I said. 'This lady is French. The French are not your enemies.' I remembered some advice Brereton had given me once. I held out my hand to him. 'Captain, my name is Owen and this is Beatrice. May I know your name?'

He stared at me for a few moments, ignoring my hand, and then he sat back in his chair again and picked up my passport. 'My name is my own, monsieur. You may know me by my nom de guerre. I am Captain Coco.'

'Coco?'

'It is my nom de guerre. My French instructors called me that. I was trained by the French, as a paratrooper. An elite force. Were I to give you my real name, it could be used to harm my relatives. I am from Équateur, which is now attacked by the foreign Tutsis.'

'I see.'

'Soon we will take it back.'

'Of course.'

He stood and turned his back to us, frowning and studying the map. Beatrice and I glanced at each other.

'You should understand this,' the captain said. 'I come from a warrior people. I and my men. Yes.' He was tapping the map now, lips pursed. From somewhere in the area of Bukavu a pin came loose. I heard it hit the floor as the captain brooded. My eyes found it in a groove between the tiles. It was blue.

The captain's frown deepened and he turned to look at us again. 'Yes, I have fought in this war. I have fought. I have fought at Goma, at Bukavu, at Uvira and – most recently – at Kalemie.'

As he declaimed his hand described an arc southwards, two thousand miles across central Africa, inadvertently following through all the way to the Cape. I glanced at Beatrice again. This time I saw to my horror that she was struggling not to smile.

The vinyl squeaked as the captain resumed his chair.

'We have fought bravely,' he said, 'but we face a great conspiracy. Even in Kinshasa now there are Tutsis and Jews poisoning our president. This cancer they talk of. And now they send *you* here as well.'

Beatrice was still.

'We're here to report on this campaign,' I said. 'This lady is French. We're reporters. We're not your enemy.'

He smiled at me. 'Spies, reporters, what is the difference?'

'Reporters don't have secrets.'

He nodded, staring at me, and his smile didn't change. 'Frankly, monsieur, if it were up to me I would shoot you now and bury you.'

We said nothing.

He nodded again. 'Indeed, yes.'

The captain picked up my passport, studied it for a few moments and then dropped it on the desk again. 'This is a meaningless country,' he said. 'I know nothing about it. You could be spying for anyone.'

'I write for a newspaper. We have laissez-passers from your government.'

'The government is in Kinshasa. This is Lubumbashi.'

He studied us both for a few more moments and then abruptly he yawned, jerking a hand up to cover his mouth. He moved the pistol a few inches to the side, picked up our documents and placed them back with all the others.

'In any case, you are fortunate,' he said. 'You are to be held here tonight and sent back to Kinshasa tomorrow. Now go.'

I let Beatrice leave the room first. As I exited I heard a clicking noise behind me. The captain was cleaning his pistol.

Outside in the dark the guards were quarrelling again. It was growing cooler. Brereton always carried some biltong and biscuits, and at least one whiskey bottle for emergencies, and the colonel watched us passing them back and forth until Brereton took them over to him in his corner. The colonel smiled for the first time since we'd been with him. 'Merci bien, messieurs,' he whispered. Beatrice gave him a bottle of water from our communal hoard.

We were stretching ourselves out on the hard plastic benches when the office door opened noisily and the captain appeared at the entrance to the passage. He looked around at us in what seemed to be puzzlement, and then he said, loudly but very carefully, 'Why are you all in here still? You should be in the other room. It is more comfortable.' And he stepped over to the dark archway and pulled aside the chair that blocked the entrance to the VIP lounge, flicking on a light.

By the heavily curtained window there was a long yellow sofa and two matching armchairs, the colours dulled by a thick layer of dust. The captain waited until we were all in the room and then he said goodnight, locked the veranda door and returned to his office. Beatrice had moved to the sofa and I saw her open the curtains a crack and peer outside. When I came up beside her I could see the empty runway silver in the moonlight.

'Why do you think the French called him Coco?' I asked her.

She paused before she answered, not turning her head. 'Perhaps he was very chic back then.'

She sat down on the sofa. Brereton and the colonel each took an armchair. Neither was tall, and the armchairs were so soft and wide that they could just about stretch out on them.

Beatrice had a bottle of insect repellent that she passed around the room and Brereton gave us the whiskey again; we stood and drank together, then handed it back.

I lay down at my end of the sofa and pulled my jacket over me to keep the mosquitoes off in case the repellent didn't work. Opposite me I could see Beatrice propped up at the other end of the sofa and beside her was a silver gap where the curtains just failed to meet. Then off in the distance the generator spluttered and died and the neon tubes in the ceiling faded, leaving ghosts in the dark for a few seconds more. The night was abruptly silent except for the barking of dogs in the distance. Beatrice's face was the only thing I could see, lit by the moon through the curtain.

The fabric of the sofa was rough against my face. The dogs barked at the moon, and a little while later, way off in the distance, there were two quick rifle shots, then nothing more. Beatrice was gently snoring. Once I woke and found our feet were touching. I wondered how she could sleep so well with the moonlight on her face.

The moon had set when someone started banging at the door of the building. It must have been almost dawn. The office door opened and feet made their way hurriedly towards the veranda door and then there were loud voices, the squeaking of rubber soles on linoleum, and men were standing in the archway flashing a torch over us. I lifted my head just enough to see past the armrest and felt rather than saw Beatrice doing the same. The torch beam steadied on one of the armchairs and two shadows moved forward and stood on either side of it.

The soldiers shook the man on the chair and an impatient voice shouted something from behind the flashlight. The colonel did not move, clinging to whatever dreams he may have had. Then the voice behind the flashlight barked again and a rifle butt cracked against something that was both soft and hard. There was a groan and the colonel sat up and tried to put his shoes on, but one of the soldiers hit him again and then they grabbed him by the elbows and pushed him from the room. The flashlight swung in the archway, picking out the colonel's stricken face as someone wrenched his briefcase away from him. Boots thundered off and a few seconds later the veranda door closed again and a pair of feet made their way, very slowly, back towards the office. Silence returned. Beatrice's eyes were wide and cold in the first light of day, which seeped along the floor from the crack in the curtains, silver and grey like the trail that a snail leaves.

'At least we gave him a drink,' she said.

Dawn crawled up the wall. Behind the terminal the generator spluttered and roared into life again, erratic, percussive, a sound like pistons backfiring. There were shouts as sentries were woken at their posts and a vehicle droned onto the apron. Beatrice rose from the sofa and opened the curtains. The sun was up now, very low in a sky void but for a single long, thin bar of pink and white cloud. The grass of the airfield shone like the sea, the sun on the spider webs.

9

I met a lot of good people in Kinshasa. Most of them I forget now, people who did me favours, but I remember the gorilla guy although I can't recall his name. Let's call him Fred. It doesn't matter.

Fred worked for the British world service as a pool reporter, based out of some office in London, and they sent him to the Congo to do all the chicken-shit stuff that Tim Drysdale and the other war lords didn't care for. He was thin and stooped, with wispy blond hair and startled brown eyes. When he talked his neck couldn't quite hold his head steady and this made him look too earnest, as if he were forever presenting a bad piece to camera. Not that he got much screen time; he was too low in the batting for that.

I came to know Fred by sight in the early days, when you could still see him at breakfast in the morning or in the bar at night. He always sat with people from his own company and he didn't seem to talk much. When he disappeared I didn't notice. We only heard of him again when Polly Vermeulen was hired to mind him.

It seems that Fred was being worn down by the news cycle. The Brits had dozens of outlets to service on both radio and television – national, world service and regional stations, all of them screaming for input every hour of the day. The corporation's bigfeet – and none was bigger than Drysdale – scorned the smaller shows while fighting like ferrets for spots on the prime TV bulletins. Bottom of the pan, halfway round the S-bend, were the regional radio stations in places like Wales and Ulster, where the local anchors were desperate to be able to say, 'And now I'll be talking to our man in Kinshasa.' Which was Fred, in his hotel room, on the end of a phone, giving round-the-clock blow jobs. When things got really busy he didn't even have time to leave the hotel; all he could do was recycle stuff that other hacks told him, or that he saw on the TV or read on the wires. You couldn't sink any lower than that –

at least, not until the internet kicked in. Fred's sat-phone buzzed angrily while his mobile bleated counterpoint. His room became his prison.

After a few days of this, Marvell Dlamini, the chief producer out of Johannesburg, flew Polly up from South Africa to help Fred cope with the load. But, instead of taking pressure off Fred, Polly's arrival merely freed him up to do more voicers, forcing him ever deeper into his cell. I imagine him sitting there, his dreary tales of second-hand horror droning in his ears like a bluebottle trapped in his head . . . And when the anchors in Bristol and Cardiff and Belfast were done with him they would have tossed him aside so casually – 'And now – sport!' – and some snotty little producer would have grunted at him and cut the line before Fred could even say anything. This would have been Fred's only human contact for eighteen, twenty hours a day, apart from visits from room service, and Polly's quick briefings.

'He's beginning to freak me out,' Polly told us in Laura's room one night. 'He never answers when I knock because he's always on the phone, so I wait for a bit and then I let myself in with my key. When I go in he's sat in a chair in the corner, always on the phone, and his eyes just follow me as he keeps on talking. The floor is covered in trays of food and wire printouts. How he reads them with the lights off, I'll never know. By the light from the TV, maybe.'

Beatrice passed Polly a drink. Polly slopped some down and then continued. 'He just stares at me while I'm briefing him. Sometimes he asks a question, but when he talks he talks really carefully, like he's trying to save his voice. If I'm lucky the phone rings before long and he's off on another blow job. The really creepy thing is that as I go out the door I sometimes hear him repeating back what I've just told him, exactly and precisely, word for word.' She shuddered.

Beatrice was fascinated. 'It's like he's not there himself any more. He's become a conduit. Some kind of portal.'

'We have seen the future!' declared Brereton.

Polly wanted to cheer Fred up so she bought him a present in the market. She showed it to me before she gave it to him: it was a wickerwork gorilla, about the size of a one-year-old child, with a round gaping hole where its mouth should have been and two smaller holes for its eyes. It was hollow inside and its hair was woven from finely shredded strips of black plastic.

The doll looked comic by daylight but Polly soon discovered that in the darkness of Fred's suite the effect was very different. Propped up on the flickering television, the doll seemed to have acquired the power of movement. When Polly first gave it to Fred he greeted it with a rare smile, but after the first day he seemed to be frightened of it. He receded further and further into his corner, and now when Polly entered the room his stare juddered on the edge of panic.

That's how things were when we flew to Lubumbashi. When we got back to Kinshasa the next evening, dirty, exhausted and hungry, Polly was sitting alone in the lobby, fretting with a clipboard. When Brereton saw her he dropped his kit in the middle of the floor and tried to jump into her arms; he used to tease her terribly, which I thought was unfair. But Polly was too distracted to be pleased with Brereton's flirting, and before he could start telling her our story she was pouring out her own.

'It's been horrible,' she said, and you could see she was on the point of tears. 'When I went to his room this morning he looked at me as if he hated me, and when I tried to brief him he told me I should leave. It's as if I did something to hurt him. He's beginning to scare me.'

'Fuck him,' said Brereton, and he stood up on his toes to kiss her cheek. I wondered if she knew about Laura.

It was Brereton's idea to eat by the pool. After Lubumbashi it seemed the right thing to do, even though it was night already. Orphan kids were squabbling beyond the wall that separated the poolside from the street and insects buzzed about our heads. The only other customers on the terrace were three French photographers laughing hoarsely with some bar girls and a pair of Scandinavian TV stars leaning carefully together in a corner, talking slowly and seriously, both at the same time.

Beatrice came down from her room wearing a light cotton dress with short sleeves. Her swimsuit was a dark curve beneath it. The hot air was trapped between the hotel and the apartment block to its rear. It reeked of chlorine. When I sat down, now wearing shorts, the plastic chair stuck to the backs of my legs. After only a few seconds it felt as if I'd already been swimming. Rasheed and Polly joined us, and the waiters brought drinks dulled by ice that had melted too quickly.

The water shone like chain mail in the lights from the hotel. I set my whiskey down on the poolside, took off my T-shirt and stepped off into the deep end. The water absolved me, cool as I sank, warm as I rose again, but there was so much chlorine in it that I had to keep my eyes screwed shut to stop them from stinging. I floated on my back, carefully opened my eyes and then quickly shut them again as someone splashed in close beside me. Polly surfaced, hooting and blowing out water. Brereton took off his shoes, rolled up his trousers and sat on the edge of the pool, dangling his feet in the water. Polly swam over to splash him and he started to churn the water with his legs. Beatrice was standing, removing her dress. She wore a black one-piece swimsuit and she stood straight above me, poising herself on her toes, swinging her arms back and forth to prepare for the dive. In her thigh a muscle tightened and softened and a bone shifted in her hip, pale beneath the dark arc of the swimsuit. I tasted chlorine in the back of my throat. The Frenchmen had turned to watch her. Then Beatrice arched her body, swung her arms up all the way and launched herself from the poolside; I saw her breasts jump beneath her suit, and when she came up close by me she was blinking back the pain in her eyes.

'Jesus, that burns,' she spat. Polly started laughing, her deep chest booming, and you couldn't help joining in, and we were all laughing at Beatrice as she spluttered and wept when somewhere in the darkness above us a window crashed open and a harsh, quivering voice called out: 'Polly? Is that you down there? Answer me, you fucking bitch!'

A dim figure was leaning from an unlit window on the third

floor, right above us, the curtains draped around its shoulders. Its voice shook with a hatred so intense that we stared at each other in shock. Brereton had stopped kicking his feet in the water. 'Who's that up there?' he demanded, but by then we could all see that it was Fred. I could even see his face working.

'I'm talking to that bitch Polly, not you,' shouted Fred, and then he spotted her in the pool. 'Why don't you tell them about your joke, you fucking cow?'

Everyone on the terrace was silent now, watching, the two Scandinavians shaking their heads as they tried to refocus. A couple of waiters had emerged from the air-conditioned lobby and were staring upwards. Polly looked close to tears.

'I don't know what you're talking about,' she called to Fred. 'Why are you being so horrible?'

Fred gave a short laugh. 'Because of this, you fucking bitch.' He vanished in a swirl of curtains, and when he reappeared a moment later he was holding a dark shape at arm's length; the hand gripping it was wrapped inside a plastic bag. He proffered it to us stiffly, like an offering for some altar, and I saw it was the gorilla doll.

'What's wrong with it?' demanded Brereton.

'What's wrong with it? Take a look: it's full of fucking cockroaches!'

Fred flicked his arm stiffly and the doll came plummeting down towards us, the plastic bag fluttering after it. The doll hit the edge of the pool, bounced and then fell in the water a few feet out, face up, floating high off the surface. The curtain swirled and Fred was gone again.

'It does look a bit nasty, doesn't it?' said Brereton. He resumed kicking his feet in the water. 'I wonder if it's got some voodoo purpose.'

'It's just a doll,' insisted Polly, looking around for support. 'I gave it to him as a present. I bought it for myself but then I thought it might cheer him up.'

'Cheer me up?' shrieked the voice from above. He must have been listening behind the curtains. 'It's infested my room with cockroaches! They're all over the place! You should smell the stink!'

'It does hum a bit, doesn't it?' Brereton remarked calmly. 'I can smell it from here.'

The gorilla was low in the water now, and indeed it did give off a musky odour, the smell of something that has been dead a long while but hasn't quite finished rotting.

Polly addressed herself directly to the curtains. 'Look, I'm really sorry if I've offended you, but I gave you the gorilla in good faith and I thought it was very nice. I don't know anything about the cockroaches. I never saw any in your room.'

Fred laughed sarcastically. 'Of course you didn't. You would say that. The place is crawling with them.'

'Try opening the curtains,' suggested Brereton. 'Try getting out a bit. I'd be seeing things too if I were a hermit.'

'Don't make me come down there.'

'The door should be somewhere to your left, you fucking stylite . . . Listen, if this thing is full of cockroaches, why aren't there any in the pool? If there were any in there, they'd be abandoning ship by now, right?'

Beatrice whispered: 'Actually, there is a cockroach there, right beside it. It's still kicking.'

Brereton glanced around and frowned. 'That doesn't mean anything,' he said. 'You always get a few insects in the swimming pool. They fall in and can't get out again.'

'How did it get that far out into the pool, then?' asked Beatrice.

Brereton shrugged. 'It must have swum out.'

'That's ridiculous,' said Rasheed. 'Cockroaches can't swim.'

Brereton turned and smiled at him. 'Since when are you an entomologist, Rasher?'

'It might have flown out there and then fallen in,' said Beatrice. 'Cockroaches can fly, right?'

'Of course,' said Polly, 'but I think it's only the male ones.'

'No, that's not true,' insisted Brereton. 'You're thinking of ants. Or is it termites? Anyway, with cockroaches you get some species that can fly and others that can't. It's got nothing to do with gender.'

'You're just making things up now,' said Rasheed.

'I'm serious. I'll bet you fifty dollars.'

'I'll take that bet,' I told Brereton.

'There was nothing wrong with it when I bought it, and it felt empty,' Polly said helplessly. 'Maybe he's been putting things in it himself. I told you before, he's crazy.'

'I am not crazy!' shrieked Fred. 'And I'm telling Marvell about this. First thing tomorrow morning I'm going to have you fired. First thing.' The curtains swirled again and the window slammed behind him.

Rasheed sighed and began wading towards the aluminium ladder. 'I'm getting out of this pool. That thing is starting to scare me.'

The French snappers turned back to their prostitutes; the Scandinavians sank into a drunken silence. Waiters appeared with food, but after a few bites there wasn't much appetite left, what with the heat and the chemicals and the stink from the gorilla bobbing about in the pool. It seemed to move in a different rhythm to the wavelets in the water, as if something large inside it were indeed struggling to escape.

'We've got to do something about Gatsby there,' said Beatrice.

Brereton went over to the entrance of the changing rooms, found the pool net and fished out the doll. Holding it at the full length of the pole, he flung the doll as far as he could over the wall into the street. He waited a moment to see if there would be any reaction, then dropped the pole and started back towards us.

'The next round's on me,' he announced. He dropped back into his chair and lowered his voice. 'I'm going to charge it to that mad bastard's room.'

Polly was alarmed. 'Please don't, Charlie. I'm going to be in enough trouble with Marvell as it is.'

'Oh, go on, Polly. I reckon he owes us all a drink.'

'Charlie, please.' She put her giant hand on his arm. He looked away from her, frowning, towards the Frenchmen and their prostitutes.

'Look at them. Fucking whoremongers. The frogs of war . . .' His voice trailed off as he watched Laura appear in the doorway and then he raised his voice again: 'Speaking of which, here comes

Africa's leading shit-magnet . . . Oh fuck, Polly, Marvell's with her!'

Laura's smile flashed for a moment, just for Brereton, and then she sat down beside him. Marvell Dlamini stood over us, staring down at Polly. He wasn't smiling, which meant things were very serious indeed.

'Where've you been?' he demanded. 'I've been looking for you everywhere.'

Polly tried to smile at him. 'We've been out here all the time. Having a swim.'

Dlamini glanced round the table, shrewd eyes sucking us all in. Then he fixed them on Polly again. 'Have you seen your correspondent tonight?' he asked, and I could see Polly twitch at the sharpness in his voice.

'Why?' asked Brereton innocently. 'Is there a problem?'

'He's gone off the air. He's already missed a dozen phoners. I've knocked on his door but there's no answer. If we can't find him I'll have to wake up Drysdale to take over. Then we'll really be in shit.'

'Oh, dear,' whispered Polly.

'Perhaps he's had some kind of episode,' Brereton suggested.

Marvell stared at him but Brereton kept a straight face. Marvell turned back to Polly. 'I'm going to take a chance on the curfew and check the Piano Bar. You look around the hotel – there might be a party on. But start with his suite. You have a key, don't you? If you find him, call me right away.'

Marvell turned and left.

'Oh, God, what'll I do?' moaned Polly. 'He's obviously still up there, gone completely doolally.'

'Maybe he'll top himself,' volunteered Brereton.

Laura stood up, stretching herself. 'You must try to find him before Marvell does, Polly. Maybe you can sort it out before anything becomes official.'

'How can I sort it out?' demanded Polly. 'I'm terrified of him! I don't want to be anywhere near him!'

Laura raised her hands. 'I've got to go and send some pictures now. If I see him, I'll tell you.'

Brereton watched Laura as she made her way towards the door. 'Maybe Beatrice could go up with you,' he offered to Polly.

'I don't think that's a good idea,' said Beatrice. 'I think he has a problem with women. Charlie, you're old enough to be a grown-up. Why don't you try to calm him down?'

But Brereton was still watching the door through which Laura had vanished. 'I don't think we hit it off very well,' he said slowly. 'Besides, I've got to do a phoner of my own in a few minutes.'

I saw Polly follow his eyes.

'Then that leaves Owen,' said Beatrice, and she smiled at me. I could only stare back at her.

Fred's room was on the third floor, like Laura's, and Beatrice's. But Laura and Brereton got out of the lift together on the second floor, and Beatrice and I went up the rest of the way alone.

The corridor was beige, its walls and its doors dimly lit on either side by gap-toothed rows of carious white lamps. Our feet hissed along the carpet together until it was time for me to halt outside Fred's door. Beatrice put a hand on my arm and whispered that she would leave her door open, in case of emergency. As she unlocked her door she smiled back at me encouragingly.

The night hummed with yellow fatigue and darkness condensed at either end of the corridor. Fred's door was dark brown, the number and peephole picked out in brass. Was that movement I saw in the darkness beyond the fisheye? After a few seconds staring into it, I knocked three times. No answer. I knocked again and waited. Nothing. I took Polly's key from my pocket and put it in the lock, rattling and scraping in the silence of the hall.

Inside the room the curtains were half open and sodium light spilled onto the floor from a gap in the curtains. A heap of bedclothes lay at one end of the sofa and a pillow at the other. There was a vegetable smell.

Fred was sitting in a deep shadow in the far corner, cross-legged in an armchair. All I could see of his face was the light from the window reflected in his glasses. He seemed to be staring at me. A satellite handset was placed on a stool beside him, its cable running to an aerial taped onto the windowsill. He sat with his hands folded in his lap, wearing a shirt and slacks, and his bare feet shone white in the dimness. He didn't move as I pushed the door further open. Fresh light from the hallway seeped in around me.

'Hello,' I said.

'Hello.' His voice was very calm and quiet, unrecognizable from the shriek of a few minutes before.

'I'm Owen,' I said.

'Hello, Owen . . . Who do you work for?'

His tone was friendly but distant. Fred seemed to contemplate my reply for some time. 'That's nice,' he said finally. Another pause. 'Do they treat you well?'

I shrugged in the darkness. 'It's basically a freelance deal, but it covers my exes . . . it's good just to be here on such a big story.'

I saw the glasses flash a couple of times before he spoke again. Fred was nodding. 'I feel that way too. It's a tremendous experience for me.'

'Really?'

I thought I heard a sigh. 'Yes, really . . . I was very lucky to be sent on this story. It's my first big foreign job. I was going mad back in London.'

'Oh.'

'Yes. I needed to get out more. I was on the desk all the time.'

I stepped into the room and almost slipped on a thick slick of newswire printouts.

'Do you mind if I turn the light on?' I asked.

'Be my guest . . . It's very dark in here, isn't it?'

I found the switch and blinked in the sudden light. Behind his thin lenses Fred's eyes were dark and sad. His bare feet stuck out from his trouser cuffs, bony and ridiculous. The rubber rat's-tail aerial of an ancient Kinshasa cell phone protruded from a waste-basket beside him and the plug for the sat-phone lay dead on the floor. The hotel phone had been wrenched from the wall, bringing the plastic socket and a lump of plaster with it. I pointed to the sofa.

'Do you mind if I sit down for a moment? I've had a couple of very long days.'

'Not at all . . . Just push that stuff at the end to one side.'

I avoided the heaped bedclothes. They smelled of sweat. 'You've been sleeping here, have you?' I asked casually.

'Yes . . . I didn't want to sleep in the bedroom.'

'I see . . . Why not?'

For the first time he moved, turning his head away to look out of the half-open window. 'You know why not. You were down by the pool, weren't you?'

'Yes, I was . . . So is it the cockroach thing?'

'Yes. The bedroom was full of cockroaches. So was this sitting room, but not so bad.'

'I don't see any.'

'They've gone now.'

'I see.'

He sighed again, and this time I could see his chest heave convulsively. 'You think I'm mad, don't you?'

I raised my hand to rub my eyes and temples. 'I'd say that you seemed a little upset.'

'Upset?' Some life was coming back into the flat voice. 'I'm telling you, this place was crawling with cockroaches, and they came from that fucking doll.'

I let my head fall back and tried to focus on the off-white ceiling. A couple of mosquitoes rested there, fat with blood, digesting their last meal and planning the next.

'You should get some insect spray,' I said. 'For the mosquitoes. You've been bitten, haven't you? You could get malaria.'

'I had a can of spray but I emptied the whole thing into that gorilla. A whole fucking can. Twelve hours later the roaches were back.'

There was a ring of light on the ceiling just above my head. I let it go fuzzy, hardened it, let it go fuzzy again. 'Really? You'd think a whole can would do it . . . Still, they say they're really hardcore, don't they? That cockroaches will be the last thing to go if there's a nuclear war?'

I felt him lean towards me. 'They operate on pure instinct,' he said, with sudden vehemence. 'They are man's exact opposite in

128

the survival spectrum. They're instinct, we're intelligence. They can grow as big as mice, and outrun a squirrel.'

Was I slipping into his crazed story now? I didn't much care. 'You seem to know a lot about them,' I said, and stifled a yawn.

'I once did a ten-minute radio spot on them, for a science programme. It almost won an award.'

'Ten whole minutes just on cockroaches?'

'There was an important new paper out about their ecological role and social behaviour. Lots of stuff that wasn't known before.'

I yawned, openly this time, then I lowered my eyes to look at him. 'Did it say whether they can fly or not? Or is it just the males who can fly?'

He blinked. 'I don't remember.'

'Pity . . .' And where was this going? Oh, yes . . . 'Listen, you don't seriously think that Polly deliberately infested your room with insects, do you?'

He looked out of the window again. 'Where else did they come from? Jesus. I sprayed a whole can of Doom into that doll . . .' He shuddered horribly.

It was better, I understood, to believe in the cockroaches. And why not? Perhaps they were real.

'Maybe there was some kind of nest in there,' I said. 'Maybe it was an accident. I'm sure Polly wouldn't have known. She's really very nice, you know.'

'You're one of her friends, aren't you?'

'Yes, I am. But I'm talking to you as one man to another.'

He glanced at me, then back out of the window. His expression was even more mournful than before.

'You really think there was a nest in there?'

'It's the most likely explanation.'

'I can't remember if cockroaches have nests . . . ten whole minutes of airtime and I don't even remember that.'

'It probably didn't come into the framework of your piece.'

He sighed again. 'Probably not. I hope not. I'd hate to think I missed something important . . . It was supposed to be a kind of complete guide to cockroaches. Comprehensive.'

'You can't get everything in. There's never enough time.'

'No . . .' There was a very long pause, and when he spoke again his voice was conversational. 'Everyone thinks I'm mad now.'

Another mosquito whined past my ear and landed on the ceiling. It too was fat with blood. I mentally consulted my ankles and felt a faint tingle behind the right one. It would itch for the next four days. Perhaps I'd get malaria. I'd long since stopped taking the pills. But maybe Fred was still on them. That might explain a few things.

'Don't worry about it,' I told him. 'Everyone's a little tense these days, what with the rebels coming and the army turning nasty and stuff.'

'Do you really think so?'

'Sure . . .' I cleared my throat. 'You can always lie low here for a couple of days, if you feel awkward. Just file from your room.'

He uncrossed his legs and put his hand to his chin in token of thought. His hand was trembling. 'I suppose I could, yes. It's more or less what I've been doing anyway, for the past few days.'

'Really.'

'Yes. I've been doing a lot of phoners.'

I yawned again. 'That reminds me. I met Marvell Dlamini earlier on and when I told him I was coming up to this floor he asked me to give you a message. That's why I'm here. Apparently someone's been looking for you back in London.'

He seemed to stiffen. 'Did he say what they wanted?'

'A blow job, probably.'

'A *blow job*?'

I'd forgotten how new he was. 'A telephone interview,' I explained. 'You know. Cheap and cheerful. Not much money but not much work.'

His face screwed into something like a smile, then snapped back into place as he glanced around the room. 'The phones are all off.'

He unfolded himself from the chair and almost fell over as he stood. He must have been sitting there for a long time. He staggered over to the corner and began replugging the sat-phone, then he stopped and turned slowly. 'The only thing is, I'm not sure what they'll want to ask me about.'

I put both hands to my temples and rubbed hard. How long since Polly had last fed him? I'd had no news myself since we left for Lubumbashi, the morning before.

'Just agree with whatever they ask you, then throw in something extra from the wires,' I said hopefully.

'I haven't read the wires since yesterday. Polly didn't bring them today.'

Of course she hadn't. I closed my eyes and tried to think.

'Tell them the rebels are advancing rapidly towards Kinshasa,' I said finally. 'Tell them they are deep in the jungle, and nobody knows quite where. Tell them Catholic missionary radio is accusing the rebels of massacres. It's always saying that.'

'What about Mobutu?' His voice was coming from a different direction. I opened my eyes and saw that he was back in his chair, staring at me, pen poised over a writing pad.

'Mobutu says he won't negotiate. Neither will the rebels. The French are demanding a ceasefire. Well, they were last time I heard, which was a couple of days ago now. I doubt if they've changed their minds in the meantime.'

'And what about the humanitarian situation?'

'Listen: fuck the humanitarian situation.'

'No, seriously. They always ask about that.'

I closed my eyes again. 'The humanitarian situation is very grave . . . Food is short in the markets . . . If clean water runs out there's a major risk of cholera, I suppose.'

'That sounds pretty bad.'

'There's always cholera and stuff when people drink shitty water.'

'Doesn't matter. This is good stuff . . . Is there anything I should say about children?'

'The UN says that children remain most at risk.'

'From what?'

'All the above, plus child abuse, I suppose. A lot of women will have been raped too, but don't say anything about that unless you're asked first.'

'Why not?' He had stopped writing.

'It might sound too eager. If they want rape, they'll ask for it.'

He was writing again, and he had the tip of his tongue tucked back over the corner of his lip. It looked yellow but it might have been the light.

'Will that be okay, do you think?' I asked.

He stopped writing and looked up at me. 'I suppose so, yes . . .' His eyes slid downward. 'I'm sorry about earlier on.'

'Don't worry about it. It'll all be forgotten tomorrow.'

I stood up, and swayed for a moment. 'Oh, and listen,' I said. 'When you've cleared your lines with London you should get some proper sleep. Tell them you've got food poisoning or something, and if they want any more blow jobs in the next few hours they should get Drysdale to do them. Apparently he's keen to get on the radio more.'

'Did he say that? I thought he only did television now. He thinks radio's beneath him.'

'No. He loves doing radio. Especially the early-morning regional shows. He reckons that's when you can really connect with an audience.'

'I suppose he's right.'

The lock clicked behind me. I was free. Down the dim corridor I saw the crack of light along Beatrice's door. It opened further and I saw her face.

'Owen,' she whispered.

She stood aside to let me enter her room. She was still wearing the cotton dress but there was no sign now of the dampness from her swimsuit. Her laptop was open on the table beneath her mirror, and I turned the chair away from it and sat down. Beatrice was over by the television, pouring whiskey into tooth glasses. She handed me one, then sat on the foot of the bed, facing me.

'Well? How did it go?'

'Not bad, I guess. I'm not sure how crazy he is. Maybe there really was something wrong with that doll.'

'He's crazy, all right.'

'I suppose so . . .' I sipped the whiskey. 'He's going to put his phones back on. I think it's going to be okay with Polly. I told him it was a misunderstanding.'

'Let's call her and tell her.'

She turned around on the bed and stretched her arm out for the telephone. I studied my glass; Beatrice was a pale haze in the whiskey as Polly answered. Beatrice waved me over and I knelt on the floor beside the bed. She passed me the receiver, looking into my face.

'What happened, Owen?' said Polly's anxious voice.

'He looked pretty rough and he'd turned the phones off. I told him it was all an innocent mistake. I think he'll be okay.'

'He's not going squealing to Marvell, then?'

'I don't think so. I told him to talk to London and then get some sleep.'

Beatrice was smiling at me. I could see my outline in her eyes.

'I told him he should get London to wake up Drysdale to help with the radio work.'

'Oh, God.'

'Sorry. Couldn't help myself. If I were you, I'd stay away from him for another day or so.' I looked at Beatrice again. 'Maybe one of the other producers could feed him tomorrow. They all owe you favours.' Beatrice rolled on her side, facing me, then raised herself up on her elbow and reached for her glass. It was on the bedside table, beyond me.

'Goodnight, Polly,' I said, and put the phone down.

Beatrice's sheets had the sweet, stable-like smell of sleep and cigarettes. Beneath her dress she was naked. Her shoulders were pale brown, with the moist warmth of fresh-made dough. I couldn't be sure if I was pulling her in or if she was pressing against me as I tried to find her mouth with my lips, but it turned away from me, somewhere amid the unmade hair, as she moved her head to listen. Outside the door, at the end of the corridor, the lift machinery had whined and stopped and its door creaked open. Beatrice's mouth could not have gone far. It occurred to me how tall she was as I measured myself against her.

Feet scuffed on the nylon carpet beyond the door. We lay there, together, listening, our heads cocked, as if fearing detection, and I felt a hand come up to rest on my hip, by the hem of my shirt. I held my breath. Beyond the door voices were murmuring, growing louder. The woman was Laura. She said something down low in her throat and her companion began to laugh, burbling like a badly choked two-stroke engine.

'It's Laura and Brereton!' I whispered. 'They're together! I knew it!'

A door opened and closed and there was silence again in the corridor.

Beatrice sighed and I felt her knees part and brush down past mine, and a moment later her lips surfaced between my jaw and my ear.

She kept the light on so I had to close my eyes from time to time to remind myself who I was with. I could see her then as I first saw her, that night at the border in Goma, hugging herself in the drizzle. Her shirt had been pulled tight about her by the strap of her camera. She told me later that she'd been a swimmer, in a previous incarnation, until bad habits prevailed. I suppose that explained it: when she moved beneath me I felt impelled onward, as if by a wave.

I opened my eyes and saw her frowning at me. What business had those other Beatrices here, with me, and with this new Beatrice, whose sweat trickled from the wispy hair by her ear, whose brown neck and shoulders faded abruptly into a pale and lightly freckled chest? If I'd found the nerve I could have watched their eyes narrow, their frowns deepen, their shoulders move faster with each breath. But I felt outnumbered. I think now that perhaps I always felt outnumbered. I relaxed my elbows and felt my mouth press against a shoulder. I felt the Beatrices resolve themselves to a common cause, and then it didn't matter which one I was with until I had to open my eyes again.

The light of the lamp showed a faint fuzz of gold hair on Beatrice's pink ear lobe. We lay there for a while, meshed together. Then she took her hands from my waist and I felt her skin hiss away from mine and her shoulders tighten as she stretched her arms out on either side of her, across the pillows, and when she yawned, convulsively, I felt her pinch almost to the point of pain. She laughed, and pulled me forward again, just once, with her legs, and then she heaved beneath me and we slipped away from each other with the sad bright pang of a parting kiss.

She moved again, turning sideways away from me, and I pushed in behind her as she reached for the packet of cigarettes lying on the table beside the lamp. She took out two cigarettes and passed one back to me, over her shoulder.

'We can't get caught,' she said, reaching back for her lighter, the muscles of her back working against me.

We slept without sheets in the warm air. Neither of us heard Fred screaming in the corridor, or the commotion when they came to restrain him. Sometime later I heard the door of Beatrice's room open, and the voice of a cleaner talking to someone behind her, and then there was an abrupt silence and the door shut softly again, and I tightened my arm around Beatrice, who was still asleep.

It was almost afternoon when I came down to the café. Laura and Brereton were drinking coffee on a sofa along the wall, beneath one of those kebab-shop posters of James Dean in a diner with Bogart and Elvis and Marilyn.

'Tell us what happened last night,' demanded Laura, and I felt as if I'd been slapped. But it was Fred who concerned them. It seemed he was already across the river in Brazzaville, heavily sedated, having been shipped out by Marvell under medical escort. In an hour or so his plane would leave for Paris.

Laura had been the first on the scene. Early that morning Fred had opened his door to come down for breakfast. It was to be his first trip outside his room in several days. Across the hall from his door, propped against the wall and staring blankly back at him, was the gorilla doll. It was still dripping. Beside it a baby cockroach scuttled uncertainly around on the floor.

Brereton denied any involvement, and I think that I believe him. Maybe the doll found its own way back: who's to say? We were in Africa, after all. Marvell later told us that Fred recovered enough to return to his desk job, although that's hardly a happy ending, when you think about it. As for Polly, Marvell refused to believe that she was entirely innocent in the affair. He gave her a full-time contract.

I felt sick for the rest of that afternoon and the sickness increased as night came on. After the information minister's daily briefing in the ballroom I went to my room and lay awake on the bed. I got up and wrote a piece, a pull-together, and later on I called my desk and had them phone me back so I could dictate it to a copy-taker. Through the chink in the curtains I saw that the city was darkening, and only street people and local residents were wandering in the dusk. The sound of the phone punched me in the stomach.

'Owen?' said Beatrice, my own name, dopplering past me.

'Hi.'

'I didn't see you this afternoon.'

'I was at Kinky's briefing,' I said.

'I couldn't go. I had to write.'

I sat down on the bed. 'You heard what happened with the gorilla?'

'I told you he was crazy.'

That was the only time she came down to my room. After that, in the time that was left, we always met in hers; she said she was old-fashioned. Once, creeping away in the early morning, I ran into Brereton as he sneaked away from Laura's room. We nodded to each other and said nothing.

Beatrice and I were silent together. Once I tried saying her name, almost for form's sake, but it came out hollow and I felt her giggle beneath me. That first time, in her room, she had surprised me with her intensity. She had learned to be serious; she was older than me. Should I be grateful or should I be jealous? Where had she acquired this gravity, and from whom? I was grateful then, though. I didn't care. She kept her eyes closed, smiling at something, and when she opened them and looked at me her smile broadened. How could you forget something like that? How could you mistake it?

She had a different laugh in bed, much lower. I remember her sitting up against the headboard one of those evenings, the sheet half wrapped around her, as I fed her some of Brereton's false confessions of moral squalor. It felt so easy. Her bare shoulders shook and then she put her arms around me again. I've never understood anything so plainly. The phone rang and it was Polly, inviting Beatrice down for supper, wondering if by any chance she had seen me. I felt her muscles shift as she put the phone down, the glide of her skin as she turned back towards me, and then she put her hands on either side of my face and kissed me on the mouth.

IO

Two days after Fred went mad there was an outbreak of street protests that the police and army put down with an oddly restrained degree of brutality. I don't know where they found the energy: with the rebels so close there was little to be lost or gained. On the second day of the troubles I found myself scrambling over a gate into an office compound in Gombe, choking and weeping from the tear gas, my snot soaking my shirt. The yard was crowded with other fugitives from the riots, local people who kept grabbing my hand, thanking me for being there, as I collapsed against a wall, gagging and gasping. A couple of kids appeared in front of me, blurred shapes, to dab at my eyes with rags soaked in water. I could see again, and I watched the yard slowly empty as the fugitives stole away, hopping walls and fences, while outside the police and army still roamed the frightened street. Alone again, I slowly climbed back over the gate and dropped to the ground on the other side.

The street was wide and lined with dusty trees. Little white dots bobbed in the haze, the helmets of civil guards blocking a distant junction, but where I stood the street was empty. A vehicle was approaching, driving too fast in too low a gear, and I flattened myself back into the gateway as a civilian pick-up truck sped past. A group of Presidential Guards was standing on the back, swaying with its motion. Between them slumped a young man who was naked to the waist.

When the truck had gone I stepped into the street again, and at that same moment another figure emerged from the next gateway, twenty yards away: it was Fine. He was staring up the street and didn't see me. I drew back into my gateway and considered what to do next, and when I heard his footstep he was almost on top of me and I had only a moment to step out of hiding.

'Oh, hello, Nathan,' I said, a tone of mild surprise. I was pleased to see him fly sideways in shock.

'Owen! Jesus! Where the hell have you come from?'

'I was hiding in there. I got tear-gassed.'

He gestured with his head towards the next compound. 'I was hiding in there.'

Fine was sweating, and his jeans and jacket were thick with the dust of whitewash. His face was smeared with dirt where he had clawed away the tears and snot. I must have looked the same. Shots sounded somewhere off towards the river.

'What the hell are you doing here?' I demanded, and fell in beside him as he started to walk again, towards the river and the shooting. 'I thought the *Chronicle* didn't want you in Kinshasa.'

'It couldn't be helped. Tommo and I jumped on the last plane out of Lubumbashi, and this is where it brought us.'

'You mean you didn't stay to cover the fall?'

He paused before answering, not turning to look at me. 'We were out at the airport with the Presidential Guards when the rebels started shelling it. We couldn't get back into town because the guards had started fighting with the regular FAZ in town – the regulars were trying to prove to the rebels that they'd gone over to their side. We figured that if the shelling didn't kill us, the Presidential Guards might, just for spite. Then this big Ilyushin landed and this little guy in a safari suit strolled off it and started selling tickets, five hundred bucks a head. The weird thing was, Jansson was already on the plane, hiding in the cockpit. They'd picked him up at some rebel-held strip.' He looked at me then, and laughed. 'Can you believe that?'

It was a good story, I thought. Better than our own adventure.

'Where's Tommo now?' I asked.

'I lost him in the crowd.'

There was more shooting ahead and a dozen young men exploded from a side street a hundred yards off and sprinted across the boulevard. Moments later an army truck careered after them, covered in jeering soldiers. It bumped right across the main street without even slowing down. A man was screaming down the side street. Two soldiers appeared at the corner and stared at us from across the road.

I felt my steps falter.

'We're heading the wrong way,' I said. 'The hotel is back that way.'

'I'm not going to the hotel,' Fine said over his shoulder. 'I want to find out what happened today.'

I quickened my steps to catch up with him. 'It's over. Kongolo Mobutu showed up with his goons and they tear-gassed Tshisekedi and bashed him on the head and then they took him away. I was there. I saw it.'

Fine shook his head. 'For all we know the other marchers made it to the prime minister's office. Maybe that's what all that shooting's about.'

We could see down the side street now. The truck had vanished, but fifty yards away soldiers were gathered in a small circle and rifle butts were rising and falling. Their comrades on the corner fingered their weapons and glowered at us. One had blood down the front of his shirt. It didn't look like it was his.

Fine's pace quickened. The breeze from the river was bitter with gas. We reached the end of the boulevard where it opened out into a wide triangle where the ways divided. Beyond the open triangle was a stand of high trees, mountains of green, beyond which curled the first foam of the cataracts. The sun hammered down on the grass and the concrete, and I stopped in the last patch of shade before the beaten zone. The shooting was still close by, still invisible; perhaps it would recede before us, always somewhere else, like the mirage that danced between the trees and the tarmac. Riot guns were popping off somewhere down the side streets, but less and less now, and little groups of soldiers and policemen were drifting back from God knows where, all tired and happy. Even Fine could see that the show was over. He stopped, out in the sunlight, and stood there for a while watching the soldiers. Then we turned our backs to the river and began to walk home.

Cars were wedged bumper to bumper in the square in front of the hotel, their drivers hooting and screaming, packed so tightly that we had had to climb over them to get into the lobby. Inside, everybody was shouting and snapping at each other, the way people do when they're angry about how scared they feel. Polly had written the names of the missing on a whiteboard inside the lobby doors, and when Fine and I walked in she rushed to gather us in her arms. My name, I noticed, was top of the list, right above Fine's and Extrastrong's. The Gardes Civiles had arrested Extrastrong and wanted a thousand dollars to release him and five thousand for his camera. I went to my room and showered and changed, then sat down and wrote for a while. I wondered where Beatrice was. Her name wasn't on the board, but she didn't answer in her room.

I was back in the lobby when Jansson walked in. He was barefoot and had no bags and no cameras and his head was wrapped in a seeping bandage. He walked straight through the lobby into the bar and ordered a bottle of vodka, and when Polly and I tried to stop him he laughed and made a show of boxing, pumping his fists at us, then turned back to the counter.

The Frogs of War gathered around Jansson at the bar and wrapped their keffiyehs and their Khmer scarves around their heads in tribute to his bandage. I went to the lavatory and on the way back I detoured to the reception desk, called Beatrice's room and listened to the phone ring for a while. When I got back the bar was even louder, lots of people shouting and laughing and being braver than they had been, and the Frogs of War had been joined by another bunch of bar girls, and Jansson was swaying on his stool on the edge of the group, looking around him, suddenly alone again. His wife had left him six weeks before.

The group at our table grew larger but there was still no sign of Beatrice. Tommo wanted to go out by the pool to eat and I agreed in the end, though the restaurant was still not full and I knew that the pool would be haunted by Fred and his phantom insects. Outside, the air wrapped around our faces like a hot dirty towel. The terrace seemed empty but as we pulled two tables together a metal leg screeched across tiles and a face popped up in the corner by the bushes and I saw that it was Beatrice. She was sitting bent forward at a table, talking to Fine. She saw me, hesitated, raised a hand, and Fine looked at us, but he stayed hunched towards her in his chair, talking intently, and did no more than nod to me, and then the others were all sitting down around our two tables – Brereton, Polly, Tommo, Laura, Rasheed, Jansson, I don't know who – and I sat down quickly opposite Tommo, my back to the dark corner.

Brereton had bought a box of Cuban cigars from the diplomatic store and he passed them around now. I put mine in my shirt pocket. Rasheed fetched a bottle of single-malt Scotch from his room and poured everyone a shot. We did that sort of thing all the time, back then. I don't think I've ever lived so well.

Food came. Once or twice I saw Tommo look towards Beatrice and Fine and then look away again. As the others grew louder he became silent, and I guessed he must also be drunk now. I leaned forward, feeling my shoulder blades draw apart.

Polly was talking about a row she'd had that morning about access to the hotel roof. Her booming voice was all throat and nose, with the spiky vowels they'd clipped for her at the second-best girls' school in Pretoria. All the other TV agencies had asked Polly to sort the problem out; she was always the one people turned to when it came to chartering planes or setting up camera pools. Polly said that the hotel manager had told her that he didn't want anyone filming on the roof because they might fall off or draw fire; he was worried that the hotel's parent company might be sued back in Belgium. Polly told him that if the TV people couldn't get up on the roof they wouldn't be able to do their live two-ways. The manager said that wasn't his problem, and she said that hotels always let TV people up on the roof, didn't he ever watch the news? He said no, not if he could help it, that it always looked so scary. She said that if they couldn't film from this hotel they would all move out and go to the Intercontinental in Gombe instead, because the manager there would let you do whatever you liked and anyway it was much taller and you could see the river much better from there. Plus the Intercon would be the first stop for the French and British marines when they came scooting across from Brazzaville in their little rubber boats to rescue the crooks and the

142

foreigners. The president's family had all moved to the Intercon, so obviously they'd had a word to the wise.

I thought of Diamond Doug. I hadn't seen him for days. I wondered if Beatrice knew anything about him but she was still sitting behind me, in the corner with Fine.

Anyway, Polly said, she told the manager that in case he didn't know it no one else was coming over the river any more so if any of his guests left now he would have trouble replacing them . . . And every guest was a gold mine, paying outrageous prices for rooms, meals and drinks, and God help you if you touched a hotel phone. When I could I used to go to Laura's room and borrow her sat-phone and get my desk to call me back. Beatrice would do the same. The day before, Laura had left us alone for a few minutes and we put the chain on the door and lay down in the corner, so as not to rumple Laura's bed.

So, Polly said, the manager suddenly remembered that if people wanted to go to the roof it would be difficult for him to stop them. The door had to be left unlocked for emergency reasons, he said, but that didn't mean the hotel said people could go up there. It was their funeral, he said.

Brereton said that the view up there was fantastic, particularly as the sun went down. You could see across the river to Brazzaville and back south towards the stadiums. Fine had almost wept earlier when Brereton pointed out the stadium where Ali fought Foreman.

'Fine went up with you?' I asked.

'No. He came up after, with Beatrice.'

I took Brereton's cigar from my shirt pocket and borrowed his cutter. Even as the blades snicked together I realized that I'd cut too much off the end of the cigar. I lit it anyway and from the first drag it started to burn down one side, not evenly, the way cigars are supposed to. I put the cigar down in the ashtray, very gently, as if I were laying it to rest, and gently took my hand away. A waiter had just changed the ashtray, it was clean, and the cigar lay there smoking for a minute or two before it gave up and died. Then I felt movement and Beatrice was standing over the empty chair beside me. Everybody was greeting each other, all mind-if-Is, and then a moment later Fine was there too. I heard his voice saying names right behind me, including my own, but I felt too tired to turn around and look at him so I watched Tommo instead. He was sitting up again, like someone making an effort. Who was Fine? I asked myself. Why should Tommo Capaldi be sitting up for him?

Beatrice sat down beside me but I didn't look at her either. I wondered if, like Tommo, I ought to be silently drunk. Fine slumped down beside Tommo, in the last free chair, and the funny thing was Fine also looked tired. He looked the way I felt, which was very different from the way I'd pictured him all evening, crouched behind my back. After I noticed that I made an effort to catch his eye.

'Tommo's been telling me more about Lubumbashi,' I said to him. 'I gather Jansson went out alone into the bush to hook up with the rebels.'

Fine shrugged. He was always shrugging, at least as I recall him now. Perhaps I'm doing it for him.

'You have to admire Jansson's balls, though,' I pressed. 'He goes to Lubumbashi, crosses over to the rebel side somehow, enters the city with them, scoops the lot of us and then gets himself out again. What an operator.'

Fine didn't say anything. At the other end of the table Laura and Brereton and Polly were arguing loudly about which Jo'burg butcher sold the best wors, with Polly taking Laura's part. Jansson sat back, smiling to himself and fingering his bandage.

'I never asked you how Rachel was,' I said. 'How is she settling in Jo'burg without you?'

Fine seemed to smile, but as he answered one hand brushed the air slowly away from him.

'She's fine. She loves the house. Her parents are coming from the States next week. She's taking them off on safari.'

I nodded. 'It'll be good for her to have some company. It must be scary for her to arrive in Jo'burg and find herself alone half the time.'

Fine brushed the air again, more slowly this time. 'I go where they tell me,' he said, and I saw him glance at Beatrice for a moment, but she was looking at me. 'Kinshasa isn't even on my beat, strictly speaking,' he said, 'but what can you do?'

At the far end of the table Laura was getting up to go. Jansson was peering at her from beneath his bandage, stained brown and red and yellow, as if he'd never seen her before. Women said that he took his rebuffs gallantly, and there was never any awkwardness next day because he never seemed to remember. Beatrice's face was half in the shadow and her eyes held me carefully, as if she were trying to mean something to me. But I was in no mood for understanding. Even as I sat there I thought, 'I can pick up the pieces later.'

I turned back to Fine, and as I spoke again I felt desperately like yawning. 'But it must make life difficult. Rachel's planning for the big wedding back home, isn't she? What if you're still here?'

He laughed at me then. 'For God's sake, Owen, I'll be long gone by then. We all will. The wedding's not until June.'

'It's April now. You never know.'

'Jesus, Owen. Have a heart.'

Beatrice was still watching me. Tommo wasn't smiling.

'She's a lovely girl, Rachel,' I said.

Tommo leaned forward. 'Too right,' he said.

Beatrice sat back in her chair. Fine gave a little smile and a shrug and raised his hands in token of surrender, and then he reached forward and took my cigar from the ashtray.

'Is nobody smoking this?' he said, suddenly businesslike. 'It looks like a decent cigar.'

'It's mine,' I said. 'I fucked it up when I lit it.'

Fine studied it carefully for a moment. 'No,' he said, 'all it needs is some trimming. May I?'

Laura said goodnight and left, Brereton stood up, then Polly. Rasheed had left already, to go and pick up Extrastrong from the police cells. Fine took out a pen-knife and carefully sliced the burned end from my cigar so that it was fresh and even again, and when this was done he lit a match and held the cigar to the flame without inhaling, evenly toasting the cut end of the cigar until it turned black. Then he shook out the match, lit another and used it to puff the cigar into life. The end of the cigar turned into a perfect disc of red, then quickly faded away beneath its first grey coating of ash. He took a few more puffs before offering it back to me. I shook my head.

'Well done,' I said.

The others were gone, and I noticed then that Tommo had slipped off after them without saying goodnight. Jansson was dozing alone at the other end of the table.

Fine was busy with the cigar, which was still drawing perfectly. The smoke curled around us, me and Fine and Beatrice, just the three of us together at the end of the table, and I found its smell sickening. Beatrice sat there, leaning back in her chair, studying her wine glass. I breathed shallowly, because of the smoke, and looked at Fine puffing on my cigar, and I thought how good it would be to get up and leave, come up for cold air, lie down alone in my own quiet room, but I couldn't be the next one to leave that table. My smile ached as I picked up a half-empty bottle of beer, now almost warm, and refilled my glass.

'So,' I said, looking deliberately from one to the other, 'any plans for tomorrow?'

Fine puffed more smoke and Beatrice said nothing, and then I heard a chair scraping and the smoke parted and Jansson dropped heavily down in the empty chair on the other side of Beatrice, catching her elbow, spilling wine on her T-shirt. He sprawled in the plastic chair, clutching a beer glass and a bottle in either hand. His hands wove around each other as he turned sad eyes to Beatrice.

'Hello, Beatrice,' he said, and set the glass and bottle on the table, more or less together, without looking, and when he glanced down at them his face broke into a smile of victory. The bandage had slipped to the back of his head, revealing a clump of black stitches on his left temple where a soldier had clubbed him. His skin was discoloured by iodine.

'Hello, Jesper,' Beatrice said quietly, watching her own hands gather her cigarettes and lighter, and then she glanced at Jansson and I saw her do a perfect double take. I almost laughed. She was staring at Jansson's head, at the exposed wound, and Jansson was smiling at her, or at least trying to, and then his eyes flickered and doubt came into them and he felt for the bandage and didn't find it, and he reached up into his hair and pulled it down quickly, covering the wound again. Beatrice was standing, and Fine after her, and I pushed my own chair back. Play to the whistle, I thought, feeling sick again.

'I think I'm going to call it a day,' said Fine, stretching his shoulders back. 'You watch yourself, Jesper. I don't reckon you can take another smack on the head tonight.'

'Those fuckers stole my shoes today,' said Jansson loudly, still sprawled in his chair. His position hadn't changed, nor even his expression, yet he seemed to be pleading now as he looked from Fine to me and back again. He didn't look at Beatrice. 'After I came back to the hotel I saw him in the lobby, and he put his foot beside mine –'

'Who is this "he" you're referring to?' asked Fine, a touch impatient, turning away already.

Jansson looked pained. 'Douglass, of course. Did I not say already? He came up and put his foot beside mine, and I was only wearing socks now, and he said to me, when a FAZ puts his foot next to yours it ain't 'cause he wants to dance with you. It's 'cause he's shopping.'

He mimicked the accent surprisingly well.

'I wondered where Doug had got to,' said Beatrice, as she made her way around the table towards the door.

Jansson looked disappointed, but plunged ahead. 'He has been hanging out with some Ukrainians at the airport. Anybody who wants to get out of somewhere in a hurry and has enough diamonds, hidden up their ass maybe, they can get in touch with the Ukrainians and they'll fly out to the bush and pick them up and take them to Brazza or Bangui or Lusaka or wherever they want to go, loot and all, even cars – they have an Ilyushin 76. They wanted Doug to work with them because he knows all the people on both sides – even the Rwandans. Doug is their greeter.'

'Really? How do you know all that?' I asked, squeezing behind his chair as I followed Beatrice.

Jansson raised his glass to us.

We left him alone there in the darkness by the gleaming pool. He made a show of cheering up as I touched his shoulder to say goodnight. I wonder how long he stayed out there, finishing off the warm beers we had left on the table.

The lobby was empty except for a cleaner mopping a pool of something from beside the stairs. I followed close behind Beatrice as we crossed the bright, naked space to the lifts. Fine brought up the rear, where I did not have to look at him. Beatrice pressed the call button, glanced at us, then leaned against the wall, frowning towards the glass doors that gave out onto the street. Behind the reception desk a clerk was totting up a pile of room tabs. The hotel was making everyone settle their bill every other day now, so as not to be stiffed when the end came.

The lift pinged to life behind us. Beatrice went in first and pressed the button for the third floor. I pressed the button for the second. The lift was small, and when Fine stepped in after me he had to squeeze against the opposite wall, away from the panel of buttons. Even with the door still open the air smelled of smoke and our sweat and of what was left of Beatrice's perfume. She was slowly rubbing her lower back against a brass handrail at the back of the lift, and gazing straight out the door, as if considering some remote problem, and then the doors slid closed and the lift lurched and Fine cleared his throat and said, 'First floor, please,' and I pressed his button for him. I had to turn my face away from him to do so.

Fine said goodnight as he left the lift. The doors came together, and Beatrice leaned back into the corner and stared at me. We reached the next floor and the door opened onto the dim corridor. I turned to face her, one foot in the door.

'Well, goodnight,' I said.

She stared back at me, wound up into the corner of the lift, her hands pressed back against its walls like springs. I thought hopelessly of how she had laughed for me only the morning before. Then she seemed to shake herself, peeled a hand from the wall and put her finger on the hold button.

'Aren't you coming?' she said, frowning.

As the lift closed its doors on us again, Beatrice reached up, pulled my face down to hers and kissed me once, on the forehead. She put her arms around me, and for a few moments we leaned together like worn-out fighters. Then the doors began to open and we moved apart once more.

Jansson had worked as an advertising executive before he packed it in one day and drove all the way to Bosnia in his own private car. He arrived in Sarajevo at the height of the siege with no contacts or saleable skills, but because he seemed cheerfully suicidal Amalgamated News put him on a day rate, running tapes and errands for its TV crews. Then someone lent him a stills camera and he started learning to shoot on the side. One night he woke up buried under tons of bricks and roof tiles, and because the shells were still falling it took them twelve hours to dig him out. By the time Jansson finally got himself properly fucked up – up in the mountains somewhere, was all Laura told me – Amalgamated News had realized he was no longer expendable. Two of the big freelance features agencies were offering him full membership any time he wanted, so his bosses reckoned that if they wanted to keep him they would have to offer him a plum.

Paris was what they came up with. Jansson, in Paris, dear God. I can still remember Laura laughing when she told me about that. The gig didn't last long, of course. The end came when Jansson stumbled late one morning into an anteroom at the Élysée Palace, where Amalgamated's Vice-President (International, London) was waiting for a long-sought interview with the president of the Republic of France. Jansson was unshaven and stinking of alcohol, and equipped only with two plastic disposable cameras, a Fuji and a Kodak, which he'd bought moments before at a kiosk on the street. He told the horrified bigfoot that he was experimenting with different formats and film saturations. In truth, his regular kit had been stolen in a bar.

Mitterrand affected not to notice anything unusual about the photo shoot: the French entertain a morbid cult of the lens monkey, and will put up with any amount of eccentricity from strange men with cameras. But the Vice-President (International, London) had a much higher opinion of his own dignity and he was determined to get Jansson fired. He failed, but by the time the dust settled his agency had learned a few things about Jansson that any of his friends could have told them all along: Jansson didn't want a career; he had left one of those in Helsinki. He didn't want to be famous or powerful, or to have to operate anywhere but on the ground he was standing on. He didn't want to negotiate with clients, fill out expense forms or plan his year ahead. He wanted to go where others sent him, take his pictures, then go somewhere else. There had been no need for Amalgamated News to try to buy him off with Paris. He was a wire man. He would never have left them for some poncey stills agency.

Jansson never tried to suggest that he was on the bottle because of anything in Helsinki, or Bosnia, or because of his marriage, or his childhood, or anything like that. In the story he wove for himself, late at night, on a hundred terrace bars, the collapse of his entire life outside his work was merely a station on the road to his destiny. Drinking for him was not an effect, it was a cause. He didn't state his case as clearly as that: dedicated drinkers send their signals not through words but through the binary codes of sins committed and duties undone; of silences and grunts; or, like that night by the pool, through the points at which they slip in and out of conversations. That night by the pool, as drunk as he was, Jansson wanted to raise the subject of loneliness, having sniffed it in the air. I call it loneliness, you call it love, maybe.

The next day Fine checked out of our hotel, the Memling, and moved across town to the Intercontinental. He told Laura that the Intercon was much the better place to be if you wanted access to diplomats and spooks and government people. He had to start working angles again because now that he was in Kinshasa he was at war with the *Chronicle*'s West Africa correspondent, whose turf it was. The West Africa correspondent was an old hand at the paper who had spent years in the office in New York, and he was using every trick he had learned there to keep Fine off the front page and far back in the book. By questioning Fine's facts and analysis and by filing a spoiler story of his own, he was able to shoot down the big Katanga feature that Fine and Tommo had worked so hard on. There was nothing Fine could do about it. Everyone gets bigfooted sooner or later.

When Fine moved out of our hotel Tommo didn't want to go with him, so Fine agreed that he could keep an eye on things at the Memling. It should have been like the old days, before Fine showed up, but of course there was Beatrice now. I didn't care to notice the way that Tommo would look at me when I left a scene early or turned up late. Beatrice didn't want to be acknowledged, and it never occurred to me not to go along with her. Before I left her room she would open the door a crack to make sure the hall was clear, then kiss me and push me out. The trick was to get out the door unnoticed; if I did run into someone on the third floor I could always claim to be visiting Laura. Brereton would know different but I knew he wouldn't mention it to anyone, except Laura, and I knew that I was safe with her . . . Anyway, it was Beatrice's game I was playing, not mine. Perhaps it was fun, in its way. Perhaps that was part of it, for her.

Kinshasa had a small community of Ismaili merchants whom Brereton knew from years back. They were staying put, and a week after Lubumbashi fell they hosted the first of several cricket matches. We played in choking humidity on the broken tarmac of a school playground, with a single wicket and a tennis ball wrapped in gaffer tape. We always lost: the Indians took their game seriously, and, apart from Tommo and Brereton, none of us had ever played cricket before. Tommo said that Fine was now spending much of his time playing tennis with a very knowledgeable man who claimed to be an assistant to the US military attaché. One day Fine and his new pal took a set of clubs from the embassy and hacked their way around what used to be a golf course near the presidential funk hole at Camp Tshatshi. That was Fine for you. I happen to know he hated golf.

Rebel leaflets appeared on the streets, and Mobutu's son doubled the guard around the hotels and public buildings. You could go up on the roof of our hotel and look down on the roof of the nearby French embassy and watch two Foreign Legionnaires, stripped to the waist, shovelling documents into blazing braziers.

Most of us were still in bed early that Friday morning when the president's motorcade drove through town and out to the airport. Extrastrong happened to be on the roof, shooting a stand-up for an agency client, and he scored a big scoop by filming the long line of limousines, armoured cars and ambulances as they blinked in and out of view between the buildings of the Boulevard du 30 Juin. The people of the city had cheered the president in December and jeered him in April, but now they just stood and watched him go. They knew that this time he would not be coming back.

The following morning Beatrice woke me early, pulling at my shoulder the way she did when she wanted to get rid of me, but when I turned to put my arm around her she was gone. I peeled open my eyes to find her standing naked by the window, staring out at the street through a slit in the curtains.

'Can you hear it?' she said, not turning.

I rubbed my eyes and came up beside her. 'Hear what?' I put my arm around her.

'Shooting,' she said.

I could only hear the hum of the air-conditioning so I slid the window open and straightaway heard, from somewhere close by, towards the market, the carping sound of a Kalashnikov. It was firing single shots, spaced out and steady like a slow drum beat, and then it was joined by another, firing in slightly different time; and then somewhere else entirely, back towards the river, a magazine was rattled off on full automatic. Beatrice turned to me with wide eyes, and we stood together and listened as the firing intensified and spread until the city ripped around us. Then Beatrice pulled away.

'It doesn't sound right,' she said. 'We should go take a look.'

When I got back to the hotel three hours later Douglass was hanging around by the reception desk. He wore a photographer's vest and a baseball cap and he listened with his head on one side as I described what I'd seen on the streets.

'Just like I told you,' he said when I'd finished. 'The calls have been made. Meanwhile the FAZ are sitting put and shooting in the air so the rebels know where to find 'em. The one thing nobody wants right now is a nasty surprise.'

'Is that what it's about? Well, someone got a surprise this morning. There're three men lying naked in the market, shot full of bullets.'

Douglass looked unimpressed. 'That ain't such a shock. You're talking about two young guys, one older? One of the young guys got lots of tattoos?'

'That's right. Did you see them?'

He wrinkled his nose. 'No, I ain't been down that way. But I was expecting to hear something about some people like that.'

'Who were they?'

'People with a bad feel for politics. You'll see a few more like 'em next couple of days.'

Douglass studied the lobby. It was beginning to calm down a little. Most of the TV crews had already set up shop on the Boulevard du 30 Juin, waiting for the first rebels to appear in the city; it was still far too risky to push further out from the hotel. Other people were upstairs filing, or in the café getting food.

When Douglass spoke again his voice was low and conspiratorial. 'So how are you and Beatrice getting on?'

The question sent me sideways. I had never been asked it before. 'How do you mean?'

'I mean, you're together now, right?'

'Well, yes. Sort of. I suppose we are.'

He nodded. 'Well, that's real nice. I'm pleased to hear it . . . But hold on a minute . . .' He began to grin evilly. 'Were you two trying to keep it a secret?'

I didn't know what to say. Douglass laughed and slapped me on the arm with his bony little hand. 'You're a hoot,' he said. 'I don't know what she sees in you . . . I'll tell you what, you want me to not tell everyone about you two and your little secret?'

I felt anger rising. 'I don't care, but Beatrice might.'

'Okay, but that means you've got to protect her honour, right? So if you want to buy my silence you got to do me a favour, right? You still got a car?'

'Beatrice does, but no driver. He didn't turn up today.'

'But she got the keys, right? Okay. You two meet me here at three o'clock and you can take me for a ride. My driver turned yellow and took off with my jeep and I got to meet someone near the airport.'

'The airport road's not safe yet.'

He lowered his sunglasses onto his nose so he could stare at me. 'It'll be safe. And if you see your friend Thomas tell him he should come along too. There might be some pictures.'

'What have you got on Tommo?'

He laughed and stepped closer. 'Mr Simmons, sir: I can get my own ride if I have to, and I don't think there's too much secret about what you got going on with that Beatrice. It's *me* who's doing *you* a favour here. If you want to see something interesting, then all be here at three.'

I ran into Tommo a little while later. I was drinking coffee with Laura when he walked into the café with Jansson, both of them red-faced and weak from the sun. A porter came in with a note for Tommo from Fine, who had called from the Intercon to say that he would come downtown as soon as the road from Gombe was clear. But Fine never made it to the Memling that day. It was a pity. If I'd known he wouldn't be coming, I might have told Tommo about Douglass's outing. I could have used his snaps.

Beatrice's car was an old Mercedes that shed thick scabs of green paint every time it hit a pothole. She'd never driven it herself before, and as we pulled away from the hotel she had to hunch forward over the wheel to see out through the cracks in the windscreen. The streets were almost deserted, and the men and boys who dared to roam abroad went in tight groups, wearing white headbands and holding aloft green branches, as the rebels had said in their leaflets. There was still a lot of shooting and somebody had set fire to a cache of ammunition in a Garde Civile depot a block from the hotel. As we turned onto the Ndjili road, cooked-off tracer bullets were lofting up into the sky behind us, fat and slow as footballs.

The rattle of the car and the roar of the hot wind through the open windows filled our ears. There was no traffic. Here and there somebody looked out through a gate or over a fence burning with flame trees and sometimes a dog would be lying out in a patch of shade on the street, enjoying the holiday, but as we went south through Limete the streets became deserted. Beatrice was silent, but Douglass sat in the back chatting away on his cell phone in what sounded like Swahili. He sat straight up on the edge of the torn leather seat, one hand to his ear and the other resting on a worn old canvas satchel. To the photographer's vest and baseball cap he had added a red silk scarf and an SLR camera. Diamond Doug had been studying us well.

He told Beatrice to turn left onto the Boulevard Lumumba, where big houses with rusty corrugated roofs peeped over ragged fences, the compounds spaced out between patches of weeds. Then the houses drew further apart and Douglass told Beatrice to turn left again, onto a side road, and she had to slow down as the tarmac ran out and was replaced by stones and dirt. Tall grass grew up around us, and I hadn't even noticed a junction up ahead when Doug suddenly snapped, 'Right here,' and the car fishtailed danger-ously before barely making the turn.

'I wish you'd sit up front, Douglass,' complained Beatrice. 'That way you could give me directions in time.'

The drawl from the back seat could have been amused or bored. 'I told you, it looks better for me if I sit in the back. A black guy in the front would look like your flunky.'

The fat old Mercedes bounced from trench to pothole to rut, rolling like a barge in a crosswind. The road passed through an expanse of high grass and weedy plots of maize and manioc. Ahead and to our left columns of smoke were rising into the sky from several points towards the airport. We were heading parallel to the river. The road curved to the right slightly, and as we came out of the bend Beatrice had to swerve suddenly to avoid a car standing in the centre of the road. It was surrounded by a black outline of dull broken glass and carbonized rubber. Two blackened lumps sat where the front seats had been and daylight shone through holes punched in an open rear door. On the edge of the road lay a still figure, half in and half out of the tall grass, in combat pants and a T-shirt black with blood. Smoke was gusting from the car's melted engine compartment.

Beatrice swerved around the wreck without braking. Douglass stopped humming, then leaned forward to tap her on the shoulder. 'You see that house up there? Pull up at the gate and honk the horn.'

The house stood on a junction between the road and a narrow, overgrown track that seemed to lead towards the river. It was like any other house out that way – a clump of sheltering trees, a tin roof, a high reed fence twisted with steel cable and crowded by weeds. White letters on the gate warned of a chien méchant, but when Beatrice hooted there was no answering bark. We waited a minute, then hooted again, and eventually the gate opened far enough to reveal a woman wearing a coloured wrap and matching headdress and bright gold earrings. Her lips were pursed and her eyes screwed up as she stared at Beatrice and me, but when Douglass climbed slowly out of the back her face straightened and I saw that she was very handsome. She could have been anywhere between thirty and seventy.

'Bring the car inside,' she said in French, and we pulled in under a tree beside the fading whitewash of a brick-walled bungalow. Two young men with rifles were standing on either side of the gate. There were gaps torn in the fence, low down, and the yard was littered with spent cartridges. The men wore wellington boots, and the jungle pattern fatigues that had been issued to them brand new in Goma were now faded and patched. They stared at us without interest as the woman beckoned us to follow her inside.

The front room was a wide, cool space with a red tiled floor. Two more soldiers were sitting together on a sofa with their rifles held between their knees, stiff and awkward like teenagers in adult company. They hardly dared to move their heads as the three of us filed in behind the woman. Before them, sitting at a wooden table set in front of the window, was a tall, very thin man in a plain olive green uniform. He was leaning far back in the chair with his hands behind his head and his legs splayed out in front of him. A walkie-talkie and a cell phone lay on the table with a lighter and cigarettes, and a rifle and a canvas harness full of spare magazines hung on the back of his chair. When he saw Douglass the soldier laughed and jumped to his feet and grabbed his free hand, and the two of them were grinning and talking away to each other in Swahili, still holding hands, while Douglass swung his satchel gently in his free hand, its weight drawing his skinny shoulder back and forth behind it. Through the front window you could see out over the fence and down the road and through the trees towards the shabby towers of Kinshasa. The sky behind them was gold and silver with the failing sun. In the foreground squatted the black hulk of the smouldering car. You could smell its acrid stink on the still air.

Doug's friend collected his kit from the table and headed for the door and Doug followed him, signalling us to wait where we were. As soon as they were gone, one of the soldiers rose from the sofa and clumped over to the window, hunching down to watch the road. He didn't dare to sit in his boss's empty chair. Beatrice tried to talk to the other one in French but he shook his head and scowled.

Douglass came back alone five minutes later, and now he held the satchel clasped under his armpit as if its weight no longer interested him. He wasn't smiling, but you could tell he was in a good mood.

'Come on,' he said, and we followed him out into the corridor and through the front door. The officer was now standing with the other two soldiers by the open gate, peering up the road and talking into his radio.

'Is this your army, Douglass, or have you just borrowed it?' asked Beatrice. 'It looks a little small.'

Douglass sniggered again. 'You might say that I've rented it.' Then he raised his arm and pointed up the road to the east; we followed his finger and saw a lone figure standing in the road, three hundred yards off, where it curved away into a stand of trees. The figure took a few steps forward, levelled a rifle, lowered it again, took a couple of steps back, as if undecided, and then turned and gestured to someone behind. Within a few seconds the road beyond was lined on either side with gunmen. They just stepped out of the trees.

'I'll introduce you properly to the major now,' said Douglass. 'If you want to go and march into Kinshasa with him, I can drive myself back. That's if you don't mind.'

I think maybe Tommo found out about Douglass's invitation. Maybe Douglass left word for him some other way, a note or something. I never asked. It was no big deal, anyway, because Tommo found his own way to the story. He was crouched there, all alone, snapping away, as the first rebel scouts moved past Ndola and into the city centre; Beatrice and I had to skip to one side to keep out of his shot. Then Tommo moved out into the middle of the road, hunkering down further to frame up the two long files of soldiers as they trudged towards and past him, down either side of the road. They were young and dog-tired and spooked by the invisible gunfire, and they marched in wellingtons and broken army boots with cloth-tied bundles of rifle grenades and mortar bombs balanced on their heads. I greeted Tommo as I skipped past him, still keeping pace with the scouts. His face twisted into what was probably a smile but he didn't look up from the shot he was framing and then I lost him in the crowd. The closer we moved to the centre of town, the more people came out on the street. The townspeople danced and sang and waved their white flags and their green branches as they crowded in on the nervous soldiers, trying to talk to them, but none of the soldiers spoke Lingala. The major got someone in a suit to shout at the crowd but there was too much noise for them to hear him, so the major pointed his rifle in the air and emptied a magazine and the mob scattered and his men pushed on, breaking into a trot, and Beatrice and I sweated to keep up with them. I saw Jansson up ahead, perched on a wall, and then we jinked to the right off the main route and were swept along a short side street and in through the steel gates of the river port, gaping and unguarded. The soldiers fanned out through the piles of junk and cargo, through the rotting sheds and office buildings, and down to the low muddy shore with its fringe of reeds and garbage. We followed the major as he strode through the gates, across the yard and out onto a floating jetty where the riverboats had docked before they all fled to Brazzaville. The old wooden jetty swayed and creaked and thundered as we marched out onto the water. The shore opened out on either side to show us a graveyard of dead boats: rotting timbers and plates of rusted steel protruding from the slimy water, a big paddle boat driven up on a beach, dugouts decaying in the mud and the hyacinth. We were at the end of the jetty now, where the river slid past with its warm kennel smell. Beyond our dark arm of the stream was another fringe of reeds dividing it from a great reach of rippled water red with the sunset, and beyond that again, several miles distant, were the lights and the towers of Brazzaville. The major halted, slung his rifle over his shoulder and stretched both arms along the railing that protected the end of the jetty. Beatrice and I stopped just behind him and some junior officers squeezed past us to join their commander at the rail. They all leaned there for a few moments, staring out over the water at the lights of another strange city, and then the major straightened up and glanced at his men and said, 'Bien commencé, bien fini.'

Beatrice nudged me, and then the soldiers turned and trudged past us, back towards Kinshasa. The lights of the fallen city crowded the shore like a flock of roosting seabirds, spooked into flight again, here and there, as silent lines of tracer.

II

The dust blows forward and the dust blows back. The dust blows from the Sahara to this northern estuary. It turns to silt; this bank and shoal. Cartwright we burned to ashes, at his own request.

You can picture the scene: you've seen it in the pictures. Cartwright had no family except this newspaper – the newspaper itself, not the people who work here – so only a few colleagues showed up for the funeral. Hugh read something that a priest of some kind had given to him, and then he said a few words on his own account. Outside the chapel there was wind and rain, plastering dead leaves against the dripping headstones. It was all most satisfactory.

Lucy Viner came out in a taxi with me, for some reason; Cartwright never liked women much. Our property editor, who couldn't make it, had commended us to the crematorium manager, his cousin, and after Cartwright's little send-off – the camp sliding door, the comically slow conveyor belt – the manager took Lucy and me for a tour.

Everything burns, he confided, apart from a few fragments of teeth and bone. Of course, he said, mourners tend to get upset if the urn rattles when they shake it – and they always do, he said, when they think you're not looking – so you have to run the ashes through a special machine that grinds everything to powder – teeth, bones, the works. He showed us the grinder, standing on a bench in the corner of the workshop. It looked like a top-loading washing machine. You put the ashes inside it together with a half-dozen large steel balls and then the machine spins them all around together. The manager reached into it and took out one of the balls. 'Here,' he said, 'feel the weight,' and he put it in my hand. It was thinly coated with greasy grey flakes. I hefted the ball for a moment, then handed it back to him. Behind his back Lucy pulled a horrified face.

'What we can't burn we crush,' she whispered as we left.

Cartwright's will had specified cremation but he left no instructions for his ashes; none of the usual mummery of scattering them at sea, or wherever. He was born crippled and grew up ugly; his body was his lifelong enemy, so perhaps he wanted it annihilated as soon as he was done with it. After that he didn't care. We could of course have dumped his ashes in the newsroom. He would haunt the place anyway.

The crematorium had one of those walls of remembrance where they stash people's ashes in little tiled-up alcoves. It looked like the pigeonholes inside the newsroom door – the old newsroom, the way it was before I went to Africa – where Cartwright used to lurk for his victims. His niche was marked by a small tile bearing a two-line inscription, and Lucy was surprised to see that his birth and death had fallen on almost the same date, sixty years apart.

They were filling the niches on a first-come, first-served basis, from top to bottom, left to right. To Cartwright's left was a little girl, only two years old. Strange that her parents could bring themselves to burn her; in cases like that people usually cling to what they can. Above him there brooded a colonel of artillery. 'What a terrible filing system,' said Lucy. 'Cartwright would never have stood for it.'

Hugh had given up on his plan to say some words for Cartwright in the newsroom, but there was still to be an informal gathering in the pub; you could always be sure of a turn-out for something like that. Our favourite corner of the bar is dark, panelled with wood and mirrors, and a stuffed fox stares out from a case in the wall. I don't care to catch its eye. When we arrived that evening the hall door was wedged open so that Francie could fetch some crates in, and outside in the alley it was raining hard, December rain, haloing the street lamps. The radio said that the wind was north-north-westerly, Gale Force 9 gusting to Storm Force 11, and the whole town felt as though it were pulling back inside its old walls, the walls that aren't there any more.

'Most people who live vicariously do it through other people,' I told Hugh, 'but what if you tried to live vicariously through yourself?'

'I'm not sure what you mean by that,' he said carefully. We'd already been there a while.

'I'm not sure either. But it sounds pretty clever.'

Because it was a special occasion Francie brought out sausages on sticks. The room began to fill with damp figures, including many of Hugh's youngsters. It occurred to me that they would never have come here while Cartwright was alive. Perhaps his spirit has been exorcized, although that fox in the box looks remarkably like him. Harry McDowell wanted to sell us another one of his unprintable stories about the sordid lives of the publicly housed. Niamh Hanrahan said the government was to blame. Ted Hetherton started telling his own yarn but soon lost the thread of it. Hugh ordered everyone another drink. The barman finished loading the crates into the dumbwaiter and closed the hall door against the rain and the wind. The room grew warmer.

Lucy Viner cornered me at the bar and started to talk to me. I emptied my glass carefully, then set it down on the bar beside the china plate that held the last of the sausages, burned, quite badly, in token of Cartwright's cremation. The stuffed fox stared down at the sausage with glassy-eyed hunger. Everyone else had been too polite to touch it. I picked it up and bit it, feeling carbon coat my teeth.

'A walk?' I said finally. The bar was crowded now, and Lucy and I were wedged into the corner by the dumbwaiter. She wore a jacket and a dark, fitted skirt and she smiled up at me seriously. Her eyes were brown.

'A walk in the mountains,' said Lucy. 'Or on a beach, wherever. To get some fresh air. You could do with it. I've never seen you anywhere but the office or the bar.'

'You saw me in the crematorium today.'

'That's what got me thinking.'

Hugh squeezed past and gave me a nod on his way to the door. It was a relief to see him go: I didn't want any more of his reminiscences about Cartwright, or any more questions. He keeps coming back to the idea that Cartwright must have left a message for us. It's almost as if he knows something.

Lucy attacked her glass fiercely, swirling gin and tonic around behind her pursed lips, then swallowing, all the time glaring at me. I had to laugh then. Seconds out, round two.

'I'll pick you up tomorrow and we can head up the mountains,' she said. 'I know some trails that aren't difficult. I'm guessing you're not very fit.'

'You're very kind,' I said, 'but the fact is my leg isn't up to it.'

She had started to nod, quickly, even before I'd finished. 'But you walk to work each day, right?'

'Yes, but it's not far, and there aren't any hills. If I had a car I'd drive.'

'Then we'll go for our walk on some nice level trail.'

'It's December. I only have these shoes.'

'Then we'll go somewhere that's paved.'

The south sea wall begins near the power plant, then runs east for three miles into the middle of the bay. Or at least that's what the guidebook says. I prefer to think of it as the other way round, of the wall surfacing out in the bay and then driving itself ashore. Why read from left to right? The wall makes most sense out in the deep water, beyond the breakers, before it loses itself amid the reclaimed land and sewage works, the abandoned wharves and batteries.

We used to walk out along the wall quite often, Hugh and me, back when we were students. Sometimes on a Friday night after the bar closed, when it was very warm or very windy, we would buy some cans and get our friend Wally, who didn't drink back then, to drive us out there. If we were lucky the tide would be in and the water would wash beneath us all the way out to the end of the wall, but often we had to walk for twenty minutes or more above damp mudflats and black pools where the lights of the city trembled in the wind. Then we would come to the tide line, creeping or roaring as the moon and wind conspired, and last of all to the lighthouse. Its beacon flashed red. Off to the north, at the end of a ragged breakwater that submerged with each tide, its rival flashed green across the deep-water channel.

At the very end of the wall you could walk around the lighthouse and look out to the wider sea beyond the headlands, with the waves hissing beneath you and the lighthouse to baffle the wind. If it was warm we'd drink our beer sitting on the stones, but on nights when the wind had fetched us we'd stand close together and shiver, talking in short phrases as we watched the breakers. The east wind blew seldom; it was cold, and the lighthouse gave no shelter from it, but it brought the best waves. A couple of times, one autumn, one winter, we had to turn back early or else be swept away. That was part of the attraction, I suppose.

That was many years ago, and I haven't been back since, not until this week. I don't think Hugh does that sort of thing any more. He's very busy with the paper, of course, and then there's his family. I'm told Wally now lives alone on the other side of town and does something with computers.

At least I was able to talk Lucy out of picking me up from my house. We met in the afternoon at a café near the bridge, the one where Cartwright used to take his victims. As I made my way there I checked the state of my limp. My leg hurt more than usual, I decided with satisfaction. I should have stayed at home.

It was Saturday, and car windows displayed flustered mothers and bawling children and spilling bags of shopping. Their cars veered witlessly from lane to lane, and whenever one strayed out in front of us Lucy would strafe it back into line with long, vicious bursts of her horn. She drove well but rather fast.

We left the traffic behind at the port roundabout. After the powerhouse the bay opened up to our right and ahead of us. There had been a frost that night, a heavy one, and even after it thawed the day remained cold and clear except for a band of fog that lay out to sea along the eastern horizon. To the south and west the winter sun hung low over the foothills, backlighting the city a dark cherry-red. Mist was forming on the slopes and the cars crawling along the coast road had already turned their lights on. The sea twitched like a landed fish between us and the coast road, pink and grey and silver. We were in luck. The tide was in.

Lucy stopped the car at the last line of boulders and I opened the door and felt the air catch in my throat. I walked on ahead as she locked the car. The car park was streaked with crusted sand blown from the beach. Off to the left a line of white foam marked the sunken breakwater on the northern side of the shipping channel. Beyond it the low dunes of the silt island obscured the far shore of the bay until it reared up into the northern headland. Beyond the headland the night was gathering. I watched until I saw the white flash from the lighthouse on its southern point. Then another one, maybe fifteen seconds later. It used to seem longer, between the lights. I stood there, slowly breathing the cold air that came off the sea.

Lucy rustled up beside me, fastening her jacket. The slight breeze was ruffling her hair and her eyes shone from the cold.

'This is amazing,' she said, stopping beside me. 'I never knew this place was here.'

'I thought you grew up in this town.'

'I did, but you know how it is. You never do the touristy things at home.'

'I don't think it's a touristy thing. I don't think tourists ever come here.'

'So how did you know about it?'

We started off along the uneven paved surface towards the distant lighthouse. 'Hugh took me here when we were at college. He grew up just over there. His dad worked for the port and docks board.'

She caught up with me. We passed the ruined battery on our right and after that there was nothing but the sea on either side of us, stirred to a low chop by the rising breeze. The wind was in the east, cold, but still too light to raise the breakers. My face tingled, and when I looked at Lucy I saw that she was pink beneath her hair. We walked in silence at first and it was only when a pilot boat droned downstream and laboured to draw ahead of us that I noticed how fast we were moving. I checked my leg and realized with alarm that it was no longer hurting. The unevenness of the flagstones, the need to step long or short to avoid the gaps between them, seemed to counteract my limp, like waves of opposite amplitude cancelling each other out. I was striding. The pilot boat picked up speed, its engine thudding, and through the dirty windows at the back of the wheelhouse I could dimly make out three figures. Soon the boat reached the lighthouse and swung right, disappearing, and when it re-emerged from behind the lighthouse it was a little toy, heading out to sea. In the fog bank beyond it the channel buoys were blinking.

'Can't you walk a bit slower?' asked Lucy. 'I thought you were supposed to be injured.'

I remembered then that I was out of breath, and that I needed a smoke. I stopped and offered her one, then put my back to the breeze so I could light them both. When we moved off again we found a comfortable smoking pace. The pilot boat had vanished.

'So what was the story with Cartwright?' Lucy asked suddenly.

The question caught me off my guard, and I wondered for a moment if that was what this was all about. I looked at her, but she was gazing away from me, towards the mountains and the ferry port, and when she turned back to me there was no intent in her expression.

'I don't think I know any more about him than you do,' I said carefully. 'He didn't exactly reach out to people.'

'I heard he was sick.'

'He was sick all his life, and he was born disabled. I assumed he'd got used to it.'

'How can you ever get used to being crippled?' said Lucy, and then added quickly, when she saw my smile, 'I mean really crippled?' She was flushing now. 'You're not crippled. You have a limp, that's all. Personally, I think you make too much of it.'

'You think I'm fishing for sympathy?'

'Don't tell me you don't feel just a wee bit sorry for yourself?'

I laughed. 'No. Why should I? I've been very lucky in my life. You'd be surprised how lucky.'

Lucy smiled. 'So if you don't feel sorry for yourself, why did you turn a question about Cartwright into a conversation about you?'

'It wasn't me who changed the subject.'

'Yes, you did.'

166

'No, I didn't.' I was smiling now too. 'You did. You said he was crippled and then you started having a go at me.'

We passed the old bathing club, a bleak concrete hut built halfway out along the wall. The pilot boat was a small light in the mouth of the bay, and in the fog behind it I could see navigation lights and the dark loom of a ship. Finally I said, 'He must have been lonely.'

'He never married or anything?'

'No . . . He did have a big love affair, with someone from the paper. At least, that's what one of the old fellas told Hugh once.' I thought about the photograph on Cartwright's floor, then put the thought away again. 'I don't know much about him, really. His family are all dead.'

We walked on for a spell in silence. We were almost at the lighthouse when the pilot boat came clattering back around it and nosed into the channel. As it passed us, Lucy waved and I saw an answering movement from inside the wheelhouse. I liked her for waving at the boat, and the boatmen for waving back to her. But Lucy was very pretty, and the wind was now strong enough to show her shape against her coat. We reached the lighthouse and came to a halt on the round mull at the end – or beginning – of the great sea wall. It was almost night, and we were standing in the middle of the sea.

Lucy stood beside me and took in the shining dark water, the flickering channel buoys and the heart-wrenching lights of a city at nightfall in winter. She said something quietly, perhaps to her-self, which was snatched away by the wind. I saw her shiver. The ship had disappeared again, which meant the fog was creeping in towards us.

Lucy tapped me on the shoulder and when I looked down at her she was miming for another cigarette. I had to make an angle between my body and the lighthouse and switch my lighter up to full flame. When I turned back to her she had moved right to the edge of the water and was standing with her arms clasped tightly about her. She accepted the cigarette and her first exhalation exploded white into the wind.

'I wish I'd known about this place,' she said. 'When I was a little girl I used to stop beneath the railway bridge downtown and stare down the river. On a clear day you think you can see the open sea. I used to wonder how many people had sailed that way in the old days, and how many had come back again.' She took another deep drag on her cigarette. 'I was a bit of a sap, if truth were told.'

The wind now carried the deep drone of an engine and the lights of a ship were pulling clear of the fog. There was a pilot on board, I thought, and wished I could watch the ship come in for just a little longer without having to talk to anyone. But I could feel Lucy's eyes on me.

'If it hadn't been for what happened, do you think you would have come back here anyway?' she asked after a while.

I realized all at once that I didn't know. I couldn't remember how I'd felt before. It was astonishing. The ship was drawing itself up above us now and I stared in wonder and envy at the dim lights from the bridge, where the pilot must be. It was some kind of freighter – I don't know ships – and its slab-sided hull was painted a flat, cheap white and streaked with rust. From the prow, above the little white bow wave, a small figure in yellow foul-weather gear stared down at us. Then Lucy raised her arm to wave, dispelling the question that hung between us, and after another second the sailor raised an arm and let it drop again. The ship seemed to pick up speed as it came abreast of us, surging ahead of the thunder of its own engines. The sides bulged out from the sharp prow and I could see dents and pits, and odds and ends of greasy gear hanging from pulleys and railings. The superstructure came abreast of us – rows of dirty golden windows, a bridge gallery whose door was dogged against the cold, a red navigation light. Then a square, ugly funnel, a lifeboat and the stern. *Daisy Chain* was painted across the stern in big black letters, and beneath that, much smaller, *Monrovia*. The ship churned away from us up the narrow channel, another small figure watching us from its stern rail. This time Lucy didn't wave. Sparks flew from her cigarette as it struck the stones beside her. She shivered again, staring out to sea.

'Do you think that ship's really from Liberia, or is it just registered there?' she asked. 'They have a big shipping scam, don't they? Down at the Free Port? Half the world's ships are flagged there to avoid taxes and stuff?'

The Free Port. What had she been reading? 'Most of the ships registered in Liberia have never even been there,' I said slowly.

'It's a pity. It would be amazing to think that ship might have just come here all the way from Africa, from the hot to the cold.'

I tossed away my own cigarette butt and turned to smile at her. 'You've really got it bad, don't you?'

Her answering smile was only a little embarrassed. 'I suppose I do, yes . . . I'm dying to get out of here.' She switched, self-mocking, to the seagull accent of the town: 'See the ould world, you know?'

In the darkness beneath our feet there was a sudden concussion and a burst of white foam. The ship's wake had followed it ashore. Overhead the sky was clear and the first stars were shining through the haze above the city. Further out the darkness grew, and the blinking lights on the headland and the channel buoys were vague. The fog must be thickening.

I took a few steps backward and leaned my back against the lighthouse. 'So why don't you just go?' I asked her. She turned, and I saw her shrug in the darkness. Her face was indistinct.

'I might, but I need to find somewhere to go, and get some work lined up.'

I smiled, although I doubt if she could have seen me. 'Were you thinking of Africa?'

She held her hands up and laughed shortly. 'It was one of the places I was thinking of . . . Tell me this, would you go back there yourself?'

The cold seeped into my back from the wall of the lighthouse. I stared at Lucy's shape in the darkness, silhouetted against the sea, standing with the poise of a diver and swinging her arms gently. Why did she include me in her question? Soon she would go off into the world somewhere and I would stay here, that much was clear and cold and banal, but still I was surprised at the stab of pain that this knowledge gave me. You should know better than that by now, said a hard, merry voice in my head.

The voice made me want to laugh at myself. 'No,' I said aloud. 'I don't think I'd go back . . . I can give you a couple of names to call, if you want. But I can't promise anything. I've been out of touch with them for a long time. I don't even know if you should mention me.'

'That would be very kind of you,' she said. Still she stood motionless, a few feet away, facing me. There was a pause, and then she added. 'You know, that's not why I asked you to come for a walk.'

I dragged myself upright away from the wall. 'Please. I know. Don't worry. But it's freezing out here, and it's time we found a bar.'

Somewhere between the lighthouse and the bathing club she linked her arm through mine. I have no idea what she meant by that. It didn't matter anyway. By the time we reached the mainland a foghorn was booming at the entrance to the bay.

12

Everyone took leave after Kinshasa, myself included. I'd some business back home, and when I flew back to Johannesburg I was met by midwinter. At Germiston my taxi tunnelled into a bank of freezing fog, and when we emerged I saw the city perched high on its stone ridge and the first rays of day shining in its windows, floating above the murk.

Closer in, the freeway ran on stilts along the played-out gold reef, between the high-rise towers and the yellow mine dumps. I looked down and saw the city reassembling itself from the cold night – figures emerging from underpasses and marshalling yards, fires burning in oil drums, the first lonely taxis standing at traffic lights, steaming in their own exhaust. Brighter now, the northern sky shone pale through the open stairwell of a tower block. Such attention to detail, so easy to miss it. Then we descended onto Empire Road.

I dumped my stuff inside the kitchen door, climbed into freezing sheets and slept until the light outside my window was yellow with the evening. The house was very cold, and I burrowed into the rubbish in the spare room to find the electric oil heaters and then turned them both up full. I put some of my stuff away and had a shower, and only then did I find the courage to phone Beatrice. Perhaps she was not even in town. Her last e-mail had been vague. Her phone rang four times and then she answered. She was having coffee at the Full Stop with a French colleague. She would be done in a few minutes. She would drop around.

I watched through the window as Beatrice parked her car behind mine at the end of the driveway. She drove an old Polo that still had the Northern Cape plates of its previous owner. Anyone driving past could see it parked out there, almost on the street. I opened the iron security gate and stood back to let her pass into the kitchen but instead she stretched up to kiss me. I was very grateful. I hadn't allowed myself to expect that.

The house was almost warm now – it was an old mine property, small enough to heat. The only lights in the room came red through the window from the setting sun and pale through the door from the lighted hallway. Would it work here? I wondered, as Beatrice lay back on the bed. So much might depend on things that were missing, or things that had changed. Beneath me Beatrice was as remote and cold and white as the moon. It terrified me. Outside I heard the evening traffic honking on the avenue and the shouts of the African maids calling to each other from gate to gate. I listened with my head back, frozen, to the cold bright sounds of the night outside, and then I looked down at Beatrice and saw that she was smiling at me, only a little puzzled. Then she turned her head to one side and bit my upper arm, quite hard. After that everything was fine. We lay in bed all evening, as the house grew warmer, then went out and had dinner, then went back to bed.

Laura was really leaving us this time, for good and for all, and that Saturday night she gave her last big party in the empty shell of her house. Her stuff was already at sea somewhere, bound for her new base in London, and she'd had to borrow Marvell's garden furniture to set up her buffet. Laura had volunteered me to come early and help, and Beatrice came too. I didn't ask her to, she just did. It was the first time we went somewhere openly together. In the kitchen Laura opened a bottle of Allesverloren, and for lack of chairs we all three sat up on the sideboard by the sink, passing nuts and olives back and forth.

Soon guests and music overflowed from the lounge into the kitchen, and out in the garden people shivered and blew plumes of smoke and breath. There were strings of coloured light bulbs running between the trees and lanterns hung from branches. Over in one corner men were gathered around the barbecue, and under the porch a DJ had set up his deck and his speakers. A long table stacked with bottles was manned by a couple of bar staff, and by the edge of the veranda stood a big tin bath filled with ice and cans of beer. A lot of our people hadn't arrived yet: they were starting the evening elsewhere, or putting young children to bed, or driving round Rivonia in search of cocaine. This was the early house, older women with jewels and hairdos and men with slacks and sweaters, a couple of diplomats and politicians, the kind of people whom Fine used to schmooze on behalf of the *Chronicle*. It was said that if you worked such people properly they might even give you stories, but I never tried.

There would be no more talking to Laura that night. She was leaving, and therefore belonged to everyone. She wore white silk trousers and a matching white shirt so that even in the dim light of the garden you could see her glowing. I observed the poise of her chin and the set of her shoulders; even as she talked she was squaring herself up to the end of one thing and the start of something else. Then somebody nudged my arm and I turned and saw Brereton, leaning in the shadows in the angle of the wall. He must have been there when I came out.

'She looks well tonight, doesn't she?' he said.

'Laura? Yes, she does.' I was embarrassed that he had caught me watching her, surprised that he acknowledged it.

We stood in silence for a few moments and then he spoke again. 'It won't be the same here without her,' he said.

'You're going to keep in touch.' I said it firmly, more statement than question. He smiled past me. 'Oh, no doubt we'll try . . .' He was still watching Laura. 'People are always coming and going. If you meet up again, you meet up again. Otherwise there's bound to be somebody new along.' He turned to look at me for the first time. 'It's a shallow life, isn't it?'

I realized with relief then that he was very drunk. I'd always looked up to Brereton.

'Some people would find it romantic,' I said.

He pulled his grin at me, the lopsided, tired one that made certain women swoon, and then, after holding the smile for a long, pointed moment, he pulled it tighter, his lips drawing thinner, his cheeks fissuring, wordlessly segueing from cynicism to sarcasm. I felt stung.

'So why not follow her back to London?'

Brereton reached over to fetch a tumbler from the windowsill.

'I did try to go back a few years ago,' he said, and took a long drink, 'but then I came back out again. I found that even when you stay in one place the people you like still leave you. Only enemies accumulate.' He took another drink. 'I also find it's best to stay well clear of the office. Hang around there for any length of time and you're bound to get rumbled.'

Laura had moved to another group now, under the jacaranda in the corner of the garden. For a moment Marvell eclipsed her and then she shone again, red and gold from the charcoal that was flaming on the braai. A sudden breeze rustled the leaves and chased a cloud of sparks off the barbecue and across the lawn. The group closed around Laura. Like me, they all owed her favours they would never now repay.

'I think you'd make a great couple,' I said, aware as I did of how lame I sounded.

Brereton laughed and pulled himself off the wall, carefully balancing his drink. 'It's very nice of you to say so,' he said formally, and lurched off into the crowd.

I watched him go, and then I went around the corner of the house to regain the kitchen: the way through the lounge was too crowded. As I neared the front door, feet crunching on the gravel, I saw two women standing together in the light of the porch, embracing each other, and when they drew apart I saw that it was Beatrice and Polly and that Polly was crying. Beatrice held her by the arms, talking quietly, and I heard a sob from Polly and saw a distant, almost hard expression steal across Beatrice's face, and then as I slowed to a halt, not wanting to intrude, my heel crunched heavily and they both turned and saw me and Polly cleared her throat noisily and told me that she'd just got a phone call to say that Jansson was dead. He'd been killed in an ambush somewhere. So we went out to the garden and told Laura and she just nodded a couple of times and said she would turn off the music and make an announcement. And that's how Laura's farewell party, which she'd been planning for ages and had repeatedly put off because of all that fuss in the Congo, became instead a wake for Jesper Jansson.

Extrastrong turned up about an hour later. He had been in the office with Rasheed, trying to find out what had happened, and he brought us a printout of a flash that Amalgamated News had moved a few minutes earlier. It said that Jesper Jansson (39), an Amalgamated News staff photographer and native of Finland, had been shot dead while on assignment in southern Sudan. There was then a line of the usual sanctimonious bollocks from whichever management type had been responsible for keeping Jansson's wages down.

The music was gone, and many of the guests with it, but the house rang to the sound of cell phones going off. After a while Extrastrong called Rasheed and then put him on to Polly, and she talked to him for a long time before she put her phone down among the empty wine bottles and overflowing ashtrays on the borrowed trestle table.

Jansson's death was difficult to deal with. You could see people shooting looks at each other that night, trying to figure out how they should react. It was a very serious business, very grave, so grave that you had that vertiginous feeling where you're frightened you might smile. There had been Hansi and the others in Mogadishu in '93, Francis in Burundi in '95 and now, almost three years later, this. Yet this was meant to be a dangerous beat. At some point the thought slithered into mind, the notion that a death was overdue, that it came as a vindication. The thought was chased away, the frown deepened. It was very disturbing. I consoled myself with the fact that I didn't know anyone who disliked Jansson, not even his wife.

And there was something else to consider, at least as time went on: Jansson had been a genuine wanderer, someone you often didn't see for weeks or months until he popped up in some airport or bar or shithole somewhere. Even before the ambush he was already an apparition, and apparitions are hard to kill. I was seeing him in bars and airports and shitholes six months later: I saw him at Lungi airport as they put the stretchers on the plane. I sometimes see him still, even here. But please don't think I'm being fanciful. I know it's a trick of the mind. I have other things to worry about.

Beatrice, on the other hand, was untroubled by Jansson's death;

untroubled in the sense that it really did grieve her. I had no idea why: they'd never seemed close. I thought, perhaps, that he reminded her of someone. I sometimes had that feeling with Beatrice, that there were other people present. It would explain a lot. Perhaps it even explained me. I wondered, once or twice, whom she was reminded of, in me, in Fine, in Jansson. She never talked about her past life except for incidental details. She melted away before questions. And how do you confront someone who isn't there? Answer: you lie in ambush.

But I told myself I was being selfless. Every night I stayed with Beatrice at her apartment in Northcliff. I fucked Beatrice selflessly each night. I crack myself up sometimes, looking back.

Jansson had been in Nairobi in one of his holding patterns, closing down the bar of the Norfolk every night, when he ran into one of those people who cover white men's wars for posh features pages and big-paying magazines and who style themselves 'war correspondent'. Apparently this particular war correspondent needed an African chapter to fill out his forthcoming memoir, and for want of anything better he'd decided to go to southern Sudan, where there'd recently been some lacklustre murdering. But the war correspondent had fallen out with his own snapper so he signed up Jansson instead. It must have seemed the right thing to do. People like Ernest Hemingway and Teddy Roosevelt used to drink at the Norfolk too. It was a good box to tick.

The war correspondent's editors persuaded Amalgamated News to let Jansson go with him, so next day they both flew to Uganda, where they fell in with a young American freelance writer who'd been travelling around by herself. In Arua they hired a jeep and made contact with a guide from the SPLA who took them across to Sudan. Jansson set up his sat-phone at Yei and called the bureau in Jo'burg to tell them where he was. Rasheed answered the phone. He and Jansson used to forge receipts for each other and play battleships on those rare occasions when they were both in the office at the same time. Later, Rasheed admitted that he could only half remember taking the call.

The local SPLA commander gave the three of them the freedom to go wherever they liked, provided they took a couple of armed minders with them. But this meant that their jeep was now more than full, and there was no hope of hiring a second one – there's nothing in southern Sudan, even by African standards. In the end Jansson's party decided to break the usual rule and leave some of their gear behind in Yei, with their driver to mind it.

The war correspondent insisted on driving. They were about two hours outside Yei, still well short of the supposed front line, when, before anyone could stop him, he swerved the jeep around a fallen tree that lay across the road. The next thing they knew they were all sitting in the wrecked jeep with their ears ringing, watching the front wheels and axle roll away up the road in a cloud of black smoke. They were unhurt but dazed, and Jansson even started to giggle. But the American girl, who was sitting in the back, said she saw that their escorts were clawing at the door handle, desperate to get out. The shooting began a moment later; the ambushers must have been dozing when their own mine woke them.

What happened next is unclear, as you might expect. The American woman remembered bailing out onto the road after the two escorts and scooting for the bush on the far side. She saw one of the SPLA guys turn on the far side of the road and shoot at something. She didn't see any more of the others and didn't wait to look.

After a few hours hiding in the bush she heard engines and crept back to the roadside. It was an SPLA patrol. They took her back to the site of the ambush, where Jansson was lying by the jeep. Jansson's door had been riddled with bullets and the upper half of his body wasn't worth stripping, but somebody had made off with his jeans and his boots and all the equipment he'd had with him. One of the two escorts was found dead in the long grass near by but it seems the nasties hadn't found him because he still had his rifle; they must have been too nervous to stick around and search. Probably not government troops, then. Maybe Lord's Resistance Army, or some other private militia. We never found out.

The SPLA wrapped Jansson in a blanket and shipped him back to Yei on the back of a Land Rover. The poor American woman had to keep him company. When they reached Yei the war correspondent was somehow there already, calming himself with Jansson's whiskey and frantically typing; he had a deadline he could just about meet, if he wasn't distracted. It was left to the American, who, unlike the war correspondent, wasn't even working with Jansson, to make all the phone calls to Amalgamated News, and later to speak to Jansson's wife, and his mother in the Åland Islands. 'Yes, I was with him at the end,' she would have lied . . . She later told Rasheed that the war correspondent had hemmed and hawed before he gave her Jansson's sat-phone, even though the phone belonged to Amalgamated News and wasn't his to withhold. Brereton reckoned that he must have been worried she might use it to file a story of her own.

We were still sitting there at one in the morning, that night Jansson died, when Laura brought in a computer printout. It was the war correspondent's story, which was about to run in syndication around the globe. Brereton read it aloud, his voice gradually rising. It was a moving, controlled, understated piece, written in the first person. The war correspondent recounted soberly the circumstances leading up to the fateful ambush, his desperate effort to drag his stricken friend from the wreckage, his own miraculous escape and his subsequent attempt to find the American woman after she fled. It touched, lightly, in passing, upon his grim duty as a combat reporter to put his own feelings aside and file on his friend's tragic death.

By the time he got to that last bit Brereton was practically shrieking. A caption indicated that the piece would run with a portrait of the author and a column head-shot of Jansson, taken years before in Bosnia, where the war correspondent now claimed to have known him.

I suppose one shouldn't blame the war correspondent, really. He'd hit the jackpot, the way things work now. Maybe I'd have done the same, if I'd been in his position . . . No, it really is difficult to blame the war correspondent. But God help him if he ever meets Polly when she's drunk.

The gear that Jansson had left in Yei arrived in Johannesburg a couple of days later – the American freelancer had brought it back to Kampala and then shipped it out by airfreight. London told Rasheed to go through the bags and retrieve any company property before sending the personal effects on to Jansson's wife in Helsinki. In one aluminium case Rasheed found a spare company-issue camera body, which he ceremoniously smashed against the wall, and a half-dozen bottles of Bushmills. We drank them there in the Amalgamated News bureau, in Jansson's honour. I'm pretty sure his wife wouldn't have wanted them.

Amalgamated flew Rasheed to Finland to represent the bureau and some bigwig came from London to deliver the eulogy. The war correspondent also turned up; I suppose he needed some more colour for his book. He wanted to speak at the service but Rasheed threatened to smack him, right there in the Lutheran chapel. We heard later that the American freelancer had also wanted to be there, at her own expense, but she was still stuck in Uganda. She'd spent all her own cash freighting out Jansson's gear, and Amalgamated News hadn't bothered to repay her yet.

The odd thing is, Beatrice would have gone to the funeral too if she'd had any money. I couldn't understand it. Instead the two of us sat in her flat all that afternoon waiting for Rasheed to call us from the service. She'd begged him to do so. Beatrice was beside me when my cell phone rang and after a few words I passed it over to her. She listened carefully, asked a couple of questions, and when she cut the phone off she was crying once more. I put my arms around her and rubbed her back, staring out of the window through dark, cigarette-smelling hair, trying to conjure Jansson's face again. At first it was beyond me, and then suddenly I was back by the pool in Kinshasa, that night when I first despaired of Beatrice. We'd left him sitting by himself in the dark, finishing our drinks. Thus had I consigned Jansson to eternal night and loneliness. For a moment his image reached out and clutched my throat, but only for a moment. I'm sure Beatrice never noticed. I hope not.

Four days after the eclipse of her farewell party Laura left Johannesburg for good. She called me that morning and asked me to drive her to the airport. Poor Brereton, I thought.

I was early, for once, and as Laura finished dressing I was free to walk around the empty house. Everything Laura owned had already been sent ahead, sold or given away. Even the cupboard beneath the sink was empty. Most people would leave some bleach and floor polish or something, but Laura had been planning this departure. It was to be significant, and not a trace of her would remain. When she appeared at the bedroom door she was wearing a sort of trouser suit that looked just slightly too small for her. She replied to my look with a smile that was almost shy.

'I was wearing this the day I arrived here,' she explained. 'It was winter then also, and I was surprised how cold it was when I got off the plane. It was my first time in Africa. I took a taxi to the Rosebank Hotel and the driver charged me three hundred rands. Can you imagine? I didn't know any better.'

Laura had only an overnight bag and a hard plastic carry-on case holding her cameras and a laptop. I made sure I was first out the door with her bags, to give her time to say goodbye to her house, but she followed straight after me and didn't look back. She left the door open behind her: it didn't matter now. As we drove out to the airport the green highway signs that had grown so familiar down the years became strange to me again, in sympathy with Laura. She didn't say very much, just watched the city as it melted away from her, humming beneath her breath. The sun was setting behind us, beyond the Brixton tower. In all the time I'd known Laura I never until that day understood how deep her feelings ran.

We parked at the airport and I hung back in the departure hall while Laura checked in. She was flying back to Germany first class, having been forced to abandon her dream of taking her final passage home by cargo ship. She'd worked out all the connections: coasters and container lines, hopping from port to port, all the way up through the Bight of Benin. But then at the last minute she was offered a big new assignment in London and her boss couldn't spare her the time.

Laura checked in, then came strolling back to me, glancing from one side to the other with the unhurried curiosity of a shopper who doesn't need to buy. When she looked up into my face she smiled suddenly and put her hand on my lower arm. 'Let's go for a drink,' she said.

The bar was in the domestic terminal at the other end of the airport, a plastic waste land where parents bickered in the cruel light while their children spilled nuts on the floor. Lone male travellers came in, drank quickly and departed, leaving contrails of smoke and wet rings on the bar. Laura found a quiet cubicle in a corner while I went up and ordered the drinks. We were both having whiskey. Laura never drank whiskey, so I understood that this was part of her rite of departure, her liturgy of me.

'Sláinte,' she said, and we clicked glasses. She swallowed more than half her drink in one go, without blinking. Never let it be said.

She started talking about the flight ahead and as I made myself look at her it occurred to me that – just for instance – we would never now make those trips we'd talked of, by ship to Saint Helena, by jeep to the Richtersveld. She flickered before me in the bar's strip lighting: the oddball on foot by the docklands in Cape Town, the stranger-to-be drinking whiskey at the airport, these in the same instant and a half-dozen more besides, blurring off at the dark edge of the frame.

Laura was asking me a question.

'What will I do next?' I echoed, and felt my eyes slipping away from her. 'I hadn't thought about it, really. What I'm doing already, I suppose.'

'So? And you don't get bored with it?' She held her glass with one hand on the table in front of her, and I almost smiled as I thought of a microphone.

'No, I don't get bored with it. Besides, what alternatives do I have? I'm unemployable anywhere but here.'

She laughed. 'You have such a romantic picture of yourself, Owen. I always find this funny about you. You like to pretend you are so old and so cynical.'

'You mean like Charlie Brereton?'

She didn't blink. 'No. Not like him. He does not pretend.'

I didn't care for that. 'I was surprised that you wanted me to take you to the airport,' I said. 'I assumed he'd be taking you.'

She turned the palm of her free hand upwards and slowly opened it and something invisible melted into the air for ever.

'So what about you and Beatrice?' she asked.

The sensation had itched away at me ever since Laura called me the day before: the impression that somewhere close behind me, just beyond the periphery of what I could presently make out, was a corner of her choosing into which she was backing me. There would be nothing I could do about it, I knew that in advance. But only in chess do people resign when they know things are hopeless. In life we use up all our pieces first.

'What about us?'

She smiled again. 'You are serious about her?'

'Well, that's a bit sudden. Maybe. Why wouldn't I be?'

'She is very nice,' said Laura, and I studied her through narrowed eyes as she took another sip of her whiskey.

She spoke again. 'I think perhaps you and Nathan are not friends any more.'

'Why do you say that?'

'It seems like you and Nathan have not been friends ever since Kinshasa.'

'That's silly,' I said.

But Laura would not be deterred. I knew that, of course.

'I think perhaps you are jealous of him,' she said, and then added more quietly, 'You should not be.'

'Jealous? What do I care if he's a big star in New York? That's not what I'm about.'

She tilted her head a little further. 'What are you about, Owen?'

Was that checkmate, or just another interim manoeuvre? I'm sure I could have thought of a reply, a way out of that one, but I never had to. The loudspeaker gonged into life, calling Laura's flight for boarding. Laura sighed, pulled herself upright, smiled at me and said, 'Well, I suppose that is it.'

The little wheels of Laura's carry-on droned along the floor. As usual, the lift for the departures floor took for ever to arrive, and when we got there we had to fight our way out through swarms of people who had come to bid loved ones farewell – there were always bigger crowds in departures than arrivals at Johannesburg's airport, I don't know why. Finally we reached the security gate and Laura stood up on tiptoe and kissed me once on the cheek.

'I'll see you again,' she said, and walked off towards the gate.

13

The next day Beatrice woke me with an insistent pushing at my shoulder. I turned into her arms, my eyes still closed, and felt her breath on my face. Her hair brushed my nose.

'Let's go away for a while,' she said.

We were both broke, as usual, but Beatrice had a plan. There was a conference starting in Durban in a couple of days – sustainable development, something like that – and she was sure that her French paper would want her to go. French editors love covering conferences and big set-piece stories, where facts needn't screw up your themes. If her company would pay the bill, for the trip we could both go to Durban and stay in the Edward, overlooking the sea.

We set out in the early afternoon in Beatrice's old Volkswagen. It was almost dark by the time we passed Villiers. Near Harrismith fat fingers of cloud reached down from a pearl sky and it started to snow. The oncoming traffic thinned out and several trucks flashed their lights at us. A few miles on we came to a roadblock where a policeman shivered in a blue bull's-wool greatcoat. The snow had closed Van Reenen Pass, he said, but if we wanted we could divert around by Oliviershoek, although that pass too might be closed before we reached it.

The night closed in behind us as we fled into a galaxy of snow-flakes, brilliant in the headlights. The snow was sticking on the short, burned grass by the side of the road but the tarmac itself was thawed by the heat of the passing trucks; the route ahead must still be open. The doors of Beatrice's car were loose with age and the heater barely managed to keep the windscreen free of our breath. The road turned pale, then white, until even the tracks of the trucks were indistinct. There was hardly any traffic now. The car grew colder until I asked Beatrice to pull over so I could get our jackets from the back. She stopped the engine and I stepped out into cold, white silence. Looking out over the edge of the road, I saw that we were parked on the lip of a steep valley, white and filled with snowflakes, and far beneath us was the black, still water of a large dam. I stood and stared for a few moments until the whiteness ahead turned red and then gold, and the silence was broken by the roaring of a big diesel engine in low gear. The truck was only thirty yards away when it broke through the white curtain. The driver slowed and tooted twice in inquiry and when I waved he kept going. When I got back in the car I saw that Beatrice had rolled down her window and was staring down into the valley while snow settled on her sleeve. She got out of the car to put her jacket on, and it was a few moments before she climbed back in and restarted the engine.

The road was open, but only just. Beatrice drove slowly and carefully, peering into the blizzard, and once or twice we skidded, just a little, on the sloping bends. Somewhere in the darkness we passed the hill of Spion Kop. The snow was thick now and beginning to drift where the wind blew free across the uplands. When we rejoined the main road we found it lined with the shadows of parked trucks, waiting for the passes to clear. We kept descending, and by the time we reached Mooi River the snow had turned to sleet.

It was raining when we arrived in Durban, hours late. We drove on to the Marine Parade and found the coloured lights of the fun fair shining, even though it was closed for the season. The seats on the chairlift rocked in the wind and the night rang with the din of halyards resonating against the steel flagpoles lining the esplanade. The rain veiled the lights of the promenade, beyond which the Indian Ocean thundered invisibly on the beach. Bits of torn palm fronds littered the road. We found a parking space half a block from the hotel, took our things from the car and ran for it but we were soaked by the time we reached the door. The desk clerk turned up his nose at us but we did have a booking, right there in the computer, and there was still enough time for a meal and a drink. Later we pulled open the nylon nets of our window and looked out towards the ocean. There was nothing to be seen but the hard glistening geometry of palm trees and promenade, the impressionistic streetlights. Beyond them the surf was an abstract line of white on the black that stood in for the sea. Beyond that again there was nothing but the solid murk of the storm, mauve in the lights from the city.

'Usually you'd see ships out there,' I said. 'They have to anchor out beyond the bar until a berth is free in the harbour . . . I suppose they're still out there, but you can't see them because of the rain.'

I felt Beatrice's teeth nip my upper arm, the pressure gradually increasing until suddenly it vanished, and then she spoke into my ear.

'What's all this bar and berth stuff? You sound like a sailor.' Her voice was amused.

'I read it in a history book. In Shaka's day the colonists had to anchor in the bay and run goods and people in over the sandbar in surf boats. The sharks would eat you if you overturned.'

She pulled me around to face her. We'd turned off the lights so we could see out the window, but her face was smiling in the glow from the promenade.

'You're such a boy,' she said. 'I bet you tell yourself these little stories everywhere you go. I'll bet they keep you company.' And she began to unbutton my shirt.

Beatrice really did have to write about the conference if she wanted to claim the trip as an expense. The alarm in her cell phone woke us both before seven the next morning. She got up and went to the window and stood there so long that I roused myself and went to join her. I saw in the mist the dark outlines of ships, a dozen or more, riding at anchor out to sea, and much closer in little black dots bobbed off the pier head waiting for waves. There were always a few surfers out there, even in the foulest winter weather. Beatrice's skin was cool and I put my arms around her and we lay back on the bed, listening for the knock at the door that would signal coffee. I drank mine in bed, watching her dress, and when she left I put the 'Do Not Disturb' sign on the door and fell asleep again.

When I woke it was mid morning and, with nothing better to do, I shaved and took a taxi to the convention centre. The storm had given way to a spell of gusty drizzle, and miserable hawkers peered from the sheltered shop fronts, wrapped in extra layers of clothing, their business ruined for another day. The weather had left delegates with little choice but to attend the conference so the convention centre was heaving with damp, ill-tempered people, all wearing identical little backpacks coloured UN blue. The press desk wanted to know if I'd registered in advance, like you had to, so I took a gamble and gave them Laura's surname. Knowing her, she'd have put her name down months ago, just in case she'd still be around. The girl on the desk scanned a list in her computer and then looked up at me.

'It says here your first name is Laura.'

'It should be Lawrence. A temp filled the forms, back at the office. She didn't know me.'

She gave me a blue nylon backpack containing a bunch of press releases, pamphlets and fact sheets, plus schedules and contact details for all the main sponsors. There was also a ball-point, a notebook, a packet of condoms with an HIV message and a king-sized Mars Bar that I ate on the escalator.

I put the pen and the notebook and the condoms in my pocket and dumped the rest of the pack inside the door of the press-room, a great barn filled with rows and rows of desks, most of them empty. There was no sign of Beatrice. Hacks were dotted here and there, singly or in clumps, like islands in a formica sea. Rasheed was bent over a desk near the top of the room, talking on the phone, so I made my way up behind him and tapped his shoulder. He smiled at me tiredly and waved his free hand into the mouthpiece of his telephone. He listened for a bit, said goodbye and hung up.

'You're back early,' I said. 'They didn't give you much time for the funeral.'

'No,' he said, and began to nod his head earnestly. 'No, bru, they did not. I landed back in Jo'burg yesterday morning and they flew me here last night.'

'I can't believe they've got you back at work so soon after a trip like that.'

He hadn't stopped nodding, even while I spoke. 'Oh, yes,' he said. 'I was rostered to cover this conference before Jesper got killed and there was no way to change the roster. At least, not without flying another producer in from some other bureau, which would cost money. And London spent so much money on Jesper's funeral that there's nothing left in our budget for this month.'

'Amalgamated paid for his funeral?'

'No,' he said, still nodding. 'The insurance paid for that. But they flew me from Jo'burg economy class. I'd a stopover in Heathrow and our big fucking laanie bossman joined me there for the flight on to Finland. Only he was in business class and I was in economy. The bastard was bringing his wife and kids to meet him the day after. I'm not supposed to know that, but I do. They're in Lapland now, seeing Santa and his fucking elves.'

'I don't think they have any snow there in summer.'

'I don't think so either but I'm not fucking management, what do I know? The lucky thing was, by having me go in and out in less than two days Amalgamated was able to save putting me up in a hotel ... On the flight back through Heathrow one of the stewardesses gave me a whole bottle of wine to myself. She felt sorry for me because she'd seen me on the flight out.'

'Are you going to see her again?'

Rasheed finally stopped nodding. 'She said she was married.'

I started to scan the room again. 'That's a really bad story,' I said.

'It surely is.'

'You shouldn't let them treat you like that.'

'I have to. I'm trying to get them to move me back to Cape Town. It's time I retired and bought a fucking wine farm.'

I left him there. Beatrice's phone was switched off. She must be working. Tides of lunchtime were flushing through the halls and vestibules. I halted on the mezzanine outside the pressroom and stared down into the flood of people surging to the food courts. From this viewpoint the mosaic of little backpacks, bobbing along on shoulders, gave the particoloured crowd a shift of blue. The solid mass of a Zulu choir slid by beneath me, its robes a shiny red slick in the stream. Above us all, the rain was dribbling down the high glass sides of the building. Warm air washed a drowsy mumble around me and I had to shake myself awake, telling myself I was still hungry despite having eaten the Mars Bar. I was about to move on when I felt a tap on my shoulder and I turned and found myself looking into the face of a slender black man in smartly pressed chinos and a new denim jacket. He looked vaguely familiar. He was half frowning, trying not to smile.

'Hello, Owen,' he said, and held a hand out. He must have seen my hesitation because he hurriedly continued: 'We met in Goma. I am Sylvestre.'

'Sylvestre?'

'Yes. I worked for you as a translator . . . We visited the camps together.'

Another day when it rained. 'Good God, Sylvestre!' I said, and grabbed his hand. 'I'm sorry. It's just I never would have thought to see you here. What the hell are you doing in Durban?'

The green tag fastened to his jacket supplied the answer before he spoke. 'I am a delegate,' he said, as he nodded down towards it. 'I work for Alarm now.'

'Really? You work for Alarm in Goma?'

'No. Nairobi. I was doing some translation work for Think of the Children and then Alarm hired me as a regional adviser. As it says in the Bible, unto them that hath shall be given.'

'Does the Bible say that?'

He smiled. 'I believe it is from the Gospels, yes. My mother used to say it, anyway, although she herself had very little . . . But how are you, and Charlie and Tommo? And Nathan? Are they also here?'

'Brereton and Tommo are up in Johannesburg and Fine is back in the States for a while. He's getting married.'

His smile broadened. 'Married? That is nice. To Beatrice?'

'No. Not to Beatrice. To someone called Rachel . . . She's also American . . . Why did you say Beatrice?'

But Sylvestre was already looking past me at the rain that pattered harmlessly on the glass above us.

'I am easily mistaken,' he said diffidently. 'If you talk to Nathan, please give him my congratulations.'

'Of course . . . Actually, Beatrice is here at the conference today. She came with me.'

'Really? That is good news.'

'We should all meet up and have a drink together. Or lunch. What are you doing for lunch now? I can call Beatrice and we'll get out of this place for a while.'

Sylvestre was shaking his head. 'We have a meeting every lunchtime – Alarm has sent a team of us and we are supposed to coordinate each day. But if you are free tonight it would be wonderful to meet you both. Since I have been here I have been nowhere but the hotel and this conference centre.'

'We've a car. We can come and get you.'

We exchanged cell-phone numbers, shook hands again and parted. I watched him ride down the escalator and vanish in the crowd and then I tried calling Beatrice again. The call went straight to voicemail. I stepped onto the escalator and descended to the ground.

Foddered now, the herd was scarcely less sullen than at the start of its break. Scores of former college activists in expensive loafers and cheap promo T-shirts lumbered about with little groups of their Third World disciples, astutely assembled from centres of poverty and gratitude, tight on the leash of short-term local-hire contracts. These were people who had started out with fierce intentions for good and who now, thanks to their success, found themselves as dependent on charity as the big-eyed waifs on their fund-raising posters. The main foyer was lined with stands and informational displays, petitions to sign and positions to ponder. Sustainable logging, desertification, species diversity, ozone depletion, indigenous crops and gene modification. Drought, famine and death. War. All would be charted, analysed, quantified, understood, addressed, confronted, tackled, combated, fought and – in principle – defeated, right here in Durban, from Tuesday morning until Friday night. It helped that it was raining. And beneath the buzz of disputation, the barking of orders and the distant crackle of amps in dreaming lecture halls, there murmured the true voice of the conference, its carrier signal: '. . . contract handling logistics for Alarm out of Abidjan . . . press officer EU election observation mission, three months in Pakistan . . . De-mining gig in Mozambique . . . the UNHCR needs a new flack in Grozny . . . teaching post in a think tank back home . . . it's full salary UN package and if you play it right it'll get you to Rome or Geneva, who knows, someday maybe to New York . . .'

You get to drive around interesting places in a big new Toyota jeep with a twenty-foot radio mast and a winch and a snorkel and live in a free house with verandas and servants, but it's still not worth it. You spend years dodging from one short-term contract to the next, chasing the funds as compassion flits from disaster to disaster, and every new job takes you one step further away from wherever you come from and whatever it was you originally cared about, until you no longer talk about your work to outsiders, not like you used to. And if you're lucky and persistent you might end up working full time for one of the big global players, with a tax-free salary and fees paid so the kids from your second marriage can go to the best international school in whatever shithole you're currently pretending you don't really live in, with an empty apartment in Paris or New York or somewhere that's meant to be home. It's not a good life, I don't care what anyone says. I don't know why anyone would want to live like that.

Two o'clock, and the crowd shuddered and heaved and began to ebb back towards the conference halls and seminar rooms. I stepped into the lee of a display stand and read for a while about northern Namibia, where some naked herdsmen were about to be civilized into extinction by some new dam or other. By the time I'd finished reading the tide in the foyer had receded, stranding little pools of gossipers and the odd scuttling latecomer. Then I spotted Beatrice. She was sitting with her back to me in a café on the other side of the foyer, among tables piled high with the wreckage of lunchtime. She was with a man I didn't recognize. I could see that he was speaking, and she was intent but half turned away from him, as if she had to listen but didn't want to.

The stranger was tall with tanned skin and dark blond hair. He was dressed like a hometown hack on an outing, complete with the survivalist pocket-vest and those bush pants you can unzip to turn into shorts, but when I got closer I saw the green delegate tag on his shirt. He was talking too low for me to hear and Beatrice was so intent on his voice that it wasn't until I touched her shoulder that she looked up at me, turning her face with the slow pain of broken attention. The stranger showed me a look of bland uncon-cern. Beatrice's face was flushed and she looked at me for half a beat before she seemed to recognize me. I glanced from her to the stranger, feeling my own smile foolish.

'Do you mind if I sit down?' I asked.

It was the stranger who spoke. 'Of course not,' he said, and offered his hand.

His name was Daniel Schoon and he was from the Netherlands. He worked as a spokesman for one of the big UN agencies. He fed me his story unbidden, in phrases of equal length, talking like a street spieler, and he punctuated his phrases with a short, unamused laugh. He and Beatrice had been good friends in Bosnia, he said. I looked at her when he told me that but she was looking away, towards the grey void in the skylights.

'Who were you working for?'

'I was a freelancer, I worked for many people. Writing and producing. There were lots of us in the Balkans like that, at that time, all very young and crazy.' He gave his laugh again. 'It was a crazy time.'

'So people keep telling me.'

'Yes. It was a lot of excitement. But very sad too.' His face was suddenly mournful. 'We lost some good people.'

'So did Bosnia, from what I hear.'

'Yes. A great tragedy. Those of us who were there will never forget it.'

'I'll bet. Do you know the one about how many Sarajevo corres-pondents does it take to change a light bulb?'

'No?' His eyes widened.

Beatrice jumped in quickly: 'Owen. I have to meet someone in two minutes in the pressroom. Do you want to walk me back there?'

I was about to say yes when I remembered why I'd come here in the first place. 'I was going to get something to eat,' I told her. 'Can't I follow you?'

'It's an interview. I'm meeting a Congo expert from the Global Disaster Group. She's taking me somewhere for a presentation so if you don't come now you'll miss it.'

I wondered why she thought I'd be interested in Global Disaster. 'Thanks all the same,' I said, 'but I think I'll get a sandwich. If you leave your phone switched on this time we can meet up when you're done.'

She stood up slowly and took her bag from the back of her chair, frowning not at me but at Schoon. 'All right, then,' she said. 'I'll see you later . . .' She looked at me and tried to smile.

Schoon did not get up when Beatrice departed but remained in his chair, leaning back and smiling at me as if we were going to have a conversation.

'I'm going up for a sandwich,' I said. 'Can I get you another coffee?'

'That would be very nice,' he said affably. 'I will have the one that they call here cappuccino, although I think the name is not so accurate.'

There were only three sandwiches left in the ransacked display on the counter. The checkout girl produced two coffees from behind the machine with alarming swiftness. Instead of foam on top there was a thick grey skin that held the steam in. When I returned to the table Schoon looked at his cup and sighed. I sat down opposite him and tore the cellophane from the sandwich, which consisted of orange processed cheese, bright yellow margarine and grey, pulpy bread. Schoon watched sympathetically as I took a first bite.

'It's horrible, yes?'

I chewed and swallowed. 'Yes, but I'm hungry.'

'The food is always so at these conferences. Normally one goes out somewhere to eat, but here there is this rain . . .' He waved vaguely towards the windows. 'Even to get to the car park is impossible in such weather.'

I bit again. The cheese tasted of sugar. Schoon sat back in his chair watching me contentedly, his arms crossed over his chest. I noticed his expensive watch.

'How long have you been with the UN?' I asked, and once more he gave his unfunny laugh.

'Five years,' he said. 'It's interesting work, with a lot of travel, but soon perhaps I will go back to reporting again. I miss the excitement.'

I nodded. Most reporters don't wear Rolexes. 'And how did you meet Beatrice?' I asked, casually, and took another bite of my sandwich.

'It was in Sarajevo,' he said, and then he frowned again at his coffee and took a ball-point from his shirt pocket. Gingerly, he put the tip of the pen into the coffee. 'You can say I got to know her through another old friend of mine.' Slowly he twisted the pen so that the grey skin on the surface of his coffee wrapped itself around it, then he glanced up at me. 'Maybe you knew him too? Jesper Jansson?'

'Jansson? Of course I know him . . . And you met Beatrice through *him*?'

The connection staggered me. Beatrice had never mentioned any prior friendship with Jansson, before Goma threw us all together. Never in all the moments that I'd presumed to be un-guarded had either of them referred to any past between them. I stared at Schoon, but he was frowning at his cup again. Slowly he lifted the ball-point clear of the surface. The slimy membrane dangled from the nib like a diseased foreskin.

'Yes, poor Jesper,' he said, studying his catch. 'To survive so much in Bosnia and then die some stupid place in Africa . . .' He sighed elaborately. 'But perhaps he would think it was funny. He was a funny guy.'

I saw a lonely man drinking slops by a swimming pool in the dark, smelled the stink of hot chlorine.

'And you met Beatrice through him?' I asked again, and Schoon gave a sad little smile, like someone detecting an impropriety.

'Yes. I met him first of all in Sarajevo. There was a whole bunch of us there, all young crazy people . . . When there was shelling we would all sit in someone's bedroom – on one of the lower floors of the hotel, of course – and pass around a bottle and a spliff.'

'And Beatrice was a friend of his?'

He began to swing the scum away from his cup, poised on the end of his ball-point, but as he did so it broke free and dropped back into the coffee. He sighed and shook his head, staring into his cup, and I felt like reaching across the table and shaking him. He looked up at me and for an instant I caught a glance of shrewd surmise. Then the blandness snapped back into place and he spoke again. 'I do not know if they were friends, as such . . .'

'You don't mean they were together?'

This time his laugh held real amusement. 'No, of course not. Jesper was supposed to get married then, to some girl from home. He missed her so much, it was quite funny.'

'She left him six months ago. They had two kids. She took them back to Finland.'

He was fishing in his coffee again, and didn't seem to hear me. He went on: 'Beatrice already had a man in Bosnia, an Englishman. Also a writer. I did not know them so well, to be true, but I used to see them go around together . . .'

He stopped talking again, staring sadly past me, and I knew for sure then that he was not as stupid as he pretended, and a good deal less pleasant. I wondered what they thought of him, when they passed the bottle around back in Sarajevo. Did they even know his surname, or was he just one of those people who appear for a day or two and then, if you're lucky, disappear again? I realized I was still smiling.

'She was alone when she came to Africa,' I said.

His face assumed a sad expression. 'It is not surprising, even after so long a time.' With a sudden flourish he flicked the end of the pen and a little grey snot of coffee skin arced through the air and onto the table between us. He gazed at it with satisfaction.

'What do you mean?'

He widened his eyes at me, the pen still poised in triumph. 'You mean you don't know?'

I didn't answer. He stared at me for a moment, then sat heavily back in his chair, puffing his cheeks, his fingers fanned with the tips pressed down onto the table. He held this pose for a couple of seconds then suddenly expelled the air from his cheeks and sat forward again.

'It was no secret . . .' He fixed me suddenly with a look that was meant to be grave. 'Perhaps it's something I should not discuss . . . You are together with her now?'

'Yes.'

He shook his head in a show of perplexity. 'And yet she does not tell you of such a thing? It's strange . . .'

And I swear to God, he actually pursed his lips again and started drumming the fingers of one hand slowly on the table. I could have smashed my fist down on them, just to hear the crack.

I was about to pick my phone off the table when quickly he sat back in his chair again, sighed, and began to talk. His tone was calm, conversational but – at the beginning, I noticed – just a little too hurried.

'I can tell you, if I want, because in fact it's my story too, because I was there . . . It was the time of Srebrenica, with all the killings, and I myself was in a village near by, which was empty. I was producing for a TV crew from Amsterdam. There were lots of us there, Beatrice and her man too, his name is Matthew, and then mortars started to fall and we think maybe the Serbs are coming, so we have to get out.'

He stopped and stared at me, as if he expected something from me. Reluctantly I dug into the cant. 'Serious shit,' I said.

He nodded, narrowing his eyes. 'Oh, yes. It was the real shit. There are mortars and shells, mostly on the road, so now the only way for us to get out of the village is a track across the hills through the forest. So all of us jump in our cars like crazy guys, all mixed up, and take off towards the mountain, and behind us the shells are exploding closer and closer, until we get into the trees and they can no longer see us. Even then they are firing blank . . .'

'Blind.'

'Blind? So? Anyway, they cannot see us. But the shells are still falling in the trees behind us, and the track is very steep and bad, all stones and mud, and it's raining – just like here now. It is very bad for driving, because on one side the mountain falls away into – you say a chasm?'

'You could say that, yes.'

'We have to drive very carefully so as not to fall in the chasm. And the worst thing is, our shooter is driving. He is a staff guy who has just come from the Netherlands – a network pussy, yes? Anyway, he is very frightened and he wants to go too fast. I have to make him stop the car so that I can drive, because of course I am used to this; I have been in shit like this before.'

Again he stopped and waited for me to nudge him on.

'Sure,' I said. 'Where is Beatrice while all this is going on?'

He blinked. 'Beatrice? She is up ahead, with Matthew and their friends. I suppose they are driving very fast too. But of course they are also old-timers by now, and used to mountain tracks in Bosnia, and they have a Neva jeep, which is a very good jeep for these roads, even if it is from Russia and very small. Did you ever drive one?'

'No.'

He dropped his eyebrows and went on. 'Anyway, because we had to stop and change drivers, all the other cars are now far ahead of us and we are the last ones on the road. Tail-end Charlie, you can say. I drive quite slowly, because the woods are very thick now, and I do not really think that anyone is trying to follow us, and I am more afraid of crashing than of being caught. So we go another kilometre or so and then we turn a bend and I see someone standing in the road.'

He stopped again but I said nothing, and after a long pause, staring at me meaningfully, Schoon sighed and went on. 'It is

Beatrice,' he said. 'We stop the car. I see that she is bleeding from her hair. In a place by the side of the road all the branches have been torn away, on the downhill side.' He looked away again. 'So of course, you see what happened . . . Beatrice could not talk properly. I thought she was perhaps emotional, but it turned out later she had been struck in the throat. Her hands are torn too, because she had climbed up the chasm by pulling at thorns . . .'

There was nothing in this scene that belonged to me.

Schoon watched me for a moment, and then continued. 'Well, we tried to put Beatrice in the car with the cameraman, who has a medical kit, but she will not allow it. Instead she comes with us down through the hole in the trees. It is very steep and muddy, and we fall more than we walk, and everywhere there is torn branches and splinters and broken glass and parts from the car, but maybe forty metres down the hill we find the Neva, smashed against a tree.'

He interrogated my face again. I was getting used to it. Then he shook his head slowly.

'One of the photographers, a Belgian guy, who is called Alban, is in the passenger seat. He is dead, with his neck broken. Matthew is in the seat behind him. He is seriously fucked up, I can say to you, but he's still alive, and he is asking for Beatrice, even though she is now holding his hand and trying to talk to him. Except that of course her voice is gone, and she can only whisper, he can't hear her, and he can't see her because of the blood in his eyes.'

He stopped again, and waited. Was this his money shot? A fly had landed on the crap from Schoon's coffee and was polishing its front legs together, preparing for bliss. Everything is loved by something, it seems.

'Who was driving the Neva?' I asked suddenly, without looking up.

'Driving? Did I not say?' The fly sat motionless, its front legs crossed. 'It was Jesper. He was driving.'

I had to think about that for a while. 'I guess that makes sense,' I said finally.

Schoon was too much in the swing of it to want to circle back now, and he waved us both onward. 'Maybe it is the steering wheel that protects Jesper, but he has only a broken wrist and I think maybe some concussion, because he has a big cut on his head, and on his knuckles where they went through the window. He is sitting on the other side of the car staring at the trees, which are very dark now. We have to shout at him to get him to look at us . . .'

'What about Matthew?' The fly was feasting on its own vomit.

'Ah, Matthew . . . I will not tell you the injuries he has' – a pause, I did not look up – 'but he is hurt really bad, and all the time he is calling to Beatrice . . . Except he cannot speak so well because he has no teeth left in front . . .' There was another long pause. 'Later they found them in the back of Alban's head.'

No. Perhaps that was the money shot. Perhaps Schoon would want to freeze it there for a while.

'I take it from the general context that Matthew died,' I said, and raised my face to Schoon again.

Schoon held his head to one side for a moment before answering. 'There was blood from his mouth and nose and ears, and a big bruise across his head, but of course we had no choice. We had to move him . . . We decided we cannot leave him there and go for help because the night is coming, and it is too dangerous to stay. He is in terrible pain. We have to pull him from the car. And when we do this he starts to scream, crazy words, like nonsense talk, and we are so frightened that we put him down again, on the forest floor. Beatrice is on the ground beside him, holding his head and trying to talk to him, but even if he could still understand anything I think perhaps he would not be able to hear her because her voice is gone. All she can do is whisper to him. And even when Matthew stops screaming and becomes quiet she keeps on whispering . . . And after a while we don't know what to do, we are just looking at each other, because who is going to tell her that Matthew is gone?'

He held the question aloft for a few moments, shoulders raised, then let it drop again.

'In the end it is Jesper who talks to her . . . Perhaps he is not so concussed after all, because he comes around the car, and his arm is hanging because it is broken, and he tells her that Matthew is dead. And she just looks back at him . . .'

When I looked up he was staring past me, across the foyer towards the grey, streaked windows. He seemed spent. Then he blinked and turned back to me and something clicked shut behind his eyes again.

'We had to leave the bodies there,' he said, in a new voice, one that was almost harsh. 'We could not stay and we could not move them . . . The hill was too steep and it would take too long, even with ropes, and we had no ropes . . .' He mimed a rope between his hands, then brushed it away into the air. 'And of course, Beatrice does not want to leave her man lying there in a forest. She wants to stay with him . . . Of course, this we cannot permit. But how do you force her? If you cannot drag a corpse up the hill, you cannot drag a woman who does not want to go . . .'

I found a voice. 'I suppose Jansson handled that too.'

Schoon was staring out of the window again. He didn't seem surprised by my interruption. 'Yes,' he said. 'Jesper talked to her . . . He was her friend . . . He told her that if she would not come with us, we could not leave her, and then maybe all of us would be in trouble. We could come back for Matthew and Alban next day, he said, because they were dead. And he checked Matthew again, and told her again, very gentle, that he is dead . . . And all the time Jesper is talking to her she is completely silent . . . And then she bent down and kissed Matthew, like a child does, very quick, and then she got up and started to climb back up the slope.'

I'd asked for it, and now I didn't want it. And still Schoon went on, in his calm, ever so slightly high-pitched voice.

'It is all we three men can do to help Jesper up the slope, because of his broken wrist, and because now he has lost his strength again, he is just staring. We get in the jeep and drive until we get to a UN position, just before dark . . . For me this is twice as scary as anything before, to approach these soldiers who are very frightened . . .'

'So that's it, then. End of story,' I said.

Schoon blinked again, then shook his head slowly. 'No. It is not the end . . . Next day some diplomats went with Beatrice to look for the bodies. They had a UN escort.' He shrugged. 'They find the wrecked car and it is how we left it . . . Alban is still in the front seat, but Matthew' – slowly he turned his two hands palm upwards on the table – 'Matthew they cannot find . . . The soldiers go looking through the trees, up and down the valley, and it is maybe an hour before they find his body, off in the woods.'

I had had as much as I could take of Schoon and his fan dance. 'Why the fuck would anyone want to drag a corpse away?' I demanded.

Schoon cleared his throat carefully. 'It seems he crawled.'

He was really watching me now. I could feel it. But above me ranks of silver beads were marching silently across the skylight, fleeing from the grey wind. Somewhere to my left, behind the counter, the serving girls were arguing in Zulu, or maybe just discussing the foulness of the day. Behind me a pair of high heels kept lonely company across an acre of floor tiles, and then off in the distance a door slammed open and voices splashed off concrete walls. They drew closer, and for a moment I shut my eyes entirely, cutting out the cold day, and allowed myself to think for a moment that life was somewhere else. But when I opened them again there was only the day, the one that we had, that day, and this man called Schoon and the story he'd told me. All were still waiting when I opened my eyes again.

'So you see,' said Schoon, and made another show of shrugging, as if it were just something he could toss away, after the life he'd had. Just one of those things.

'That's quite a story,' I said finally.

'It is terrible.'

'You tell it very well,' I said.

Schoon was staring blandly back at me. His smooth face, the smooth face of his story, left me nothing to grip on. I pushed myself back and away from the table. My plastic chair scraped harshly across the floor, and for a moment it seemed as if my leg would become entangled in it.

'Thanks for the story,' I said and walked away.

I could not go in search of Beatrice. There was another break in proceedings in the main conference hall and I had to thread my way through the thickening crowd to get to the exit. I could have gone off walking in the rain, I suppose, but it was raining too hard. I hailed a taxi and went back to the hotel. I looked out of the window for a little while, to where a few straggling dots still bobbed in the sea, waiting for their last wave. Far beyond them the line of anchored freight ships loomed dark in the mist, their riding lights extinguished. I wanted to think about Beatrice, and about this new thing, this Matthew, but my mind kept sliding away from them. Finally I gave up. I turned on the television and settled down to wait.

'Your friend Schoon told me about Matthew,' I said quietly, but Beatrice didn't look up from her typing. 'I'm very sorry,' I said.

Without turning to face me she leaned sideways from the chair to reach into her bag, then straightened up again. I watched her face in the mirror as she put the cigarette in her mouth. I could see my own reflection, sitting up on the hotel bed, but her eyes never betrayed her. She lit the cigarette, exhaled a funnel of smoke, dropped her eyes towards her keyboard and started to type again.

I watched her for a while, thinking about Matthew. And then I thought about Fine, and at some point my train of thought was interrupted by the ashtray from the bedside table, one of those heavy, chunky crystal ashtrays, exploding against the wall. There were butts and bits of glass everywhere, and I felt suddenly as if an elephant were sitting on my chest, my eyes, ears and throat swelling from the pressure.

Still she said nothing. Her head jerked when the ashtray smashed, and for a second her eyes met mine in the mirror, but that was all. She started writing again. I got to my feet, picked up my jacket and cell phone and went out onto the promenade. The rain had passed, and beneath the palm trees the bricks were faintly steaming in the red light of evening. I walked all the way to North Beach and back, very slowly, half believing she might call me. When I finally went back to the room her stuff was gone. I walked quickly around the block but I couldn't see her car. And then I remembered our appointment with Sylvestre and I actually did cry for a moment or two, with something like anger, because we were going to let him down.

14

Cartwright never approached his victims directly, back in his prime. He liked to work his way around the newsroom, coldly making small talk, until by process of elimination you pretty much knew whom he was stalking. He preferred to catch his victims at the far end of the newsroom, by the pigeonholes beside the water-cooler, so they'd have to follow him, watched by all eyes, as he slowly limped the length of the room to the exit. Thus were the damned taken off to be coffeed.

Like most people starting out back then I was terrified of Cartwright, so I studied his methods closely. I imagined that he'd have to work hard to sneak up on me, and I sought further security by switching to a desk near the door. But of course I'd underestimated him. While I'd been studying him he'd been studying me, and he struck at a moment of weakness.

They had put me on the police beat, which was supposed to have a hard, seedy glamour. Really it meant spending long hours in bars with policemen, pretending we were friends. So it was that I came into the newsroom one Friday morning half an hour late, with a cheap sausage roll and a takeaway coffee. I switched on my terminal and tried to read my e-mails, but it hurt my eyes to turn the pixels into letters. Giving up, I unwrapped the sausage roll and took a queasy bite.

It was at this point that Cartwright announced himself, speaking right into my ear. Startled, I swivelled my chair around to face him, but my mouth was too full to say anything. You had to admire him for that: he never wasted tactical advantage, even when he didn't need it. Economy of effort, that was his thing. I had to sit there dumbly staring back at him, chewing too quickly, while he stood above me, smiling dreamily over my head at something in the middle distance, playing with his watchband. He had a blue folder clamped under his arm.

'I said, Owen, why don't you come across the road for a coffee?' he repeated.

I swallowed – too soon – and straight away I felt the lump of meat paste rising up again. He watched, still smiling dreamily, as I fought back my gag reflex.

Finally I was able to speak. 'I've already got one here, thanks.'

His smile broadened. 'It's better across the road.'

I trailed behind Cartwright as he bullied his way across the busy street, heedless of the buses and cars that hissed past only inches away. Inside the café the air smelled of warm wet wool and of coffee and stewed tea, and the floor was streaked with damp grime from the street. We queued together in silence for mugs of coffee, and Cartwright took a flapjack wrapped in cellophane from the counter by the till. He paid for us both and took the receipt.

There was a table free beneath the stained-glass window. I preferred the booths in the backroom, where you could smoke, back then, but I knew that Cartwright couldn't stand tobacco. In any case, I consoled myself, I was less likely to see people from work out front. Cartwright fussed with his coat on the back of his chair, and as I waited for him to sit down opposite me I felt a sudden thrill of impatience, that feeling you get as a kid when you're trapped with your parents in public. Apart from that I was too hung-over to care, even as Cartwright placed his little blue folder in the centre of the table and I saw my name written on it.

Cartwright's grey, dry little eyes expressed his being exactly. They scouted slyly around the room as he found my range with a few preliminary rounds of small talk, and it was only when he had lulled me enough to let my own eyes wander that I sensed, rather than heard, that his subject had switched abruptly. He was firing for effect now. Jolted back to him, I found myself mirrored between the plastic frames of his glasses, skewered by the dry, grey little eyes.

'I beg your pardon?'

He held my eyes for a moment and then when he was done he dropped his gaze to supervise his fingers as they unwrapped the flapjack. The oatmeal was half coated in chocolate, much of which stayed glued to the plastic as he peeled it away. With a little flourish he separated the flapjack from the wrapping, glanced from one to the other, sighed, then let both fall to the surface of his tray.

'I said the editor is very pleased with you,' he said. 'He thinks you're doing a really good job on the police beat.'

'Really?'

Cartwright nodded without looking at me. 'He thinks your approach is very fresh. He likes the way you've developed contacts so quickly and the way you dig out original stories.'

I had only three contacts – two alcoholic detectives and a lawyer who'd made a lot of money from legal aid by persuading poor defendants to plead guilty straight away. She used to help me out sometimes because she despised her clients and was running for the council on a socialist ticket. I didn't know any criminals and I didn't really want to. I seldom broke new stories and never any big ones.

'That's very flattering,' I said.

Cartwright's eyes traversed slowly back towards me like the turret of a battleship. 'It is, isn't it?' he said mildly. He paused on that note, then went on: 'The editor says he knows young talent when he sees it, and it's important not to let it go to waste.' He was actually rolling his eyes now. 'It's very soon, but he wonders whether you'd be interested in moving up.'

I wondered who Cartwright felt more contempt for – the editor or me.

'Promotion?' I asked, secretly fingering the three aspirins that lay loose in my pocket.

The closer Cartwright hunched towards me the less inclined he was to look at me. The mid-morning flood of customers was seeping from the café and I recognized nobody in the great room, but Cartwright leaned right over until his ear was only two feet from my mouth. His thick black hair was flecked with dandruff and slightly greasy.

'The editor is planning some changes,' he murmured, staring at an elderly lady as she unloaded her tray onto the table beside us. She caught his eye for a moment, flinched and quickly looked away from him. A smile ghosted across his lips.

'For a start,' he said dreamily, 'there'll be an opening in Moscow in a couple of months when Luke Murphy comes home, and soon after that there'll be another vacancy in either Brussels or Washington. Mary or Burt will be coming back to be a deputy editor – we're not sure which yet – and whoever doesn't come back will switch to the other bureau. That leaves two foreign posts to be filled and a few other changes to be made in the shuffle.'

'How does this affect me?' I asked, forcing myself not to sit forward.

Cartwright sat back slowly in his chair and folded his arms. 'Well, it's all subject to internal advertisement and interview, of course, but I wouldn't be at all surprised if Burt goes to Brussels. As for Washington, the editor is thinking of giving everyone a bit of a shock. He wants to send a young high-flyer – someone who's shown he can write well and operate by himself but who's also got the youth and energy to really make a mark out there.'

I felt my breath in my throat. Cartwright stopped, smiled and went on. He reached out one hand towards the folder on the desk and began to slide it back and forth, a couple of inches at a time, with his index finger.

'So, although it's of course still subject to the usual in-house advertising, I wouldn't be at all surprised if Washington went to someone completely unexpected.'

I leaned towards him, despite myself, and his smile broadened further as his eyes drifted back to me.

'Someone, for instance, like Hugh Rainsford.'

'Hugh?' *Hugh?*

'Yes. Indeed. Hugh. The editor feels he's been doing a very good job on the politics desk. Wise beyond his years, the editor says. And I have to say I agree with him. I think Hugh will do very well in the Washington job – subject to interview and internal procedures and all that.'

He spoke deliberately, all the while staring at me, making sure

I completely understood my own inadequacy. But something was still glinting at me through the gloom.

'So you want me to move up to politics to replace Hugh?'

Cartwright smiled sadly. 'No, no. Good heavens, no. No no.' He folded the smile away, pursed his lips and then continued. 'No, I wouldn't be surprised – subject to the usual conditions and the interview and all that – if the politics spot goes to Patricia McNulty. She's wasted as education correspondent.' He paused to clear his throat, getting the timing right again. 'Which is where you come in. We'd like you to take over from her.'

'You mean as education correspondent?'

Cartwright didn't nod so much as shrug, his attention wandering again. 'It's a full-time speciality, grade three, and you'd be staff of course, not contract any more. And you'd have a much higher profile in the paper. You should see all the mail Patricia gets each day from parents and pupils and interested members of the public.' A sneer flashed for an instant and was gone. 'Plus there's all the page-one stuff you'll do whenever the university admissions are announced or there's a teachers' strike. And once you establish yourself you'll never be off the current-affairs shows on television – they always want panellists to discuss things like falling standards and declining discipline in the classroom and all that. You'll go to all the big teachers' union conferences and see a fair bit of the country.' He paused, that timing yet again. 'It's a solid career move. A big slot to fill.'

Cartwright was openly bored with this already. He'd had as much fun with me as he could, for the time being, so now he was just doing the editor's bidding. And it wasn't a hard sell or a soft sell, it was take it or leave it. They could easily find someone else for the job. Of course, said Cartwright, I should take all the time I wanted to think about it. There would be plenty of time, he said.

I spent the rest of that day dodging assignments, gazing into the slot that had been opened for me. It was rectangular, and to be lowered into it I need only admit that I was rectangular too. I typed my name into my computer and added 'Education Correspondent' – and then I stared at the screen for a long time. Did the byline suit my story? And meanwhile Hugh would be off to Washington . . .

Lucy Viner says that according to office legend I jacked in a high-flying career here and went off to freelance in Africa because I was young and bold and in search of adventure. Maybe I did want adventure. I wanted a lot of things, without ever doing much about them. But now that I don't have to tell myself stories any more I can admit that it was envy, vanity and – above all – stark terror of the known that sent me into Cartwright's cubicle the following Monday to say I didn't want the education job. He seemed strangely pleased, and shook my hand. But Cartwright was still Partridge's creature and he made me pay for my ingratitude. I learned soon afterward that my contract would not be renewed when it came up again, although I might yet be given the odd casual shift. There was, for instance, some work coming up in the near future on the exams desk, fetching and carrying for the new education correspondent. I became very brave and adventurous when they told me about that.

15

It's hard for me to think of Johannesburg in any season but winter. It was winter when I first went there, and stood on the top of the Carlton Hotel and watched the droning, dirty, grey-brown grid of the city stretched out beneath me, thirty storeys below, winter colours bleeding into a gold horizon. In winter it never rains, and the bare trees stand black against a sky filled with pale gentle light. Mist boils off the Emmarentia dam in the morning and evening, and you can drive up Brixton hill and stop beneath the broadcast tower and look out over the city as it lights up in the night. Almost none of it was there a hundred years before. I wonder if it's there now. They closed the hotel down.

I called Beatrice a few times, standing in the chill of my kitchen, but she'd never recorded a message for her cell phone so all I got was the beep. I think maybe she went away for a while. I didn't ask and nobody told me. One night a few weeks later, driving through Greenside, I thought that I saw her, walking with a strange man towards the restaurants. Perhaps you'll understand me when I say the feeling was exquisite. I'm pretty sure that it was her.

Timothy Drysdale's latest book was called *Not Untrue and Not Unkind*. It was a memoir of sorts of his recent visits to Africa, very well written, spare and almost honest. There was a moving chapter about Jansson, even though he had died only months before the book came out, and even though they scarcely knew each other. A lot of other familiar figures also turned up in the book, if not always by name. Brereton – named only as 'Charlie' – featured in several passages as a foul-mouthed heart of gold. I bought a copy of the book in Johannesburg airport when I set out for Sierra Leone that last time, and I was halfway through it by the time I landed in Liberia. I finished it on the mercenaries' helicopter as it flew from Monrovia to Freetown, looping out over the sea as a precaution against ground fire. The next morning, when Brereton and Tommo walked into the deserted breakfast room of the Cape Sierra Hotel, I took the book from my bag and pushed it across the table at Brereton. He stopped grinning when he saw what it was. He'd received an e-mail from Polly that warned him about the contents.

Brereton fucking hated that book. He hated it for several reasons, but most of all he hated it because in one particularly moving section 'Charlie' wept as he helped to bury a murdered Hutu kid in Goma. Maybe he did cry, although I didn't see it. And I, unlike Drysdale, was there.

'I've been turned into a plot device,' Brereton complained that night in Paddy's Beach Bar, when he'd had a chance to look through it. 'That bastard Drysdale has made me his proxy, so he doesn't have to spell the feelings out himself.'

'Better proxy than poxy,' said Tommo, who was also referred to in the book. 'He could have made you have syphilis, like that count in *Out of Africa*.'

'Count von Blixen really did have syphilis,' protested Brereton. 'He was a real-life character!'

'So are you, according to Drysdale,' I said. The book made no mention of me.

'Relax,' Tommo told Brereton. 'Nobody's going to know that it's you.'

'Yeah,' I snorted. 'The book's only the number two bestseller in Britain.' Brereton sank for a time into silent misery, then suddenly jumped in his chair.

'Jesus!' he yelped. 'What if they make a fucking movie out of it?'

Tommo half swam along the bar towards Brereton until their faces almost touched. He was smiling as if to himself.

'Who do you think they'll get to play *you*?' he hissed.

Beyond the woven walls of the bar the wind hissed in the palm fronds and the waves washed invisibly on Lumley Beach. Paddy's was empty apart from a few hard-faced whites and mestizos who sat at the counter talking Afrikaans and Portuguese. The curfew didn't apply to mercenaries and spooks or, we hoped, to us. A couple of bar girls haunted the dark corner by the dance floor where Valentine Strasser used to sit with his guards. The girls spent a few minutes trying to pick us up and then went back to dancing together.

Brereton and Tommo had arrived the day before me by a different route, an overnight sea voyage from Guinea in an open pan-pan. We'd assumed that this Sierra Leone story would be big, but when Tommo and Brereton landed at Kissy they found Rasheed and Extrastrong and a few others waiting on the dock for the ferry back across the estuary to Lungi airport. The wire agencies were pulling their people out already: the Americans were again threatening to bomb Iraq over weapons inspections, and the market for African wars had suddenly vanished. But here we were now, the three of us. The Nigerian peacekeepers said that in a few days they would be finishing the job they'd just started by taking Freetown back from the military junta. Their commander told Brereton that we were welcome to come along on their next operation. We would have the story to ourselves, if we wanted it. Nobody else did.

The air force of the lawful government of Sierra Leone consisted of a single Soviet cargo helicopter flown by South African mercenaries. Its pale green skin was streaked with soot and stray oil, and De Wet and his mates had to spend hours each day with their heads in its engine just to keep themselves alive. Occasionally the helicopter would whine and bang into life and we'd wake up and lift ourselves off our old sofa by the apron to watch De Wet clatter away from Lungi airport on some secret little mission. Sometimes the helicopter came back with bits of trees stuck in its landing wheels; De Wet had learned in Angola that it was better to go fast and low.

Sometimes when De Wet tilted his head back you could see a quick blue glint beneath the peak of his Gauteng Lions baseball cap and sometimes, though more rarely, teeth would flash from deep inside his beard, but, unlike his mates, De Wet never spoke to us.

I suppose he had reason to be shy: his paying clients, whoever they were, were in the process of restoring Sierra Leone's elected president, a process that involved cutting a few corners in matters of strict international law and that, when certain details leaked out several months later, almost brought down another, much grander government in Europe. But we had nothing to do with leaking that story; the arrangement we had with De Wet and the other South Africans, an arrangement that was entirely unspoken, was that we wouldn't stare too hard at anything they might unload at Lungi airport, that we wouldn't write them up or take their pictures, and that they in turn wouldn't ask their Nigerian friends to throw us off the apron.

So the Fijian door-gunner would smile and wave at us – though he smiled and waved at everyone – and Koos, De Wet's manager, even took the odd beer with us at the local shebeen. De Wet himself seemed to spend all his spare time – the time that he didn't spend maintaining or flying his own helicopter – on fixing up the Hind that had been recaptured from the rebels.

The Hind gunship had originally been leased by the last Sierra Leone government but one for use in the war for the diamonds. But then nine months earlier the army had switched sides, cutting a deal with the rebels to carve the country up between them, and the Ukrainian pilots had fled. As had the president, and anyone else with the sense and means to get out: the Revolutionary United Front had entered the coalition on a platform of voodoo, amphetamines, mutilation and rape. So the gunship had sat rusting at Camp Cockerill, twenty minutes' flight-time from Lungi across the broad estuary of the Sierra Leone River, until the Nigerians had recaptured it the week before. Having nothing better to do with it, they gave it into De Wet's keeping. There was talk now of bringing another pilot up from South Africa to operate it, and meanwhile De Wet could use it as a run-about whenever his own helicopter was being serviced, hopping back and forth across the estuary with a belly full of Nigerian officers or British diplomats or those mysterious people who were deposited on the further edge of the apron by light aircraft that took off again without having stopped their engines.

It was one of De Wet's shuttle flights that brought us Captain Fuck 'Em Up. Brereton gave a low whistle as we watched the young officer squeeze himself out of the little passenger bay in the belly of the Hind; he wore green Nigerian fatigues but US army webbing with all the bells and whistles – GI torch, camel-back, combat knife, the lot – and he had one of those low-slung pistol holsters that you strap to one thigh and that make you walk like you're saddle-sore. Behind him a servant staggered under the weight of a Desert Storm duffel bag.

The new arrival blinked in the light of the apron and then he spotted Brereton and Tommo and me lounging on the sofa in the shade of the hangar, which had been our base for the past week.

'I'm just sorry I missed out recapturing Freetown,' he told us, in perfect Texan, absent-mindedly stroking the brand-new Glock that his father had given him. 'But this next phase of the war is gonna be sweet. We're gonna fuck 'em up for sure.'

Captain Fuck 'Em Up was the son of a very rich general who ran a southern Nigerian oil state, and he'd come back from college in Texas to claim his share in the family business. So the Nigerian army sent him off to its peacemaking mission in Sierra Leone, to see if he was serious.

But Captain Fuck 'Em Up was in the wrong movie. He got his first inkling of this a week later when the Nigerians finally pushed inland from Lungi and he found himself forced to ride with us in our hired Mercedes. Apart from the armoured scout cars at the front and rear of the column, there were only two working radios in the entire brigade. The colonel had one and the captain had the other – it was his own personal kit – and because we had the only vehicle that wasn't full of troops or towing a gun we were pressed into service as a staff car, driving up and down the line of trucks to pass on orders from the colonel. The colonel placed his jeep right behind the armoured car at the head of the column, driving himself while his driver sat in the back and sulked. Tommo was delighted with how things had worked out – he'd always dreamed of having this kind of access to a military operation, any operation at all – but it was a big disappointment for the captain. This was not at all how things were done in the US army field manuals he'd read. And he'd wanted to take point, to ride on the leading armoured car, to be up with the action, such action as there was.

The fleeing junta forces had abandoned lots of cars and trucks in the road for lack of fuel, but the lead scout car would just nudge them aside: the nasties weren't grown-up enough to have left anti-tank mines or booby traps. Sometimes we'd hear the chug of the scout car's .5 machine gun and all the trucks would halt, and Tommo and Captain Fuck 'Em Up would jump from our old Mercedes and sprint on ahead to see what was happening, and Brereton and I would go jogging after them and by the time we'd get to the head of the column all we would see would be the colonel looking bored in his jeep and a few distant figures running into the bushes, a trail of discarded bundles, maybe a cooking fire or a couple of logs laid out across the road.

Sometimes there'd be hostile fire, wild shots from a long way off, and then the colonel would order his men to line up on both sides of the road, facing outwards, shoulder to shoulder like musket infantry, and their NCOs would stalk back and forth behind them to watch as they shot off branches and shredded leaves. After a minute or two of this the colonel would shout something and they'd all skirmish off into the bush, although not so far that the colonel couldn't see them.

The column would drop off a little garrison at every village or crossroads along the route, five or ten soldiers with a sack of rice and a machine gun: the Nigerians only cared about the road north to Guinea and the big towns along it; everything else would be left to the RUF and to Major Johnny Paul's mutineers, who would wait far out in the bush until some invisible tide turned and everyone sensed it was their time again. Which happened, and not for the last time, a few months later.

Captain Fuck 'Em Up was quickly disillusioned and Tommo went into a sulk. It wasn't blood lust, not with Tommo: I knew what he was thinking. It was always the same thing with Tommo. He was thinking, was this thing for real? So it was almost a relief, the evening we reached Lunsar, when a Nigerian corporal was shot through the head.

The soldiers had charged in among the shacks and houses, shouting and waving, hammering on shutters and shooting at shadows, and amid all the clatter and low comedy a bullet came whirring out of the wood smoke and the bright evening air and hit the corporal right in the forehead. You could hear the smack. The corporal was still frothing at the mouth when they carried him back to the roadside. They set him down outside the schoolhouse, beside another soldier who'd been hit in the forearm and who sat with his back against a tree, holding his shattered arm out stiffly to avoid further staining his pants. Blood pattered to the ground from a spreading damp patch on the elbow of his shirt, dripping fast and irregular, like a message in Morse. The wounded man watched the corporal until the corporal's breathing stopped and they covered his face, and then the wounded man sighed and closed his eyes and slid over sideways. Perhaps he bled to death there. I forgot to check.

When the shooting was over, the townspeople came out to greet their new saviours and settle old scores. Groups of men and boys were dancing around on the points of their toes, shouting and laughing or talking in whispers. When they spotted a target there'd be a flurry of movement, and if their quarry was quick enough he could escape for a while among the houses and the huts, darting and weaving until they finally trapped him. Then for a while you'd hear begging and screams.

There were two of these marked men who doubled back towards the road, dodging and ducking, so that a crowd of all ages had time to join the game. The men were both half naked, as if they'd been asleep when events overtook them, and their sweat glistened as they hurled themselves around and about between the trees and junk and houses, dodging clubs and stones. A girl in school uniform trotted up with a rock in either hand.

'We are going to kill them,' she announced, and then she blushed and giggled at the sound of her own classroom English.

The crowd drew in closer, the noose tightening, until someone stuck a foot out and tripped one man as he fled. The RUF guerrilla, or junta soldier, whatever he was, smacked the ground hard, face first, and you could hear his teeth snapping. The crowd was laughing even louder now and a flurry of stones bounced off his back where he sprawled on the ground, and then miraculously he was up and running again, off around a hut, and people were cheering.

You could see that he was about done. The man was shiny with his own blood. His face was still twisted in horror but his eyes were losing interest, turning to other things. Then I suppose he must have caught one last glimpse of something worth hoping for because with a sudden turn of speed he dodged a swinging axe handle and burst through a gap in the mob. Perhaps he knew what he was doing, maybe he was just lucky, but he was headed straight for the schoolhouse, only fifty yards off, where the colonel was making his billet. And then there was a blur behind him and a sound like a wooden block dropping on a hard tile floor and a stone the size of a grapefruit curled up and away from the point in space through which his head had just passed. The schoolgirl was giggling again. The fugitive kept running for a few yards and then he swayed and staggered and his legs gave way and he pitched forward on the ground, right where I was standing, and the crowd came roaring in around him, because if he couldn't play any more it was time to finish the game.

I'm not proud of this. I've had time to think about it. Who was I? The man lay there stinking of his own redundant fluids, disgusting, like roadkill, and people were lifting rocks and hoes and heavy sticks, angling around me so they could finish things off without inconveniencing me, their new foreign guest, by making me move. And I stepped over his body, putting a leg on either side of it, and lifted my arms, shouting some crap about how this man was under arrest, or something, that ECOMOG wanted him for questioning. Can you imagine? And the strange thing then was that some of the older people in the crowd joined in, shouting yes, we must arrest the criminals. And part of the crowd was forming an escort and old men were reaching over and patting my back and saying that's right, we've had too much killing, leave this man to justice, stuff like that. And we were close enough now to the schoolhouse to see the Nigerian sentries turning towards the racket, only a few yards to go, and then the stricken man's feet gave way and I had to pick him up and carry him in my arms like a child. He wasn't big, and though he was muscled like a boxer he didn't seem heavy. I saw Tommo take a snap of us and then put his camera down, looking disgusted, with which of us I don't know, himself or me. And we were only ten yards from the soldiers and they were taking steps towards us when I felt the crowd surge behind us and something whooshed past my head and there was a sound at once sharp and dull and I felt a strange, catching little vibration through the bones of my arms and the man I was carrying twitched and let out a breath. People behind me were laughing while others were shouting in anger, and when I turned I saw a young man who looked like a teacher – shirt and tie, wire glasses – and he was shouting back at the others and holding a small hatchet up in the air. When he caught my eye the teacher smiled at me, quite friendly, still shouting his case to the others, as if I didn't factor into this one way or the other, just a well-meaning tourist. And I suppose he must have known why he did what he did. Who was I to interfere?

Brereton came past leading the other fugitive by the arm. His man didn't look too bad, considering. Brereton must have used his strongest language to get him out in such good shape. I laid my own man on the ground at the feet of a Nigerian sergeant. He was still breathing, short and shallow, but thick dark blood was oozing from a neat little slit in the top of his shaven skull and his eyes were goggling off in different directions. That's how I left him. I don't suppose he made it. He could have been a rapist or a killer or a thief or anything. Fuck him. None of us mentioned that business again.

There was a mechanic in Lunsar who'd managed to hang on to an old petrol generator and that night we parked in his yard. Brereton and I spent hours chasing rumours around the town, buying up hoarded petrol at five bucks a bottle or more, and when we returned the mechanic started the generator and Tommo plugged in his laptop and his scanner and his sat-phone and the little electric kettle that he used to heat his developing fluids. He worked out in the yard by the stuttering engine and a crowd of children sat and watched. Every now and then he'd drag his eyes from his screen and notice them and smile.

The mechanic's house was built of concrete blocks and wood and thatch and it had four rooms, bare but for a couple of mattresses, a few stools and a chest of clothes. The nasties had taken everything else. We gave the mechanic's wife some dollars, and after a long expedition she came back and cooked us fat chewy grains of swamp rice served with a hot peanut sauce. The children got the leftovers. It was our first hot meal in a week but Tommo ate his in the yard, sitting vigil over his equipment. After dinner Brereton and I washed ourselves from a bucket in the corner of the yard and the children whispered together at the whiteness of our bodies. Then Brereton took out his whiskey and we sat out the back and watched the moths dance round the porch light. It flickered in time with the misfiring generator.

The mechanic wouldn't drink whiskey but he had some palm wine hidden in the thatch and he took it down and sat beside us on the porch. Below us Tommo hunched ever closer to his computer, his face blue, staring at the 'send' bar as it crept across the screen. The palm wine was stored in a clear plastic bottle and it looked like semen. After a while the mechanic began to tell us stories about what had happened after the coup, when the kids without parents started to side with the rebels. Every few days, he said, a new group would come from the bush and go door to door, even though all the good stuff had been taken in the first week. So long as you found something small for them you were probably okay, he said, but they liked to rape the women. Fortunately, he said, he had no daughter, and his wife was growing old.

Tommo stood up and breathed out and closed his laptop and switched his phone off. The batteries were all charged so we switched off the generator, and the mechanic's children went to lie inside the door of the house on a thin cotton mattress. I passed

Tommo a plastic cup of whiskey and he sat down beside us, and it was a while later before I remembered that I needed to make a call. When I switched on Tommo's phone it asked me for a number so I keyed in the PIN, but the phone said it was the wrong number so I checked it with Tommo where he sat on the porch and he told me the PIN again and it was the same number I'd put in already. So I entered that number again, and it didn't work, and then I tried again a couple of times, and next thing I knew the LCD was flashing a message that said 'access denied' and 'please contact manufacturer'.

At some point the phone must have started asking me for a back-up number but I hadn't noticed. And if you put in the wrong number more than three times the phone assumed it had been stolen and shut itself down. Brereton set up his own phone and called his paper's systems people, and they called back a while later to say that the only way to reset Tommo's phone would be to take it back to the dealer.

Tommo took it pretty well, considering. Yes, he said, the PIN thing was a major design flaw. And yes, if he had to file again he could work off Brereton's equipment. It was not like New York would be looking for him anyway; Fine was still on leave somewhere, and Iraq was all that anyone seemed to care about.

The column formed up again next morning on the northern edge of Lunsar, the trucks lining the shaded roadway as they waited for the colonel to lead them on to Makeni. The soldiers climbed up and down the wooden sides and joked and sang, and women came out to sell them oranges and mangoes and meat skewered on old bicycle spokes.

Brereton was fidgeting in the back seat behind me. 'Look at these idiots,' he remarked. 'We're supposed to be in bandit country here and yet they don't even get off their trucks when they're halted. I'll bet one RPG would kill fifty for sure.'

The air was scented with wood smoke and grilling meat. I heard Brereton yawn, and Tommo's door open and shut again. The chatter of the women and the laughter of the soldiers became an indistinct echo of the waking world. Sometime later Tommo's door clicked again and I opened my eyes and saw him standing beside the car, grinning to himself. When he saw I was awake he lifted something for me to see.

'Like it?' he said. I wiped my eyes and looked more closely.

It was a T-shirt made of black cotton. In the middle of the chest was a crude rendition of a human face, with orange skin, a long thin nose and eyes as clear and blue and dead as a poisoned lake. Tubular lips were twisted in a red lascivious leer and the short, Afro-like hair was impossibly golden; the hair seemed to have been embroidered onto the shirt with synthetic silk thread. The whole ghastly image was surrounded by a silver spray effect.

'What the fuck is that?' demanded Brereton's voice behind me.

'It's a Princess Diana T-shirt,' said Tommo proudly. 'My mum still isn't over her. I bought it from that stall over there in the market. They've got loads of them. That and Manchester United.'

My seat lurched as Brereton grabbed it to lever himself forward. 'You must be joking,' he said. 'That's not Diana. It looks like Harpo Marx.'

Tommo shrugged. 'Maybe we all look like that to them.'

'What the fuck did you go and buy that for?' You could hear the admiration creeping into Brereton's voice.

Tommo was still twisting the garment back and forth, considering it fondly. 'This cotton's really pretty good quality,' he mused. 'I needed another T-shirt. I've only got the clothes I'm wearing.'

Brereton opened his door. 'I told you not to give that bloke our laundry . . .' The car rocked slightly as he got out. 'I'm getting one of those T-shirts too.'

Tommo moved around the front of the car to block him. 'No way, Brereton. I don't want you stealing my look. Get the Man United one instead.'

But Brereton dodged past him. 'Fuck off, Tommo,' he spat over his shoulder. 'I hate football. Anyway, we owe it to her memory. It was us who killed her.'

The column moved off, the soldiers singing martial chants and gay farewells while bare little boys ran gamely alongside. The sun was halfway up the sky already, and as the road curved round into the east, escorted by long files of palm trees, the hard light splintered off the surface ahead, burning a star on my retina.

Now there was only the bush again, the raised highway running naked above it beneath the milky cataract of an overcast sky. We passed a Toyota pick-up truck, twisted and carbonized on the side of the road, and beside it lay an anti-aircraft gun wrenched from its mounting on the truck, its fat brass rounds black in the burned grass. Perhaps De Wet had got it with his Hind. Beside me in the back seat Captain Fuck 'Em Up studied the wrecked Toyota as we passed it. Something about the set of his face, turned half away from me, told me he was humming again, the sound lost in the wind through the windows. Brereton was driving and Tommo, who had claimed snapper's privilege, made him work his way up the column until we were almost at the front, with only the scout car and the colonel's jeep ahead of us. The bush smelled like old pennies. The world was empty again. There was no one to be seen.

Two hours after we left Lunsar a rusty metal tower reared up above a clump of palm trees ahead. From it steel cables straggled like creepers. Then there were red galvanized roofs and a water tower, a metal sign advertising soap, and the trees and weeds gave way to patches of bare earth littered with plastic and poisoned by sump oil. Huts of mud and sticks and metal rose up from the earth and came leaping down to the roadside, sucked in by the speed of our arrival, and we could have been back in Lungi or Port Loko or Lunsar again except that here in Makeni there was no welcome, nothing moving at all except for a yellow dog that came trotting down to the side of the road wagging its tail. We passed an empty tree-lined side street, substantial bungalows built of brick and cinder instead of mud and wattle, and I watched, feeling sleepy now, as a kid in shorts and flip-flops stepped out from between two houses fifty yards ahead and raised a hand to us, and then metal barked and flame sprang from the hull of the armoured car and dark shapes spun off into the road.

Tommo almost lost his camera out the window as Brereton swerved to avoid the remains of a Nigerian soldier and then again

222

to dodge the scout car, now smoking in the road. We swung in behind the colonel's jeep as it screeched off the road to the right and bucked and leaped across a waste of pitted dirt and orphaned tree roots that filled the angle with the next side street.

The colonel's jeep bounced up a low bank onto the road again and swerved off down the street to the right. Our Mercedes hit the bank with a flat, final crunch, slamming belly down onto the rough ground and bouncing up in the air. When it landed again in the roadway the engine was roaring, much louder than before but with a dying rattle. The brakes came on, throwing us all violently forward, and before the car had even stopped I was lying in a deep gutter and Tommo was with me and Captain Fuck 'Em Up was striding off past the smoking engine of the Mercedes to where his commander stood by his jeep, staring thoughtfully back towards the junction.

Behind us the armoured car was stranded in the crossroads, its left front wheel twisted out at right angles to its hull like a broken limb. Its body spasmed and strips and stars of razor-sharp light danced from the heavy machine gun in its turret. Bits of gravel leaped like sand flies from the road around it. The shooting from the ambush was continuous now, with the sound of canvas tearing.

Brereton was hiding behind the shredded rear tyre of the Mercedes, curled up like a pangolin, peering back at me from under his arm. Tommo was up on one knee taking pictures of the armoured car. Its machine gun stopped firing but still the turret jerked peevishly from side to side, like a slap-happy drunk trying to work out who hit him. A footstep crunched close by my ear and I looked up and saw the colonel's driver lean down to peer beneath our car, where a pool of oil was spreading.

After a moment he straightened up again. 'You have broken the sump,' he said, and shook his head.

The street was lined with trees and reed fences. Beyond them the ambushers, out of sight around the corner now, had found something else to shoot at. The crippled scout car was firing too, and then one of the commandeered jeeps came into view in the junction, still towing its howitzer, and it made a slow and sedate turn towards us, part-sheltered by the hulk of the armoured car, with dirt and stones flying from the roadway, its indicator piously winking. It cleared the junction, somehow still moving, and drove past our car to pull up behind the colonel's jeep. The gunners jumped out with their rifles ready and dodged round their vehicle, pointing and chattering. There were three neat holes high up in one of the side windows.

Tommo was reloading his camera, using his body to shield its innards from the fine grit drifting down the street. Brereton took out a cigarette and tried to light it but the gas in his lighter wouldn't catch. He hurled it to the ground.

'Cunt,' he said, and then he threw the cigarette away too.

Ten yards from us, across the road from the colonel's jeep, a gout of earth detached itself from the roots of a tree and rose into the air. Then another. The colonel's driver placed himself carefully on his stomach, grunting with the unaccustomed effort, and began to fire single shots back across the junction, past the armoured car, off into a blur of blue smoke. Every time he fired, a spent case would eject from his rifle, bounce off the Mercedes and ping back against his helmet, striking just above his ear. He didn't seem to notice. It occurred to me that this was probably the funniest thing I'd ever seen in my life, and I made a sober note to try to remember it. I wanted to show Brereton but my mouth was too dry to call to him.

The gunners took a mortar tube from the back of their jeep and set it up on its base plate and bipod, in the cover of a tree trunk, while the colonel and Captain Fuck 'Em Up stood behind the colonel's jeep as bullets smacked into the roadside only yards away. The colonel was talking into his radio, presumably to the armoured cars. When the mortar was set up the colonel gave a command and the gunners, who hadn't even clamped the sights on it, dropped a round down the barrel, and there was a terrible thonk that I felt in my sinuses, like being kicked in the head by an invisible giant, and the base plate rang on the hard ground. The street filled with bitter-sweet smoke and twigs and leaves and little bits of burning plastic, and a few seconds later, somewhere up ahead, there was an answering thud and the sound of stones and steel striking metal and wood.

'Come on,' shouted Captain Fuck 'Em Up, and he charged off across the street alone. The gunners watched him go. Tommo hesitated, then he went as well, the fence on the far side of the street lurching as he crashed into it, his face turning back to us, and just as I pushed myself away from the tree trunks and the vehicles and the roadside clutter there was shooting again, off to the left on the other side of the junction, and the street became a chasm of light as I threw myself across it. Four, five, six steps, and faces turned to look at me from the shelter of the fence. Seven, eight, and the angles seemed good again, the street closing out on me. And then something caught my foot and the ground swung upwards and dull pain thudded through my shoulder and I slammed into the ground. The world flashed, and as I twisted on the ground another blow struck me hard in the stomach and all my breath rushed out of me and I couldn't see any more. I began to struggle against the weight that was crushing me and I heard screaming, and, although I couldn't breathe, I had the strength to kick and claw until the crushing went away. I heaved myself onto my hands and knees, gasping in pain, on the point of puking. Beneath me, indifferent, tiny red ants were quartering the dust. Somewhere behind me Brereton was moaning.

The fall had sent me crashing through the fence and into the yard beyond it. To the right rose the whitewashed brick wall of a bungalow and to the left bare dirt stretched off to the far wall of the compound, bricks topped by a fringe of reeds. By the wall of the house there was a jumble of plastic buckets made from old drums of cooking oil with coat-hanger handles. The yard was shaded by the branches of two big trees whose trunks anchored the fence in the corners.

Brereton was squatting with his back against the fence, his face and chest covered in blood.

'You punched me,' he quacked angrily, putting his head back

and holding his nose. I didn't answer him: I was still winded from when he had fallen on me.

Captain Fuck 'Em Up stepped carefully in through the gap we'd made in the fence and placed a foot on the collapsed section and tested it to see if it would remain flattened. He glanced at me and then at Brereton and Tommo, squatting together in their matching T-shirts. Blood and snot were dribbling from Brereton's chin and down the face of Princess Diana. The captain stared at him for a long moment, blinked, then padded over to the far corner of the yard and thrust his rifle out through a hole in the fence. It was easy to pull the reeds apart and look down the street to where the ambush had been laid, in a cluster of small houses set among a grove of trees. Behind us, back towards the edge of town, there was heavy firing, the distant roar of engines, voices of men loud but muffled, as if shouting in another room. Brereton pushed his head in beside mine so he could look through the same crack. I could smell his blood.

About two hundred yards off, beyond the huts where the ambushers had lain, a cloud of smoke and dust hung in the air near a further street of houses. A gaggle of tiny figures was fleeing full tilt across a stretch of waste land, and Captain Fuck 'Em Up began firing after them, his rifle snapping only inches from my head. I could hear the bolt singing between the shots. The fleeing figures disappeared among the houses, only to flash into view again some moments later, flitting off into the bush on the edge of town.

The mortar fired again and this time its bomb burst in the waste land – a white flash, red sparks, brown dirt, grey smoke. Brereton had grown a beard where the dirt was sticking to his bloody lip and chin. Captain Fuck 'Em Up was still shooting but at what I don't know. The second scout car appeared in the street, creeping forward, its machine gun tearing pieces from the houses and the trees, with a squad of soldiers hunched down behind it.

Tommo snapped away a bit more and then when his film ran out he slumped with his back to the fence and began to fumble in his pouches for a fresh roll. He caught me looking at him.

'That's probably as good as this is going to get,' he said quietly.

226

Brereton was trying to spit. 'I'm going back to the car for some water,' he said.

'Me too,' I said, and the *m* tore skin from my lips.

16

The colonel went back to Lungi to collect more troops and supplies for the final push to Kabala. We moved into the Catholic mission centre, where a few foreign missionaries had been holed up with a crowd of refugees since the crisis began. The head of the mission was a worldly Italian monsignor who had somehow persuaded the RUF not to harm any of his people. Perhaps the rebels had reasons of their own not to violate the sanctuary. Perhaps they too believed in its magic.

We had already been in Makeni for three or four days when some Kamajors appeared at the crossroads in the middle of town. They had come north on foot from Bo, looking for stragglers from Johnny Paul's evaporating army. There were about forty of them, little bird-like men and boys with magic charms fastened to their clothes in parcels of bright cotton thread. Their spears and bows and one-shot hunting rifles looked more like theatre props than weapons. Each wore a mirror fastened to his hat or chest. The mirrors would reflect bullets back at the enemy who fired them.

Their leader was a small, very dignified man in his eighties. His men were in awe of him. He wore a plain white smock, befitting his status as a prophet, and a round shaving mirror hung from his neck like a pendant.

He explained to us that his people did not believe in modern weapons. They were hunters in an old tradition, he said. Kalashnikovs had no power against a Kamajor, but a Kamajor had power against those with Kalashnikovs. 'Believe me,' he said, 'you could take his rifle' – he nodded at a listening Nigerian sergeant, who commanded the guard at the crossroads – 'and point it at me and pull the trigger, and I would not be harmed. This is a power I have.'

The Nigerian sergeant was a believer too. He offered to lend Brereton his FN rifle and the old Kamajor insisted that Brereton have a go. When Brereton refused to shoot him the old man smiled faintly. The sergeant was delighted, and the other Kamajors nudged each other and laughed. It was proven: not even a white man could kill a Kamajor.

The old man spoke English very well and he carried himself warily. Many years before, he told us, the British Empire had sent him halfway round the world.

'I do not fear these people, these RUF,' he said. 'They are like children. *I* have fought the Japanese.'

Then he gathered his men and boys and led them off north past the edge of town, a jilty little corporal of the Royal West African Frontier Force.

One evening Captain Fuck 'Em Up came to the mission to tell us that the colonel's convoy would be coming from Lunsar the following morning. Instead of stopping in Makeni it would be heading straight on through to Kabala, the last town before the roads broke down in the deep jungle towards the Guinea frontier. And that would be the end of the war for us: even if the Nigerians decided to extend the operation to Bo and to Kenema, or the diamond fields at Koidu, we no longer had the cash or the energy to follow them. Besides, our papers didn't care.

By now a few private cars had reappeared in town but none of the owners would rent to us. The story of what had happened to our Mercedes had already got around. We would have to wait for the convoy in the hope of a lift.

There was gunfire that night, in the small hours. First a whole flurry of shots, spitting and hissing off in the distance, and then a few seconds later a single shot, an afterthought, or the last hurtful laugh. I lay awake for a while and listened. The three of us were sleeping on blankets spread on the concrete porch outside a schoolroom in the mission, away from the sighing mass of refugees in the mission's dining hall. A meteor streaked across the sky, or perhaps it was something else. Perhaps my eyes weren't even open any more.

We carried our gear down to the crossroads in the false dawn before the sun edged up over the circling trees. An old Bedford army truck stood in the junction, its windscreen starred by bullets. Someone had sprayed *who bear* and *war niggaz* across the front in silver paint, and matt-black swastikas had been daubed on the doors, which were also punched through with holes. Beside the truck was a pile of captured rifles, and two young men lay face up on the dirt verge of the road, one dead and one dying. A few Nigerian soldiers were standing close by, whispering and watching.

The dying man wore combat pants and a dirty white shirt pulled open to show a small hole in his lower right ribcage. With each short painful breath a little red bubble vanished into it, then popped out again. His left trouser leg had been ripped open and a field dressing was pulled tight around his upper thigh. The dressing was already black and shiny. He lay with his head tilted back and to the side and his arms stretched out above it, his eyes squinting up at the dull red globe that now rose above the trees. When we stood over him his eyes flickered towards us for an instant, then turned back to the dawn. You could see he was fascinated by it.

The sergeant in command was a friend of ours, the one who believed in the Kamajors. He said that late in the night the truck had come north along the road from Magburaka. It seems nobody had told its occupants that Makeni was no longer theirs. Most of them escaped into the darkness when the shooting started. The sergeant shook his head and said 'Ay!' a couple of times while telling the story, as if unsure whether it was funny or sad. Then the man on the ground coughed, as if to get our attention, and when we looked at him he was already showing his teeth in that stupid snide grin that dead people have, staring wide-eyed at the sun.

There were no officers about and nobody knew what to do with the bodies. The sergeant posted a guard over them but as the sun climbed higher and the town awoke the passers-by ignored them. They'd seen plenty of dead people already. But the dead men lay under the best shade tree, where we'd planned to wait, so instead we had to cross the road and sit with our backs against a fence, trying to doze with the sun in our faces.

The corpses were still there a couple of hours later when we heard the growing rumble of engines and an armoured car appeared around the curve to the south, followed by the colonel's jeep and then the trucks with their soldiers.

The armoured car rumbled past and the colonel, who was driving again, slowed his jeep, staring at us through the windscreen as we waved to him, and then he noticed the bullet-ridden truck and he braked so suddenly that his driver shot forward from his place in the back. The convoy concertinaed to a halt and doors opened and slammed as officers jumped out to join the colonel, who was standing over the dead men and listening with one ear as the sergeant stood to attention and stammered an explanation. The colonel nodded, almost smiling, and then he turned and deigned to notice us.

'Gentlemen,' he said. They must teach them to talk like that at staff college. They always call you 'gentlemen'.

Brereton launched into his spiel, asking politely for a lift, but the colonel was staring at the truck again. I could have sworn he was counting the bullet holes. There was a moment's silence and then he turned back to us, puzzled. 'But would you not be more comfortable with your friends in the car?' he asked.

Brereton looked at me, confused, and I looked at Tommo, and Brereton started trying to explain about our dead Mercedes again – the colonel had been there himself when we killed it – but Tommo was staring at something off down the street, starting to smile.

'Jesus Christ,' he said, and laughed.

Beatrice was walking towards us along the line of halted trucks and their staring passengers. She wore a T-shirt and khaki jeans and her hair was much shorter than when I last saw her, stiff and spiky with the sweat and the dust of the road. Her arms were red from the sun and when I looked at her face I saw that she was smiling.

'Hello, Owen,' she said, and she put a hand on my right shoulder and pushed her face up to kiss me, once on each cheek, and then she turned to Brereton and Tommo and made the usual joke about presuming and Brereton hugged her and wanted to know how she'd got there and Tommo was laughing and I was standing there with them all, smiling, sharing the joy of the meeting, and I saw an old green station wagon – no, it must have been blue, Tommo's camera wouldn't lie, not about something trivial like that – pull out from between the trucks and drive slowly towards us down the wrong side of the road, the sun blazing off the windscreen, and Beatrice was pointing to it and then the car moved in under the shade of the tree and the sun died in the windscreen and there in the driver's seat was Fine.

Fine jumped out and now everybody was shaking hands and hugging each other and backs were slapped, and Beatrice was standing in front of me again, asking me how I was and I smiled back at her and told her I was great, that this had been the trip of a lifetime. Fine shook my hand and I wondered how it was that he now had no trouble looking me in the eye. He wanted a picture to mark the occasion and he herded us all over to stand with our backs to the Mitsubishi, with the Bedford looming over it. And when Tommo didn't want to take the shot I stepped in and did it for him, because that way I wouldn't have to be in it. And Beatrice looked at me, but I didn't notice that at the time, when I was taking the picture, not until years later, two weeks ago now, when I saw it again in Cartwright's blue folder, clipped from the spread in the *Chronicle*'s magazine. The one that they finally gave Fine his prize for.

The armoured car's engine spattered to life again and the colonel was back in his jeep with Captain Fuck 'Em Up, who'd appeared from somewhere, and we had to grab our stuff in a hurry and somehow pack it all into Fine's car, which was smaller than our old Mercedes. Brereton was the undisputed driver now, after how well he'd handled the ambush in Makeni, so he ran his seat forward and Fine, who was the tallest, sat behind him. Of course Tommo claimed snapper's privilege and sat in the front. That left Beatrice and me standing by the car and then Beatrice said, 'You sit by the window. You always get carsick.'

So that's how we travelled to Kabala. Tommo was twisting in his seat to talk with Fine, laughing at everything that was said, even by himself. Everyone was delighted, of course. Unexpected meetings in unlikely places – they make us feel so pleased with ourselves, so destined, like characters in a novel.

Fine's bosses had been very taken with the pictures that Tommo had sent them from Lunsar and the fall of Makeni, so they asked Fine to cut short his vacation by a couple of days and join him in Sierra Leone. The hope was that between the two of them Fine and Tommo could come up with material for a big spread and a few shorter pieces. They'd already decided a theme for the trip, back in New York, Fine's old shtick about African solutions to African problems, the one he'd been touting since Goma.

Fine's bosses had been e-mailing and telephoning Tommo for the past couple of days to tell him Fine was coming, but being desk-bound types they'd only thought to try Tommo's sat-phone, which I'd killed in Lunsar, and his in-house e-mail address, which didn't work with Brereton's computer. Which was a shame. Things might have turned out differently, if I hadn't killed that sat-phone, if I'd known that they were coming and had some time to think.

I began to feel sick, despite my place by the window, and whenever the conversation came my way I was aware of Beatrice's eyes on me, and beyond them of Fine leaning forward to listen, grinning at me with an eyebrow halfway to his hairline. That trick he had.

Kabala was – is, I suppose – almost a hundred miles north of Makeni. The lowlands rose into low wooded hills, vivid green from the night mists, and the road snaked back and forth in long curves, rising and falling, and as the car heeled into the turns Beatrice swayed against me. Her thigh was pressed against mine and her shoulder pushed under my ribs. If I turned my face from the open window I could smell the sweat in her hair and the soap she always used, one that smelled of oranges.

She had flown to Abidjan directly from France, and on the plane she met Laura, who had begged to be sent back to Africa on a special assignment. The two of them spent a couple of days in Monrovia, just as I had, trying to find a way into Freetown, and then Fine turned up, having picked up their trail in Abidjan. He'd already made contact with De Wet and his friends – no doubt the US embassy helped with the introductions – and arranged a lift to Freetown for them all next day. But they had left the hotel to eat seafood that night and next morning Laura was too sick to move. They had to leave her at the Mamba Point Hotel, in the care of the manager, but she would join us when she felt well enough to travel. Brereton said he hoped not: Laura was a shit-magnet, and we'd had enough of that. Fine, on the other hand, was very keen to see some trouble; he needed the colour. Tommo told him about the lynch-mob at Lunsar, and the ambush at Makeni, and about Captain Fuck 'Em Up and the colonel, and Fine leaned forward, half across Beatrice, so he could hear Tommo in the front, frowning and nodding.

Little wisps of smoke floated here and there along the wooded valleys or high up on the hills, but no one appeared by the roadside. We drove on for a few more miles and then at Makakura crossroads the colonel halted the convoy and called his officers together and made them look at maps to try to work out a way to get around behind the nasties. But once again they had known we were coming, and when the column entered Kabala at dusk the rebels had already skipped. The streets were clogged with cars and trucks abandoned for lack of fuel, or because they wouldn't stand up to the forest tracks that were now the only escape routes. The townsfolk used the abandoned trucks as stages on which to perform the rites of liberation, the singing and dancing, and Fine and Beatrice had to make the most of it; this was the end of the road, the only colour they would get now, having come all this way. Tommo went off to shoot it, for Fine's sake, while Brereton and I stayed in the parked car, slumped against our doors. Feet churned the dust outside and eager hands reached in to pat our shoulders and grab at our hands, until we rolled up the windows and sat in the hot stuffy car, eyes closed, ignoring the hands that drummed on the roof. Finally the column began to move again, and Beatrice and Fine and Tommo trotted back to the car, and we followed slowly through the crowd as the trucks climbed a steep winding slope to a broad hill overlooking the town. At the top of the hill was a plateau where a group of single-storey administration buildings stood beneath some peeling gum trees. The highland evening cooled rapidly and stars hardened in the haze.

Brereton parked the car on the southern edge of the hilltop, as far as he could from where the trucks had formed a laager around the colonel's new billet. It was dark, and we got out our torches to eat a meal of tinned tuna and stale pitta bread and the last tube of potato crisps that Brereton had bought at the Lebanese supermarket in Freetown. We laid the food out on the roof of the car and ate standing up but I wasn't hungry, and after a few bites I stepped back into the darkness and washed the oil from my hands with some of our drinking water. Tommo had collected it in plastic bottles from a spring in Lunsar, mixing it with twice the recommended dose of chlorine. It made me think of the pool in Kinshasa.

I wandered off a few yards and lit a cigarette. The night was moonless and the town beneath us was black apart from the glow of cooking fires in backyards, smothered by their own smoke. At long intervals there were bursts of shooting, past the northern edge of the town, and the echoes washed off invisible hills. Tommo had screwed off the end of his torch and stood it up like a candle on the roof of the car and I could see Fine's eyes flash whenever there was shooting. Then off to the north, not more than a kilometre or two, a heavy machine gun began to stammer on a hilltop. A line of sparks whirled into the sky like water from a hose, followed three or four seconds later by the hammering of the gun and the hiss of fat bullets rushing off into the night. One burst passed high over our hilltop and then the weapon fell silent again.

'What do you think, Beatrice?' said Fine's voice, dry in the darkness. 'Does that qualify as bang-bang?'

'It'll have to do,' said Beatrice.

Her face flared for a few moments in the flame of a lighter and when it went out I could no longer see her, just the glow of her cigarette.

I said goodnight and moved a little way off into the darkness, taking my laptop bag for a pillow. I lay on my back on the wiry grass and pulled my jacket over me and listened to my friends bid each other goodnight. Springs creaked and a door clicked carefully as somebody settled in the car. Further off, by the Nigerians' laager, men murmured around the flames of a fire, and later the flames died back and the voices grew silent. The stars burned relentlessly above the hilltop now, wheeling westwards across the sky, but the hard ground bore into my back and the crickets could not lull me. Satellites ran noiseless errands. Once, high above, I saw the lights of a plane, followed a long time later by the remote rush of its engines, and with a shock I felt again the stab of wonder and envy which that sound had inspired in me as a child, the sound of a jet, or the sound of a train, late in a sleepless night. And when the aircraft had passed I was left with the cold, sure understanding that I would rather be anywhere but where I was now. This story was done for me. I sat up, cross-legged on the ground, and felt for a cigarette. For a few moments my lighter surrounded me with a halo of ragged grass and dirt, and then I sat for a while in the scent of my own smoke. The crickets had fallen quiet and the night was very still. A shoe scuffed the grass and a shape moved against the stars.

'Have you got a cigarette?' asked Beatrice.

I took the last one out of the packet and held it up to her, and somehow in the dark she found my fingers and took it from them.

I flicked the lighter and now I could feel her hair in my face as she leaned forward to suck the fire in. Then she sat down on the grass before me, a dim ghost flashing red whenever she drew on her cigarette. She smoked with short, avid puffs, as if for the cigarette's sake and not her own.

'It's good to see you again,' she said.

I didn't know what to say to that. She couldn't see me, or hardly at all. After a while I said: 'How long do you think you'll stay?'

'Well, we only just got here . . . Rather late, I suppose . . . We should look around for a couple of days and then see where the story goes next. There must be some feature stuff to do here . . . Rebel atrocities . . . Rebuilding.'

'I reckon I'll bail tomorrow,' I said. 'I've already got all I'm going to from this trip.'

She didn't answer for a while, and then said: 'Are you serious?'

I said nothing. She drew on her cigarette again. 'Is this because of me?' she asked, very quietly. I wondered if the others could hear us, if they were awake.

'No,' I said. 'Not just you.' It occurred to me then that I had waited months for this conversation and now I was having to whisper it. It's easy to smile about that now.

'Well, what, then?'

'Fine.'

'What about him?'

'You travelled here with him.'

Her cigarette cut a red slash in the night. 'For God's sake, Owen. I met him in Liberia on the way here. It wasn't planned. And anyway, Nathan has nothing to do with anything there was between you and me.'

'The way you say it you make it sound like there never was anything.'

'Owen, I'm sorry.'

My fingers burned. I sent my cigarette to die a little way off, a shower of sparks on the hard ground. There was a long silence.

'I wanted to talk to you,' I said finally, very quietly.

She drew on her cigarette, deep enough for me to see her eyes as pools of darkness. 'Please believe me, Owen. It really had nothing to do with you.'

I sat in the dark and thought about that. The fear that had sickened me resolved itself into a remote, bright emptiness, infinitely cold and comforting. Nothing to do with me.

She sat and watched me for a while. I wonder if she could see my face. She took one last drag on her cigarette and I saw that she looked calmer now, and then a red meteor arched through the night and exploded into stars. She stood up.

'I wasn't fair to you, Owen. I'm sorry about that.'

It occurred to me that my packet of cigarettes was empty, and that the rest of my carton was back in the car, where someone was sleeping. I wouldn't have enough cigarettes to see me through to morning. It was too much.

Go out on a starry night and lie on your back on the ground, somewhere flat and bare, with no trees or buildings anywhere near, nothing to anchor the corner of your eye and remind you of the earth that holds you, and perhaps for a few seconds the flat dome of stars, small and large, dull and hard, will be magically transformed, shot through with perspective, and you'll see the universe in its real dimensions, a silent lattice of stars and galaxies, some near, some vastly distant, and your head will swoon and you'll feel that you are falling upward into infinite depths. How long can you stand it before you close your eyes and shake your head?

The stars sank back into greyness and night receded from the hilltop to reveal the town, straggling in its valley, and stranding the form of Tommo, over by the car, wrapped in his jacket and lying face down on his Princess Di T-shirt. Over by the bungalow a sentry paced silently. The air was almost chilly.

Presently the car door opened and Brereton climbed out and stood peering crossly around him. Tommo sat up and stretched, and then a few moments later Beatrice's head rose from the ground on the far side of the car. I couldn't see Fine.

Brereton was incredulous when I told them I was bailing. Tommo looked unhappy but there was nothing for him to say, so he sat there with his back propped against the car wheel, slowly stirring his cold instant coffee. Fine tried to look puzzled, but to me he was always going to look pleased. I rummaged in the boot of the car to find my cigarettes, and not until I'd lit one did I answer Brereton's objections.

'I'll hitch a lift back with the Nigerians,' I said. 'They're bound to have some transport going back to Freetown today, now that this operation is over.'

Beatrice sat on the bonnet of the car, rubbed her face in her hands and then stared at me. Her face was tired and grey.

'I still don't see what the big hurry is,' said Brereton. 'In a couple of days we'll all bail together. There's still plenty to do here.'

'I talked to my people last night,' I said. 'They've had enough of this story. It's all Baghdad, Baghdad, Baghdad. They want me to get out.'

'You talked to your people last night?' Brereton had his head on one side.

'Yes. I used Tommo's phone.'

'Tommo's phone is dead. You killed it yourself.'

'It must have been yours, then. They both look the same.'

'For fuck's sake, Owen.'

I had to give them something more. 'Look, don't worry about it,' I said, and smiled as best I could. 'I'm also feeling a bit sick, to be honest. Since yesterday. It started in the car. Captain Fuck 'Em Up says that if I get to the airport by tonight I might be able to hitch a lift out tomorrow morning on the next C-130.'

When I actually did go to see Captain Fuck 'Em Up he was in the yard outside the colonel's bungalow, stripped to the waist and shaving from a tin mug, studying his work in the wing mirror of the colonel's jeep. He seemed embarrassed when I caught him. He said that a supply convoy was due to arrive from Lunsar in the afternoon and that it would be heading back to the airport tomorrow, or maybe the day after.

'If you're leaving town you should wait and go with the convoy,' he warned. 'It has an armoured escort. There are still some RUF making trouble near the road. Johnny Paul's guys too. You heard the shooting last night?'

'That was all to the north of town. I want to go south, and I need to go today.'

He shrugged. 'No road is safe. I'd advise you to be patient.' He turned back to his mirror.

Outside the bungalow an elderly lieutenant was dismounting a guard detail. The men stood in a gently swaying line and ported their rifles, breeches locked open, and the officer walked up and down behind them checking for live rounds. He smiled anxiously when he saw me watching him. I quickly turned away.

When I got back to the others they were packing their gear in the car. Beatrice was hunkered a few feet away, checking her e-mails over Fine's sat-phone. Brereton caught sight of me and raised two eyebrows. He was beside the car, fiddling with the fastenings on his old leather satchel. 'You don't have to worry about hitching a lift,' he said. 'We're going back too.'

'Really? Why?'

'Fine got a message from his desk in New York. The State

Department says that President Kabbah is flying back from exile tomorrow and they're going to have a big restoration ceremony at the football stadium in Freetown the day after. General Abacha's coming from Nigeria and lots of other African heads of state. We need to get back to cover it. But it would be best not to drive back alone – did Captain Fuck 'Em Up say whether there's a convoy heading south today?'

'No . . .' I answered slowly.

'No, there's no convoy today or no, he didn't say?' interrupted Fine. He was squatting down beside Beatrice, helping her do something with his sat-phone, and he tossed the question over his shoulder at me.

I looked at him coldly. 'No, there's no convoy today,' I said.

'Shit,' mused Brereton. 'That doesn't help us much. Perhaps we should wait until tomorrow, if there's going to be a convoy then?'

'Ideally we should go today,' argued Fine. 'To be on the safe side – get to Freetown tonight and get set up tomorrow. We need to allow for unexpected delays.'

They were all looking at me now, waiting for me to solve their problem for them. I thought about the long road back to Lungi, the deserted stretches, the hills and the woods creeping up to the roadside, and I thought about the shooting in the night, and the convoy that might go south tomorrow, but then I looked at Fine and Beatrice, squatting together over the sat-phone, heads almost touching, and tomorrow seemed like a long time away.

'Captain Fuck 'Em Up wasn't sure that there would be a convoy south tomorrow either,' I said slowly. 'But the road south is quiet – the shooting last night was all to the north of here. If we go today you can let me off at Lungi airport this evening. I need to catch that plane.'

And strictly speaking it was true, what I told them, every word of it. I've thought about it a lot, for ten years now, and I can still tell myself that. Every word I said was true.

Beatrice had stood and turned to look at me. 'You should come with us to Freetown,' she said quietly. 'I'm sure your people will want coverage of the celebration too.'

I hadn't thought of that. 'We'll see,' I said to her. 'Like I say, I think I'm coming down with something.'

As we loaded the car we heard an engine starting up beyond the bungalow and then the colonel's jeep appeared and drove off down the hill towards the town. At the bungalow they told Fine that the colonel had gone to meet some local chiefs and that Captain Fuck 'Em Up was with him. So we wrote them a quick note thanking them both and hoping we might see them again at the ceremony in Freetown.

A hot wind had risen in the gum trees, shaking the hand-me-down leaves and tugging at the hanging shreds of bark. The wind stripped dust from the dirt on the hilltop and the town below us vanished. As we pulled away the colonel's servants were running back and forth to rescue the wet clothes that they'd hung on a truck.

We wove our way down into the hazy grid of back streets, where brightly clad figures lurked in porches and round corners, hunted by the wind. Brereton leaned forward to peer through the murk, and as the wind rose and the dust turned to grit we had to close our windows. The heat was hard to bear.

The wind chased us to the edge of town and there it halted. It was the strangest thing. Looking back, I could see a brown spire rising over the hills and rooftops, flecked with shreds of paper and plastic, and dust devils played like stray children on the scrub at the edge of town. But ahead of us the hot vacant road shimmered in the sun and there was no wind to trouble the massive indifference of the bush. Beatrice was shifting around beside me, trying to make herself comfortable. I wound down my window and sucked in the air.

We drove on for a while. A car passed us, coming the other way, a crowded old Renault with bundles of goods tied to the roof with string.

Brereton cut through every bend as we wound down through the hills, gambling on his reactions and the lack of oncoming traffic. Tommo had his right arm out the window and every now and then his fingers would start drumming on the roof and then he'd recollect himself and stop. Fine was talking to Beatrice in a low voice, not loud enough for me to hear above the wind rush from my window. But it didn't matter, I reminded myself a couple of times. They could talk if they wanted.

The car dropped down a sharp hill, swinging left, and at the bottom was a narrow river and a little bridge, and as we approached it a soldier stepped out into the road and held his hand up. Fine and Beatrice grew silent and Tommo drew his hand back inside the window, and then we got closer and saw the man's cap badge, and just beyond him the piece of string that was stretched across the road as a symbolic barrier. A couple of other Nigerians were sprawled on a bench beneath a shade tree by the road.

We slowed, almost stopped, while the soldier in the road bent down to stare in at us, and then he straightened up and waved us on and one of the other soldiers flicked his wrist and the string lay flat in the road and we crossed it and pulled away again.

'I never thought I'd be glad to see the Nigerian army,' said Fine.

'They're lovely people,' said Brereton. 'Just so long as they're not in Nigeria.'

'Or Liberia,' said Fine.

Up another ridge, then down again, and the wooded slopes fell away into a sea of trees and shrubs and dried marsh and untended fields and the road snaked above it on its narrow little causeway.

We came to a village with signs of life, children playing, cooking fires, and a few more bored Nigerians guarding a piece of string. This time they waved us through without making us stop. One of them even saluted us, which Fine thought was funny. Brereton began talking about what he wanted to do if he made it to Freetown that night. First, he said, there would be a cold Star at the bar in the Cape Sierra – provided they had fixed their fridge. If not, he was prepared to wait until he'd had a real shower – hot, for preference, although cold would do, provided there was soap. Then he would head down to Paddy's. In Paddy's the beer was always cold. Tommo reckoned that Paddy would have fresh fish again by now, barracuda, grilled, in that spicy sauce they had, with chips. Brereton wanted cheeseburgers and tomato ketchup, perhaps a steak. On our last night in Freetown, Paddy had told Brereton about a shipping container that was en route from Guinea, full of wine and whiskey and gin to restock his looted bar. It would surely have cleared Kissy docks by now.

Fine, who had only been in the bush for three days, had to point out that there was a curfew in Freetown. They would be confined to their hotel. Brereton said curfew or not he would still go to Paddy's, but that just to be sure he'd force Fine to go on ahead of him to draw any fire. Beatrice told Brereton that this wouldn't be necessary. Brereton would be quite safe: her father had told her once that soldiers have a natural tendency to shoot high in the dark. Brereton told Beatrice to fuck off.

We came to a place where palm trees rose at intervals from the low bush. Many were just bare blackened poles, killed by lightning during the rains. They looked like the columns of a burned temple. The road curved sharply round and dipped into a broad, lightly wooded watercourse, and Brereton steered the car to cut a chord through the bend. Ahead there was a little low bridge, more of a culvert, and as we sped towards it another soldier emerged from the tall grass just beyond and raised his hand to halt us.

Brereton tutted and the car began to slow. Then Tommo said quietly, 'This bloke's not wearing boots.'

The car's gravity shifted backwards as Brereton's foot came off the brake. I felt Beatrice coiling beside me.

'I don't think we should stop,' said Brereton, his voice flat.

'We have to,' said Fine. 'He can't miss.'

The man in the roadway swam towards us. He was very close now, close enough for me to see the dirty fatigue shirt open to the waist, the shiny chains he wore around his neck, the eyes wide and hard as headlights. He was holding his rifle across his body, elbows raised and body twisted into a parody of some martial arts pose he'd seen in some video. His shaven head was tilted back and his face set in a mask of blank disdain. And the road pulled us smoothly towards him. Then Brereton swore, under his breath, one word I couldn't hear, and the car pitched forward as he began to brake again. My stomach lurched away from me. We were only yards away from the figure in the road. And then the gunman's face transformed itself into a different mask, a kind of grimace, and in one quick movement he swung his rifle up until it was held above his shoulder in a strange overhand grip, like a fish spear, pointing towards us, and I knew then that he wasn't alone, that he was performing for someone, and the rifle flashed and the windscreen ticked and my face stung and we were all flung back as Brereton floored the accelerator, aiming the car at the man in the road.

The gunman was firing on full automatic, the barrel of his rifle jerking up into the air. It amazed me how slowly the car was now moving, how long it took for each flash of the muzzle to follow the last, how the shining spent cases seemed to hang in the air. His face glided past my window and it was screaming something at me as he fumbled with his magazines, a big bunch of them all taped together.

It took a long time for me to turn and look at Beatrice. She wore the face I'd seen before in a refugee camp, on the porch of Laura's house, in a hotel room in rainy Durban. There was more than one weapon firing now and I couldn't hear what Fine was shouting. His words came much too slowly. Then the car swerved abruptly and Beatrice was thrown across me. Brereton was leaning out of his seat and with his right arm he was struggling with Tommo, who was hunched forward in the passenger seat. There was blood on the windscreen and dashboard.

Fine was shouting. Help Tommo. That was it. Beatrice leaned forward between the seats, trying to pull Tommo back by the shoulder, and I reached out a hand to the back of his head. There was blood running out from under his hair.

There was a flash and ringing silence and the car seemed to glide for a while and when it crashed down again there was choking smoke and a grinding sound.

The car was at a halt, diagonally in the road, the engine still running. A door opened, a white hole sucking out the smoke, and Fine was getting out of the car, his hands raised, calling to the shapes that ran from the bush. Then he slammed back against the car, right into the angle where the door met the body, and he bounced off hard and came down on his knees, making a choking noise. Then they shot him again and he fell face down in the road.

Beatrice was struggling and I held her by the shoulder. Don't go, I tried to say, stay here, but I could hear no sound above the ringing in my ears. The back of Tommo's seat was smouldering in front of me. The passenger door was gone, and so was Tommo. Brereton's head was twisted away from me, face turned towards his window, his right ear blackened and bleeding. Stay, please, I tried to tell Beatrice. But I had no strength in my left arm and my right arm couldn't go to her.

Brereton was fighting with the gear stick. The car lurched a couple of feet, stopped, then began to grind forward again, and Beatrice pulled herself away from me and I saw her go through the door that Fine had left open. I wanted to follow her but my body wouldn't answer me. I shouted at Brereton to stop the car but he didn't seem to hear. We were moving again as bullets pick-pocked through glass and sheet metal. My neck and shoulders stung.

Something punched my right shoulder and threw me sideways and forward against the back of Brereton's seat and I thought I heard him scream.

I remember that my ears were still ringing. I was sitting in the dust, surrounded by torn branches, watching the car burn. A shadow moved over me and I looked up, and Laura Guenther took my picture.

17

Because Cartwright and I shared an office and sometimes took a drink together – though only when Hugh was present – people often assumed that we were friends. So when he failed to turn up for work one Sunday morning it was me they sent out to check on him. Cartwright was often sick but it was unheard of for him to miss a shift without phoning in, and even then he would usually work from home. But today he wasn't answering his telephones. The duty editor made a point of looking grave as she gave me my taxi vouchers. Faces turned as I walked to the lift. Perhaps the old bastard is dead, the faces said. Alone in the lift it occurred to me that few, if any, of them had any first-hand reason for disliking Cartwright. Hugh had seen to that, by forbidding him from talking to them. They disliked Cartwright for the sake of tradition.

The taxi took me over the canal basin, past the greyhound track and across the slimy black tidal creek, and then it swept round a curve of pebble-dashed houses and shops and out into the cold sunshine by the coast. It was late morning, fine and still, and I looked to my left, past the new playing fields and up the wide road that led to the docks. The streets up there, I remembered, were named after ships; it was there that Hugh had been raised. Pencils of steam rose vertically from the chimneys of the power plant. Then the park on the left vanished and there was nothing but a low grey stone wall between the road and the strand. The tide was a spring low, and it was impossible to tell where the wet grey flats became the flat grey sea. The sharp line of the horizon ruled an end to the confusion: all that really mattered, it said, was the bright void of a clear December sky.

The taxi slowed and stopped. I signed the voucher and stood with the bay behind me, staring across the whizzing traffic at a low terrace of nineteenth-century houses, red brick and grey slate, with stone steps leading to front doors with fanlights and with basement windows trying to rise above their station. Hedges grew out through wrought-iron railings, and clumps of ill-assorted doorbells showed that most of the houses had devolved, bit by bit, into separate flats. I checked the address they'd given me and saw that Cartwright had the end house on my left. He must have come by it a long time ago; nobody in our trade could afford to buy out here any more.

I skipped through the first lane of traffic, balanced a moment on the white central line, then finished the crossing. The railing in front of Cartwright's house was painted black. Beyond it the little square of lawn, bisected by a concrete path, was neat and featureless apart from a few stalks of dry seaweed left by some recent storm. No flowers for Cartwright, I thought, opening the gate. I walked slowly up the path and the bright certainty of the day receded, until all that was left to me was the flat green paint of the front door and my broken reflection in a frosted-glass pane. An antique brass button, mounted in the middle of the door, made a bell ring somewhere far inside, too far away for a house of that size. I waited a minute, hearing the cars and trucks drone past behind me, then pressed the bell again. There was a large brass knocker beneath the doorbell and I tried that for a while, for form's sake. Then I pushed the door a couple of times, quite hard, but it didn't give.

I went back down the steps and into the garden. There were two downstairs windows, one on either side of the front steps. A solid white basement door was set into the side of the steps on the right, barely head high. It was locked. The first window was screened inside by a thick grey net curtain. I pressed my palms against the pane and tried, just for interest, I told myself, to see if the sash would move upwards. It moved a fraction and then stuck, to my relief. I couldn't see if it was latched on the inside. The second window gave onto a dark space full of boxes and what might have been furniture covered in dust sheets. I stared in through it for what seemed like a long time. There were seashells scattered beneath a thick layer of dust on the windowsill. A child would have put them there, I thought.

I could think of nothing better to do than to try the front door again so I reclimbed the steps. The upstairs windows were set on either side of the raised doorway but too far out to reach. Both were shuttered on the inside. I rang again, again nothing happened, and I was wondering what to do next when I saw a movement to my right. An old woman was staring at me from the steps of the next house, thirty feet away. Her eyes were washed out like the sky above us and she wore a wine-coloured woollen cape that looked like a tepee and a wine-coloured felt hat that almost matched. She was poised, as if for effect, holding one hand up to the door in front of her. A key glinted in the darkness of her glove. Then another gloved hand popped out of a slit in the cape and gestured to me – the kind of twitch that once might have summoned a waiter.

'Are you looking for Mr Cartwright?' she called across the space between us. Her voice surprised me: it was the voice of a much younger woman, so strong that she didn't have to shout.

'Yes,' I said. 'Have you seen him today?'

She looked suddenly disappointed. 'I never see him. He keeps odd hours.' She had the key in the door now.

'But you do know him?'

She stopped and turned to me again, frowning. 'I remember the night he was born,' she said. 'I heard his mother shouting. My mother wouldn't tell me why. They brought me in to see him the next morning.'

She was looking at Cartwright's house, not me. I noticed then that, like Cartwright's, her door had only one big brass doorbell.

'I'm from his paper,' I said, and smiled at her. 'I've come to visit him.'

She might tell me more about Cartwright if I didn't spook her. But she narrowed her eyes and took a step back into the darkness of her doorway. She paused there, head on one side.

'There's something wrong,' she said, matter-of-fact. 'He never has visitors . . .' She considered me for another long moment then shook her head. 'You could always try around the back. There's a door into the back garden from the alley.'

Then she vanished, leaving her door half open.

Cartwright's house stood on a corner where a little side street met the coast road. Behind it a narrow mews opened onto the side street and beyond the mews another terrace of brick houses stretched off inland. The side street was quiet, lined with parked cars. I recognized the nearest as Cartwright's old Ford. Because of his condition they let him park behind the office, in one of the spaces that were normally kept for directors. I took a few steps and peered into the car. A newspaper was sitting on the dashboard on the passenger side, carefully folded with the masthead and date clearly showing. It was our paper, yesterday's edition.

I checked to make sure that no one was watching before I turned into the mews. Hard on my right was a door made of crude planks, painted the same flat green as Cartwright's front door. I gave it a push and it clicked and swung open.

The back of the house mirrored the front except that the back door gave directly onto the garden without any steps. A council refuse bin stood on a square of concrete just inside the alley door, its hinged lid open. It was empty. The rest of the garden was given over to the same flat waste of grass as the front. When I tried the back door it opened easily, and I stepped from the hissing daylight into the silence of the house.

I was standing in a small and very neat kitchen, old deal cupboards lit by light strained through the nets on the windows. Beneath the nearest window was a big square porcelain sink, the kind you find in old farmhouses, with a teacup and saucer inverted on a draining rack beside it. In front of me was the grey rectangle of an open door and beyond it bare wooden stairs led up to a dim light.

'Hello?' I called, half-heartedly, and waited for a while. I started to close the back door but then changed my mind and left it open. As I climbed the stairs my feet thundered in the silence. At the head of the stairs was a small hallway dappled with broken daylight from the frosted glass of the front door. I thought for a moment, and then I stepped softly to the front door and turned the catch, opening it just enough to let the traffic in. Then I allowed myself to look around me. On my right another door stood open, and beyond it another light was burning. There was no hurry. I pushed the door open the rest of the way and slowly stepped inside.

The room was a study of sorts, lit by a single fringed lamp standing in one corner. The lampshade threw Chinese patterns on walls lined with leather-bound books and fading paperbacks and cardboard-backed adventure novels of the old school. Some of them must have belonged to Cartwright's parents once, to the mother who screamed for him.

Her son was sitting behind a leather-topped desk, his head leaning back and his chin tilted towards the door. His mouth was open in its own scream, choked off by the same black matter that crusted the shoulders of his old blue suit. I stood there inside the door and stared for a while, and then I put my hands in my pockets and took a couple of steps sideways and leaned forward to look more closely. The back of Cartwright's head was gone. A thick black smear, still glistening in the middle, ran down the back of the leather swivel chair in which he sprawled. I straightened up again and took another step forward. I could see the pistol now, lying in his lap, still wrapped in his fingers. It was one of those old Webleys. You'd be surprised how many of them are still about, hidden away in attics and cabinets, heirlooms from the old wars. I took a step up beside the desk and leaned forward to look at the pistol more closely. Through the open front of the cylinder I saw the dull pitted tip of a soft-nosed bullet. I straightened up again.

'You messy old fucker,' I said, deliberately loud. And then, after a pause, more quietly, 'I always took you for a poisoner.'

Cartwright's eyes were almost closed but a sliver of white made it look as if he were having one last squint at the world before they screwed his lid down. It occurred to me that the room was cold, and much too dark. I straightened up again and looked behind me. Heavy wooden shutters blocked the window and I had to wrench hard to pull them open. There must have been a knack to it, or perhaps Cartwright always left them closed.

Outside it was still late morning. A bus moved past, its roar dulled by the window pane. Far out on the sand a few seagulls were fighting over something I couldn't see. I shivered and turned back to Cartwright. I could see in the daylight how white and dead he was, but the thick slick of blood that pooled on the floor was vividly black. I looked at the bookshelf behind him and saw a splash of putty-like tissue and clumps of hair and bone: Cartwright had plastered his brains all over a set of antique encyclopedias, which was a nice touch, it seemed to me.

The desk was bare except for a big cream-coloured Bakelite telephone, a small stack of papers and a blue cardboard folder. The papers and the folder were aligned exactly with the edges of the desk. Tiny spots of blood were flecked across the folder, the papers and the telephone. I leaned against the windowsill and stared across at the folder, and then I put my hand in my pocket and took out my cell phone. Then I put the cell phone back in my pocket and walked across the room and picked up the folder, curling my fingers beneath it to avoid the dried blood spots. The police would forgive me for having a look, I told myself. I was held to be his friend. And my name was written on it.

The phone on the desk rang, a shrill mechanical summons. It didn't make me jump. Somewhere downstairs another, louder bell echoed the ringing handset. I have never heard any sound so lonely. For whom was Cartwright still alive? After the fourth ring I picked up the heavy receiver, ignoring the faint speckles of Cartwright's blood. It was dry now anyway.

'Hello,' I said, and closed my eyes and waited.

'Owen?' said a woman's voice. It was Hugh's secretary. I put the phone down before she could say any more.

I opened the folder. It contained a thick stack of A4 pages loosely bound with treasury tags, copies of articles that I'd written myself, back in my reporting days. Those at the top of the stack, the most recent, were computer printouts of pieces I'd filed for my various strings from Africa, taken from the web or from LexisNexis, but as I leafed on through the sheaf these gave way to yellowing photo-copies of older cuttings from our own newspaper, dated by stamp and classified by hand. Some passages had been underlined in red or green ink, but the margins were bare of praise or blame.

I felt tired and my leg was sore, and I had already been sitting on the corner of the desk for several minutes before I realized what I was doing. I stayed there anyway, until my good leg started to swing.

When I was done I gathered the pages between my hands and tapped them on the desk to square their edges again, but as I picked up the folder to put them back I felt more papers rustle inside, and I saw that it contained another, much smaller sheaf of pages, actual clippings cut from newspapers and magazines. I almost didn't bother to look at them. I knew they would be from the *New York Chronicle*, and from Beatrice's magazines in France and the US, and from Tommo's old paper in Sydney. But I riffled through them anyway. The last item was a photocopy of an article I'd never seen before, from an academic journal in South Africa. It was the byline that struck me: Spencer Armitage, it said. The piece was dated only two years before.

I read through it slowly, and when it was done I put everything back in the folder and replaced the folder just where Cartwright had left it, guided by the little square of desktop that was free of minute bloodstains.

I looked at the stack of papers. The topmost, stippled with blood, were envelopes containing bills from the phone and electricity companies, both very small. The postmarks showed that the bills had arrived on Friday, when Cartwright would have been at work, too late for him to pay that week. He would have had to wait until Monday. Beneath the bills was a petition from the local residents' association, proposing a package of traffic-calming measures to protect children on the street. There were two little boxes to tick, one for 'yes' and one for 'no', and a couple of lines of broken dots where people could write in their own suggestions. Cartwright had voted 'no'.

Next was a letter from a mass-circulation magazine, advising Cartwright that he might have won a major prize, and beneath that was a clipping from our newspaper, from two days before, carefully removed with a scissors. It was a piece from the op-ed page, one of my sections. Two punctuation errors and a typo had been circled in red, and there was a note of complaint in the margin written in ball-point, in Hugh's handwriting. Cartwright must have brought it home with him.

I looked at Cartwright again. The newspaper on the dash of his car, the back door left open, the folder on the desk . . . Cartwright's open mouth and half-closed eyes suggested a snore now. He might even have been smirking. I wouldn't see him again.

'Is this your idea of a joke?' I demanded aloud, and waited for an answer.

His left hand was hanging straight down outside the arm of his chair, and when I moved around the desk I saw a waste-paper basket lying on its side. His hand must have knocked it over when it swung free of him at last. A few balled-up pieces of paper had rolled from the basket, and when I went to pick them up I saw among them a crumpled photograph, black and white on the front, yellow on the back. The picture showed a young woman with dark hair, dressed fashionably if one assumed that the picture was taken in the 1960s. She was standing by a low stone wall and smiling at the photographer. She had very crooked teeth, and you could tell from the way she held her lips that she usually tried to hide them but that right then she couldn't help smiling. It made up for the fact that she wasn't very pretty. In the background there were mudflats and a still, hazy grey sea. I looked out of the window and there it still was, all of it, just the same.

I put the photograph on the corner of the desk behind me, where blood had not splattered, and then I straightened out the papers from the bin. Just a few bills stamped as paid, some crumpled envelopes, another circular from the residents' committee, this time asking people to fix their cats. When I was done I set the bin back on its base and crumpled the papers up and put them back into it, and then I looked at the picture again, and finally I picked it up and crumpled it again and put it in the bin with the other papers. It was not for me to redeem her.

I looked at the folder again, and then I picked it up and looked around me. There was a leather bag on the floor by the bookshelf, one of those plain envelope-like ones with simple loop handles and a zip fastener along the top. I'd seen Cartwright with it once or twice in the office: it was the one he used to transport his folders. I put the folder into it and then, after a moment's thought, I added the traffic petition that I'd left on the desk: there would still be time for me to post it before the votes were counted.

I tucked the bag under my elbow and walked into the hall, out of the front door and onto the top step. The seagulls had vanished. Far off in the distance a tiny figure notched the horizon where the sea must begin. Digging for worms. I stared across the see-sawing traffic at the waste of sand and water. Had anything out on those flats changed since Cartwright first set eyes on them with a child's wonder, or through his long awkward life? For an instant I saw him, just across the road there, playing alone with a bucket and spade. I seemed to take it for granted that he had been an only child.

Carefully I eased myself down until I was sitting on the top step. A container truck halted in front of me, blocking the view. As it was pulling off again the phone in my pocket began to buzz. It was Hugh's secretary again. She sounded angry but I ignored her and told her to connect me to Hugh. He was at home with his family. It was supposed to be a Sunday.

'Oh,' said Hugh, when I told him. There was a long silence. I heard him clear his throat, and then he spoke again. 'Today was meant to be his last shift. They were making him retire but he didn't want any fuss. He said he'd tell you himself today. He knew that you were on duty.'

I tried to remember if Cartwright had said or done anything strange on Friday. The truth was I couldn't remember seeing him at all.

Hugh said he would telephone the police himself to make sure the thing was handled with whatever finesse was required.

I stretched my bad leg out below me. The cold stone burned through my trousers. I took out a cigarette and lit it, and I was looking out to sea again when I heard a voice calling me. The old lady had re-emerged from her house and was standing on her top step, still wearing her tepee but without the hat.

'Is it bad news?' she called. I nodded.

She disappeared inside again, then re-emerged a moment later wearing her hat. I watched her make her way slowly down her steps, gripping the iron railing, then out through her gate and in through Cartwright's. For a moment I thought she was going to try to slip past me and enter Cartwright's house – a ghoul will try anything for a thrill – but she stopped halfway up the steps and peered up at me. I eyed her back, still smoking my cigarette. Neither of us spoke for a while, and then finally she put her hand up to brush a wisp of thin hair into her hatband.

'I remember when he was born,' she said shyly.

'I know.'

She smiled suddenly. 'Of course you do. I told you, didn't I? His mother was a lovely woman . . . I didn't like his father much, though.'

Gripping the railing, she turned and slowly eased herself backwards until she was sitting four steps below me. When she was done she twisted around as far as she could and turned to look up at me, with the expression of a child who has done something clever.

'We shouldn't really sit on the cold stone,' she confided. 'It gives you piles.'

I laughed. 'I'll bear that in mind,' I said.

'How did he die?'

I looked back to the sea again, and thought for a while before answering. 'He shot himself,' I said.

'I see . . .' She found another stray wisp of hair and sent it back into hiding. 'That *is* unusual.'

'I suppose it is.'

I finished my cigarette and lit another. We sat there together and didn't speak again until the police car drove up onto the pavement outside the gate and two officers got out. Then the old lady pulled herself slowly to her feet and turned and smiled at me.

'I'd better be off to church now,' she said. 'I'll say a prayer for him.'

'That would be good.'

'And for you too, of course.'

'Thank you.'

She stepped to one side to let the policemen pass her in the gate. They went past her as if she weren't even there. I got to my feet and stubbed out my cigarette and waited for them, battling a sudden and almost overwhelming impulse to smile. The police were brisk. I told them where to look and waited outside while they went to check for themselves. They were still in the study when my phone rang. It was Hugh again.

'I forgot to ask you,' he said. 'Did Cartwright leave a note? Any kind of message?'

'No,' I said.

18

The Nigerians' northbound convoy came across our car about a mile from the ambush scene, where Brereton had finally crashed it. They gathered us up and put us in the back of a truck, which they sent back to Lungi under a detached escort. The truck's tailboard was broken, and without lifting my head from the floor I could see the scout car following behind us, the commander's head protruding in its leather tank-man's helmet. I thought he was a cosmonaut.

Laura was talking to me. She was telling me how she'd flown into Lungi airport the night before and hitched a ride north with the Nigerian convoy. There were other people lying around me, bouncing about beneath the canvas awning. There were holes in the canvas and shafts of sunlight flashed about like disco lights. The floor of the truck was sticky.

I was numb at first, but not for long. At Makeni an Australian nun-doctor gave me some morphine that she'd kept hidden from the rebels. That was good.

When I woke up again I was back in the truck. I had a mattress now. The morphine was wearing off and I tried not to moan. My right arm pulsed and burned as if someone had wired the nerves to a strobe machine. I couldn't feel my right leg.

I heard Laura talking to somebody behind me. I started to cry again and Laura appeared and gave me more morphine. I wondered where she'd learned to do that. Maybe she'd already told me.

At Lungi airport they lined us up in the mouth of the hangar where Brereton and Tommo and I had spent such a happy week once, lounging and napping and waiting for our story to move. A small twin-engine jet taxied up on the apron, and I watched as the other stretchers were carried over one by one and slid on board.

Laura held my hand and told me not to worry. Then she was talking on a sat-phone. She seemed very angry. A while later somebody put me in a helicopter.

Later Diamond Doug, who came to see me in the hospital, told me that De Wet had flown me across the estuary to Freetown free of charge, which was nice of him. I wish I could remember the trip. I'd always wanted to fly in a Hind.

Douglass also gave me a message from Laura. She said my own people had refused to pay for my evacuation. Management was worried that if they helped me now it might be seen as an admission of liability. Her company had ordered her to go to the Gulf, but she would have stayed to look after me if Douglass hadn't turned up. I never saw her again.

'You're lucky you were hurt cheap, boy,' said Douglass, perched like a sparrow on the end of my bed. 'Nothing the surgeons here couldn't deal with. Just a lot of it.'

The ward was hot and crowded and it didn't smell of antiseptic. On the floor beneath my bed a cardboard box held some of the shrapnel that they'd taken from the right side of my body. There was more in my leg, they said, but it was too hard to get at. The box also contained one of Tommo's cameras, the FM2, with a 50-millimetre lens. There was even some film in it, according to the counter: sixteen exposed frames, twenty to go. The Nigerians must have thought that it was mine.

Douglass told me he'd come back to Sierra Leone to reopen his branch office. Freetown was safe for him again, now that Charles Taylor's friends had been driven back into the bush. They still held most of the diamond fields, but not for much longer. Anyway, he said, he always did good trade, even when he was on the wrong side of the line, because he paid the best prices. In dollars, not guns, he added, and then he repeated it.

He acted like it was the biggest joke in the world to see me again. He didn't mention the others. I found out later that he'd squared my bill with the doctors. He didn't tell me that himself. He did say, though, that in a few days he and some friends would be bringing in an Ilyushin full of something or other and that when it was empty it could take me back to Abidjan. From there I could go where I liked.

He had brought me a couple of tubes of potato crisps from the Lebanese supermarket. The owner was a friend of his, and when Douglass mentioned that he was going to see me in hospital the owner gave him the crisps as a gift for me. He remembered how Brereton and I had bought a whole box of them to take with us when we headed up-country. I gave them to the little boy in the bed next to mine, along with all my shrapnel. I'd seen him admiring it; the mine had blown his legs clean off, so he'd no shrapnel of his own.

As it turned out, I didn't need to take Douglass up on his offer of a free flight to Abidjan. He went to Bo on business for a few days, and the morning after he left an American showed up in the ward and said he was from the *Chronicle*. He was young, about my own age, but very grave. He had short combed hair and he wore a beige linen tropical suit that looked as if he'd bought it just for this assignment. His face had that keen, stupid look that speaks of squash and postgraduate study.

He told me he was a writer – American hacks often call themselves that – and from the way he paused when he mentioned his name I guessed he reckoned he was a star back home. His name was Spencer Armitage, and the *Chronicle* had sent him out to pull together a big magazine feature about Fine's last days. To get the full story he needed my memories. Also, he added smoothly, his paper would like to fly me out of Freetown. They felt really bad that their air-ambulance company had left one of Fine's wounded buddies on the tarmac at Lungi, just because I didn't have insurance or anyone to guarantee the cash. At the time, Armitage said, his bosses hadn't known about me.

I lay back on my lumpy grey pillow and thought about what Armitage had told me. Fine had finally done it: his story would run at great length off the cover of the *Chronicle*'s glossy weekend magazine. It would be under his own byline: Armitage said there was enough stuff in Fine's diary, notebooks and computer to cobble together a few thousand words of first-person reportage. In the coming days Armitage would travel up-country with his own monkey, retracing Fine's steps and talking to people who'd met him, and then he would weave Fine's stuff into a story and write a side piece of his own. Tommo's pics would carry the whole thing. They were really very good, Armitage confided; there was one of me, carrying that rebel away from that lynch-mob in Lunsar, which had a sort of Michelangelo composition to it. They might even give a whole page to it, for Tommo's sake.

'You're going to be a hero,' said Armitage, as if he were offering me a payment.

The following morning Armitage came back and propped a mini-disk recorder on my chest. Across in the next bed the legless kid stared at us with his mouth open. Armitage pulled a chair to the side of my bed, took out a spiral notebook and drew a line down through the middle of the page. He was wearing a different suit today.

'So tell me,' he said formally, 'what did your friends mean to you?'

Once, when I had some money, I took Beatrice for a weekend at a bushveld safari camp. We drove east from Johannesburg for three hours, crossed the Long Tom Pass and then threaded north through the hills of Gazankulu. The road wound through plains and valleys strewn with one-storey shacks. Livestock grazed between the houses, leaving broad patches of bare earth for the wind and sun to harrow. As we drove, we realized that the fields of scattered houses formed great conurbations, unmapped suburbs for towns that were hundreds of miles away. Goats were climbing the thorn trees to strip the hard green leaves.

Young people swarmed everywhere along the tarred road and its unpaved tributaries. Girls and boys in uniform hurried for appointments with school clocks, cutting brisk paths through drifting clouds of older siblings. The idlers shuffled along in their flip-flop shoes and watched the traffic as it passed. Minibuses halted and knots of people nudged up against them like puppies looking for suck. Suitcases went into the taxis; bundles of goods came out.

'What are they all doing here?' murmured Beatrice, slumped in a corner of her seat.

'They live here,' I said. 'It was a homeland for Shangaan people. Back in the old days the whites wouldn't let them live anywhere else.'

'Sure. But what do they actually do?'

She must have been teasing me again, but again I didn't notice.

'The children and older women live here, and everybody else goes to the Reef to get work. They send money home when they can and they come back for weddings and funerals and holidays.'

She stared across the waste of shacks, where rusting wire fences enclosed red gardens of carefully brushed red dirt. I looked across at her but her face was turned away. Then, as I shifted my eyes back to the road ahead, she suddenly leaned over and hugged my knee where it curved above the clutch pedal. I looked down at the fine brown hair that ran down to the nape of her neck. Then she straightened up and smiled at me.

The safari camp was suitably rustic, an unfenced cluster of wooden chalets in a stretch of low bush. Our chalet had a rhino motif, which Beatrice thought was rather funny. Although we'd arrived in the early afternoon, she insisted on lowering the mosquito net before she pushed me back on to the bed. We were still asleep at 4 p.m. when they called us for the game drive.

'Can't they just drive the game past our hut?' Beatrice mumbled to the pillow, but I was insistent. I told her I was paying for the trip and I wanted to see all the animals I had coming to me.

An open Land Rover was waiting for us behind the huts; we were the last ones to arrive. Our fellow guests were a pair of Afrikaner newlyweds and two middle-aged English women. As we climbed onto the truck the English women glared at us from joyless faces and muttered loudly to each other about some schedule or other.

The honeymooners were scared of them and in awe of us. They were barely twenty years old and you could tell that they didn't have much education or money, that this really was the trip of their lifetime so far, and you wouldn't bet that anything much better would come to them in the future. She was small and neat and rather pretty apart from her bleached, frizzy hair. He was a big fit lad with short hair and slow eyes, and when our guide turned up with a hunting rifle the boy asked to examine it before we set off. The rifle was unloaded, and the guide allowed him to work the bolt and sight it at a tree and pull the trigger, and then he took it gently back from him. The boy was displaying for his female in the manner of his kind, and as she watched she fought to keep the pride out of her face.

Our tracker was a thin Shangaan in a German army parka. He perched on a padded stool welded to the front of the Land Rover, which made Beatrice laugh. She called him the hood ornament.

I don't remember what animals we saw. Impala, I suppose. At last light we stopped beside a dam where hippos grunted and blew, and the guide offered us drinks from a cooler box. The Afrikaners wandered off a short distance to murmur to each other while the English women stayed in their seats on the truck, accepting with bad grace the gin and tonics that the tracker passed up to them. They seemed to resent the delay.

The sun had set and somewhere in the grass close by an insect whirred like a faulty transformer. The dusk drew fanciful shadows from the bushes and thorn trees, and the first stirrings of the night ruffled the surface of the dam. Apart from a rim of gold along the distant, jagged edge of the Drakensberg the western sky was a silver infinity. A phrase came to mind – the peace that passeth understanding.

The moment was broken by a ghastly commotion somewhere across the dam. There was a series of booming, rasping barks, followed by a prolonged shriek of pain and fear. I felt Beatrice move in close beside me while the guide and the tracker jerked their heads towards the noise.

The guide spoke after a long moment. 'It's just baboons,' he said. 'They're in that big tree to the right of the dam, see? You can see the branches moving.'

The tree was heavy with leaves, and as we peered through the gloom we could see the branches whipping back and forth. There was another storm of grunts and shrieks and the thrashing re-doubled. The honeymooners drew in beside us and the two English women gave up their crabbed conversation.

'It sounds like they're being attacked by something,' said Beatrice doubtfully.

The guide slowly shook his head. 'Nah, it's not that. It's the big fellow . . . He's having some problems with one of his girlfriends . . . I'm afraid baboons are old-fashioned about women.'

The barks broke out again, mounting in an almost human crescendo of hatred and spite. The upper part of the tree convulsed as if in a hurricane and the female baboon screamed again, in mortal fear or pain, until its voice abruptly choked off into silence. There was a momentary pause and then many other voices started shrieking in the tree. Beatrice took a step away from me, towards the guide and the tracker, her eyes wide. She looked as if she might even be about to say something, but the guide shook his head and chuckled. 'It's just nature's way,' he said.

One of the English women spoke up, a supercilious smudge in the half-light. 'You're not supposed to get involved with them,' she said. 'It's not like they're people.'

Beatrice didn't answer. At the other end of the Land Rover the newlyweds were kissing.

19

They're making me work some early shifts, now that Cartwright is gone. It doesn't really suit me but I'm in no position to complain. The newsroom is becoming 'integrated', which means the reporters have to file all day for the internet as well as for the print edition, more work for the same money, and for those who don't like it there'll be another round of lay-offs soon. Most of the reporters never get to leave the office any more, because they're too busy rewriting stuff they've just heard on the radio or read on the internet, stuff that the radio and internet just lifted from us. And then they wonder why we're losing our readers. Me, I wouldn't care about any of this if it weren't for the early starts. Plus I'm worried that Hugh might resign. He thinks it's all bollocks.

Before I went to work this morning I took my coffee to the park behind my house and sat on a bench by the basin, watching the ducks through the rails. The ducks swam towards me, hoping for bread, but I never bring any, so they milled about in front of me for a while, quacking politely, then chevroned off towards an old man who was waiting on the opposite side of the water.

It was cold and grey, almost raining, and the wind seized the old man's crusts and hurled them back in his face. He had to bend down to gather them up again, then lean out through the railings and jab the bread sharply down onto the water a couple of feet below, like someone throwing darts. Even so, the wind blew the bread in against the brick side of the basin, and the ducks churned about some more before they found the courage to take it from within the old man's reach. He eased himself upright again and stood there, smiling to himself, and when the ducks had finished and moved away he put his hands in the pockets of his blue raincoat and stood hunched in on himself. He looked like the heron that stands all day long on the tiny island while the wind plays in its feathers. It was there again today.

The wind sucked the heat from my coffee, but I've come to like it cold. The old man shrank further in on himself, then turned and moved towards the gate, expelled by the wind at his back. I turned up the collar on my jacket, resolved to tough it out, but the dankness turned to drops and the rain hissed across the lake, driving me along after him, into the blind, decaying street that leads towards the city. I should have gone home to put my mug in the sink but that would mean facing back into the wind, and anyway the mug was old and chipped and stained. There was a skip full of rubble outside one of the old Georgian houses and I tossed my mug into it and smiled as it smashed. I would replace it, I decided, by stealing Cartwright's mug. It was sitting there on his desk, the desk that has still not been reassigned to anyone.

Buses grunted and roared all down the wet hill. Grey stone buildings turned dark and shone, and the wind on the bridge whipped the morning crowd sideways. The rain came and went like a sub-plot, and I was wet right through when I got to the office. There was no one else in yet. The newsroom was bright with electric light and the wind whistled outside, vainly seeking entry. I took a newspaper from the pile by the newsdesk, warm from the press in the print-room below, and went into my alcove. Cartwright's plain white china mug was standing there on his desk in its usual place, between his computer and the telephone. There was dust inside it.

I took Cartwright's mug out to the deserted coffee room, washed it and filled it from a big urn of last night's coffee. It was almost cold. Here the window gave onto the cluttered mass of air vents and fire escapes and ad hoc extensions at the back of the building. A seagull floated between the brick islands of the chimneys, its wings trembling, facing into the wind. It hung there for a full minute and then it made some minute alteration to its trim and in an instant it whipped back and down to plunge beneath the shining sea of roof tiles. The office filled slowly with murmuring voices and the gentle buzz of telephones.

It was almost eleven when Lucy came in. She was always a little late. She wore a dark, close-cut suit and a pearl-coloured silk blouse and business shoes, and a couple of heads turned as she walked to her desk. I'd finished the paper and was doing the crossword. A while later I saw her walk out again. I thought again of the seagull. Then presently my phone rang, the first time that day. I looked at my watch and saw that it was lunchtime.

'I'm downstairs in the lobby,' said Lucy's voice. 'Can you come down for a minute?'

'Why?'

'It's a surprise. Just come down for a minute.'

Lucy was waiting under the hostile eyes of the security desk. Her suit made her look even younger than she was. It came to me why: it made her look hopeful. Someone was standing behind her in the mouth of the little cubbyhole where, back in the old days, we used to interview the paranoids who came in off the street. Back then we always gave them a hearing before we eased them on their way again, but now we use an outside security firm and the lost and the lonely are told to fuck off.

Lucy smiled at me uncertainly. 'Please don't say anything to Hugh just yet,' she murmured, and then she touched me on the shoulder and ran up the stairs.

Charlie Brereton stepped out of the alcove and took his right hand from his pocket and held it out to me. He wore an expensive-looking raincoat, damp at the shoulders, and from his shoulder hung his worn old leather satchel.

'Hello, Owen,' he said.

'Hello, Charlie.' I took his hand carefully. It was still white from the burns.

'I'm in town for the day and I heard you were here,' he said. His smile didn't change. 'Go on. Get your coat.'

'I didn't bring one today.'

It was no longer raining much but the cars and buses sprayed water ankle-deep across the pavement. Brereton paused on the corner, unsure, while a council lorry drowned his shoes.

'Maybe you can suggest somewhere,' he said. 'I don't know this town at all.'

'There's a bar down there we could go to,' I said, and nodded towards the river.

'Not a works pub, is it? I was hoping for somewhere quiet.'

'Don't worry. I'm ashamed of you too.'

He laughed.

We crossed the roaring street with the wind at our backs and turned left around the corner into a sudden space of calm. Outside the cinema the copper gnome stood with his torch dripping. People flitted by with their heads down, the women shielded by umbrellas whose spokes slashed past at eye level. I kept having to duck away from them but Brereton was beneath it all. He skipped sideways for a couple of yards, studying my gait.

'Is it just your leg that's still bad?' he asked. I noticed he was a little breathless.

'Pretty much,' I said, without slowing down. 'And you?'

'Full recovery. My bullet was almost spent, apparently. They reckon it hit something else first. Probably you.'

'Well, there's a bond for you.'

He laughed again. It was the same old broken-nosed snigger, like he was snorting beer through it. Then he came to a sudden stop.

'Is that the river through there?' he said, nodding down the street. 'Can we go and take a look?'

I led him across the road to the breast-high stone wall that topped the embankment. Behind us the self-important stream of traffic hissed and moaned along the quay while in front was the pent-up force of the half-tamed estuary. We were back in the cold of the wind. It picked through the damp wool of my jacket and whipped the thin hair off the back of Brereton's scalp as he leaned on the wall and stared into the flood tide, three feet below. Billows of angry brown water swept away from the bridge piers then eddied around again, like drunken tramps reeling back to a fight.

'Must be nice in summer,' remarked Brereton.

'It's usually much the same as this.'

He wanted to know about the various buildings along the river. I told him what I knew. Far off to the right the lift bridge was opening and beyond it the low grey shape of a naval vessel stood out from the fug.

'Is that the sea down there?' asked Brereton, as if surprised. 'Can you walk down there from here?'

'It's too far,' I said. 'You have to walk for miles. But it always looks closer from here. I don't know why.'

'Let's take a stroll that way anyway. Just for a bit. I love old docklands.'

He turned his face downriver and I had to follow him. 'So does my boss,' I said.

Brereton's eyes were back on the flood. 'Hugh Rainsford? I've heard good things about him.'

'They're probably true.'

He glanced at me. 'Don't tell him, for God's sake, but my boss would quite like to poach him. They knew each other in Washington.'

'Forget it. Hugh hated being abroad. He's a home bird. He'll never go away again.'

Brereton smiled thinly. 'Unless he gets the sack.'

I looked at Brereton then but he was gazing innocently past me.

'So how about you, Charlie?' I said after a pause. 'What has you over here? Business, I hope.'

'Of course. I didn't come to see you.' Another snigger. He was laughing a lot today. 'We're looking for a new super-stringer here so I came over to see a couple of people. It's a break from the desk.'

'I take it that Lucy Viner is one of your prospects.'

He flashed his teeth again, then turned back to the river. A plastic bottle slithered downstream, blown along the surface by the wind, leaving a brief wake behind it.

'To be honest I think she might be wasted as a stringer here,' he said.

'Yes.'

'I thought I might give her a trial somewhere more lively. See how she gets on.'

'Africa, by any chance?'

'Maybe. What harm can she do there?' He looked at me over his shoulder. 'If we do pick her, she could well be the last one we ever send to Jo'burg. There's no money for foreign news any more, Africa least of all. Most of our rivals have already pulled out.'

The quay broadened out and the wall dropped away so that there was nothing between the river and us but a low metal railing. Lights flashed along the side of the old steam-packet terminal across the swirling water. A black mass of wheels and girders showed where the dead canal once fed its commerce to the river.

Brereton slowed and turned to me again. 'Let's sit down here a minute,' he suggested. 'I get tired quickly.'

The corporation had planted fresh saplings on the quayside and put long stone benches between them. As he sat on the damp bench Brereton was careful to pull the tail of his raincoat in under himself. Then he began to cough, very carefully, as if trying to avoid moving his chest.

'I thought you said you were okay,' I said.

He raised a hand for a few seconds before speaking again. 'There's other stuff. We didn't live well back then, did we?'

'No. We did not.' I sat down at the other end of the bench, upstream of him, facing him from ten feet away. The wind was at my back. After all, it was his party.

'And I'm older than you too. It catches up.' He laughed again. It occurred to me that, for all his laughter, he had yet to say anything really funny, and nor had I.

He watched me for a few moments, still smiling, and then he glanced off past my shoulder. From behind me the wind carried the sound of a train on the railway bridge.

'How is Laura?' I asked finally.

Brereton was smiling again. 'I haven't kept in touch. You know how it is . . . I've got two kids now, you know.'

'You must be joking.'

'For real. A boy and a girl.'

I had to fumble for the name. 'Not with Polly?'

'You should see the size of the fuckers. They're huge.'

That I did find funny. Brereton waited until I'd finished laughing and then he spoke again. The wind was tugging his lapels.

'I did see Laura about a month ago,' he said.

The ship had vanished and the lift bridge was closing. The wind pushed the river away from me, sped the tide towards the sea, silver and black and grey. Beyond the bridge there was no horizon.

'Really?'

'Yeah.' He waited.

'Where?' I asked.

'In Paris.'

Beyond Brereton's head a little forest of masts rose from the tiny, brick-walled boatyard that stood between the river and the traffic. They gleamed in the grey sky.

'How is she?' I asked. The steel halyards were dinging in the wind. I remembered that sound in Durban one night.

'She looked okay. I didn't talk to her.'

'Why not?'

He shrugged. 'I saw her on an escalator at Charles de Gaulle. You know that bit where there are some slanting up and others slanting down? I was down, she was up. I don't think she even saw me.'

'So you didn't actually meet her?'

He did the laugh again. 'Oh, no. Nobody's seen her since Sierra Leone. She did one last job somewhere and then she gave it up. Apparently she'd had enough.'

'Still, I'd have thought that someone would be in touch with her.'

He bounced up and down a couple of times on his end of the bench. 'I tried to get hold of her a few times after I got out of hospital, to say thanks and all that, but I couldn't find her.'

'Shame,' I said, but Brereton didn't seem to hear me. He began to bounce again, just a little at first, then faster. A tight smile spread onto his face as he gazed past my shoulder.

'I did hear something about her, though,' he said dreamily, looking past me. 'It was from a chap called Armitage, who wrote for Fine's paper. He came to see me a few months later, just before I got out of hospital, and he mentioned that he'd tracked Laura down to some place in Alberta. She's shooting wildlife stuff now, apparently. He said he'd managed to get a number for her but when he called her on the phone she told him to fuck off.'

I looked at him carefully. 'What did Armitage want?'

'Oh, the usual. Information. Quotes. Colour. He was trying to write a book about Fine – he must have thought he was on to a good thing, what with all those books and films they'd already done about that Eldon kid in Somalia. But I suppose he must have missed the boat. I never heard about any book about Fine coming out. And loads of American hacks have been killed since then.'

'You have to work fast,' I said.

Brereton snorted. 'Yeah. It's a saturated market.'

Neither of us spoke for a while. I listened to the wind moaning in the masts and the dull roar of the traffic on the road behind us, rising and falling like the sea. I stirred on the bench. Maybe Cartwright's neighbour was right about the cold.

'So Lucy gave you my name as a reference?' I said finally.

He stood up and stretched himself, swinging his satchel out in front of him, then letting it fall to his side. Stiffly he did a half-turn, looking first out across the river, then down the river to the sea, until he stopped with his back to me.

'Is it really like this in summer too?' he said over his shoulder, his words barely audible in the wind.

'I exaggerated. It's nice sometimes. Sometimes it sparkles.' I pushed myself up off the bench. 'I used to come down here a lot. There's a good pub across the road there.'

Brereton turned back to face me. When he spoke again his voice was casual. 'This Armitage bloke, he told me that when he went to Makeni just after it happened he met that Nigerian officer. You know, the good soldier?'

I shrugged, still smiling. 'Captain Fuck 'Em Up, we called him. I don't remember his real name.'

Brereton nodded quickly. 'Captain Kanta. That was his name. His name was Captain Jibril Kanta.'

'If you say so.'

'That was his name. Captain Fuck 'Em Up was a joke name. Actually, I think it was you who gave it to him.'

271

'No. I came up with Diamond Doug. I don't know who thought up Captain Fuck 'Em Up.'

'I think it was you.'

'It's not a very good joke. It was probably yours.'

He sniggered, and came slowly towards me, swinging the satchel. 'Captain Kanta told this Armitage bloke that he was surprised that we all took off that day without an escort,' he said. 'Captain Kanta thought we would wait until the next day, when we could have gone back to Lungi with an armed convoy. He reckoned he told one of us that the road was too dangerous for us to go it alone.'

He stopped and stared down at me where I sat on the bench. Eventually I looked away.

'He didn't put that in his big piece in the *Chronicle*,' I said.

Brereton stopped swinging the satchel. 'No. It would have made the story too complicated right then,' he said, grinning tightly at me. 'It wasn't what they needed.'

Foam was oozing out around the stitches of his soaked shoes. They must be pretty new, I thought.

'And I'll tell you something else Armitage told me that he didn't use in his article,' Brereton continued. 'He was a real chatty bastard, that one. I'm glad I didn't give him anything he was looking for . . . He told me that when he spoke to Rachel back in the States she broke down in tears and told him that just before it happened Fine asked for a divorce.'

He was still standing over me, still staring me down. I felt I ought to give him the pleasure of going along with this; I at least owed him that.

'So?' I asked.

'So they'd only just got married.'

'So?'

'So draw your own conclusions.'

'It mightn't mean anything.'

'It might.'

Some of the air had gone out of Brereton. He stood there but he wasn't looking at me now. He seemed to sag, and after a while

I scooted back along the bench a couple of feet and motioned to him to sit down beside me. He did, folding his coat beneath him again. We were both looking out across the river. They were building a new hotel over there, but the big yellow cranes stood silent over the skeletons of steel and concrete, swaying gently in the wind. I suppose the weather was too bad to operate them.

I let the river run past as I examined the story from different angles. Brereton let me sit in silence as I stepped back ten years and looked at the story from there, and then I came back to the present, and looked at it again, snatching quick squints at it, too hard and bright to look at for long. Beatrice in bed, cool and naked, that final night in Durban, that first night in the Memling. White and frightening on a winter night in Melville. And as I'd never seen her, on a hillside in a fir wood, as Schoon had described her, and that was still the worst thing, when all of us had lost her. And then I tried to picture her with Fine, and I realized, almost with sorrow, that he too looked merely ridiculous.

Brereton had straightened his legs out in front of him, hands deep in his pockets, like a man unwinding after a difficult job.

I looked at him. 'Did you tell me these things because you thought they would hurt me?'

'Of course.'

'I don't think they do, much. But they might later. I'll have to think about them some more.'

He took out a box of cigarettes and offered me one, and we looked at each other for a moment and almost smiled.

'I wonder what Beatrice thought of us all,' I said. But Brereton was having difficulty lighting his cigarette. The wind kept snatching the flame from his lighter, and I saw that he couldn't bend his burned hand to cup it. I put my hands around his to shield the lighter, and when his cigarette was lit I used its tip to light mine. He took a deep drag, puffing his cheeks out, then fed his smoke to the wind.

'How should I know?' he answered finally. 'I never really knew her that well.'

We watched the river in silence for a while.

273

'I didn't used to think of Fine as having any problems,' I said finally.

'He made his own. You know, when he came to Kinshasa that time he didn't have permission from his office? He'd been ordered to stay in the south. Armitage said Fine nearly got fired for it.'

'Fine's stuff from Kinshasa was very good.'

'One of several reasons why they didn't fire him.'

Brereton was drawing his feet in, preparing to stand.

'I already knew that Armitage had found out about me and Captain Fuck 'Em Up,' I told him quietly, and he turned slowly back to me.

'Yeah? How? Did he tell you?'

'Oh, no,' I said, slowly getting to my feet. 'I read it in his big Fine story. As it happens, Armitage did actually publish it. Just not as big as he'd hoped. It was in the *Rhodes Review* a couple of years ago.'

'Really? You're joking. What did it say?'

'It was about taking stupid risks for stories. Which showed how much he really knew. It wasn't very good, to be honest. I guess the *Chronicle* mustn't have wanted it. Or anybody else with real money to pay for it.'

'I never heard about it and I'm running a foreign desk in London. How the fuck did you come across it?'

It would be difficult to explain about Cartwright, I thought. 'A friend gave me a copy,' I told him. 'A couple of weeks ago.'

Brereton shook his head. 'Jesus,' he said. 'So that's all that our lives were worth in the end. The *Rhodes Review*, eh? And I'll bet you've been sweating all these years that people here would find out what a fucked-up fuck-up you are.'

'Not really. I'm safe. We still have a union.'

Brereton stretched again and looked at his watch. 'I suppose it's time for lunch, then,' he said. 'You mentioned a pub.'

There is a town in Namibia called Gross Barmen. In Zimbabwe you can stop your car and have your picture taken outside the Great Dyke Butchery. There's a bar in downtown Jo'burg called

Die Fisterman, or there used to be, one time. Did I really waste my time in Africa? Jansson had children, now Brereton does too. Fine's last story made the front of the magazine and won a big prize and the *Chronicle* endowed a foundation to commemorate him at Columbia University. Tommo's old paper in Sydney sponsors a workshop in his name. Every summer it teaches poor kids to take photos. With a bit of luck it might even get them killed. Nobody really claimed Beatrice, though. She was too many things, not enough of anything. Armitage barely mentioned her.

Cartwright will be the first to go. That old lady next door can't last much longer, and she has more of him than anyone but me. Perhaps I should go round there some afternoon, invite myself in for a cup of tea, do a little digging. See if I can drag him out a bit longer. It would be like going on the road again, except minus the notebook. But can you imagine how Cartwright would feel if he thought I was prying into his secret little griefs? After he had had the last laugh? Then again, he might just think that it was funny. It might even be what he wanted all along.

Twenty years ago there was a very bad summer here, nothing but rain and wind, and lots of religious people went to pray all night at certain churches and shrines because, as they shivered and stared in the wet and the gloom, they thought they could see the holy statues moving. Other people laughed at them, and psychiatrists went on TV and said that it was a natural phenomenon, a design flaw in our vision, that if you stare at anything long enough it will seem to move about. I think maybe there's more to it than that. I think that if you stare at anything long enough you'll start wanting to believe that it might be staring back.

I still have Tommo's camera. I keep it, unused, just the way it came to me, under the stairs, where – as it happens – it is always cool and dark and dry. There is a chance, then, that the film it contains might not yet have perished. Sixteen exposures, and twenty more to go.

Maybe I should rip the film out now and ruin it. Or I could have it processed, maybe even start using the camera myself. Of course

I'd have to learn how it works first. And you can see why I'd be frightened. There could be anything at all in that camera, until I open it up, and learn differently.

ENDS

F
OLO

6/23/10